outtakes vol 2: the commission world

bethany-kris

Published by Bethany-Kris
www.bethanykris.com

ISBN 13: 978-1-989658-62-8

DEDICATION & A NOTE FROM BK

For my readers, as always. I hope you find your favorites and rediscover what it was you loved about this world and characters of mine within the pages of this collection. The only reason these continue to exist in some form, paperback now, is because of you and because I know you deserve them because while it took me years to write all of this, you were also along on the journey with me.

I get asked often if I am planning more books for these "families" and the truth is, no. I will not be going back to write old characters in new situations, because they've had their turn, but that also doesn't mean the world is dead. Maybe just a few people, though …

But I'll save that for another day.

Hugs and happy reading.

Xo,

BK

CONTENTS

MARCELLO

ANTONY OUTTAKES

FATHERS DAY OF '93

Antony/John POV

"Shut *up*, Gio!"

"Knucle John says—"

"*Shut up.*"

Antony cracked his eyes open just enough to stare at the ceiling of his bedroom. He didn't know if his sons were just waking up and trying to sneak past their parents' bedrooms, or what was happening. All he knew was that once Gio learned to start talking around two years old, the kid *never shut up.*

Oh, God.

He loved his son.

So much.

Both his boys, really.

But Gio incessantly talked all the time. It never ended. He could talk for an hour about a certain flavor of ice cream if someone didn't rein the kid in before he really got going. He liked to talk, and it was impossible for the boy to do anything without talking while he did it. Which made things like playing Hide and Go Seek with his brother impossible because …

Gio never shut up.

"Papa, you up?"

In his bedroom, then. He didn't answer Dante back right away because a part of his brain was still asleep, and he was trying to figure out why he felt like he'd just slept twelve hours. A good sleep, yes, but a *long* one.

That was unusual for Antony. He rarely felt this rested when he woke up. He was typically the one in their house who was up at the ass crack of dawn because work never ended as a made man. If it wasn't one thing, then it was another.

1

Antony looked over in the bed to tell his wife the boys were up, but he found an empty bed staring back at him. He blinked at the spot where his wife should have been, but quickly realized something else.

The window.

And the sun.

The sun was way too high in the sky for it to be early morning. Antony darted up in the bed, and instantly reached for the alarm clock on the nightstand to check the time. Ten-fifty-five, it read.

In the *morning?*

"Hi, Papa!"

Antony didn't even get to wonder why he'd slept so long or where in the hell his wife was because the next thing he knew, Gio had climbed up on the four poster bed, and launched himself from the footboard right onto his father's lap.

And *almost* hit the family jewels in the process.

"Jesus Christ," Antony grunted, laughing under his breath.

Wiggly little three-year-old Gio rolled to his back, and beamed up at his father with a bright smile that could light up anybody's fucking life. How a person could be sad when there was a kid like Gio around, Antony would never understand.

"Ma says—"

"Not to be a *shit*," Gio interrupted.

Antony pressed his lips together to keep from smiling. He was not supposed to encourage the cussing, but he found it really hard. Especially when the kid used it in the correct terms.

"She did not say shit," Dante grumbled.

His oldest son climbed up on the bed, too, but unlike Gio, his first move was not to act like a bird that could fly across the bed and land on his father. He did get close enough to let Antony pull him into a hug.

"Where is your Ma?" Antony asked.

"Cooking," Dante said. "Waffles—your favorite."

Antony smiled. "Oh?"

For a moment, Antony reclined on the bed with his two boys. Dante on his right, and Gio in his lap because he couldn't convince that kid to do anything else. Once he got his mind set on something, that's all that would be happening.

It wasn't very often Antony got to have moments like these. Quiet, peaceful moments first thing in the morning with his two *principes* because life liked to get in the way all the damn time. So, he soaked it up.

Late morning sun, white sheets, and two little boys who kept looking at him like he was king of the whole world. Someday, they'd figure out he was just a man. And not a very moral or good one at that, but a man nonetheless. Their father ... but for now, he enjoyed being the very large sun in their small world.

"And she said I don't have to go to school," five-year-old Dante pointed out. "Because it's a special day."

Antony glanced at his son from the side. "Is it?"

Fuck.

Antony's mind scrambled to figure out what day it was. Not his anniversary, and not his wife's birthday. Not one of the kids', either. Not somebody important. No holidays, he was sure.

What had he missed?

"Yep," Dante said, pushing himself off the bed using two hands. "For you, Papa. Happy Father's Day."

Gio flipped himself over in Antony's lap and beamed up. "Happy Father's Day!"

"Breakfast is ready."

Antony found the owner of the sweet voice standing in the bedroom doorway. His wife, already dressed and ready for the day, looked like she had a secret to share. He loved her best when she looked like that. His greatest memories were pulling those secrets from his wife in a way only he could do, too.

"I had work to do today," he said.

Cecelia shrugged. "John said he would handle it, actually. We pulled some strings. A break is good for *everybody*, Antony. Even when that man is you."

Well, then ...

"Waffles!" Gio shouted. "I want waffles!"

Waffles it was.

*

Twelve hours later ...

John *tried* closing the door of the apartment quietly but that was

3

the thing about the goddamn door. Nothing about it was quiet. It squeaked, and when it latched, it echoed in the silent apartment.

Didn't matter.

The place didn't stay silent for long.

"Papa!"

It was way too late.

Eleven at night.

Lina was pretty strict about keeping a bedtime routine for Luciano, so he had thought by the time he was able to make his way around today, his boy would already be sleeping and out for the night. John just planned on staying til morning, waking his son up, and then heading across the state to deal with the woman who hadn't stopped calling his phone all damn day.

His wife, that was.

Fuck, he hated her.

Kate made that easy. Hating her, that was.

Not the time, John.

It couldn't be the time when little Lucky was heading his way with a big smile, and arms wide open. John was already kneeling down to greet his son with a hug, and a kiss on top of his dark-haired head.

For a second, John took the moment to admire his son. All those familiar features, and bright hazel eyes. Just like his dad. Lina liked to joke that there was no way John could deny Luciano because they might as well have been twins.

But fuck him because he saw Lina in their son, too.

In Luciano's sweet ways. In the happy glint that always shined in the boy's eyes. In the way his hugs always felt like home and love.

He was John's son through and through.

But his mother was there.

"Little late tonight, huh?" Lina asked. "He wanted to stay up."

John touseled Lucky's hair, and smiled at his boy. "Yeah … stuff came up."

"I bet."

He ignored the way she said that. He let her have her moods, and feelings. Lina was due them. After everything … all the choices he made that should have ruined whatever this was between them, the woman was still here.

She loved him despite of it.

Despite the fact she was a mistress.

4

That she raised their son practically alone.

That her name was ruined.

She loved him.

"We'll watch that show you like, get some popcorn, and whatever else you wanna do, all right?" John asked his son.

The boy nodded. "Okay."

He wanted to apologize for not being there. It was Father's Day, and instead of being with his son, he made sure his best friend could spend the day with *his* sons.

Because that's just how shit went sometimes.

Luciano never seemed to care that John wasn't here as much as he wanted to be. He just cared that John was there when he *was* there. Nothing else mattered then.

"Did you miss me?" Lucky asked his father.

John's gaze dropped to his son again. "More than you know, my boy."

Lucky grinned in that way—the Grovatti way.

No, he couldn't deny this boy at all.

He just wished he didn't have to hide him.

"Happy Father's Day, Papa."

John kissed Lucky's forehead, and dragged him in for a tight hug. Grabbing his son's face, he tipped Lucky's head back so that the two of them could stare at each other.

"I'm always gonna love you, yeah?" he asked. "You know that, my boy, don't you?"

Lucky nodded. "Yeah, Papa."

"No matter what, Lucky. Someone is always going to love you."

John didn't know then, that time was ticking down. That this whole thing was just a bomb waiting to blow with a clock that was running out of seconds. He'd be the first to go, and then Lina. He wouldn't know anything until it was too late.

But he hadn't lied.

Someone would always love Luciano.

John, even dead.

The boy's mother, in Heaven.

And a whole family across the state who, in those moments, hadn't even known Luciano existed.

They would love him, too.

When John and Lina couldn't …

When it counted the most …
They would love him.

A FATHER'S WORRY

As a father of boys, Antony tried not to do one thing too much: *worry*. It was basically impossible because considering who he was and the life he lived, well ... didn't he have more things to worry about than most?

He certainly thought so.

Nonetheless, he did try not to let his worries overcome him. His boys were good—*great*. They came from him, after all, and with just enough of their mother coloring them up to make sure they had a decent conscience while he took care of all that pride they often stumbled over, he thought it would be okay.

Mostly.

And there was Lucian.

Who was not the same.

He couldn't be.

Months after finding Lucian and moving him into the Marcello mansion with the rest of the family, and Antony found himself worrying over the boy that didn't share his blood more than he did his biological sons. He'd asked a friend if that was normal—or was it just because Lucian wasn't really *his*, and he felt a need to overcompensate for that fact? His friend said more the first than the second. At the moment, Lucian took over Antony's worry because he was the one who needed it the most out of the three boys. Another day, it might be Gio.

Or Dante.

Who knew?

It might help if Lucian actually ... *talked*. Or rather, if Antony knew that the boy was listening when someone else tried to speak to him. That was the thing, though. Lucian often seemed like the more one talked or the busier life seemed to be around them, the more he retreated into himself and the things around him.

Like now.

"Okay, Dante," Antony said in the bedroom doorway, "as long as you're reading, then you're good to stay up. You hear me?"

Under his big comforter, Dante nodded. "Kay."

"And you're sure you don't know where Lucian—"

"He hides all the time, Papa. It's what he does."

Right, right.

Dante wasn't wrong.

That didn't make this any easier on Antony, though. Because now, Lucian had been hiding for most of the evening and it was bedtime. Thing was, it was fine if the kid didn't go right to bed but that wasn't the goddamn problem. The problem was that Antony could not find the fucking boy and *that* was concerning.

Usually, Lucian had a myriad of hiding spots that he liked to tuck away in. A therapist said it was probably because everything was still so new to Lucian and *big*, that he was just trying to make everything a little smaller and easier to process. As if *that* was why the kid liked to hide in closets, cupboards, in showers … basically wherever the hell he could fit.

He didn't leave the house.

Not that it mattered—one of the guards or cameras would see him if he did. Hell, *that* would be an easier way for Antony to find Lucian than what he was trying to do right now. Because not only did he have Lucian to worry about, but he also had his other two sons to take care of.

Because he was *sure as shit* not calling Cecelia away from her girls' weekend with the handful of friends she actually did care to spend time with just to have her come home and help him find where Lucian had hidden himself now. Besides, his wife worried about Lucian all the damn time. So did he. Antony really didn't want to add to it.

Sighing, he murmured a *night* and *love you, kiddo* to Dante before turning around to leave the boy to his nightly reading. Closing the door behind him without much of a sound, he found a younger Giovanni staring at him from across the hall.

Surprise.

Gio got out of bed.

He always did.

About fifteen times a night.

"It's bedtime," he told Gio, grinning a bit.

He didn't want his kids to worry. Lucian did this a lot and while the boys had helped him look for a little while earlier, when he noticed they started to panic because they couldn't find their brother, he sent them off to do something more appropriate for *kids*. His boys would have plenty of years to worry about their brother and other adult problems. They didn't need to start with that shit today.

Gio didn't move from the doorway even when his father came to kneel in front of him. "Lucian knows it's bedtime, Papa."

Antony nodded. "Yeah, he does."

"He'll go to bed, too."

Goddamn.

"You think?"

Gio shrugged. "Yeah, 'cause he always follows the rules, you know?"

Which was *so* unlike what Gio did.

God.

Antony loved his boys.

Gio gave a bright smile before he hugged his father all at once. Tiny arms wrapped around him like bars and squeezed for all they were worth. Pressing a kiss to the top of his son's head, he took a single second to breathe in the scent of his kid and his life. Because someday, these hugs wouldn't come as often, and he certainly wouldn't get to kiss them on their foreheads, either.

Nature of boys, he knew.

He'd accepted it.

"Night, Papa," Gio said before turning back to the darkness of his bedroom.

Antony swallowed back the thickness building in his throat to reply, "Night, buddy. Love you."

*

Gio was right.

Antony wouldn't tell his kid that fact very often.

Nonetheless, this time, he'd been right. Lucian did know what time was bedtime, and though he probably wanted to just keep hiding, Antony found the boy *under* his bed. The only reason he suspected he might be there was because when he walked past Lucian's bedroom, he noticed one of the pillows and a blanket had been pulled from the bed. Twenty minutes earlier, the bed was still made when Antony checked the room for the tenth time.

With only the bedside lamp on, Antony could barely see Lucian's legs under the side of the bed. He could have easily left the boy to his thoughts—or dreams, if he was already asleep—but he just couldn't do it.

He wasn't mad that Lucian liked to hide. He wasn't even *sad*, though he did hope eventually it would change and his boy would join them a bit more.

Antony just ... needed to see him. So, despite knowing the floor would feel *nothing* like his own bed, he got down there and stretched out along the hardwood to peer under the bed. Bright hazel eyes stared at him from under the bed where Lucian had dragged his pillow and blanket to sleep.

"You know," Antony murmured, "the bed is *way* better to sleep on."

"It's very big," Lucian replied simply.

Ah.

"Did you have a good day?"

Lucian nodded. "Did you know there's a cubby under the right wing's third staircase?"

Goddammit.

"It would be so much easier if you just told me all the hiding spots," Antony said, chuckling.

"Sometimes, I don't want to be found."

"Yeah, I know, kiddo."

Lucian sighed, and pulled his comforter tighter around his neck before he whispered, "I miss Ma."

That took Antony a second.

Mostly, because he wondered how to respond. Of course, the boy would think about his parents. They'd not properly sat him down and explained *everything* that happened with Lina and Johnathan, but they did explain that Lucian's parents were in heaven. He seemed to understand that well enough.

This, though ...

Well.

"So," Lucian said in a sigh, "when is she coming home?"

Oh.

Cecelia.

He meant *Cecelia.*

Antony grinned, deciding he wouldn't make a big deal out of this. Didn't seem like the right way to go about it, honestly. "Ah, yeah, she promised you cupcakes, didn't she?"

"*Chocolate* cupcakes."

The kid's favorite.

"Tomorrow," Antony said. "She's coming home tomorrow, Lucian."

"Good. I'm gonna go to sleep now."

"Okay. Night, love you."

THE BOYS

Life was good.

But life at the top?

That was even better.

Antony supposed that was one of the many pros when it came to being a Cosa Nostra boss. Nobody said the life wasn't stressful, but at least sitting where he did allowed him the ability to redirect things he didn't want to deal with, or delegate a task to someone else.

Yeah, life at the top was—

"Gonna beat your motherfucking ass, Dante!"

"You can try, Gio."

Antony blinked as he stepped inside his home, and glanced upward to the upper wings of the mansion where his sons were currently in the midst of yet another one of their rows. One of their many rows, if he were being honest. He was lucky if he could get those three teenagers to go a week without them falling into some kind of battle with one another.

And people say girls are hard.

Fuck that noise.

Boys were rough.

And that was putting it mildly.

Boys were messy and loud and difficult. Boys talked with fists and sneers and fuck yous right on the tips of their tongues. Boys had no concept of personal space, and they shared too goddamn much, and sometimes they didn't share nearly enough when they needed to, or when it counted.

Too tall, filling out, hormone-riddled little monsters. And then you add onto that the fact his boys had access to all sorts of things given their life, and where they came from—not to mention money to burn—and it was just …

A little too much.

Sometimes.

"Did you just throw a fucking book at me?" Dante snarled.

Antony let out a sigh.

"And what are you going to do about it?" Giovanni taunted.

"I'm gonna kick your—"

12

"Hey, Papa."

Antony raised a brow at Lucian coming around the corner with a half-eaten apple in his hand. He looked like he didn't have a fucking care in the world, and right then, he probably didn't. After all, it wasn't him upstairs in the midst of a shouting match that was two seconds away from turning into violence with one of his brothers.

Give it three minutes.

Lucian would join in, too.

It just was what it was.

"What are they fighting about?" Antony asked.

Lucian shrugged, and headed for the grand staircase. The oldest at sixteen, he was all too often aloof, or he tried damn hard to act like it when something was going down. Antony figured that was Lucian's way of trying to keep himself out of trouble.

It rarely worked.

Once one started, the other two soon followed. Like a fucking trainwreck of testosterone, teenaged angst, and too much trouble for their own good.

"Gio acting like a puke, probably."

"Lucian, be nice."

"Where's the lie, though?"

Antony frowned. "How about, where's your mother?"

"Kitchen."

Really?

That made Antony's brow lift a bit. It was not like Cecelia to hide away in the kitchen while her sons acted like fucking hyenas fighting for the last scraps on a carcass. She was usually the first one to step in, and calm them the hell down. Cecelia wasn't the least bit frightened by her boys—she could wear a dress, heels, and have her face done up with her hair in curls, and still step in between flying fists when the time called for it.

"Stay out of that mess, huh?" Antony said, nodding upward.

Lucian glanced over his shoulder. "Yeah, sure."

Mmhmm.

He sure sounded like he fucking meant it, too.

Antony sighed.

All that lightness he'd been feeling strolling up to his home was practically nonexistent now—his stress levels were up sky-high all over again. He could delegate a lot of responsibilities to someone else, but not his family.

This was all him.

And Cecelia.

Soon enough, he found his wife in the kitchen. He expected her to be cooking something—she did that more often than not when she didn't want to deal with something, or she needed to whisk away the stress she felt.

Cooking was her reprieve.

The kitchen was her haven.

Those boys knew damn well they better not bring that nonsense into this area of their home—he wouldn't stand for it.

Except ... his wife wasn't cooking today. No, she sat behind the island with a magazine spread out on the counter, and a cup of tea sitting beside her. A bang echoed from upstairs followed by Gio's shout, and she simply glanced upward with a tight-lipped frown.

He knew it, then.

She was pissed.

"How long has that been going on?" he asked.

Cecelia didn't even look at him. "Since they got home from school."

Antony glanced at the clock, and winced. Shit. Three hours ago.

"That long?"

"Started before the gate to the driveway even opened," Cecelia muttered.

"I'm—"

"Don't apologize, Antony. I just want one single day this week where they don't fight. Anything, really. You can't even get them to sit down at a table and play nice for a meal. Even when their mouths are full, they're still trading insults with one another. It's ..."

"Tiring," he murmured.

Cecelia glanced at him, and her gaze showcased exactly how she felt right then. Useless. Like there was nothing she could do, and she had finally had enough of this. Antony knew that feeling well, but damn if he hadn't hoped their teenaged sons would figure this out on their own.

Appreciate one another.

Respect one another.

Make room for one another.

Something.

"I just wish they wouldn't fight, that's all," Cecelia said.

Antony nodded. "Yeah, I know, Tesoro. It won't always be like this, though. I can promise you that."

Cecelia laughed quietly. "You think?"

"I know, actually. I fought all the time with my brother. It's just how boys handle things. They don't talk, Cecelia. They force their space, and make room for themselves. It's how they work, and eventually, they learn that's … not the right way to go about it."

"Hmm."

She still looked sad.

God.

He hated that.

His sweet wife couldn't—would not—be upset over her sons. That was un-fucking-acceptable, and he just wouldn't let it continue.

"Give me five minutes," Antony said, spinning on his heels to leave the kitchen.

"Wait, what are you—"

"Five minutes!"

Antony made it upstairs in record time—funnily enough, by the time he did get upstairs, the fighting was all but settled. He didn't hear a peep coming out of Dante's room, and Gio was just coming out of the bathroom with a reddened mark under his cheek.

"Your brother hit you?" Antony asked.

Gio shrugged. "Maybe he did, maybe he didn't."

Yeah.

Because that's also how these fucking boys of his worked. Even when they acted like they hated each other, they still watched each other's backs like nobody's business. Someone tried to mess with Giovanni once at school—even though the boy was more than capable of handling himself—and his brothers took it upon themselves to beat the hell out of the kid causing the issue.

Just because they could.

And it was their brother.

Part of Antony was happy his boys were like that—they were going to strengthen that bond, and make it into something no one else could touch.

Eventually.

Another part of him wished they were already at that point.

Except they weren't.

"Did you deserve it?" Antony asked.

Because that was a damn good question, too.

Gio shrugged again. "Maybe I did, and maybe I didn't."

Dio, save me from these kids before they make me go gray.

Antony drew in a deep breath, and released it slowly. "Go get dressed—something appropriate for that restaurant your mother likes in Manhattan."

Gio scowled. "I don't want to go to that stuffy fucking—"

"I'm sorry," Antony said, cocking a brow, "did I start that statement with if it pleases your spoiled ass? Because I am pretty sure I did not. Now, march yourself to your room, put on something respectable, go downstairs, and apologize to your mother for this nonsense. And if we have another spell like we did today, Gio, I will not be this fucking nice. Got it?"

His son nodded once. "Got it."

"Good—get."

Antony didn't wait for Gio to move his ass before he headed into the bedroom belonging to his second oldest son. Unsurprisingly, Lucian sat on the edge of Dante's bed and flipped through a stack of CDs while Dante worked on the laptop at his desk. Neither of the two looked up at Antony's entrance.

"What?" Dante said.

Okay.

This was quite enough.

Antony was done.

"Try again," he uttered.

Dante stiffened before shooting an apologetic look over his shoulder. "Sorry."

"Yeah, I thought so. Hit your brother again, and I will have you cutting the grass with scissors, Dante. Do I make myself clear?"

Dante's brow dipped. "That's like ... ten acres!"

"Try five."

Give or take.

"But I'm sure it'd be a fun project, if you want to test me and give it a go," Antony added.

"But he—"

"You'll have to sharpen the scissors every hour or so, but maybe you'd get it done over a weekend."

Lucian snorted from the bed, but never looked up from the CDs.

16

"And you are another one," Antony deadpanned.

Lucian glanced up with wide eyes. "I didn't do anything!"

"You do enough, son."

After a second, Lucian shrugged.

Because yeah, it wasn't a lie.

"You're making your mother sad," Antony said quietly, "and what happens in this house when Cecelia gets sad?"

It took another second.

And then two.

Both boys jumped up from their respective seats, and headed for the door.

"Get dressed first," Antony shouted at their backs. "Something nice."

Lucian kept going—likely heading for his room.

Dante spun back around, and went for his walk-in closet without another word.

Because hell yeah, they knew.

When Cecelia got sad …

Antony got pissed.

And nobody wanted that.

BOYS WON'T BE BOYS

"Is this what you were looking for?"

Antony grinned at the woman standing to his left, and took the Tupperware container with his secret sauce from her outstretched hand. Cecelia winked when he said, "Maybe I was."

"*Maybe*. Maybe says the man who stayed up until one in the morning getting the sauce *just right* because apparently he can't cook burgers on the grill without it."

Sucking air through his teeth as he popped the top off the contained and the smell of spices and all his hard work the night before drifted into the air and mixed with the bit of smoke from the barbeque. "Are *you*—queen of her kitchen; first of her domain—telling *me* I was being ridiculous last night making my sauce?"

"No, I think the way you covet that sauce is ridiculous."

She even added a pat to his cheek for good measure. Before he could think better of it, he leaned forward and caught hers lips with his own in a burning kiss. At least that way, he got something good out of this conversation *and* it quieted his woman.

God, he loved his wife.

Only Cecelia could make Antony playful, and he adored her for that, too.

"But you are a little ridiculous about it," she whispered against his smirking lips.

Well…

"You only say that," he murmured, straightening back up and readying to prep his burgers with a good dose of the sauce, "because I won't tell you how I make it, Cecelia."

"I don't barbeque, Antony."

He gave her a look from the side, arching a brow. "Are you saying you couldn't use this sauce for something else, then? It's quite flex—"

"Just cook your damn burgers."

Antony's laughter rung out over the mansion's backyard that was currently filling with more people. After all these years, he still wasn't one for entertaining, but Cecelia loved it. He'd do anything to indulge his wife—even barbequing for fifty people in the neighborhood who he swore only came to the Marcello party because they were curious what they might see behind closed doors. As though they were a fucking circus act.

But who was he to say what people thought?

"Oh, there's the Martins," Cecelia noted, "I'll go say hi."

Antony sighed, not even bothering to turn and look at the new guests his wife mentioned. He didn't need to see the husband and wife, and their arrogant sixteen-year-old teenage son who regularly tested his patience whenever he was put in the same proximity as the boy.

"Keep Gio away from the kid, yeah?" Antony muttered.

Cecelia shot him a look. "I didn't notice him. There's ... a problem there?"

Antony shrugged. "Always has been, I think."

Not that he could explain it.

It just was.

Sometimes, that's how boys worked. He wanted to avoid a real problem before it became an issue and keeping the teenagers separated seemed like the right way to do it when Gio's anger could come quicker than a blink, and he had no qualms with acting out from it, either. Antony was still working on that with his fifteen-year-old. He had a feeling he'd be *working on it* for the rest of his fucking life, too.

"Oh, never mind," Cecelia said under her breath, taking her first step away from Antony, "there's their son. Worry about your burgers, Antony."

Right.

The burgers.

*

"I'm proud of you," Antony said.

From the end of his bed, Giovanni looked up from where he was kicking off his shoes to a careless pile on top of the clothes that rested down below. In nothing but his boxers, and looking like he'd probably had two or three glasses of wine when someone wasn't watching—maybe something else, too; *fuck*, Antony really needed to keep a better eye on his youngest—Gio stared at his father in the doorway.

"What?" he asked.

"You heard what I said. But in simpler terms, thank you for not pounding the arrogant shit out of the Martin kid today during the barbeque."

Gio rolled his eyes and fell to his back on the bed with his arms spread wide. "Okay, but that was *really* hard. He never shuts the fuck up, Papa—he's always going on about one thing or another like he knows what he's talking about."

Then, all at once, Gio sat up on the bed and gave his father a look. "He'd probably be a lot easier to deal with if someone did knock his stupid ass out. Did you see how he wears his fucking hat?"

Yes, with a wide brim, and off to the side, usually with a bandana underneath it. If that was Antony's kid—thank God it wasn't—he'd burn every fucking hat.

Antony grinned. "Nonetheless … I'm proud of you for holding it in check."

He fell back to the bed again. "S'was still hard."

Yeah, Antony bet.

"So, why didn't you?"

Gio made a noise under his breath. "Because then Ma would be sad, you would bitch, and Lucian and Dante would glare at me for the rest of the week while I walked around on eggshells. Honestly, he's not worth the trouble, so …"

"You know, I think that's called maturity. *Growth*."

"Stupid fucking shit, *that*."

Raising teenage boys was all about the give and the take. Sometimes Antony had to give a little, and sometimes he had to take. Gio's mouth and bad language was something he ignored a lot of the time—like now—unless they were at the dinner table.

He had more important things to focus on.

Antony chuckled. "Part of growing up, *figlio*."

"Besides," Gio said, waving one hand high, "if I really wanted to mess with the asshole, I'd just fuck his girlfriend. I feel like that's good enough for me."

It took Antony a second to respond.

His brow lifted high. "Gio."

"Hmm?"

"Are you safe?"

"Like—"

"I'm not fucking around with you right now, Giovanni David. I swear to God if someone brings a pregnant girl to my doorstep, I will have you neutered like a goddamn dog. I hear they'll do that in Tijuana. Imagine flying through turbulence to come home with stitches in your fucking nuts. I can have you there by next weekend."

"Jesus. Yes, I'm *safe*."

Okay, that was good to know.

"Gio?"

His son tipped his head up and met his father's stare from across the room. "What?"

"Women aren't trophies or weapons and we don't use them like they are. Don't you *ever* do that. Boys will be boys—but not my fucking boys. My boys will be gentlemen who behave how I taught them. Do you understand me?"

Gio sighed. "*Well ...*"

"*Gio.*"

"Yeah, Papa, I hear you."

Antony's shoulders sagged a bit with his next breath. "But do you?"

Tipping his head to the side on the bed, Gio met his father's gaze and he smirked a bit. "I always hear you—even when you think I don't."

Yeah.

Antony certainly hoped so.

KILLING

"Tell me he didn't just walk out of this office without as much as questioning you on who would do the job."

Antony righted the papers on his desk and carefully replaced all the documents of John's will back into the file.

"Antony," Paulie pressed.

"He's tired," Antony said in explanation, "and he just spent hours in interviews with police detectives who treated him like a criminal because of his last name instead of a victim after nearly being killed. Lucian isn't stupid, but he's needing something. Something I can't give him."

Jordyn.

Antony didn't need to say it to know his friend would get the hint.

"Thank you for playing along," Antony added.

Paulie pursed his lips, unhappiness shining through brightly. "He's my Godson, just like Giovanni."

Antony sighed. "I'm aware, old friend. I was there for the Christening. He's my son, remember. I picked you for the job."

Although, Antony wasn't sure if Lucian had ever been baptized under a different religion when he was a baby. Antony, knowing what John would likely want for his son, had Lucian Christened by the same man who had performed the rites on the other two Marcello sons.

"Then you know how I feel about lying to him," Paulie said simply. "I don't and never have."

Antony's sons might as well have been Paulie's own children, too. Paulie and his wife never had children, but the man had an active role in helping Antony raise his sons. Grateful wasn't a good enough word.

"Dio," Antony prayed quietly, "forgive me."

Paulie laughed darkly. "God is not the one you should be worrying about, Boss."

Antony nodded. "Cecelia."

"Cecelia," his friend echoed.

But …. God, too.

Antony would ask for clemency and forgiveness from God as

much as he would ask for the same from his wife simply because he knew no different. When he did wrong, when his life and his choices and his sins were overwhelming, Antony prayed.

"How many more?" Antony asked.

Paulie quirked a brow. "How many more what?"

"How many more sins do I have to commit before the forgiveness runs out?"

"It doesn't work that way, old friend. God is a—"

"Vengeful God," Antony interjected. "He's a loving God, but a vengeful God, too."

"I suppose."

"I've had a great life."

Paulie smiled briefly. "We all have, Antony."

"Then where is the punishment for my wrongs?"

"I told you, it doesn't work that way. You ask to be forgiven, to be absolved of your sins and misdeeds, and so you are. That's what we've always been taught."

"Funny," Antony murmured.

Paulie eyed him from the side. "What is?"

"That's how you see it. I don't, I suppose."

"Because that's what we were taught," Paulie repeated quietly. "Confession and forgiveness walks hand-in-hand. With repenting comes absolution."

"If we intend not to commit those same sins again, Paulie. If we intend to change our ways, deeds, and thoughts so the sin doesn't reoccur."

Paulie frowned. "Your point?"

"Who knows when my sins will stop?"

"Jesus died on the cross for our sins, Antony. We're creatures of sin. We're incapable of being perfect."

True.

But God was still an angry God.

He was still wrathful.

Antony feared that his inability to change his ways and the fact that he had yet to be punished by his God for his sins meant that it just hadn't happened ... yet.

Maybe it would.

Someday.

Paulie picked up this briefcase from the floor as he snuffed out the cigar he'd been puffing on. Antony always found it odd how a doctor like Paulie could smoke, knowing the risks. Antony enjoyed a good Cuban every once in a while, so he couldn't say much.

Popping open the top of the briefcase, Paulie pulled out a few items and set them aside on a small table. His friend went about checking the glass vials, each filled with a different clear liquid.

All different medications.

A deadly concoction.

"Opioids are popular on the streets at the moment," Paulie said as he shook a vial.

"I'd heard."

"It's mostly safe when used in-hospital or under supervision as prescribed, but we both know how addicts can be. Nonetheless, it's popular." Paulie grabbed something inside the case and then flashed an orange bottle filled with circular pills. "Oxy. Shove a couple in her mouth and leave the bottle by the bedside."

Antony nodded but said nothing.

"Overdose is an easy explanation. Make sure she swallows the ones you shove in. I'll make sure Charles is the coroner on call for the district," Paulie added.

"How much will that cost you?" Antony asked.

"Enough. Smart move on your part making sure Jordyn heard the phone call earlier. She'll pass that info along to Lucian, I'm sure. He'll never look to you."

Antony frowned. "I don't like lying to him, either, but he'll be angry if he knows it was me. I have to do this—I've had to do this for years."

"I get it."

Paulie withdrew a syringe from the case and popped off the cap. He went about filling the needle with doses from each bottle, cracking the syringe with his finger each time as if to mix the concoction. Once he was done, he replaced the cap, packed everything back into his case, and walked over to Antony's desk, holding out the needle.

Antony took it. "Thank you."

Paulie gave a single nod. "Ask for forgiveness. Better to ask and know then to never do and always wonder."

Antony smirked. "From who, God or my wife?"

"I think both would surprise you."

*

Antony was careful to let the front door close without a sound. Adjusting the black leather gloves he wore, Antony glanced around the dark foyer. He hadn't noticed an extra vehicle in Kate's driveway, so it was likely she didn't have any male guests over for the night. Antony couldn't be too careful.

And he didn't trust Kate.

He hadn't trusted her for years.

It pissed him off more than he cared to admit that he'd allowed Kate to live for all these years after what she did to John. Her death had been more than warranted back then, but Antony had been stuck in a place where he felt like he had already taken too much from his wife.

Her sister, too?

Antony couldn't do that to Cecelia. Not then.

Now, he didn't have a choice.

But he would enjoy this.

Kate earned it. Even God had to know that.

She'd hurt his son—tried to, anyway. Lucian would come out on top, he always did.

But she still tried.

Vile. Bitch.

Gone.

Antony had bided his time. He was done waiting. It was time for Kate to answer for her wrongs.

And of course, good bosses did their own work.

*

The door to Kate's bedroom was opened about a foot. Antony pushed it the rest of the way with as much force as he could muster. Luckily, there was no doorstopper to prevent the door from crashing into the wall with a bang. Kate Grovatti jerked up in her bed with wide, confused eyes. She instantly found a smiling Antony leaning in the doorway.

Cold.

He knew he looked so fucking cold.

"Kate," Antony said near soundlessly.

Her stare, usually cold enough to burn, was filled with fear and a dawning understanding.

Antony smiled again. "I know it's late."

Kate swallowed hard. "I did nothing."

"Funny, you have no idea why I've come here. But those who feel they need to defend their non-actions without merit usually have something to hide."

Water glimmered in Kate's eyes. Antony didn't let her show of emotions affect him in the least. Kate was false—every bit of her screamed fake. She would find no sympathy from him, not after all she had done.

Then, Kate sneered through her fear, likely realizing Antony wasn't leaving and was there for only one thing.

Her life.

"You've waited a long time for this, haven't you?" Kate taunted. "Why are you just standing there?"

Antony stepped forward and Kate shrunk into the bed. "Because I can. And you're right, I have waited a long time to finally end this. You had a good run, Kate. But my son? That wasn't just a line you crossed, that was fence jumping."

"He's not your son," she spat. "He's the grown bastard of a man who was worthless."

"Spoken from the mouth of a woman who would know first-hand how it feels to be exactly that—worthless."

Kate's bottom lip trembled.

Antony just grinned. "Are you going to cry now? I always liked it when they cried."

"No," Kate mumbled.

"Too bad." Antony withdrew the needle from his jacket pocket and popped off the cap. "I had to lie to my son tonight. He wanted to do this. Perhaps I should have allowed it after all the hell you put him through over the years. But I'm selfish, Kate. I needed to do it. I'm sure you understand."

Antony stood beside the bed, ready to grab Kate if needed. Kate clutched her blankets with a white-knuckle grip.

"Go to hell, Antony."

"I'll meet you there, Kate."

With that, he struck. The needle disappeared into Kate's scalp, a place where tracks could rarely be seen without shaving the head. Kate screamed and clawed at his arms.

Antony pushed the plunger down and kept on smiling.

*

Antony didn't expect to find his wife awake and waiting for him when he returned home. Maybe he shouldn't have been surprised. Cecelia sat on the edge of their familiar bed with a family photo album in her hands and tears in her eyes. Antony took note of the fact that the photos were the ones he'd found in Lina's apartment of Lucian, his father, and his mother.

"There was a time once," Cecelia said quietly.

"When what?" he asked, pulling off his leather gloves and then his jacket.

"When Kate was different."

"I can't remember one."

"Me, either, really. But she was."

Antony sighed as he dropped to his knees in front of his wife. Silently, he closed the album and tossed it to the side before squeezing Cecelia's thighs gently.

"I'm not sorry," he murmured.

"I am," she whispered.

"For what, Tesoro?"

"For not asking you to do this sooner."

NEVER ENDS

Cecelia lifted her head a bit at the sound of footsteps echoing from … *somewhere.* That was one of the only problems with having a home as large as their mansion. No matter how much stuff she used to fill the nooks, crannies, corners and walls, well, any noise still echoed. It sometimes made it hard to distinguish how close someone was to any one spot or where they were coming from.

And then again …

Cecelia knew her home.

That's why when the footsteps came a little closer and began to *thud* a bit more with each one, the noise getting progressively higher and higher, she knew. It was Antony taking the staircase that led to their floor and master bedroom.

This wouldn't be the first night she waited up far beyond a decent hour for her husband to return home from … work. Over the years, it had become slighter harder for her to call the mafia *work*, as though it was just another nine-to-five like everyone else's. Because it wasn't and she was unwilling to pretend like it, either.

They couldn't play make-believe.

Nobody won in the mafia's games.

At the edge of the bed she shared with her husband, Cecelia sat while tapping an envelope against the palm of her hand. Inside the envelope, waited a letter that she had already read, but that Antony didn't yet know about. She had a feeling she knew what his response would be, and how he would deal with it because *he* always did.

Whenever their boys had issues—problems with school, people, or even the law … Antony dealt with it. When they were younger, it was always Cecelia handling out lessons to their boys whenever they stepped out of line.

Time in a chair. Extra chores. A hand-written letter to apologize for one thing or another. A hug and a handshake when things had gotten a bit too rough. She was the type of mother who parented with a tone and an expectation.

Her kids tended to get in line.

But then the boys got older. They started following their father around more and more; or other men that stuck close to Antony.

Accordingly, their actions and behaviors started to mirror their father's and he stepped in where Cecelia could no longer manage with three teenage boys who only wanted to walk the same path as their dad.

She decided a long time ago ...

She loved her boys—they could be whatever they wanted to be and she would support them, no matter what. It was one thing her sons would never have to worry about.

"You're still up?" Antony's cheery tone dipped a bit at the end, making Cecelia glance toward the bedroom doorway where he stood. His gaze was locked on the envelope in her hand. "What's that?"

"The boys' Headmaster sent Dante—and Lucian but they saved an envelope and paper by just combining it into one—home with a disciplinary mark on his record, a one-week suspension that will end when we go in for a conference, and a letter explaining why. Of course."

Antony cleared his throat, the grunt as dismissive as his expression when he headed further into the bedroom. *Yeah*, see she hadn't expected him to be very concerned. The boys were smart; their grades were great, at least two of out of the three were considering college—Gio was still too young to care—and for the most part, they toed the line in their private school.

It wasn't often they stepped over it.

"Well, what'd they do?" Antony asked before disappearing into the connected walk-in closet.

Cecelia sighed. "Running some scheme ... banned items or some ... listen, it's all in the letter if you want to read it."

Maybe it was the distance in her tone that caught Antony's attention, but his figure quickly darkened the doorway between the bedroom and closet. She glanced over her shoulder at him but just as fast, put her attention back on the envelope in her hand.

"What's wrong, *Tesoro?*"

"Nothing. You know how I am—I get stuck in my head sometimes over silly things when they shouldn't matter to me anyway."

"Since when do your boys *not matter?*"

"Not like *that*, Antony. I meant ..." Frustration washed through Cecelia, but like she had always been taught to do by the women who came before her, she tampered it down. Antony never demanded or expected her to, of course, but she didn't like to be irrational or angry. Her husband heard and understood a great deal more from her when she wasn't. "They're fourteen and fifteen and already running a *scheme* at school. How quickly is it going to jump from this to something else?"

Antony made another one of those dark noises. "*Well …*"

Cecelia rolled her eyes, refusing to face him. "See, silly."

"Not silly. And quickly … if they're good at what they do, it happens rather quickly."

Huh.

She always appreciated that her husband offered her blunt honesty with nothing held back. Even if the weight of the truth took away her breath from the force of it slamming into her heart.

Cecelia didn't bother to turn at the soft approach of her husband's footsteps. She felt his presence the moment he was at her side, though. Leaning over her back, he pressed a soft, warm kiss to the curve of her shoulder before plucking the envelope from her hand.

"And I will take care of this," he added. "Don't even give it another thought."

"Antony?"

"Hmm?"

She did peer up at him then, forever willing to drown in a happily ever after of their own making with him. Until the end. "It doesn't bother you a bit, does it? That they'll be just like you."

"It can't."

"Why not?"

"I spoke my oath—I promised everything for it. Even them."

Cecelia blinked at that. "And then they'll do the same thing … make the same promise."

"Well—"

"Because this never ends, does it? This life of ours, there's no way out."

Antony smirked a bit, and despite the weight in her heart, she couldn't help but smile back at how *content* and pleased he seemed when he replied, "But it's a wonderful life, Cecelia."

She had to admit …

He wasn't wrong.

FULL CIRCLE

Antony Marcello stopped counting his birthdays when he turned *eighty*. He refused to have another birthday party after that age, too. He didn't see the point, and everyone else enjoyed it far more than he did. He rarely remembered his birthday anymore unless his wife thought to tell him it was that specific day, but that was just fine, too.

Still, despite his age ... and *no*, he refused to even think his age, now, he'd not forgotten a single thing about his life. From his earliest memory, that one of his father giving him the red pocketknife like the one he gave to all of his sons, too, to the sweet words his wife told him before she fell asleep next to him in bed the night before.

He forgot *none* of it.

Ever.

Antony considered that a gift, all things considered. When his body began to show his age, and so did his health, his mind stayed the same. People joked that couldn't possible be true when he told them, but they were wrong.

He knew it all.

Remembered *everything*.

And he told those stories over and over again. To every and any Marcello that cared to listen—they all listened—and to anyone else they brought home to be a part of their family, too. He told their stories, their *history* ... that legacy he'd started all those years ago, and he kept talking. Because when he was no longer here, who was going to tell those stories?

Who would remind them?

They needed to carry it on.

Like he had.

"Have a blessed day, everyone."

Antony glanced up from the bible in his weathered hand, realizing Sunday mass was over. Unlike years ago when he would have made sure to listen throughout the entire mass, now he did well to not fall asleep after the first fifteen minutes.

He still came, though.

Cecelia made sure of that.

Speaking of which ...

"Come on," Cecelia said beside him, smiling at him from the side. "Catrina is making dinner for everyone tonight, and I promised to help her."

Right.

It was more like his sweet wife would bark orders, and Catrina would follow along because she loved her mother-in-law. The same way the rest of their sons' wives loved Cecelia. Antony gave himself credit for that, and his sons, too.

They picked the right women.

"I need to make a stop first," he said.

Cecelia's brow dipped. "For what, Antony? You have a cold. You don't need to be lingering—"

"I'm fine."

"Antony."

"I *am*," he promised, standing from the pew. "Besides, Lucian will come with me. Won't you, son?"

Down the pew, already standing with his wife and oldest son, ready to leave the church, Lucian didn't even hesitate to say, "Sure, Papa."

"See," he told Cecelia. "I'll be fine."

"But what do you have to do?"

"I thought I might go say hello to John."

His wife stiffened a bit, but quickly nodded. "Okay."

*

Lucian lingered a few steps behind his father, and Antony was grateful. They all hovered too much, and he hated that. Like another reminder that he was no longer a young man, and he needed help occasionally.

And then there was Lucian ... one of his only sons who seemed to have a good grasp on the fact that Antony wanted to keep as much of his pride as he possibly could throughout the rest of his life. He didn't get too close, he never grabbed his father's arm to help him up the stairs unless Antony asked for it, and he didn't once mention his father's age.

"Do you want me to come up to the headstone with you?" Lucian asked quietly.

"If you want to speak with him," Antony returned.

"It *has* been a while."

"I'm sure John knows that, too."

"Thanks for that."

Antony chuckled. "And I'm sure he is also happy that you live your life, Lucian. What more could he want for you than what you've become, hmm?"

"Right," Lucian replied quietly.

Silence followed them through the old graveyard. Past the newer section that had been added over the last decade, and through the middle section where a good portion of Antony's family and friends had been buried over the last twenty years. He recognized a lot of the names on the headstones, but he kept walking.

One slow step at a time.

Until he found *him*.

John.

Standing in front of the gravestone that marked his best friend's final resting place, on one side of John was Lina, Lucian's biological mother, and on the other side, Paulie had been buried with his wife. Next to Paulie's stone was a section of grass, untouched, and with no stone.

That was where Antony would be buried.

And Cecelia, too.

They'd decided that a long time ago. It hadn't been a sad thing, and he *so hoped* that when the time came, his sons, and the rest of their family, wouldn't cry for them. He, and Cecelia, too, wanted them to *celebrate*.

They had lived a good life.

He had the memories to prove it.

Lucian stayed behind a couple of steps as Antony moved forward.

"John," Antony murmured, bending down though it took far too long to do so, and he would need help to get back up, "it's been a while, old friend."

Too long.

But like everything else in his life, he remembered John vividly. From the time they were boys, still too young to be called men, until the day he put John in that hearse for his final ride. He couldn't forget the lines of his friend's face, or the color of his eyes. And he remembered him as he was, because Antony had never gotten the chance to grow old with John like he had with Paulie, or even his wife.

Would he have had more kids?

Married Lina *someday?*

He didn't have enough memories, even if his mind was full of them. He didn't get that lifetime of friendship with John, so he was hoping heaven would give him that chance. And if nothing else, that was why he wasn't afraid of death now.

He had people waiting for him.

And he *missed them.*

"It's finally happened," he told the gravestone.

He reached out, and brushed the bit of dirt from the letters of John's last name, the *Grovatti* staring back at him in thick, block letters.

Proud letters.

He'd needed to come here today and tell his old friend, just in case John wasn't watching—although Antony believed he was—that the *son* of *his son* had taken back what had been stolen from him all those years ago.

His family name.

His *legacy.*

All of it.

John, the one that had come after the one murdered long before his time, had taken it back for them. With the help of the son of *Antony's* son. Because sometimes, if one was lucky enough to live as long as Antony did, then they were also lucky enough to see life come full circle.

What went around, came back around.

"They did it, John. They did it for us."

THE LEGACY

Antony didn't know if he was unique in the way that after his eightieth birthday, he stopped counting the years. At first, he thought it was because he knew he was closer to his death than he was his better years. Now, he didn't know if that was entirely true.

Sure, when he was younger, he had the glory of watching his wife bloom into a mother. The world had been at his fingertips. Power was his drug of choice, and he indulged just enough to make an empire. Loyalty had always been at the forefront, his honor always intact, and never challenged. He'd had the benefit of watching his sons grow from babies, to men, to husbands, and fathers ... *grandfathers*.

And yet, as he sat in the large leather chair, the backdrop of their photo shoot the family mantle covered with gold, and the crown molding intricate over a portrait of their family seal ... Antony thought perhaps these years were his best.

Yes, he needed help.

Yes, his body was tired.

And sore.

And *old*.

Yes, his mind was not as quick, even if it was still just as sharp. And yes, he had more family and friends buried than he did alive now ... but look at what he had. Look at all that he had done.

It was never more on display than in that moment. His wife smiling across the room from her chair. She didn't like to stand as much as she used to, and she didn't even wear her kitten heels anymore. That hair of hers had long turned white, and the years wrote lines on her face that matched his own in many ways. Hell, they'd spent their whole lives looking at each other, after all ... things were going to begin to match.

Surrounding her, however, were his sons' wives. Each balancing a different child on their hip, grandchildren of varying ages for them— *great*-grandchildren for him. The children's mothers, his grandchildren, did their best to wrangle the older ones into a group to keep them all out of the shot.

"Almost ready?" the tattooed blonde said. *Haven*—who surely would have made his father faint at how *different* she was from what had always been accepted as a wife for a made man. And yet, all these years and all these stories that carried through his family's lineage made Antony think ... no, it was the changes in his family, the bending of the rules ... the *rulebreakers* of his blood, who made this family stronger.

If they didn't change, they would stay the same.

Things that stayed the same were doomed to repeat the past. Somethings needed to just stay in the past, because the present and the future would always be better.

He could have died young.

Time and time again.

He felt death.

Saw it.

Heard it.

Touched it more than he should have.

Antony Marcello could have died *so young*. And he would have missed this. He might have never made this.

So yes, these were most definitely his best years. Even if his body had felt like giving up *eons* ago. He still had to be here.

At least, for this.

"Yeah, almost ready," the photog shouted.

Antony didn't miss the way Andino, his second eldest grandson, gave his wife a lopsided smile. Haven, to her benefit, was doing the best she could just out of range of the shot to hold their walking nine-month-old. *Never* had Antony had the pleasure of seeing a baby walk so early on in life. Until his great-grandson.

"Ok, let him go to his daddy," the photog said, standing up to his tripod while waiting for Haven to let her son down to the ground.

Laughter lit up the room, because as soon as she put the boy down, he darted, chubby hands out and reaching, for his father who stood next to where Antony sat on his large, ornate chair. Andino bent down, hands out to catch the oncoming boy—who hadn't quite learned to *stop* yet, but always wanted to run as fast as his fat little legs would take him to his father—while the photog did his thing.

Behind Antony, Giovanni stood with his hands resting on his father's shoulders. Gio squeezed, and Antony reached his own, weathered hand up to pat over his son's. His silent acknowledgment back.

"And look at me," the photog said.

All eyes went to him.

The man took the shot.

Four generations.

Four generations of Marcello blood.

Of Marcello men.

Of the best things Antony ever made—his most important accomplishment, he said, when a recent reporter somehow managed to get his home phone number, and called for a statement about book deal an unauthorized biographer had just received after pitching the life and legacy of Antony Marcello.

Was he mad, they asked.

Was it lies, they questioned.

Don't you want your say, Mr. Marcello?

"And one with a smile," the photog said, "before we let the rest of the family join in and have our large shot taken, too."

The four generations smiled.

Even the baby.

Did he want to have his say?

No.

His legacy would always speak for him. For itself.

He was glad he hadn't missed this.

LUCIAN OUTTAKES

NEW WALLS

"Hi."

"Hello ... Jordyn."

Jordyn shifted on her feet, smiling but still seeming uncomfortable. The man across the foyer from her wasn't in any better of a predicament, really. Lucian felt ten shades of awkward standing beside his wife, but only because he didn't know what to say or do to make her feel better about the situation they were currently in.

This wasn't easy for her.

It would never be easy.

But she deserved to know her father.

"Uh," Roland mumbled, clearing his throat. "Do you drink coffee or something? You wanna drink?"

"Water," Lucian said quickly.

He was pretty sure Jordyn wasn't supposed to be drinking coffee in her condition, but since she didn't know, he didn't want to spoil the news this way. Especially in front of a man who neither of them knew all that well.

Even if that man was her father.

Jordyn nodded. "Water is fine."

"Sure, sure. You can take your shoes off or whatever. Drop the coats." Roland pointed to an entryway. "Living-room is in there. I'll bring you the drinks."

Without waiting for Lucian or Jordyn to respond, Roland turned on his heel and left the couple alone in the entryway.

Jordyn turned to face Lucian with sadness in her gaze. "This is ..."

"Awkward," he supplied quietly.

"Not what I was expecting."

Yeah, that, too.

Lucian frowned. "We can go, Jordyn. If that's what you want, bella, we can go right now. Just say the word."

Jordyn shook her head as she toed off her suede boots. "No, Lucian. I want to talk to him, at least. I need to do this."

"Fine."

Lucian slipped his coat and boots off, placing them in a closet with Jordyn's things. He couldn't help but notice the empty hangers inside the closet. Roland's coat was in there, but no one else's things happened to be except a couple of American Eagle sweaters.

Where was the man's wife and kids?

*

Lucian kept Jordyn's hand firmly tucked into his as she conversed with her father.

Well, conversed was a strong word.

Mostly, Jordyn talked and the man awkwardly replied or assumed something of a reply.

Maybe it was the time that had separated them. Maybe it was the fact Jordyn was grown, now, and not a child. Maybe it was the fact that Lucian had informed Roland of Jordyn's childhood growing up in an MC with an abusive man front row and center, and then her mother's subsequent death.

Who knew?

Lucian hadn't told Roland those things to guilt or shame the man. He'd done it because the guy deserved to know the sorts of stuff Jordyn's mother had put her through. He deserved to know why Jordyn might not be willing to open up or why she might hold some lingering resentment toward her father.

Lucian wouldn't blame Jordyn if she did, but apparently, that wasn't the case at all.

Roland, on the other hand, felt like a wall of bricks.

Impenetrable.

"This, uh, isn't the house you came home to after Sandra had you," Roland informed.

Jordyn raised a brow. "No?"

"No, we lived in a rental. Shoddy little place, but that's all we could afford. I stayed there for a while after ..."

"After she left," Lucian finished for the man.

Roland shrugged. "Yeah."

Jordyn frowned. "Did you keep anything of mine? Like pictures or something?"

"A couple. Whatever your mother didn't take or ruin on her way out."

Jordyn kind of looked around the room. Lucian followed her gaze. There were lots of framed photographs on the walls, showcasing Roland and a woman and two children. Family photos, candid photos, and everything in between.

Lucian had seen the few baby pictures Jordyn had of herself that her mother managed to keep. He'd recognize a picture of his wife's infant self. Not one of the pictures had Jordyn in them.

Roland seemed to notice Jordyn's displeasure. "When I bought and moved into this place with my wife, I let her have the rule of the house. She did all the decorating, you know. I just nail and hang where she tells me."

Lucian swallowed the awful feeling welling in his gut.

Jordyn's hand tightened in his, like she was holding back something.

He did not want her in pain. He did not want her bitter and sad.

This was not supposed to be about that at all.

"And mine didn't make the cut?" Jordyn finally asked.

Lucian tugged gently on his wife's hand. "Jordyn, hey."

Hurt reflected in her blue eyes.

He didn't know what to say.

"Well," Roland drawled.

"What?" Jordyn asked.

"Mostly, my wife wanted to move on from all that—start our family with the memories we'd make and let go of what was gone. I understood. I'd tried to find you the best I could but I didn't have a whole hell of a lot of money to get where I needed to go. I figured your mother had moved on to someone else and maybe you had a man raising you. That was my hope, anyway."

"Well, your hopes were wrong," Jordyn muttered under her breath.

Okay.

Lucian knew Jordyn had hit her limit for the day. Just the way anger twisted at her mouth and her hand kept squeezing inside his, she was over it.

That was just fine, too.

"I think we'll head out for the day," Lucian said, standing from the couch.

He tugged Jordyn up with him.

"There's a nice little seafood place a few miles away. Follow the signs into town, you can't miss it," Roland informed.

"Thanks," Lucian said.

Jordyn sighed, rubbing at her forehead. "Can I … can I ask something else?"

Roland nodded. "Sure, anything."

"Where is your wife and kids tonight? They're only teenagers, right? So, it's not like they live away from home. You knew we were coming for more than a couple of weeks now. We had everything planned—you were contacted ahead of time. This wasn't like … an ambush on my part or anything."

Roland looked stunned. "I … well, I—"

"I wanted to meet them," Jordyn interrupted softly. "When I found out I had half-siblings and that you had remarried, I thought it would be nice to meet a part of my family. I didn't have that growing up. I had nothing growing up."

"Jordyn," Lucian murmured, tugging her a little closer to his side. "It's all right, bella."

"No … no it's not," Jordyn said, turning back to her father. "I had nothing except a mother who didn't care for me very well, but I was okay with that. I was fine with the fact you might have moved on with your life because I'm an adult now. I'm married and I've lived through hell, and that was perfectly fine. I just wanted the chance to meet you, to meet them, too. Where are they? Why aren't they here today to meet me, too?"

Roland looked like he wished the floor would swallow him whole. "My wife didn't want to be here and didn't want the kids mixed up in it, either. Dee took them to a movie for a couple of hours. I think they were going shopping after."

"Me, you mean," Jordyn said. "She didn't want to be mixed up with me."

"Essentially, yeah." Roland sighed heavily, adding, "I'm sorry, but she was content to leave it all behind. You're right, you're an adult. We both figured that by now, you'd have moved on in life, too. If you hadn't come looking for me by now, I didn't think you ever would. You were young enough when your mother took you that I suspected maybe she hadn't told you where you came from. You wouldn't have known better."

"She told me," Jordyn said faintly. "She didn't lie—she was a lot of things. She was an addict and neglectful; selfish, too."

Roland frowned. "I'm aware of what Sandra could be like."

"My mother was a lot of things," Jordyn repeated. "But a liar was not one of them."

*

"How did it go?" Antony asked.

Lucian felt the tightening in his chest return. "Awfully."

Antony blew out a puff of air that crackled in the speaker. "Yes?"

"Yeah," Lucian confirmed.

"I'm sorry, son. I know … she was looking forward to this."

"She was," he agreed. "And I don't think it's him so much as his entire world right now. The fact he's practically said his goodbyes to her without ever even actually saying it. He's left her behind—the two year old her. His life has moved forward."

"And parts of hers is still stuck back there, waiting for her father to catch up," Antony finished for his son.

"I'd say so."

Antony hummed a sad sound. "Do you feel that way too, sometimes?"

"About what?" Lucian asked.

"Us, I guess. Or rather, your mother and father. Do you feel like there's a part of you that's still stuck in your six year old self, waiting for the world to tell you they did you wrong or made unfair calls? Are you waiting for the rest of us to catch up with it all?"

"Do I want John and Lina, you mean."

"I suppose that's what I'm saying."

"So say it," Lucian said.

Antony sighed. "Do you, Lucian?"

"I miss my parents."

"I know."

"And I love them, especially my mother," Lucian added quieter.

"I know that, too."

Lucian smiled. "So yeah, but I don't worry about it too much because I know when I get back to New York, they'll be waiting there for me. I can always go home—you're still waiting."

Antony fell silent for a moment before saying, "You know we're not who I was talking about."

"But you're who I'm talking about, Papa."

"Is it really that simple for you, Lucian?"

"It wasn't," he admitted, "not for a long time."

"But?"

"But I have a family—I always have. I don't need to focus on the past."

*

"Lucian?"

Lucian slipped into the bathroom doorway and leaned against the jamb, watching his wife surrounded by bubbles in the hotel's tub. "Hmm?"

"I'm sad," Jordyn mumbled.

He didn't need her to tell him that.

Not at all.

He could see it written all over her pretty face. It only hurt him more.

They'd been in Maine for five days. Each one was a little more difficult than the last, as far as Lucian was concerned. Jordyn was trying to break through her father's walls and Roland was holding strong, for whatever reason. Roland's wife and children still weren't attempting to cross the bridge to meet Jordyn. On the four occasions Jordyn had gone to meet with her father after the first time, it was made clear her half-siblings and step-mother wouldn't be included.

It broke her heart.

That, in turn, broke Lucian's.

He was trying to keep it together, but it was really starting to piss him off. Didn't they understand what Jordyn had suffered growing up? Didn't they know what she had gone without?

She wasn't trying to corrupt their folds or insert herself into their life unwanted, but she did want to know them. What was the goddamn problem? What was so wrong with her?

She was beautiful—a happy, loving soul.

When life had done her wrong, she still came out selfless and wonderful.

"Lucian?" Jordyn whispered.

He glanced down at his wife again. "Yeah, bella?"

"There's nothing wrong with me, right?"

"Why would you even say that?"

Jordyn shook her head. "Never mind, it was stupid. I know that. I just mean … I'm not like some terrible person, right?"

"No, you're amazing."

Lighting up his fucking life every time she smiled.

She wasn't doing that nearly enough here in Maine.

"We have a family, right?" Jordyn asked.

Lucian's brow furrowed. "I'm sorry?"

"Your brothers and mother and father," Jordyn clarified. "We have a family."

"We do."

"And they love me."

"All the way around the world and back," Lucian agreed.

Because she loved him.

Because she made him happy.

Because she settled and grounded him like no one else ever could.

She wasn't Italian.

She hadn't been fully Catholic.

She didn't have pedigree or money.

She wasn't what the rest of the world would consider acceptable for a man of his status to marry, but she was perfect for the only people who mattered in his life.

The Marcellos.

"We're going home," Lucian said. "Tomorrow, we'll start the drive back to New York."

Jordyn blinked up at him. "But we still have a couple of—"

"I know, but you're not happy here, Jordyn. It's killing me. I want to take you home to people who love you."

Jordyn smiled. "You love me."

"More than you know, bella. Home?"

"Home."

*

"Thanks for meeting up with me this morning," Lucian said.

Roland nodded once. "No problem. The best thing about retirement is not needing to make plans every day for something."

"I wouldn't know."

"You're still young. You've got years of work ahead of you."

Lucian chuckled. "Something like that."

"Where's Jordyn?" Roland asked.

Lucian's expression turned passive. "She's packing up the rest of our things at the hotel. We'll be heading back home before noon. I wanted to let you know, which was why I asked you to meet me for coffee."

Surprise and sadness colored Roland's features. "But I thought—"

Lucian held up a single hand, interrupting the man. "I get it isn't you, Roland. As far as that goes, I understand you made an effort. You invited us here, you spent time with her. I know you care, but for some reason—namely your wife, but I'm not the kind of man who throws stones—you're unwilling to go any further or try with Jordyn. And that's just fucking sad. She wasn't asking for much when she came here. She wasn't even asking for a father figure. She simply wanted to know you and your family. Something that would make her a little happier.

"That woman is absolutely everything to me," Lucian continued, his voice darkening with his anger. "Everything. She is the only thing on my mind in the morning and before I go to bed. So when something that should be good for her hurts her, you can bet I'll take notice and stop it before it can take another chunk. You've taken enough. We'll be on our way."

Roland took a moment before he spoke again, like he was trying to gather his thoughts or something. "I do love her."

"I would hope so. You made her, after all."

"I'm glad she has someone like you."

Lucian laughed darkly. "Well, be happy she has someone who loves her. Someone like me is an entirely different matter."

Roland shrugged as he rested back into his chair, unbothered. "No, I said it as I meant it. I have access to the internet, Lucian Marcello. You're not the only person capable of doing a search on someone, as far as that goes. I didn't tell my wife the kinds of things you and your family are rumored to be involved in—it would only have set her on edge further. The motorcycle gang was enough where Jordyn was concerned."

"She didn't choose that," Lucian growled.

"I know. The fact remains, you are who you are. I'm glad."

"Why?"

Wouldn't most fathers want their children with a safe man?

"I suppose," Roland drawled, "because you know how to keep what's yours, don't you? That's the whole point of your ... business."

"Something like that," Lucian agreed.

Roland pulled out his wallet and flipped it open. He turned it for Lucian to see a picture of a dark haired, blue-eyed baby smiling back at the person taking the picture.

"I keep her close," Roland said. "I have always kept her close."

"I keep her closer," Lucian replied quietly.

"I hope so." Roland replaced his wallet and asked, "Would you send me an update from time to time? About her or whatever is going on in your life? I'd like to know."

"You have a phone," Lucian replied.

"And I'll use it whenever she wants me to. But I need her to use it first. From a distance, it'll be better. I might not agree with my wife on her opinions and actions, but I have two other children to think about, too. I don't want them to grow up separated from me like Jordyn did, so I make my wife happy however I can."

"I can't understand that, or empathize."

"You don't have to."

"I'll see what I can do," Lucian said.

"Thank you."

*

"Ugh," Jordyn grumbled, tossing her purse onto the bed.

Lucian walked out of their master bath with a grin. "Tired, bella?"

"Exhausted. No more road trips. Not anytime soon."

"You like driving."

"I do … but this time was just too long."

Or maybe it was something else.

"Come have a bath. I'll draw it for you."

Jordyn made a face as she fell back to the bed. "Can I sleep instead?"

"After you have a bath and relax."

"Sleeping is relaxing."

Lucian pursed his lips, holding back his knowing smile. "Jordyn, get in the damn bathroom."

Pushing up to her elbows, Jordyn eyed Lucian with a quirked brow and annoyance writing lines on her pretty features. "Excuse me?"

"I promise something good if you just listen and play along."

"Play along, huh?"

"Mmhmm," he hummed.

Sighing dramatically, Jordyn pushed up from the bed and kicked off her heels. "You're impossible."

"I am fucking wonderful."

"That, too." Jordyn pushed past him in the doorway to the bathroom. "And you better make sure there's lots of bubbles, Lucian, or I swear to—"

Lucian turned, watching his wife's gaze fall on the pregnancy test on the counter.

"Oh," Jordyn whispered.

"Oh, is that all?"

"Well …"

"Well?" he pressed.

Speechless was a good look on Jordyn.

Lucian laughed as she kept staring at the test, lost for words. "Take it. I'll wait outside."

"Take it," she echoed.

"Are you …. Okay with this?"

Jordyn nodded slowly. "I think so. Just surprised, mostly. Really?"

"Yeah. Things were adding up."

She glanced up to the ceiling, her lips moving silently. "Things add up."

"We've been busy."

"So busy."

"I'm happy," Lucian informed. "In case you were wondering. I am more than happy."

"I didn't wonder," she replied. "I know you want children."

"But if it's a boy—"

"We'll name him Johnathan," she interrupted quietly.

Yeah, perfect.

She was perfect for him.

Their life was like a home, he realized. Walls from the past, present, and what would be had already set them up. They were just starting to make their own.

New walls.

This was just another one to hold them strong.

TINY MARKS

"You're not serious," Lucian said, his hand resting against the wall as Jordyn jiggled the handle for the upstairs bathroom. "Bella, tell me you're not serious."

Jordyn flicked him with a look. "Is this something you think I would joke about?"

Well ...

Not really.

Dio, he hoped not.

"Didn't we use shit for this? Or, you got that weird looking thing put in a few years back, right?"

"Sometimes, they fail. Besides, this could have been avoided had you just went in and got—"

"Not happening," Lucian interrupted his wife quietly. "No one goes near that area but you and me."

Jordyn smirked, shook her head, and then pulled a bobby pin from her hair to poke inside the lock on the doorknob. Their two daughters had a terrible habit of locking themselves in the bathroom for however long they felt was necessary to feel like they'd done their faces and hair up for the day.

At eleven and nine-years-old, his daughters Cella and Liliana were without a doubt, two of the most diva-like females Lucian had ever come across. They could throw a right tantrum, they knew fashion like nobody else, and they scared the hell out of him on a daily basis. They were the proper Marcello principessas.

And Lucian didn't know how to handle that.

He figured at their ages, and with their kids being as old as they were, any more kids were out of the question. Besides, he had two daughters and one son. They kept trying after Cella was born just to see if they would have another boy. Then Liliana came along.

Lucian was terrified of having another girl. Another woman to grow up and have boys chasing after her. Another little girl with eyes of la famiglia all on her and her family, waiting to see who she would choose, or if her family would choose a husband for her. Another daughter for Lucian to give away.

Jordyn managed to jiggle the lock just right and pop the door open. "All right, girls, that's enough."

"Jordyn, wait for a sec—"

Lucian found the bathroom door being closed in his face. Girlish giggles answered him from the inside.

"Hush," Jordyn muttered. "Cella, if you're done, get out and go downstairs to eat."

"But, Ma—"

"You're going to be late," Jordyn said to their daughter. "And who in the hell are you trying to impress with all that makeup on, anyway? You know what, we're washing that off. Liliana, get out."

Makeup?

Makeup!

Lucian's mind had completely forgotten about the bomb Jordyn dropped on him when he heard that. He allowed Cella and Liliana to do their hair however they wanted, wear whatever clothes they preferred as long as it was appropriate for their age, and even have a little lip balm and eye shadow if it was neutral and simple.

But full-out makeup?

Hell no!

Lucian banged his fist on the door. "Wash it off right now, Cella!"

His daughter laughed.

So did his wife.

Even Liliana was smirking like she knew the hell going on inside her father's head when she stepped out of the bathroom in a pink dress with her dark curls pulled back into a neat braid.

"Hi, Daddy," Liliana said, grinning.

Lucian looked her over for makeup. There was none. Jordyn slammed the door closed before he could get a peek at Cella.

Goddammit.

"I'm hungry," Liliana informed.

"Me, too," Lucian grumbled.

"Get a move on cooking, then," Jordyn said, her voice muffled. "Or nobody will eat anything."

"We have things to talk about, Jordyn," Lucian replied.

"Not right now we don't."

Fine.

*

Lucian's hand smacked the back of his thirteen-year-old son's head when John tried to sneak a cigarette from the pack inside Lucian's suit jacket hanging off the dining room chair. He'd just walked into the dining room and his son hadn't heard or seen him approach.

John rubbed at the back of his head, glaring at his father while Lucian crossed the space to enter the kitchen. "What the hell, Papa?"

"Don't smoke. It's bad for your lungs."

Jesus, he had to put a stop to John's bad behavior before it got out of hand. Smoking was just one thing. John also had sticky fingers when it came to vehicles, liquor, and any cash his father left lying around. Antony liked to call his grandson a rebel—one that didn't have much of a cause. Dante called his heir to the Marcello thrown a little difficult and looking for a reason to be who he was. Giovanni called his nephew and Godson a kid, one Lucian needed to take a step back from and let John make his mistakes.

Lucian wasn't sure if he agreed with any of them.

John was just ... John.

Liliana skipped at her father's side, her little hand tugging on his arm the whole way. "I want waffles."

"That's going to take forever to make," Lucian argued.

"But I want them."

"Lili—"

"Pancakes then?"

That took just as much time.

At the sight of his daughter's pleading little blue eyes looking up at him, Lucian caved.

He was so weak when it came to his daughters.

So weak.

"Fine," Lucian muttered. "Pancakes it is."

"You smoke," John said when he sauntered into the kitchen.

Lucian was already working on pulling shit out of the cupboards. "Your point?"

"You know my point."

"That's not a good argument, John."

"Why can't I smoke if you do it?" his son asked.

"Because I said no and your mother gives me enough shit about smoking as it is."

"Bad language," Liliana said in a sing-song fashion as she pulled syrup from the fridge.

"Five bucks in my wallet on the inside pocket of my suit jacket," Lucian said, waving his daughter off.

Liliana practically danced out of the room in search of her hush money.

"Can I come with you today?" John asked.

Lucian side-eyed his son. "You have school."

"It's just a day, Dad."

"School is important, Johnathan."

"What am I ever going to use it for, though?" his son asked, crossing his arms and leaning against the entryway wall. "I'm going for something else and there's nothing inside the walls of that school that's teaching me anything that I need to know for the streets, right?"

His son was far too quick for his own good.

Nothing was hidden in their family. Lucian's status as the underboss to his brother in their crime family wasn't off-limits to his children. It was hard to hide those kinds of things when their names were commonplace in New York, the internet was readily available, Lucian had spent some time behind bars for weapons and assault charges relating to the mafia, and his son was a boy.

Maybe everything else could have been brushed off.

Not with John being a boy.

"I finished high-school top ten in my class," Lucian informed quietly.

John cocked a brow. "So?"

"I graduated college Cum Laude, son."

"I don't get it."

"No?"

"Nope," John said.

"Then maybe you need a few more years of school to catch up to speed, son."

John's gaze narrowed. "That's really un-fucking-fair."

"Watch your mouth."

"You don't."

"John, listen to me. I managed to graduate high school and then college with honors and all the while, I was still involved in the family. I still got my button. I worked my ass off. You're not going to get this life handed to you, kid."

"But—"

Lucian held a hand up, stopping his son. "But nothing. I don't care what any of the ass kissers on the streets tell you when you're hanging around with those cafones you seem to like so much. They don't know a goddamn thing. You might carry the Marcello name, but you're going to earn your right to have it, John. Mark my damned words, you will earn it."

Liliana walked back into the kitchen with a scowl. "There is no money in your wallet, Daddy."

Lucian turned away from the stove, facing his son. "John?"

John pulled out the missing five-dollar bill and handed it to his sister without another word.

Lucian wasn't surprised.

*

"Okay, okay, bye, bye," Jordyn muttered, turning around to give Liliana a kiss on the forehead before their youngest daughter climbed out of the SUV.

Cella was too quick for her mother. She got out without the kiss.

Once the doors were closed, Jordyn heaved a sigh. "Long morning, Lucian."

With three kids?

Yes, it was.

"John gave me hell again," Lucian informed.

Jordyn frowned. "Is it only going to get worse the older he gets?"

"Probably."

And the kid reminded Lucian of Giovanni when his youngest brother was just a teen.

"I think he has a girlfriend," Jordyn said, buckling her seat belt as Lucian pulled away from the drop off at the private school.

John went to another school with his cousin Andino. Giovanni usually picked John up in the morning and took his Godson over with Andino.

Lucian didn't know what in the hell he was going to do when he had even less control over his son than he did right now. How would it be when John could drive, had his own vehicle, or God forbid, began getting access to the trust funds his dead biological grandfather had left for him that Lucian wasn't allowed to have any say in?

"A girlfriend is the least of my worries," Lucian admitted.

"What if Liliana had a little boyfriend?"

Lucian's hands clenched so hard around the steering wheel that his knuckles turned white. "That's not even funny."

Jordyn snorted. "Kind of funny."

"Stop it, bella donna."

"Fine. Maybe a girlfriend will cool him down."

"Or maybe he's thirteen and needs to get his di—"

"Finish that sentence and I will bust your mouth, Lucian."

Lucian shut up.

"Will you talk to him?" Jordyn asked.

"About what?"

"You know, condoms and things."

Lucian glowered at the road ahead of him. "I already have."

"And?"

"And he's got a pack in his book bag and a smaller one in his dresser. Plus, he knows where to find mine."

Jordyn did not look pleased about that fact. "Lucian, that's essentially giving him permission to go out and have sex."

"No, it's not acting like a blind fool, Jordyn. It's realizing my son is more likely to have sex because he's been exposed to a different lifestyle. It's knowing that when he does, he has more than enough access to stuff to keep him safe. I'm not going to lie down and play dumb, all right. Do that if you want, but I won't."

"He's just a kid."

"Gio was fourteen the first time he had sex," Lucian blurted out.

Jordyn's brow rose high. "Really?"

"Yes. I was fifteen, so was Dante."

"Jesus Christ."

"Do you want to know how old the woman was that Gio messed around with?"

Jordyn's brow furrowed. "Woman?"

"Yeah, woman, not a teenaged girl. A woman. Do you want to know?"

"Not really."

"Well, I'll tell you anyway. She was twenty-four. It might as well have been somebody using him for things he didn't even really understand at the time. Some people would call it rape, but Gio won't. He got sex—he knew that. But he was hanging around someone who didn't look out for him and the woman thought he was an easy way in to the Capo who was looking out for Gio at the time. So yeah, Jordyn, I won't play dumb just because it makes you uncomfortable."

Jordyn made a noise under her breath. "Okay."

Lucian sighed, rubbing at his forehead. "I'll talk to John again."

"Okay."

Taking a turn-off into a drive thru for a Starbucks, Jordyn glanced over at Lucian.

"What?" he asked, seeing the question in her eyes.

"It wasn't like that for you, right?"

"My first fuck, you mean?"

Jordyn scowled. "You're so crass."

"You asked."

"Whatever. Was it?"

"No. It was messy and fast and full of fumbling and laughter. She was the same age as me, it happened in the dark, under the covers, and in a bed. Pretty normal, considering everything."

"Considering everything?"

Lucian coughed, feeling more uncomfortable than ever. "Well, her father was a Capo and all. Probably wasn't smart of me to be messing around with her."

Jordyn laughed.

"What?" Lucian asked.

"So really, John gets his nonsense from you. You were just better at hiding it than Giovanni was."

Lucian didn't grace that with a response.

*

"Well, what's the news?" Lucian asked his wife.

Jordyn tossed her purse to the bed, rolling her eyes. "Give me five minutes to settle in. I just got all the kids home from school, Lucian. No stress. This is relaxing time."

"Jordyn, I've been dying all day."

His wife made a face, her nose scrunching up. "If I was, would you be okay with it?"

"I thought we were done," Lucian admitted. "We said we were done."

"Apparently, we're not."

Not.

Because she was.

Pregnant, that was.

Lucian fell back on the bed. "Yeah?"

Jordyn nodded, smiling slightly. "Apparently. Just about nine weeks, according to the scan."

"Shit."

"You don't sound happy."

"I am," Lucian assured.

Of course, he was.

His life was full of marks. The biggest ones, he'd made himself and Jordyn had cut a few of her own into him, too. The smallest ones, the tiny ones, had come from his children. There were far more marks on his life and soul from his children than from anyone else. He loved those marks. He wore them with pride.

He didn't mind a few more.

"But?" Jordyn asked.

"I told you, I'm happy."

"But?"

"But … God isn't going to give me anymore boys, Jordyn."

"You don't know that."

Lucian knew.

He knew.

John was all he could handle.

"We'll call her Lucia."

Jordyn lifted a single brow high. "Oh?"

"Yeah, I think so."

"Lucia it is."

WAITING GAME

Jordyn wouldn't look at him.

She wouldn't talk to him.

She blamed him.

Lucian didn't need to have his wife say the words for him to know.

She blamed him for this ...

For Johnathan's kidnapping.

Lucian was three seconds away from burning down New York to find his only child. He was barely keeping control of his emotions and he couldn't fucking breathe. One of the reasons he did breathe was somewhere out in the city in the hands of people who cared nothing for his child, nothing except to use the boy to hurt his family.

Lucian's fingernails bit into his palms the harder he squeezed. He could feel them break the skin and blood pool at the wounds.

He didn't feel the pain.

He didn't feel the sting.

He barely even blinked when a skinny red line dribbled down his life line on his hand.

Nothing.

Lucian needed Jordyn to talk to him. He needed the strong, forgiving, loving wife he married to show herself and reassure him. He needed her support to be his cornerstone in the hurricane that was his mind and heart in that moment.

She gave him nothing.

"Jordyn—"

His wife stood from the couch and left the room before Lucian could get another word in edgewise.

She didn't realize it, but that only pissed him off.

Not at her, but the whole situation.

Lucian was raving mad and getting worse by the second.

"Jordyn!" Lucian shouted after her.

The slam of a door answered him back.

Wait for her, his mind whispered.

Lucian didn't have the sense to listen.

*

He wanted to fucking kill her.

Wrap his hands around her throat and squeeze the very life out of her body.

Make her bleed.

Make it goddamn well hurt.

God ...

She deserved it.

The more Dante explained about Catrina and her involvement with Johnathan's current predicament, the angrier Lucian got. Until his blood turned too hot to be inside his body and his thoughts were practically incoherent.

He wanted to kill his sister-in-law.

And when Catrina got home after being questioned by police ... when Lucian's brother stepped between him and that woman to stop Lucian from doing what every inch of him begged to do ... Lucian wanted to scream.

He might have wanted to hurt his brother, too.

This was his son.

His son!

Dante kicked him out instead.

Lucian understood why.

*

"Where are you?" Lucian demanded.

"I'm not telling you that."

Lucian rubbed at the throbbing headache beginning to form in his temples. It'd been like that, beating and pulsing, promising a hell of a lot of pain, from the very moment he had heard his son had been taken. Nothing made it go away.

"Gio, for Cristo's sake—"

"Lucian, let me do my fucking job," his brother interrupted sharply. "Let me talk to some people, let me see some friends, let me act normal. Do you think it'll help any to get your crazy ass on these streets right now, demanding answers and threatening people when you get nothing?"

Lucian opened his mouth to speak.

Giovanni beat him to the punch. "No, asshole, it won't. You're not in the right frame of mind to do this kind of thing properly. People will react better to someone they won't find threatening just by looking them in the eye. You're not here right now, Lucian, you're somewhere else entirely."

Why did his family keep pushing him out of this, like they didn't want him directly involved in this situation? Didn't they realize there was no choice there? He had to be involved.

"My son—"

"Let me do my job."

Giovanni hung up the phone.

Angrier and more frustrated than ever, Lucian was overwhelmed by his emotions. He was known for being in control. He could handle any situation. He could be cold, callous, and cruel with a look and a word.

He'd been a killer ever since he bashed in the skull of a well-dressed man who'd tried to molest him when he'd been living on the streets and saw him as an easy target. He knew death. He understood pain.

Others, mostly.

His was not the same.

Before Lucian had even realized what happened, he'd smashed his iPhone into the steering wheel of the Lexus until it was beaten into bits and pieces.

Shattered pieces.

Like his mind and soul.

A sharp piece of the screen cut his hand when he smashed it into the steering wheel again. Blood flowed from the wound, staining the white leather and carpeting inside his vehicle. Physically, he felt nothing. Emotionally, he was stricken and useless.

Lucian didn't give a damn.

His blood was okay to spill.

His son's was not.

Where was little John?

*

Lucian found himself in a comforting place. It was a place he spent a lot of time in, a familiar place where mornings and afternoons of his life had been dedicated to. A place he'd never sought out before for solace simply because he felt there was nowhere else to go. There was always somewhere else.

Not tonight.

Pushing open the main doors of the church, Lucian was assaulted by the scent of oils, burning candles and the old musk of wooden pews and silent prayers. The congregation hall was dark, lit only by the lights at the altar and the flickering flames of candles.

Nothing more.

Father Peter turned in the front pew, far away from where Lucian stood, to see who had entered the sacred place at such a late time.

Lucian didn't move when the Priest's gaze met his. The man stood, moving gracefully into the aisle and down toward Lucian.

"I'm sorry," Lucian whispered when he knew the Priest was close enough to hear, "I shouldn't have just barged in here tonight."

Father Peter's brow rose. "Lucian, these doors are always open."

So he'd been told.

Repeatedly.

"Has something happened?" the Priest asked.

Lucian nodded, but didn't speak.

"What do you need, Lucian?"

"I need him back," Lucian said.

"Hmm?"

"I need him back—I need Him to give him back to me."

Rambling words that made no sense fell from Lucian. The Priest handled it in stride.

"Do you want to sit?"

"No," Lucian said.

"Stand then?"

Lucian nodded once.

"Then I'll stand with you."

"I need Him to give him back to me," Lucian repeated.

God had given him everything else.

Family.

Happiness.

Money.

Success.

Love.

His child.

Lucian stared at the large wooden cross hanging beyond the altar. "Please give him back to me."

*

Lucian felt terrible as he unlocked the front door to his home. At four in the morning, the street was still dark and the sky was still sleeping with twinkling stars. He wondered what his son was seeing. It sure as hell wasn't the large, colorful mural on his wall, painted by his grandfather and uncle. It wasn't the soft bear John liked to call Butter because it looked like the bear on the peanut butter jar. And it wasn't his mother and father, who played and talked and sang to the boy until he was too tired to keep his eyes open.

People said Lucian and Jordyn spoiled John.

Loving a child wasn't spoiling them.

The house was quiet as he stepped inside and closed the door. Without bothering to kick off his shoes or take his coat off, Lucian followed the silence to an empty living room, kitchen, and dining room. The downstairs was devoid of light, sound, and his wife.

Lucian's heart fell and little further into his stomach.

He'd come home because he'd realized far too late that with his phone damaged and rendered unusable, his wife and family had no proper way of contacting him.

Mostly Jordyn, though.

Lucian was still pissed at Giovanni for not letting him question people on the streets. Lucian still wanted to kill Catrina.

As for Dante, Lucian still wanted to kick his ass, too.

"Jordyn?" Lucian called up the stairs.

His voice came out hoarse and tired.

His steps were sluggish and slow.

He wouldn't sleep until his son was home. His exhaustion mattered little. Lucian had long ago taught himself how to ignore his need for sleep when his nights were plagued with dreams he'd rather not relive.

"Jordyn," Lucian said again when he was closer to the stairs.

Still, nothing answered him back.

Lucian briefly wondered if his wife had left, but he quickly pushed the idea away. His father had taken his mother out of the city without much notice to Cecelia as a way to keep her from finding out something had happened to John. Giovanni had Kim set up in a hotel for the night, safely tucked away from any chance of harm.

There was Dante and Catrina, but Jordyn wasn't likely to go over there after everything.

Surely she wouldn't.

Jordyn didn't have a lot of friends. Neither did Lucian, really. The couple tended to stick close to one another. They were each other's best friends and their family filled in the friendships they might find in outsiders if they looked for them.

They didn't have to look.

They had enough now.

Lucian followed the soft glow of light filtering down the upstairs hallway. It streamed out from beneath John's nursery door. Pushing open the door, Lucian found his wife sitting with her back resting against Johnathan's crib. Awake but looking like she was ready to fall over, Jordyn blinked up at Lucian.

"I'm sorry," she said.

Lucian stilled in place. "For what?"

"Earlier."

"Don't be."

Jordyn shook her head, tears slipping from the corners of her eyes and making tracks down her cheeks. "No, I—"

"Don't be," Lucian interrupted softly. "You were right."

"I didn't say anything."

"You didn't have to."

Jordyn swallowed hard. "I wasn't right."

It felt like she was.

He took all the blame for this.

His life put his son in this place.

Jordyn reached out a hand and Lucian took a few steps forward before catching in with his own. Squatting down, he tugged his wife into his embrace and buried his face into her messy curls.

Home.

Love.

Safe.

"We'll find him," Lucian assured.

Jordyn hugged him tighter. "Do you want me to say it to you, too?"

"Yes," he admitted.

"We'll find him, Lucian."

The final straw fell and his back broke. This waiting game was a killer.

He was just one of the victims. Lucian didn't know how to be a victim. He'd sure been labeled one a long time ago, but he never felt that way before. He didn't know how to do this—be helpless.

So, he cried.

THE CHAT

Johnathan ignored the banging on his bedroom door, and continued to stare out the window where someone had left his curtains opened.

"Get up, John!"

His mother kept hammering.

John kept staring.

The snow was coming down in heavy flakes, now. Not that it fucking mattered. Usually, he liked winter, and the holidays. Christmas was right around the corner, which meant presents, and time with his family. He kind of liked that, too.

Except not so much this year.

Not at all.

"John!"

He thought to shout back at his mother, to tell her to leave him the hell alone, but didn't bother to even open his mouth. It wouldn't do him any good, really. And he knew the truth—his mother was having just as rough of a time as the rest of the people in his house.

Maybe more so.

It was just his dad in jail, after all.

It was her husband.

John rolled to his back when his mother finally stopped beating on his door, and stared up at the ceiling. He kind of wished it would swallow him whole, and then maybe he wouldn't have to deal with the day at all. Not his mother who looked sad all the time, or his sisters who constantly asked for their dad, or when Lucian was coming home.

He hated the way the teachers at school knew about his problems at home without even needing to be told. So was the way of their life—being a crime family had downfalls. Like your fucking business being all over the goddamn news.

People knew.

John didn't like it.

It was only when his full bladder made itself known did John

63

finally push out of bed, and pad into the connecting bathroom. Like his bedroom, the bathroom was dark, too.

He preferred it like that.

Didn't like the light.

Especially not in the mornings.

Once he was done in the bathroom, he shot a glance at the alarm clock on his nightstand only to see why his mother had been so constant on trying to get him up. He forgot to set it again—they were probably going to be late for school again.

Oh, well.

So, he'd miss homeroom.

Big deal.

It was only the sound of his mother's voice in the hallway—and not yelling for him—that made John edge closer to his bedroom door.

"Okay, that was a little sad," he heard his mother say.

John's brow furrowed.

Who was she talking to?

Definitely not one of his little sisters.

And then John heard, "Let's not do that, Lucian."

He knew, then.

His dad.

She was talking to his dad.

John didn't even think about the fact he really just wanted to hide away in his bedroom for as long as he possibly could anymore. Not when the chance to talk to his father was practically dangling in front of his face. He didn't get to talk to his dad nearly enough since Lucian had gotten arrested, and hauled off to jail.

Damn, John hated cops.

Especially for taking his dad away.

Pushing open the bedroom door, John moved into the hallway behind his mother who was holding Cella under her arm, and the phone in her other hand.

"Hey," he said, "that's Dad?"

His mother spun fast on her heel to face him, making Cella's head full of curls spin in every direction. The relief in his mother's eyes when her gaze landed on him kind of made John feel like crap. Or maybe that was guilt.

It was all interchangeable, he was learning.

Maybe he shouldn't have given her such a hard time about getting up. And maybe ... just maybe ... he had been giving his mother a hard time ever since his dad got taken away. It wasn't really that John meant to do that to his ma, but ... everything sucked.

He missed his dad.

All the time.

"It is," his ma said. "Do you want to talk to him?"

John's father must have said something to his ma, because Jordyn said into the phone, "It's all right, we have tomorrow."

She handed the phone over, and John didn't hesitate to snatch it from her grasp. As soon as he had the phone in his hand, he darted back into the safe darkness of his room. Before he could shut the door, though, he heard his mother call something else after him.

"Make sure you're dressed before you hang up that phone, John."

"Got it, Ma," he called back.

Then, he let his door slam.

John put the phone to his ear, but he didn't move to the dresser or the large closet that was practically another small room to get dressed. Instead, he pressed his back to the door, and put the phone to his ear. He swore his father must have heard him breathing because no sooner had he done that, then his father started talking.

"I miss you, my boy," Lucian said.

John frowned. "Miss you, too, Papa."

"You're being good for your mother, right?"

He didn't want to lie.

He didn't want his dad to be pissed, either.

"Kind of," John settled on saying.

"You gotta be good for her, John," Lucian said. "She's all alone right now, and trying to deal with all of you on her own. So, give her a little bit of a break, huh? Be good to your sisters, and eat your fucking vegetables. Whatever it takes. She wants you to do something you don't want to do, then you just do it and give her a damn smile. And do you know why you do that?"

John sniffed a bit. "No."

"Because you're her son—her only son, John. She's not ever going to have another, and certainly not one like you. You were the first baby she ever got to hold, and love. Do you think she wants that boy of hers to give her trouble all the damn time?"

"Probably not."

"Exactly. Be good for her, all right?"

"All right," John mumbled.

"I'm sorry," his father added after a moment.

"For what?"

"Being here, I guess. In here, and not there. First Christmas without me, and I bet you're feeling it, too."

To say the least … John didn't say that out loud. He didn't want to hurt his father, either.

"I know you're having a hard time with all of this, John," Lucian added. "With me not being home, I mean."

"A little," John agreed.

"But I will be soon."

"Not soon enough," he mumbled.

Lucian chuckled. "Yeah, it's never going to be soon enough, I know."

"Miss you, Papa."

He'd already told him that. He figured he should say it again.

"Love you, my boy," Lucian countered.

John smiled. "Yeah, that, too. I guess."

Lucian scoffed. "You wound me, son."

"Only a little, though."

"And don't you ever change, either."

Never.

FOR LOVE

"Daddy?"

"Hmm, yes?"

Lucian glanced down to find his six-year-old, Lucia, grinning up at him in that sweet way of hers. A way that reminded him *so much* of her mother. More than she, or even Jordyn, would ever know. Sure, Lucia looked a lot like him, too, and she was his namesake until the very end. He made sure of that. She took his eye color, her hair was all him, too—*damn*, he was sorry for those unruly curls—and even some of her attitude was definitely right from his own mouth.

But her sweet nature?

All that kindness?

Every part of her that was good?

It all came from Jordyn.

And thank God for that.

"Nothin'," Lucia said, still smiling that toothy, girlish smile of hers. "Just wanted to say I love you."

His hand tightened around hers as they continued walking down the Manhattan street. Him in his three-piece suit, and her in her pretty pink dress and stark white shoes with the *very* small heel. She had to have shoes like her ma, after all.

Someday, she was going to stop letting him hold her hand or even picking her up to carry her across a busy street. Someday, she'd stop looking up at him just to tell him that she loved him at the most random of times.

Someday, she would be older.

Different.

He'd miss these days. And God knew he made lots of time to have these days with each of his four children. A day once a week that was spent just on them. Maybe it was an evening—a movie on the weekend, or even lunch at their favorite place. It didn't matter. As long as he was spending quality time with one of his kids, that's what counted.

But he'd *really* love the new days they would have, too.

"I love you, too, Lucia," he murmured. "Always."

"Can we stop at *The Shop*?"

"They don't even have clothes for little girls there. That's for big girls like ma."

"Yeah, but, *please?*"

Lord.

He did not know how to tell his kid no.

"Yeah, we'll stop. See if we can find something for you."

"And if we can't?"

Lucian grinned down at his girl. "Then, we'll find something to bring home to Ma."

"*Yas!*"

Lucian made sure to keep his promise to his daughter, but then again, he always did. It was the one thing he wanted all his children to be able to count on where he was concerned. It didn't matter what he promised to them—he *would* make it happen.

He was their dad.

Dads never failed.

His never did.

After they'd gotten Lucia's gelato, stopped at *The Shop*—which they ended up finding something for Lucia *and* Jordyn—Lucian buckled his youngest daughter into her booster seat while the sky started to darken overhead. By the time he got on the highway and headed home, he bet Lucia would already be asleep. If she was tired, she could barely stand to stay awake in a moving vehicle. It was sweet, really.

All over again, like earlier in the day, his tired little girl looked up at him with her wide eyes that matched his but a face that matched her mother's and asked, "Daddy?"

"Hmm, yes?"

"What's that one for?"

"What do you mean?"

Lucia reached out and grabbed his hand in her much smaller one. Before he really understood what she wanted or was doing, she flipped his hand over and then pointed with her tiny index finger at the black heart—smaller than a penny—tattooed on the inside of his palm.

As Lucian had gotten older, he tattooed his body less and less. Instead, he found himself maintaining the tattoos he loved the most, or otherwise, covering ones he wished he had never gotten in the first place.

"This one—the little heart," Lucia said. "What's it for? Your wings are like Uncle Dante and Gio's, right?"

Lucian grinned. "Something like theirs, yes."

"Did you just like hearts, Daddy?"

Kids, man.

So innocent.

"It's where I hold my love the safest," he told his girl, "right in the palm of my hand."

She peered up at him. "Oh."

Once, a long time ago, Jordyn asked Lucian why he didn't have a tattoo for love. So, he got one. And there, in the palm of his hand, he kept it safe.

Lucia bent down and kissed the little heart.

Lucian kissed the top of her head.

"Love you, Daddy."

"Love you, Lucia."

THE KIDS

"Absolutely *not*."

"But *why*, Daddy? Aren't I pretty?"

Lucian pressed his lips together, and glanced sideways to catch his wife's eye from across the kitchen table. How did one tell their eight year old that, *no*, she didn't look pretty after getting into her mother's makeup—for the *tenth* time, at least—and hell to the fuck no, she would not be going to school the next day looking like a clown.

His mother had once told him that fathers were the first defense in their daughter's lives. The men they watched around them set the tones for the rest of their lives. How they treated their little girls could affect *so much*. He tried to remember that in times like these, referring back to his ma's statement as a reminder, but also as a reference.

He didn't think *this* fell into that category of things he shouldn't say, but as he didn't grow up with sisters, he wasn't a female, and he sure as fuck didn't wear makeup, he wasn't sure what he should say. Instead, he looked to his wife for help.

Jordyn stayed stone-faced.

Because *of course*.

He hoped she saw the pleading in his eyes.

The *terror*.

And that she was happy.

"Daddy?"

Lucian let out a sigh, and turned to face his daughter. Leaning down a bit so the two of them could be pretty much eye-level, he said, "You always look pretty—*always*."

Liliana beamed.

"But you can't wear that to school, and you need to go wash it off your face."

"*But why?*"

"Pimples."

Lucian glanced up as his fourteen year old son waltzed into the kitchen when he was supposed to be upstairs studying. But as he just helped his father, likely knowing it too, he chose not to tell his son to get his ass back upstairs.

"*What?*" Liliana gasped.

She was a good five years or so away from even having to *worry* about a fucking pimple … but John was in full blown puberty, which meant his younger sisters got to see him battle with all the fun shit that came along with it.

Liliana's greatest fear?

Pimples.

Putting her fists to her hips, Liliana turned to face her brother who was currently heading for the fridge—*fuck*, he never stopped eating. *Ever.* Like never. Lucian couldn't remember if he and his brothers had ate as much and as often as his son did, but he made a mental note to ask his mother, eventually.

"Why would wearing makeup give me pimples?" Liliana demanded.

"Well, 'cause if you don't wash it off your face, and give your skin time to breathe, I guess. Ask Ma," John said, shrugging, "she wears makeup all the damn time."

"Language," Lucian muttered.

"I don't wear it *all* the time," Jordyn said.

"*Okay.*"

"Ma!" Liliana swung on her mother in all her eight year old glory, looking like someone had just betrayed her, and she would *never* forgive them. "Is that true?"

"Well," Jordyn drawled.

"I am *never* wearing makeup!"

Just like that, Liliana spun on her heels, and stormed out of the room muttering something about washing her face *right now*. Lucian managed to keep a straight face until his third child was gone from his sight before a slow, sly grin spread over his face, and he turned back around in his chair at the table. Across the way, Jordyn simply shook her head.

"Battle won," he said.

Jordyn nodded. "For now."

He lost that smile.

Fuck.

*

"I mean, it's not that hard to just *tell* the boy, right?" Cella asked.

"That'll make him stop, won't it? She should just tell him she doesn't like him, that's all."

Lucian glanced over at his oldest daughter of the three—out of all his kids, Cella, at ten, looked *most* like her mother. And already, she was all arms and legs, with a long torso that told him she had taken *his* height. Same with her sister, really.

The last thing any man wanted to be doing at eight at night was listening to a ten year old girl gossip about her friends, but Lucian didn't mind. Sometimes, these chats were all he got out of his kids, but especially his girls as they got older. It seemed like he blinked once, and overnight, his kids just turned into *mini people*. If that made sense. With lives and interests of their own, and only occasionally was he let inside their tiny worlds.

Like at night.

Now.

Before they went to sleep.

"You know," Lucian said, "if that's how he shows that he likes her, by pulling her hair and taking her things ... that's now a very good way to like someone, right?"

Cella made a face. "No, I guess not."

"I mean, you wouldn't hit me or Ma to tell us you love us, would you?"

"*No.*"

Lucian nodded. "So, we shouldn't let other people do bad things to us, just so they can say it means they care about us. That isn't how it works. It's a bad excuse for people to do mean things, that's all, Cella."

She nodded.

"And your friend," Lucian added, climbing out of his daughter's large canopy bed so she could finally go to sleep under her white and pink blankets, "should let her own daddy know that some boy is doing things he shouldn't."

Cella peered up at him. "I'll tell her."

"And you'll me, won't you? If someone acts that way with you?"

"I *will.*"

Lucian smiled, pleased with that answer, and the conversation as whole. With kids whose minds were easily distracted, and prone to jumping from one thing to the next before they even absorbed what they had just been told, he figured they needed to have these conversations with their kids, but especially his daughters.

Again and again and again.

Until they remembered.

Until they *got it.*

"Night, Daddy," Cella said, rolling over in her bed, "love you."

"*Ti amo, principessa.*"

He closed her bedroom door without a click, heading past Liliana's which was already closed, and hopefully ... if he was lucky enough, she was asleep after their storytime an hour ago. Down the hall, he turned to head into his youngest child's room just to check. Lucia went to bed, no excuses, at seven every night. She should already be asleep, but he just wanted to make sure.

Pushing the crack in the door wider, he found the light was spilling out into the hallway from the lamp set up next to her toddler bed. Lucia wasn't asleep, but only because she was currently wrapped in her favorite pink blanket, and sitting on her brother's lap while John read from her favorite book.

The Princess and the Pea.

That kid could have that book read to her fifty million times, and she would still ask for one more. He bet, no doubt, she had woken up to use the bathroom—training her had been easy, but he attributed that to the fact she had such older siblings to help out— and found John awake in his room. Lucian didn't know what it was about those two ... John and Lucia, that was.

They just ... fit.

Best friends.

It didn't matter that there was twelve years between them. The fact that John often struggled with outbursts and his emotions never really bothered or affected Lucia like it did his other girls. It didn't matter that she liked those ugly dolls with the big heads, and he listened to grungy punk bands that hadn't been popular in two or more decades.

"One more?" Lucia asked, her voice still babyish.

John laughed. "You have to go to sleep, Lucy."

"*Lucia.*"

"Yeah, still Lucy to me, though."

Lucia sighed.

John grinned. "Fine, one more."

"Yay!"

Lucian slipped back out of the room.

No need to interrupt the kids.

Sometimes, they didn't always need *him*. They just needed each other.

A WOMAN'S ANGER

Women had phases of anger, Lucian had come to learn over his life span. It usually started with a warning—a look from one's wife, or if a man was *really* pushing his limit, she might even give him a verbal one. When that warning didn't work, and a man wondered if he might have crossed a line because the attitude came out to play, the dangerous things started to happen.

The *it's okay*.

And the *I'm fine*.

Women were not okay.

And they were certainly not fine.

The thing about men was that they were notoriously stupid. If they knew that those *I'm fines* meant a woman wasn't really fine, they tended to push. Far more than they should. As if repeatedly asking their wife if they were sure, or what was wrong, would somehow magically fix the problem.

It never ended well.

And then came the silence.

When all else failed, when a man *really* fucked up, a woman's anger turned into something else entirely. Something more painful than her anger formed in words and actions. Something far more worse than all of that put together.

She simply went quiet.

And that wasn't just dangerous.

It was downright terrifying.

Especially when a man loved that woman.

It had been eight days, twelve hours, and twenty-four minutes since Jordyn last spoke a word to Lucian, and he was dying. Not that he would know whether or not she cared about how he felt, because even when he sat in the same room as his wife, she refused to even give him the grace of her stare.

Her attention?

Not for him.

Her time?

He didn't fit into the schedule.

She wasn't fucking around now, and he was going crazy. There

75

were only two times in his long marriage to Jordyn that Lucian could remember making her *this* mad at him. Once was the first time he'd been arrested, and spent a couple of months in jail, missed one of their kids' birthdays, and their anniversary. Every single phone call he made from jail was ignored, and all communication went through their lawyer, for the most part. She brought the kids to visit him, but she didn't speak.

Eventually, he figured out that his wife wasn't so mad at him as she was pissed off at the entire situation. That it happened at all. That he put them in that situation. And he understood entirely, so he let her have that moment.

They moved past that time.

Another time had been over something far more petty. A simple argument that just became worse and worse until she all out refused to speak to him, and Lucian finally gave in, and went back to his wife on his knees, begging to fix it, even though he still didn't know what exactly she was mad about.

Because *compromise*.

Wasn't that what marriage was all about?

This time would not be the same.

Lucian knew that much.

It couldn't be the same when Jordyn's anger had been brought on by the one thing in their life that she loved above everything else. The one thing she protected, even to the detriment of herself. *Her entire life*.

One of their children.

Lucia, specifically.

"Jordyn—"

All it took was Lucian saying her name, and his wife's fiery gaze turned on him from where she sat at her vanity. It was the quick pull of her lips falling into a scowl that told him all he needed to know about what was going to happen tonight.

He would plead for her to listen.

To hear his point of view.

She would dead-stare him.

He'd continue talking.

Like a fucking idiot.

Lucian would sleep alone.

Fun.

"I know you're pissed at me," he muttered, "but I'm doing what I think is best with Lucia and this whole *Renzo* situation. Better I keep her in the house where we can watch what she's doing, than let her run free with him, yeah? Who fucking knows what trouble she'd find with him because she can't seem to stop chasing him around all the damn time."

Jordyn kept staring, saying nothing.

Lucian felt his anxiety spike.

He hated that.

Her *stare*.

With nothing more than a look, he understood everything there was to know about this situation, and his wife's current state of mind regarding him. She was *very* close to wanting to just tell him to get the hell out of her face. And if he got too close, he'd be lucky if her anger didn't make her punch him right in the balls.

Not that she'd ever done that before.

She looked like she might right now, however.

Perfect.

It meant she was so exasperated with him that she didn't even have the energy to form words. And he was just stupid enough of a man to think that if he talked enough for the both of them, then he might be able to fix this.

History taught him nothing.

"I mean, what did you want me to do, huh? I tried *everything*. And you saw how much she's changed since meeting him. Not for the better, either. I did what I had to do. You don't have to like it."

Jordyn surprised him then.

By *talking*.

However, what she said didn't bode well for him.

"You're right about one thing, Lucian, I don't like it."

He blinked, still standing like an idiot in their bedroom doorway because he knew better than to fully step inside the room. It might also be *his* personal space—filled with things he and his wife loved and picked together. Their large king-size bed dominated the middle with its four posters, and the canopy of dark gray fabric pulled toward the ends and held back for them to climb into the inviting bed.

A bed that he was not currently welcomed in.

"Years ago, we made an agreement about our children," Jordyn said, turning back to stare at her reflection in the vanity. "What was it, Lucian?"

He didn't even have to think about it.

Not really.

"We agreed not to step in on their personal lives."

"And what are you doing?"

He sighed. "Jord—"

"How's the guest bed across the hall, Lucian?"

His jaw ticked. "Doesn't feel like *mine*."

"And yet, guess who's sleeping in it?"

Yeah.

He knew.

BREATHE

One breath after another.
A breath in, and then out.
Inhale.
Exhale.
It seemed like an easy thing to do. Lucian felt almost ... *unsure* that breathing had always been this easy when suddenly it seemed like he could just do it without the weight that had accompanied the action for a good year or more now.

He stared at the phone in his hand—the screen had long turned blank, the device going into sleep mode because he hadn't kept the touchscreen active. Not that it mattered because while the reflection of the blackened glass only showed his face—weathered with age and *life*—he could still see what had been there just moments ago.

The phone number.
His doctor's name.
Not the office number. His oncologist's *personal* cell number that should have been entirely unrelated to work. But somehow, over the period of time in which Lucian had been diagnosed with cancer, headed straight into surgery followed by treatments ... and then *today*, he'd made a friend in his doctor.

Ralph knew how much had been riding on today. How on edge Lucian would have been waiting for the man to call because they suspected the results of his *final* tests would finish on the weekend. Which meant they were going to have to wait until Monday rolled around before anything would be properly filed into the systems.

But Ralph had pull.
Some contacts.
Doctor shit Lucian didn't understand.
The man promised to get him the results of the tests the very second the computers spat them out. With a shaking voice, though he'd not acknowledged it, Lucian told his friend that it was fine to wait until Monday.

It really wasn't.
Ralph said as much.
"Lucian, you okay?"

From the passenger seat, his wife's hand snaked across the vehicle and found his arm. Her fingertips—still warm and soft and *familiar* after all these years—drifted over his wrist before locking tight around his hand and the phone.

She stared at him, waiting.

Brows knitted.

Not quite smiling.

Eyes so wide.

She was worried.

Still trying to process.

So was he.

After *all* of it?

It came down to a thirty-second phone call that would determine what felt like the rest of his life. Because cancer did that—it stopped everything in its tracks. A lot of things around a person became unimportant when faced with a diagnosis that would absolutely mean death if not treated. And even after ...

Lucian took in another breath.

Jordyn waited him out.

"I just ... I'm breathing," he murmured.

That did make his wife smile. It reminded him of a lot of things— their entire life together, all the promises he'd made her long ago, and how it all eventually came true as one day after another passed them by. All she ever had to do was look at him and smile for everything to instantly get so much better.

He still wasn't great at *emoting*.

She more than made up for it.

"He said—"

"Cancer free," Lucian interjected quietly.

Jordyn nodded fast. "Yeah, and that's *good*. It's *great*."

"It's everything we wanted."

And needed.

Jordyn let out a burst of noise in a breath. "So why are you over there—"

Quiet?

Stunned?

About to jump out of his fucking skin?

All of that and more.

"I'm just breathing," he said.

Because he was.

And he knew she didn't understand. Although she'd had a scare a few years after Lucia was born when her doctor found a lump—that turned out to be nothing concerning after an initial biopsy with unclear results—Jordyn couldn't understand.

He didn't blame her.

She had been everything to and for him throughout this entire process. The rock to hold him down every step of the way. And when she needed a break, because she was human too, he had others who stepped in to get him through the worst of all of this.

His kids—becoming a father gave Lucian purpose he didn't know existed—kept him laughing and looking forward to what was yet to come. And then there were his brothers ... who let him be weak because his body didn't give him a choice. Late night chats and some of the best bud he'd ever smoked had him chowing down greasy fast food when he was doing chemo once a week and hadn't been taking in nearly enough calories before.

He didn't wonder how he got through it ...

Just that he did at all.

"What is it?" Jordyn asked him.

All at once, he thought he might know exactly how to explain what that call did for him.

"I didn't realize how hard it's been just to breathe. It's not so hard right now."

Her gaze met his and she slumped back into the passenger seat. Lucian stared out the street, their car still running on the side of the road where he'd pulled over to take the call from Ralph.

He could breathe.

It was like he could finally breathe.

GIOVANNI OUTTAKES

FAMOUS LAST WORDS

"Ma!" Catherine barked. "I wants that, now!"

"No," Catrina replied.

"MA."

"Catherine Cecelia, the answer is no."

"But, Ma—"

Catrina gave her daughter a raised eyebrow and that was it, the girl scampered off with a pout that could rival any puppy dog.

"Find Daddy then," Catherine mumbled on her way out of the kitchen.

"Do that," Catrina said.

At nearly two-years-old, Gio's niece was her mother all over. Gio knew better than to tell Catrina that, though, not unless he wanted one of those looks to be leveled on him.

"The attitude from that one is strong," Kim said.

Catrina pursed her lips and tapped her nails to the tabletop. "I know."

"Wonder where she gets it from," Jordyn said with a sly grin as she turned away from the stove. She was heavily pregnant with her third child and ready to go any day. Why Lucian wasn't hovering over his wife like a hawk, Gio didn't know. His brother was bad for that whenever Jordyn was pregnant.

Catrina simpered with a smile. "Not me, of course."

"Of course," Gio drawled.

"Watch it, Giovanni," Catrina warned. "Or I'll have you washing the dishes with Dante later."

Gio shot the stainless steel dishwasher a passing look. "What's that there for, to look pretty?"

"I just cleaned it," Catrina defended.

"It's supposed to get dirty. You wash dirty dishes with it."

Jordyn snickered into her hand.

Even Kim laughed.

Catrina shrugged. "There's a man in my kitchen talking. You'd think after all these years, they would learn to stay away."

Gio smirked. "I'm not very good at following rules."

"Where's Andino?" Catrina asked as she surveyed her nails.

Gio swore his sister-in-law only did that shit to annoy people. She was the only female he knew who could act as sweet as sugar with the evilest intentions behind it. He supposed that was why Dante adored his wife so much—people misjudged Catrina Marcello and then were left picking up the bloody pieces when she was done with them.

He'd quickly learned to tread carefully whenever her smartass came out to play.

"With Dante," Gio replied.

Or at least, that's where Andino muttered about going when they arrived. The toddler was quiet for his age, Gio liked that about his son. The boy was also terribly attached to his uncle Dante, for whatever reason. Gio didn't mind that, either.

"Dante is working on changing the oil in my car," Catrina informed.

Grease.

Oil.

Dirt.

Shit.

Gio could see the look of horror on Kim's face starting to form before Catrina even got the words out. Andino could slip the eye of any man, even if he was in a room full of them. It was even worse when he was told not to touch something and the kid knew he could make a mess of it.

Andino found trouble that way—he was damn good at it.

"Dammit," Gio grumbled.

"Language in my kitchen," Cat chided.

Just like his mother …

Gio scowled and flipped his sister-in-law with the middle finger as he left in search of his—likely messy, now—son.

"That was easy," he heard Cat say.

Kim laughed. "He's learning."

*

"Stop fighting, Andino."

"But, Papa—"

"Stop it. If you get that crap all over me, I'm not going to be very

83

happy, kid."

The toddler's squirming ceased. Gio continued his trek down the hallway toward the bathroom, holding Andino under his arm like the kid was a football.

"Did you see the picture I made, Papa?" Andino asked.

Gio tried to hold it back, but he still laughed. "On the side of your uncle's nice white Mercedes? Yes."

Poor Dante.

He'd just had that car painted, too.

Once Dante realized what Andino had done while Michel watched on and said nothing, Gio's brother looked like he was ready to explode. Gio kindly pointed out that the toddler couldn't be blamed when the adult was less than twenty feet away with his head stuck under a car. He then proceeded to point out that Michel couldn't be blamed either, considering the kid didn't have a lick of grease or oil on him.

"I mades Cain," Andino said.

Well, it looked more like blobs of grease with tiny finger lines all through it but if his kid saw his dog, then a dog it was.

"It was a good picture of Cain, Andino." Gio smirked, adding, "But you're still not supposed to play in grease and oil, buddy."

"Not supposed to mark on Ma's car."

Yep.

Because this wasn't the kid's first time making conceptual art on the closest flat surface with whatever he could find.

"Or Papa's car," Andino added.

Gio would take it.

His son was learning.

That was all that mattered.

Dante could suffer with cleaning his car as long as it wasn't one of Gio's vehicles. Compromise. Gio was all about the compromise where Andino was concerned. It was the best way to get his kid to follow the rules, anyway.

Lucian popped his head out of the living-room entryway with a grin. "Find him, did you?"

Gio scowled. "Shut up."

"You should have known better; he always gets into something."

Ignoring his brother's teasing, Gio walked right on past toward the kitchen. His plan was to find Kim and see if he could convince her to clean up Andino. It was no easy task—the kid didn't like to be scrubbed, but the grease needed to come off.

Andino always reacted better when his mother laid down the law.

Gio didn't like to be the bad guy.

Sucker, his mind taunted.

"Bye, Zio Lucian," Andino called as loudly as he could manage.

"We're not leaving," Gio told his son. "We're going to find your mother and then you're going to have a bath."

"Oh."

Andino's wiggling started up again.

"Stop it, if you get stuff messy, Zia Catrina will have one of her hissy fits."

"Was a ... was a hissy fit?" Andino asked, turning in the football-like hold to look up at his father.

Gio thought about the question for a minute. "Zia Catrina when she points and talks a lot. Especially if she's not smiling, but mostly when she is smiling."

Andino nodded, taking the words in. "Okay."

"Jesus, don't tell him that," Lucian said, coming up behind his brother as Gio continued his trek with the squirming toddler down the hallway. "Kids repeat everything."

Gio smirked. "I know, look at your son."

Lucian smacked Gio in the back of the head. "That's because of you."

"Yeah, well, live and learn."

"That's bad word," Andino said like he was just catching up to speed. "Only say Jesus in church and when we eats, Zio Lucian."

Andino's little hand popped out at his side.

Gio laughed when Lucian grumbled under his breath.

"Pay up, brother. The kid spoke."

You'd think Lucian would learn to curb his mouth, but nope. Gio's entire family thought he would be the one struggling to keep his language under check, but he found it easy. You know, because he liked his goddamn money and all.

Lucian didn't, apparently.

Andino earned himself a five-dollar bill.

*

"Andino, my God," Kim said, exasperated. "Stop it, you're getting it all over your little peepee."

Gio hid his snickers into his hand. He sobered quickly enough when Kim gave him a look that could have melted him into the wall.

"Sorry," Gio mumbled, still hiding the smile.

Needless to say, the bathroom was a mess. Grease and oil was not an easy thing to clean. Andino had managed to make streaks of muddy brown and black all over the tiles and bathtub. Even the floor had a few stains from where his little Nike sneakers had taken some of the mess.

"Oh, my God," Catrina said from the doorway.

Gio cringed when his sister-in-law took in the bathroom and the mess.

Catrina was slightly anal about cleaning. Just a bit.

A lot, really.

It was kind of crazy.

Even Dante pointed it out a time or two.

"What in the hell did he do," Catrina asked, "bathe in it?"

"Well ... he is now," Gio said, shrugging. "Or rather, the water looks like it."

Kim sighed. "Shut up, Gio."

"All right."

Cat made a noise under her breath that sounded entirely overwhelmed. "I ..."

Lucian poked his head in the bathroom as well, saying, "Steaks are done. Dante's just cleaning up in the other bathroom."

"We'll be down in a minute," Gio informed.

Catrina didn't act like Lucian had said a thing. "Did you let him fingerpaint on the walls, too?"

"It'll clean," Gio said.

Cat smiled and nodded.

Andino looked up at his aunt with curious eyes.

Gio knew it ... he knew it was coming.

Nothing could have stopped it.

"Are you hasing a hissy fit, Zia Catrina?" Andino asked sweetly.

Gio caught his brother's eye at the same time Kim's head swung around to glare at her husband, likely knowing that had come from him.

Catrina raised a single brow high. She looked happy enough, but

Gio knew better. When Cat smiled, nasty was sure to follow. She'd wait until there were no kids around, but she got people back big time.

Claws, the woman was full of them.

"Who told you that?" Cat asked her nephew.

Famous last words ...

Gio caught Lucian's eye again.

There were only two men in the world who could withstand or cool Cat's anger, and one was just a child who never made her angry because she adored him. The other, her husband.

"Dante," Lucian and Gio said together.

He could clean the mess.

That's what bosses were for, after all.

ONE AND DONE

Gio watched Kim hold tiny Andino as the quiet hum of the doctor's waiting room surrounded them. His son was content there, snuggled in his mother's arms. Andino slept despite the lights and the noise.

He was an easy baby.

A happy baby.

Oh, Gio adored his son.

He'd worried that the job of fatherhood would be one that might not treat him nicely. He'd worried that his instincts wouldn't kick in and that he'd be inept at the duty of protecting and caring for someone other than himself and his wife.

Gio couldn't have been more wrong.

Sure, he had his moments, the ones where he was left stunned and confused and calling his own parents for help. He had the choking moments—the ones that scared him enough to choke him silent, but those had come mostly before his son's birth.

And a few times after.

But he knew ... staring at the distance in his wife's eyes, the tiredness in her features, and the despondence in her posture as she held their boy ... one and done.

Andino would be their only child.

Gio couldn't do this again, not to Kim.

It wasn't his wife's fault, that Gio knew. Kim's pregnancy hadn't been an easy one, but she had been happy and excited all the same. And then the birth happened. The trauma of the hemorrhage she suffered that nearly killed her and their child was enough to take away anyone's spirit.

This wasn't what Gio had been expecting when it came to being a father and having a child.

No one talked about this kind of stuff. No one talked about the sadness his wife couldn't shake or how she handed Andino off to him more than he wanted to admit. No one talked about the quietness or the shadows under her eyes, never mind disinterest in almost anything.

No.

One.
Talked.
About.
This.

It was taboo, maybe. A topic that was whispered between women and doctors but not openly discussed at a dinner table. It was overlooked—ignored.

Depression. Gio knew it. He recognized the signs of it, especially in his usually upbeat and happy wife. PPD, they called it. Yeah, he went looking. It was likely that Kim didn't even know what the problem was herself.

She was not to blame.

Gio was worried.

Kim's soft sigh had Gio turning his head upward from their son's peaceful features to find his wife looking at him.

"I love you, Gio."

Gio smiled. "I know, bella."

"I'm tired," she whispered.

He knew that, too.

"It'll get easier, right? That's what everyone keeps saying."

Kim nodded. "I love him, too."

"Hey," Gio murmured, catching Kim's chin in his palm and forcing her to look at him. "You don't have to tell me that, Kim. I know you love Andino."

Kim's gaze glimmered with unshed tears. "I want to be happy, Gio. I should be happy right now."

"Kim—"

"I had to sit outside on the doorstep yesterday," she interrupted quietly.

Gio frowned. "Why?"

He'd worked yesterday. It was the first time in the two weeks since their son's birth that he left the home to resume his Capo position.

"Because he kept crying," Kim said softly. "I couldn't make him happy. I tried. And when he wouldn't stop, I just got angry. I got scared. And I just …. I couldn't do that, Gio. He's a baby. I shouldn't get angry with him—he doesn't understand."

Her words broke his heart.

And confirmed what he already believed.

PPD.

Gio searched Kim's face for any hint of a lie of for something that said she might be hiding more from him. He found nothing.

"There's something wrong with me," Kim said.

"With you?" Gio asked, smiling sadly. "Nothing, babe. You're just … a little mixed up right now."

Kim laughed bleakly. "Is that what you want to call it?"

"We'll get it sorted out."

"I don't want to do this again."

Gio sucked in a hard breath. He knew what she meant without asking. His decision had already been cemented, but he wanted to wait until whatever was going on with Kim blew over and then talk to her about the idea of only having one child.

"Just Andino," Gio murmured.

Kim shrugged. "Yeah."

"You're worried this is going to happen again."

"Aren't you?" she asked.

A little …

A lot.

"Yeah," Gio confirmed. "And I'm worried the tear might reoccur and the next time, we might not be as lucky as we were to get the bleeding stopped in time. Yeah, it worries me, Kim."

"Some Italians we are."

Gio scoffed. "Not every Italian has a large family."

"You loved having lots of siblings."

"I loved kicking their asses, sure."

Kim smiled, but it was faint. "Cute."

"Andino will have lot of cousins. Lucian is having an army. He makes up for what Dante and me won't have."

"You're awful."

"You love me."

"I do," Kim murmured.

*

"I would tend to agree with what you said," the doctor told Giovanni after the door was closed and Kim had left with their son to schedule the baby's next appointment. "It's definitely Post-Partum Depression. But the fact you recognized it and she agrees there's a problem is a huge relief for me. We'll try the meds, Giovanni, and see how it goes from there."

"All right."

"And this isn't uncommon for a first birth, not to mention, a traumatic one like Kim experienced."

"It's not a permanent thing, right?" Gio asked. "This medication and shit."

"No."

"Good."

"What else did you want to discuss with me?" the man asked.

Gio shifted on his feet, uncomfortable. "A vasectomy."

The doctor cocked a brow. "That's a little early to be thinking about this, isn't it?"

"No. It's what I want. You can do it in-office, right?"

"Yes, but—"

"I'm not here to argue," Gio interrupted calmly. "I know what I want—what my wife wants. This is … it."

The doctor sighed. "You're sure?"

"Absolutely. One and done."

*

"Mmm."

Kim's moan was soft and heady. It rocked Giovanni inside-out. Her sweet, sensual little smile as she hid her face into the blankets while he kissed all the spots on her that he could find was teasing to him.

He wanted to see her.

See her smiles.

Her happiness.

Her bliss.

"Kim," Gio whispered, kissing the swell of her ass.

"Hmm?"

"Turn over."

"But this is good, too."

"Kim."

Gio smacked his wife's ass with his hand just hard enough to earn a yelp. Without any more argument, Kim turned over on her back. Now, a sassy little grin split her lips. Nearly thirteen weeks after their son's birth and finally … finally … sex had been approved by the doctor.

"Beautiful," Gio murmured, licking a path down Kim's stomach.

She squirmed under his teasing.

"God, how long are you going to make me wait?" she asked, breathless.

Gio found her slit wet and hot under his fingertips. Kim hadn't been expecting his touch, because she jerked with a quiet cry. Softly, he stroked her sex with light touches that were sure to get her shaking and soon. Her arousal smeared under his motions up to her clit as he circled the hardened little bud.

Kim was soft and silky under his hands and Gio loved it. She was goddamn gorgeous, especially when her skin was flushed with the need to come and she was chasing that bliss. So fucking gorgeous. The more she canted her hips into his hand, the fast he circled over her hot clit. She was wetter than ever and soaking him beautifully.

So sensitive.

Fucking hot as hell.

"Come," Gio demanded. "Come for me, Kim. Let me taste that fucking honey of yours, Tesoro. I want it—come."

"God," Kim breathed.

She came trembling and mumbling his name in the sweetest way. Gio was harder than fucking steel and aching to be buried as deep as he could get into his wife. Kim trembled from head to toe, her lips parted with the quietest whine.

"So good."

Gio chuckled. "Been a while."

"Too long," Kim mumbled.

He let Kim tug off his shirt and then help push his cotton sleep pants down until he could kick them off. His cock rested at the junction of Kim's thighs and every time she moved even an inch, she rubbed over his length in the best fucking way.

He needed to find a condom and quick. Despite having the vasectomy, he still hadn't gone back to have his spunk tested to be sure everything was good.

"Condom," Gio said as Kim grabbed him and pulled him in for a kiss.

His thoughts were lost.

Just like that.

Soft lips.

Wet heat.

Her nails scored across his back as he seated his cock against her sex and pushed in with a long groan. He could feel every inch of her sex holding him tight and soaking him with her fluids.

Yeah, too long.

Heaven.

Jesus Christ, she was heaven.

Kim sighed a shaky breath when Gio cupped her jaw and forced her head back. He wanted to look at her—to see the pleasure darken her blue eyes and how her lips trembled the closer she came to orgasm.

Nothing about this was new to Gio.

He knew everything there was to know about Kim.

But nothing could ever be better.

She was his drug.

"Fuck," Kim whispered.

Pulling out so that just the tip of his cock was stretching her pussy open, Gio slammed right back into his wife. Kim's lashes fluttered as a soft oh fell from her mouth.

"Missed this," Gio grunted, repeating pulling out and holding there for a second before thrusting back in again. "Love the way you open for me—you're so fucking full of me, Kim."

"Stop talking."

Gio smirked. "I thought you liked my dirty mouth."

"I do," she moaned, pushing against him and canting her hips up into another thrust. "But I just want to fuck."

Shit.

Yeah.

"We can do that."

*

Gio spluttered over his words, feeling his fingernails cut into his palm. "What in the hell do you mean, not a success?"

"I mean, the procedure didn't work. It's rare, but it happens. The vasectomy will need to be performed again and in eight to twelve weeks, we'll check again."

Jesus.

Holy mother of sweet hell.

He knew better—he did.

Condoms should have been used while he waited between the first procedure and the checkup, but Gio had never been very damn good at following the rules for anything.

All he could think was that there was a possibility Kim would have to go through months of hell again if his fuck up ended up in another pregnancy, and then after, would she have to suffer again, too?

Gio couldn't breathe.

"You're screwing with me," Gio mumbled.

The doctor shrugged. "This isn't a situation I find funny, Giovanni."

Yeah, him either.

"We can do it—"

"I have to go," Gio said, standing from the chair and grabbing his jacket. "I … have to call my wife."

Once Gio was inside his familiar SUV, he snatched the phone out of the glove compartment and dialed his wife's cell. Kim picked up on the second ring.

"Hello?"

"It didn't work," Gio said instantly.

"Um …"

"The fucking vasectomy, Kim. It didn't work. And I can have it redone, or whatever, but you might—"

"Giovanni, chill."

Gio sunk into the driver's seat. "I'm sorry."

"My God, for what?"

"Screwing up."

"Gio, it's fine. We both knew what we needed to do between the procedure and the final checkup. We didn't, so whatever."

"Whatever?" Gio rubbed at his forehead. "Kim, do you realize—"

"I realize that everything started normally this morning, as I expected since I couldn't breastfeed Andino. We're good, Gio. Calm down."

Gio could read between the lines. The medication she started taking for the PPD could have adverse side-effects on babies who were breastfeeding. Kim suspected her cycles would start within a couple months of Andino being born since breastfeeding usually held it off a while longer.

We're good.

Relief flooded Gio like never before.

"Yeah?" he asked.

"Yeah. And I want some damned chocolate."

"Chocolate," he echoed.

"And a book. Pick me up a book on the way home, too."

Gio nodded, even though his wife couldn't see it.

"You're going to get it redone, right?" Kim asked.

"The vasectomy?"

"Yes."

Gio cleared his throat, wondering if this was their sign for something. "Do you want me to? I mean, it didn't work. Does that tell us something?"

"Yes, to get a better doctor," Kim muttered, laughing. "I love Andino, Gio. I am so happy with him. He's perfect, okay. And the thought of doing this all over again scares the hell out of me."

Good enough.

Gio smiled. "I'll have it redone."

"Good."

"Do you want me to get the refill done for your meds before I come home, too?"

Kim sighed. "Gio—"

"I don't mind, bella. I have time."

"I didn't have them filled last month. I've been without them for a while. The doctor knows—he suggested it when I mentioned how I was feeling when he lowered the dose."

Oh.

"Why didn't you tell me?" he asked.

"I didn't think I needed to. You make everything better, anyway. And Andino. He makes it better, too."

In the background, Gio could hear the quiet cooing of his son.

Andino made everything perfect.

"All right," Gio finally said.

"Do you not want to have the procedure redone?" Kim asked quietly.

He thought of Andino.

And his wife.

Maybe he could afford more time and love to another child. Maybe he'd like to see his last name carried on with another boy, or see his features reflected in a little girl.

Maybe.

But he was happy now.

So happy.

"One and done, right?" Gio asked.

"One and done."

SKIP

"Skip, what's this?" Gio asked.

The Capo glanced up from the papers on his desk, eyeing the shadow box Gio was peering into. "What, that old thing?"

Gio shrugged. "Yeah. There's a note inside."

"And that's it," the older Giovanni replied.

"Looks like it." Gio read the words: Thank you. That was it. Nothing more. "Who's it from?"

It must have been important if the Capo kept it. Fourteen-year-old Gio didn't know Skip to be sentimental about much. He did know this was the man he had gotten his namesake from but his father Antony didn't talk much about how that happened. For whatever reason, Antony didn't show a lot of favoritism to any of his men, but especially his Capos.

"Skip?" Gio asked, turning around.

Skip cleared his throat and stood from the desk. "Well, it's from your father."

"Yeah?"

"Yes."

"Shit, I didn't know that," Gio muttered, eyeing the words again. "Why?"

The Capo laughed. "No wonder your father sends you over here with me, Gio. Your mouth is never going to cut it in a boss's seat, kid."

Gio shrugged like it didn't make a difference. "I don't want to be like Dad, anyway."

There was nothing about being the leader of a major crime family that appealed to Gio. He had better things to do and worry about. He was just a kid, right. That wasn't his life.

The Capo nodded. "Which is why you spend your days under my feet, kid."

Maybe.

Gio liked the Capo, though. Skip didn't treat him like he was just a hot-headed teenager. He didn't act like Gio was stupid, either. Gio knew what his family was—Cosa Nostra—and who is father was, but a lot of people liked to pretend he didn't. The Capo never did, he treated Gio like an equal, or as much as he could. Sometimes, the guy let Gio tag along for stuff, too.

"What's it for?" Gio asked, jerking his thumb at the note.

"Because I saved your life once," the Capo explained. "And your father was kind of fucked up that day what with you and your mother being like you were, so he scribbled that off on a notepad at the nurses' station, ripped it off, and asked them to give it to me. I kept it."

Huh.

"When I was born?" Gio asked, knowing there had been some complications for his mother with his birth.

"Yeah, then."

"Oh."

"Don't get fucking sentimental or anything, kid. It's just a note."

That the Capo kept.

Gio smirked. "Does Dad know you have it?"

"Yes," the Capo said. "But we don't talk about it."

"Why not?"

"You ask a lot of questions."

"You don't mind," Gio said, sure of that fact. "You always answer."

The Capo reached out and poked Gio hard in the forehead. "Not this time, kid."

Gio scowled, batting the Capo's hand away. "Asshole."

"So I've been told. Go get me a rum and coke from the bar, would you?"

"Can I have one, too?" Gio asked.

The Capo barked a laugh. "Not if you want to live tonight when I take you home to your father."

Gio wasn't surprised. The Capo never let him try anything fun.

"And not if I want to live," Skip added, smiling. "Go get me the drink, kid. We've got things to do today."

"Like what?"

"Like none of your fucking business, Gio. You'll find out when we get there."

Gio grinned. "Are we doing the rounds again?"

He liked doing that with the Capo. He learned a lot about how money was made on the streets and the ins and outs of being a Capo. Gio never got to do much, because he was always kept far enough away from anything that might cause him trouble, but it was still decent fun.

"Fair enough," Gio said.

With a two finger wave, he left the back office. Gio made his way through the club to where the large bar waited with two bartenders working behind. Pushing his frame up onto a stool, Gio rapped his knuckles down on the top to gain their attention.

"Skip wants a drink?" the larger of the two asked.

"Yeah."

"All right. You want a soda?"

"Sure," Gio said. "Seven Up."

"Pussy drink, kid."

Gio gave the guy the middle finger. "Get me a rum and coke then."

The bartender scoffed loudly. "Only in your teenaged wet dreams, Gio. I know the fucking rules."

Seven Up it was.

Gio sipped from his Seven Up and balanced Skip's drink in his other hand as he made his way back through the crowd filling the joint. There was always lots of movement and lights. The music was good, too. But he wasn't allowed on the floor a lot when the club was open for business.

As he walked down the back hallway leading to Skip's office, Gio took it slow. He could hear the Capo arguing with someone, which was new. Skip never let people come into his office and shout when Gio was in the club. He always kept things clean and quiet, or as much as could be expected in Cosa Nostra.

Gio pushed on the office door with his hand and found it wouldn't budge. It wasn't latched completely, but it wouldn't move, either.

"I said get the fuck out," Skip barked. "And don't bother coming back until you've got your shit cleaned up. I've got nothing for you— nothing. Go look elsewhere for money, you're not getting it from me to feed your fucking habits, Red."

Gio stepped back from the door in just enough time to miss the person who stumbled out. The woman looked wild with her flaming red hair a mess and angry, dilated pupils focusing on fourteen-year-old Gio's face.

High.

He knew that look.

She was raving mad and high as a kite.

The woman sneered. "This your newest little recruit, Giovanni?"

Before Gio could blink, the Capo was out in the hallway and pushing the woman away from Gio.

"Get out of here, I said," the Capo growled. "Goddamn it, Red, have some respect. You're acting crazy."

"Crazy?" Red barked out a laugh. "You made me fucking crazy, Giovanni. I know you've got money stashed in here. You've always got money. That's what you do, right? You handle money for the big guns. I'm not asking for much."

"I won't deal with your nonsense anymore. It's bad every way you look at it and you do nothing good for me, Red. And I asked you to leave. Now."

Gio swallowed hard as an enforcer stepped down the hallway, probably having heard the commotion. The Capo gave a single wave in Red's direction and the enforcer nodded. Then, Gio found himself being pulled back inside the office. The door was shut before Skip grabbed the drink Gio held out for him.

"Thanks," the man said, his tone tired and rough.

"Who's that?" Gio dared to ask.

Skip blinked as he downed half of the glass in one go. "My biggest fucking mistake."

*

"Tired?" the Capo asked.

Gio nodded and fell onto the couch with a comic in his hands. Skip had picked it up for him to read as they drove around the streets of Little Italy. The Capo would disappear into businesses and come back out with envelopes and nothing else to say. It was a long night.

"Club is just closing, so I'll take you over to your father's office soon."

"Okay," Gio mumbled.

"Did you learn anything today?" Skip asked.

"How to be patient," Gio replied tiredly.

Skip chuckled. "Yeah, this life is all about being patient, kid."

Gio also learned a little more about the woman Skip called Red. She'd been Skip's girl one time, apparently. She got mixed up in bad people who were mixed up in bad stuff. Skip said it just like that—

stuff.

How much worse could someone be than a mobster like Skip, Gio asked.

Snorting shit up your nose bad, Skip had said.

Gio stopped asking about Red.

Gio felt his eyes turn even drowsier and he was nearly asleep when the first bang woke him up. He jumped at the volume of the noise, eyes wide and the comic falling to the floor. Instantly, he found Skip's panicked stare from across the room.

Without a word, the Capo was up from the desk and moving across to Gio. He said nothing as he grabbed the boy, yanked him off the couch and then dragged him across the room.

"What—"

"Shut up," Skip ordered. Then, he stuffed Gio into a small coat closet. "Get down, be quiet, and stay there."

Gio dropped down to his knees, his shaking hands finding the cold floor. "But—"

"Gio, do what I say." Skip dug in his pocket and tossed a flip phone down into Gio's lap. "Call someone—your father, call him and don't talk. Just call."

What was happening?

"Call, Gio."

"O-okay, Skip."

The door closed, shrouding Gio in darkness.

Gio fumbled with the phone, unable to see much as the light from the tiny flip screen didn't offer much. The first shout outside the closet made him freeze, the second caused him to drop the phone to the cold floor.

"Hey, hey, Skipper," came a slurred, dark tone.

"Friends of Red?" Gio heard Skip ask.

"You know it."

"I don't have—"

"Shut up, we know you do, Italian. You even smell like dirty money, fucker."

Gio swallowed hard and heard someone shuffle against the door, like they were covering it or something. Strangely, Gio didn't feel nervous by that fact. He figured it was probably Skip.

"Got something to hide behind there?" someone else asked.

"Nah, go look in the drawer of the desk," Skip said. "Top right hand side."

Gio heard footsteps and then more shouts followed.

And bangs.

Loud, harsh bangs.

Pops, actually.

Gio was so stunned by the noise and the sound of a body thumping into the door that he fell backwards, his hands flying upward to grab something—anything—for stability. Coats fell down on him. Gio froze as more shuffling and mumbles followed.

Light filtered in through the coats.

Gio didn't move a fucking muscle.

"Nothing in here," someone grunted before the door was slammed shut again.

"Get out of here then?" the first voice asked.

"Red's a fucking cunt. I'mma cut her for lying, the bitch."

"Take his ring—it looks real."

"The club's closed and the guy we saw earlier is cut, too. Let's get out of here."

Gio squeezed his eyes shut and tried to keep his heart from finding his throat. His fingernails cut into his palms as he clenched his hands into tight, balled fists.

Skip.

Skip.

Skip.

When Gio heard the office door, he grappled for the cell phone. With shaking hands, he managed to dial his father's phone number. Antony picked up on the fourth ring.

"Giovanni, you were supposed to bring my son home a half hour ago."

"D-dad," Gio stuttered.

Antony sucked in a hard breath, likely hearing the panic and fear in Gio's voice. "Son?"

"Something happened … something happened."

"Tell me where."

Gio could hear the sounds of doors slamming and his father yelling in the background of the call. Yelling for people—Paulie, Dante, Lucian, another man Gio knew to be a Capo. Where was his father? Wasn't he supposed to be at the office? How long had Gio been sleeping on the couch before he woke up again?

"Gio, where?" his father demanded again.

"The club," Gio whispered.

"Where are you inside?"

"Skip's office."

In a closet, he forgot to add.

"Don't move, Gio … don't you fucking move."

"Okay."

Gio dropped the phone.

*

Don't look, Gio remembered his father telling him when he pulled him from the closet.

Don't look, Giovanni.

Don't look.

Don't. Look.

Gio looked.

He saw the bloodied, blown apart head of a man he spent nearly five days a week with. He saw the blood that had covered the closet, the one Giovanni couldn't move from because he'd hidden someone important behind.

Gio saw it all.

When Antony demanded Gio talk, he wouldn't. When Antony asked how his son felt, Gio wouldn't tell the truth.

He wouldn't talk about how it took them thirty minutes to get to the club and how in that time, Gio heard Skip struggle for his last breath and felt blood seep under the door and soak Gio's shaking hands and his jeans. He didn't talk about how he could still see a man's death face when he slept or the cold whiteness of someone's dead skin when he looked at his own.

He didn't talk about those things.

"Where's Dad?" Gio asked, leaning in the kitchen entryway.

Dante glanced up from the textbook he was looking through. "Out, I guess."

"Where?" Gio asked again.

"I think he was getting some stuff settled."

"Where?"

Why was his brother being so fucking difficult?

Dante was a couple years older than him, but that didn't mean shit.

103

Gio would still take is brother outside and lay an ass kicking down on him. Or try, anyway. Dante had fast fists.

"Uh," Dante said, clearing his throat, "Skip's old club."

Skip hadn't even been buried yet. As far as Gio knew, nobody was allowed back inside the club because police had stuck their noses in.

Gio's gaze narrowed. "What kind of stuff?"

"Someone's taking over the work there. You know, Skip's work. Dad said the tape is coming off, soon."

Did Dante think Gio was stupid? Gio knew what Skip did there. Gio knew why Giovanni had been called Skip. He knew he was a Capo. He knew.

"I want to go," Gio said.

Dante shrugged. "Dad would have taken you along if he wanted you to go."

Lucian sauntered in the kitchen from the opposite of Gio. "Hey, little brother."

Gio punched Lucian in the shoulder. "Take me downtown."

"Nope."

"Lucian, I want to go see what they're doing to Skip's office."

"Not his office anymore," Lucian said, turning to face Gio. "And if you hit me again, I'll make you bleed."

Fine.

That was the first night Gio stole one of his father's cars.

Fuck his brothers for teaching him how to drive when they got their licenses.

Idiots.

*

"Where in the fuck is it?" Gio heard Antony roar.

"Mr. Marcello—"

"Shut up, you useless excuse for breath. I asked you fools for one thing—one! I let you come and go in this place long after you needed to be here for the investigation. I let you have your say and do your investigation even though I could have paid you to get the fuck out. And you didn't even do what I asked!"

Gio hid in shadowed part of the hallway as his father raged on. Rarely did Antony Marcello yell, but when he did, something was seriously wrong. Or someone had done something seriously wrong.

Gio was thinking this was the latter of the two.

"One of the Rookies took a few bags out to the back and put them by the dumpster for a pick up. It's probably in there, Antony. Fact is, everything on that wall was ruined or stained with blood."

"It was in a goddamn shadow box," Antony growled.

Gio stilled, knowing then what his father was looking for.

The note.

The one he'd given to Giovanni for saving his son and wife's life all those years ago.

"Useless," Gio heard his father spit again.

Gio just managed to slip out of the hallway and into the men's room before his father stormed out of the office. Once he was sure Antony wouldn't see him, Gio sneaked out of the bathroom and across the club. He went out the front and found an alley that led to the back. There, he found his father tearing open garbage bags and tipping them over. Antony continued his search through five black bags.

"Shouldn't they have taken that stuff for evidence or something?" Gio asked quietly.

Antony's back stiffened. Without even looking back at his son, he asked, "How'd you get here, Gio?"

"Took a car."

Sort of.

"Which car?"

"One of ours."

Sort of.

"Who drove you?"

"A guy," Gio said.

Sort of.

This lying thing was easy.

"No, they didn't need this for evidence," Antony finally said, sighing. "It was things on the walls and inside his desk. Garbage, they said."

Gio flinched at the heat in his father's tone. "Oh."

"Go take a walk, Gio. I'll find you. Don't go far."

All right.

Gio left his father alone.

Walking through the streets, Gio found a few kids he recognized in front of an pizzeria two blocks down. The heavy smell of smoke in the air was thick and pungent. The tallest kid took a hard drag from the joint and blew a large cloud at Gio as he stepped up to the group.

He'd hung out with them before.

Skip always kept an eye on Gio, though.

"Hey, Marcello," Ronnie said.

"Hey," Gio muttered.

"Heard your friend got clipped."

Gio shrugged his shoulders, but it hurt all the same. "Yeah."

The kid held out the joint.

"Wanna smoke? It'll take your mind off shit."

Did he?

Skip wouldn't be poking his head out of the pizzeria to tell him to stop.

Gio took the joint.

Antony found his son an hour later.

Gio was high.

Antony had the note in his hand.

THE CHURCH

"Merda," Dante said low under his breath, "you're looking rough today, little brother."

Gio was grateful for the dark aviator sunglasses that allowed him to roll his eyes and glare at his older brother without Dante knowing he was doing it. All that likely would have earned Gio was a punch from Dante—not that he blamed him. He would probably hit him for the same kind of shit, too.

Except not today.

Gio didn't have the energy today.

"Don't need your comments on how I look," Gio muttered as the two climbed the stairs of their family's church. The Bishop was already standing at the top and shaking hands with thier mother, and then their father, too. Cecelia always came first, though—something Antony demanded, likely. "Just let me get past Dad without him noticing—"

"That you came to church wasted?"

Jesus Christ.

"I'm not wasted, Dante."

"Hungover, then," Dante said. "Same fucking difference."

Was it?

Gio found it hard to tell, now.

"At least you managed to throw on something relatively decent," Dante added when Gio refused to respond to his last statement. "Ma will appreciate that you managed to find a suit for today."

Yes, she would.

But very little else.

Cecelia would worry.

And fret.

Antony would rage.

And worry.

Same shit, different day.

Gio was fine. It didn't matter how many times he said that, though, his parents still had some kind of hornet in their ass about his choices. And the more they tried to figure out what was wrong with him inside—nothing was wrong with him—that made him party like he was going to die tomorrow. Given his life, that was a real possibility. The more he wanted to forget he was going to wake up the next day regardless.

Because that was the fucking thing about this whole shit show—he could drink and drink and drink until he couldn't think straight or see two feet in front of his own eyes. He could take pill after pill, or smoke whatever was going to make him feel good for the night.

Gio was still bulletproof.

Nothing was killing him.

Not yet, anyway.

He really was fine.

Too bad they wouldn't figure it out, too.

"So, head's up," Dante murmured.

They were just ten steps away from their parents now, but neither Antony nor Cecelia had noticed the brothers' arrival.

Thank Dio.

"What's that?" Gio asked.

Jesus.

He couldn't even hide how gruff and hoarse his voice sounded. He was so fucked—he should have just stayed in his bed, and ignored Dante when the asshole came around to get him up for church. Antony would have been pissed, sure, but he preferred it when Gio didn't show up ... well, all right, wasted.

Plus, his father probably already knew.

If he didn't suspect.

After all, Gio hadn't showed up at his parents' place the night before like he usually would—figured he could probably get away with it being Lucian had his dick in a knot over the chick he was shacking up with ... or fucking ... or saving ... or—what was he doing with that Jordyn girl again?

"Are you even listening to me?" Dante asked.

Gio passed his brother a look, and shook his head. "Not really."

"Figures."

"What was it?"

"Lucian is bringing her to church today," Dante said. "That's the important bit."

Her.

Her ... like Jordyn, her.

The only her his oldest brother would be bringing around at the moment, although it took Gio's wasted brain a minute to catch up to speed with what his brother was trying to get through his thick fucking skull.

God.

He needed to lay off mixing molly and liquor.

It was bad news.

Gio's brow flew up high. "Like, here?"

"Where else do we go to church?"

"Yeah, but ... with Ma and Dad, and ... here?"

"Big thing, huh," Dante muttered.

To say the least ...

The Marcello brothers knew the rules—their father had been repeating those same rules to them since they learned to look at Antony and listen. They weren't to be bringing females around their parents unless it was women they intended to keep around their parents.

Simple as that.

"Do you think he—"

"I think Lucian is crazy," Dante said.

Gio rolled his eyes upward. "Yeah, but that's because everybody knows you're not the marrying kind."

"I'm the marrying kind. I just don't want to fucking get married. See the difference?"

"Bite my fucking head off. Point is—do you think he's really caught up in something with this Jordyn chick?"

Dante shrugged. "Who the fuck knows?"

Well, that was that.

"Giovanni."

Ah, shit.

Those last ten steps went quickly.

Cecelia was frowning.

Antony was as cold as ice.

"Care to have a word, Gio?" his father asked.

"Not par—"

"Get in the church," Antony snapped.

"Yeah, all right."

*

"Jesus," Antony grumbled as he dropped into the pew beside Gio, "you couldn't even manage to put on a tie this morning?"

Gio cringed. "Well …"

"What, son?"

"I did try."

His hands had just fumbled too much, and he got pissed off. Especially when Dante started barking that they were going to be late, and … yeah.

Antony sighed, and glanced over at Gio. "Take those damn sunglasses off, would you?"

"You probably don't want me to."

He could see his father's deepening scowl out of the corner of his eye, but Gio figured if he just kept staring straight ahead, then he could pretend like he didn't see it. A little stupid, maybe, but it served him well over the years.

"Bruises, or something else?"

"I just look … like shit, according to Dante," Gio admitted.

His father was quiet for a long while before Antony finally reached over, and took the sunglasses off himself. Antony stared at Gio without saying anything, and then handed the sunglasses back.

"You don't wear them in church regardless of what you look like—it's disrespectful, Gio."

Great.

A longer stretch of silence passed on between the father and son before Antony was the one to break it again. He usually was—Gio just tended to let his father speak until he didn't have anything else to say.

It was easier.

"You're scaring your mother," Antony murmured.

Gio glanced down at his hands in his lap. "There's nothing to be scared of."

"I would think the constant belief that she's going to wake up to a call some morning that they believe her son's body is in a morgue is something to be scared of, Gio."

"Low blow."

"Tell me where I lied."

Gio sighed. "I could die being a made man, too."

"Is that what it is?"

"Hmm, what?" Gio glanced at his father. "You lost me."

"You're just restless and so reckless that it doesn't matter to you either way—you're going to die, and you know it—so why not speed the process along a bit?"

"I never said that."

Antony frowned. "I wonder."

"Don't."

"I also know when this all started for you—this partying and fast living and rebellious nonsense," his father added quieter. "And I know you don't want to talk about him—about how he died, and how you were there, Gio, but you know as well as I do that Giovanni worked damn hard to keep you away from this kind of thing. He didn't want you getting messed up in drugs, or—"

"All right, that's enough," Gio said thickly.

He didn't talk about his mentor, and the man who he'd been named after.

He didn't want to.

He didn't want to remember.

"You know," his father murmured, "it's okay to say that might have messed with you a bit, and that you need—"

"I need you to drop it," Gio interjected firmly.

Antony did, thankfully.

"Fine; remember, I did try, Gio. Today, and before today. I will try tomorrow, too. I could have been outside greeting your brother as he made a choice that would change his life, and this family and his future—a choice I want to let him make—but instead, I am in here. Trying to help you."

"Wrong choice, then, huh?" Gio asked. "We all screw up sometimes, Dad. We all make mistakes. Isn't that what you keep telling me every single time I fuck up? Well, that and also that we can fix mistakes ... sometimes."

Antony shook his head. "This wasn't a mistake. It can't be—you're still my son, Gio."

Sometimes, he wondered, though.

How much was it going to take?

How far was he going to have to push?

Would there come a time when his father finally said enough was enough, and washed his hands of Gio for good? Antony seemed to believe there was something in Gio that was good—something that could change.

He hadn't found it yet.
And he had to live with himself twenty-four-fucking-seven.
Shame, that was.

KING IN WAITING

"Well?" Dante asked. "What do you have to say for yourself, then?"

Giovanni stayed quiet near the window of his brother's office. His favorite place in any office or room, really. Unlike most men in his business who refused to put their back to a window or doorway, Giovanni was not quite the same. He figured he'd cheated death so many times in his life that it was not going to creep up on him from behind. Besides, like this, he could pretend to be distracted.

Even if he was anything but distracted.

"Andino!" Dante barked.

Gio finally let his attention drift away from the window. His sixteen year old son stood in the middle of the room with a blank expression on his face even as he faced the wrath of his uncle. He was quite a sight, this son of his.

Built like a brick shithouse, and fully capable of proving he was as tough as one, too ... Andino was something else.

Gio had seen bigger, older, and maybe even better men, cower at the sight of Dante's rage when it turned on them. And yet, there Andino stood like he was facing a summer rain storm that was about to be a fucking nuisance to his evening and not his very pissed off uncle.

It amused Gio like nothing else. People kept saying this boy of his was more like his uncle than him, but Gio didn't know if that was entirely true in all cases. Andino was just really good at being fucking sneaky.

God knew Gio and Kim tried as hard as they could to let this kid of theirs live his life how he wanted to, and without too much of their—or any outside—influence. Their lives had been so controlled, and strangled by rules. He didn't want that for his son, too. How the hell was Andino supposed to learn who he was or who the fuck he wanted to be when too many other people were telling him who they wanted him to be?

Seemed simple enough to Gio.

Besides ... Andino had enough people trying to keep him in line.

Like Dante.

"Well?" Dante demanded yet again.

Andino sighed.

He was quite a fucking sight—busted mouth, bloodied knuckles, and an eye already starting to blacken. Kim was going to flip out about her son's swollen lip, for sure, and probably the cuts on his hands from where he'd broken a few teeth on the other guy. He'd taken a good beating, but Gio knew for a fact his son had given the other guy an even worse run for his money.

It wasn't the fighting that was the problem—sort of. Made men weren't supposed to fight with one another, but Andino wasn't technically made. He had a few more years yet to go for that. Still, Dante held these principes of their family to the same fucking standards as any other made man in their family.

After all, Andino—like John—was a fifth generation made Marcello man. Where else was his kid going to go but straight into the life like the rest of them?

They didn't fucking know anything different.

This was their whole world.

No, the fighting wasn't the problem. It was who Andino decided to lay a beating on that was the issue at hand.

"He's a twenty-eight year old enforcer of the family, Andi," Dante said. "A good made man who handles his business, and is looking at a Capo position in a couple of years if he plays his cards right."

"How's that Capo thing going to work out when he's drinking his meals from a straw for the rest of his life, huh?" Andino asked.

Gio literally had to press his lips together to keep himself from laughing. Because fuck yeah, that was a smart ass response, but it was a damn good one, too. Credit where it was due, and all that shit.

Andino wasn't lying, either.

The enforcer would be lucky to wake up.

Dante's jaw clenched, and he acted like Andino hadn't spoken out of turn at all. "And that alone means you know better than to be fighting with him. What were you thinking?"

"That he shoulda shut his fuckin' mouth," Andino said quietly.

Dante arched a brow at that statement. "I beg your pardon?"

"I said what I said."

Gio tipped his chin up, and nodded to himself. Andino also had balls which was more than he could say for a lot of people. Gio didn't really take credit for that because a lot of the Marcello men were arrogant fuckers that could drive a saint crazy.

Dante leaned back on his desk, and rested his hands against the wood top. "I said, I beg your pardon, Andino. Try again."

"And I said—he shoulda kept his fucking mouth shut. Popping off like that about John when his back is turned because he thinks he can get away with it. Nobody's going to say shit about John whether he's looking them in the face, or not. Not while I'm standing right there to listen to it, too. I warned him. If he could talk, you could ask him. I warned him, zio."

Gio cleared his throat, and glanced away when Dante's gaze slid in his direction. He was asked not to step in on this. Right now, that was taking a great deal of his patience, but fuck him if he wasn't at least going to try.

But he couldn't pretend like he didn't know how goddamn protective Andino was over John. Especially now with John's recent diagnosis. Andino was most sensitive to someone trying to hurt his cousin in some way. He'd always been like that even before they knew John was bipolar. He'd been inseparable from his cousin since the two were in diapers.

"What did he say, then?" Dante asked.

Andino's jaw stiffened. "You don't care. You care that I almost killed him."

Dante nodded, and gave his nephew a look. "Yes, in your grandmother's garden, Andino. You don't see the problem there?"

"Next time I'll lure them away from the house, then."

Gio's brother sighed so loudly that he couldn't help but snort. He had to look away to avoid Dante's glare that was surely coming his fucking way. Dante was predictable like that.

"I do care," Dante murmured, "now tell me what he said."

"Called him crazy. More than once, too."

The shift in atmosphere was palpable. It took a beat in time, and then two before Dante said, "All right, go on, then. Go clean that fucking face of yours and your hands before your mother lays eyes on you, Andi. Get."

Gio turned in just enough time to see his son's back disappearing out the office doorway. He glanced his brother's way to find Dante was staring at the floor, and a hell of a lot calmer than Gio expected him to be.

He almost looked … contemplative.

Gio wasn't sure he liked that.

"You'd have done it, too," Gio was quick to say, "had that been me or Lucian someone was slandering, you would have—"

His brother had done things exactly like that growing up, too. They all had. Gio didn't think he needed to bring all those events and times to the conversation, though. He was sure Dante remembered them without Gio pointing them out.

"I know what I would have done," Dante uttered, "so don't bother."

"Then, what—"

"I think I want to move Andino to mentor under Lucian, if you wouldn't mind."

Gio's brow furrowed. "He's mentored under me since he could walk, Dante."

"I think he would be a better fit for Lucian."

"Because why ex—"

"And then under me, by-proxy, and without directly saying so," Dante added quieter.

Gio's eyes widened, and he made a noise under his breath. "Mentor to ... take over?"

Dante passed him a look. "It took me an hour, Gio, to get that kid to even admit he'd beat the shit out of that enforcer. A whole fucking hour of him standing there looking like he needed to go to the emergency room. I think the only reason he did decide to talk was because he was fucking bored of ignoring me."

That was ... fair.

"I don't know what that had anything to do with changing mentors for him, though."

"Don't you?"

Well, maybe he did. But maybe he also wanted Dante to say it.

"I mean, if you're going to change his whole life," Gio said, "and be the man who does that to him, then at least be the man who can look at his father and tell him that same thing, Dante. Look at me and tell me it."

"I don't want to change his life, or what he's doing," Dante countered fast. "I know what it feels like to grow up knowing every single day this is the seat waiting for me, and what that does to someone, Gio. I know it's not easy. But he is the best fit—in the end, he's going to be the one making the right choices when it comes to this family's legacy. This was John today. Imagine when it is our name he's standing in front of like a brick wall that won't be moved."

"Then, what are you planning on doing?"

"When it's time for him to know he'll take over after me, then it's time. And I will tell him."

That … sounded messy as hell.

Gio wasn't the boss, though.

He was just Andino's fucking father.

Gio had never been a king in waiting.

Apparently, he was going to raise one.

DANTE OUTTAKES

THE IMPOSSIBLE

Dante hung back in the office, his gaze locked on where the doctor's hand was a little too low on his wife's body than he was comfortable with, but he kept his mouth shut. The man kind of had to be checking lower on her pelvis, anyway. The little wand moved the gel on Catrina's stomach around, and a *whooshing* noise filled the room. It reminded Dante of the white noise on a television channel that had gone out late at night.

The longer that sound filled the room, the worse Dante's nerves became. His fingers twitched, and he couldn't seem to stand entirely still. He wasn't the type for anxiety—that wasn't his thing. Always calm and in control, he felt like the exact opposite in those moments.

It didn't escape his wife's notice, either. She wasn't like him—nervous, sure, but she kept it to herself. Her gaze locked on his, and he heard her silent, *It's okay.*

Loud and clear.

It still didn't feel okay to him.

What if they couldn't find it?

What if it wasn't there?

What if—

All at once, that white noise became quieter as it faded into the background of the sounds coming out of the speaker. It was still there, yes, but faint. What came to the forefront was a galloping beat—that was the best way Dante could describe what he was hearing. It sounded like a hundred horses' hooves beating against the group.

Constant.

Steady.

Strong.

Catrina relaxed on the bed a bit, and Dante finally stopped his fidgeting. All his nerves—for this moment, anyway—were gone just like that. They had heard the heartbeat before. Several times, actually, but that didn't this moment any less important or nerve-wracking to Dante. Each time he knew they were going to be looking for it ... it was like his mind went to the worst thing possible first as he waited for them to find those galloping hooves again.

He had other things to worry about, of course. Getting through his pregnancy. Having his only biological child born. Those were things that hadn't yet come, and he still felt more anxiety over than he really wanted to admit, but it would come. And he had no doubt that he would panic the entire time.

Just like he had done for this moment.

The doctor smiled. "And there it is, everyone. One heartbeat. One-fifty-three beats a minute, if I'm hearing it correctly."

"Can I record that?" Dante asked.

"Sound, not video, if you wouldn't mind," the doctor replied.

Dante nodded, pulled out his phone, and brought up the recording app. The doctor held the wand steady as Dante recorded maybe fifteen seconds of his baby's heartbeat. His wife was still looking at him—*watching* him. Only now, her silent words had changed to, *See, I told you.*

"Thank you," Dante said after he turned it off.

"No problem."

The doctor took his time putting his equipment away, pulling off the gloves, and helping Catrina wipe off her stomach before his wife was sitting straight on the bed. The curtain closed out the doctor and Dante for a minute so she could slip off the hospital gown, and put her clothes back on instead. Once the curtain was pulled back again, Catrina was back in her knee-length, body-hugging dress and sky high heels.

No matter how many times he told her the heels could be shortened a bit to make it easier for this pregnancy, she just gave him one of *those* smiles. A smile that simply said, *Men.*

Like he couldn't possibly know better, and she was just going to pat his head like a silly little puppy who was cute, but was also still wrong. That was his wife in a nutshell.

She was amazing.

She was giving him something amazing.

And he loved her for it.

Penning something in the file he held, the doctor turned to Catrina with a smile. "Everything looks great, Catrina. And as of yesterday, you were beyond the first trimester which is really the only thing we were concerned about. It isn't you that has the fertility troubles, after all, so I don't consider you high risk for the rest of this pregnancy. Resume normal activity, within reason if it feels fine. And the ladies at the front will make your next appointment. Another five or so weeks, and we'll be able to find out the gender ... if the baby wants to cooperate when we put him or her in the spotlight."

Catrina smiled. "Great, *grazie*."

Once the doctor was gone from the room, and Dante was alone with his wife again, he crossed the room to go to her. She was just picking up her Gucci bag from the chair when his hands found her neck, and he pulled her in for a kiss. Long, and lingering, and *sweet*. He really just wanted to kiss her because that always made everything better.

Catrina smiled as he pulled away. "You know, if this makes you so nervous every time we come to listen to the heartbeat, you don't have to come to these, Dante. They're standard appointments."

He shook his head. "No way."

Nope.

He wouldn't miss one.

Even if he almost had a heart attack each damn time.

Catrina stroked her thumb along his jawline. "Well, the first hurdle is over with now."

"First thirteen weeks, hmm."

She smiled. "You know what that means, don't you?"

It took him a second.

And then two.

"Time to share the news with everyone else."

Catrina's smile turned into a full-blown grin. "Are you ready for that?"

Terrified, maybe.

Not because his family would do something to make him feel that way. They would be just as excited and happy for this as he was. His brothers—his parents, too—knew how badly he wanted children, but over the years, they stopped talking about it with him. By his choice because frankly, it fucking hurt when it just wasn't supposed to be.

It was the impossible for Dante.

And now it was real.

That was the thing, though ...

Telling everyone ...

"It's going to make it very real," he murmured.

Catrina nodded, and stroked his cheek again. "This Sunday, then?"

"After church, I think."

Done deal.

*

Catrina passed a wiggling Michel over, and Dante finally got the boy settled in his lap in the pew. He could have sent his son down to Sunday school like a lot of the other children, but he didn't trust *anyone* except family with his kid. Besides, Michel would much rather stay with his mother and father, anyway.

They wanted him with them, too.

"Here, play with Daddy's phone," Dante said, giving Michel the device to keep him occupied while the priest at the altar finished up his service. Michel pressed all the buttons on the screen, lighting it up, but unable to unlock the device. Not that it mattered—he didn't keep much on his phone, anyway. No photographs he didn't want seen, and certainly not videos. He had the recording of the baby's heartbeat that he'd listened to that morning, but he doubted Michel was going to somehow get that turned on with the phone locked. "A few more minutes, Michel."

The baby chewed on the phone as down the pew, Antony glanced at his son. "I heard we have news to share. Someone want to let me in on that?"

Catrina gave Dante a look.

He just shrugged. "It came up."

"How does it just *come up*?"

"I didn't tell them what, Cat."

"Mmm."

Chuckles passed over the front pew, but it only took a single look from the priest to quiet the Marcellos. It didn't matter, really. Dante could still feel the eyes of his family on him and his wife. He had thought that mentioning they had news to share would help with his nerves a little bit. Like prepping himself for the big moment.

It had, sort of.

Dante's phone buzzed, taking his gaze down to where his son was holding the device. A call lit up the screen, but because he had it on silent, it made no noise. It didn't matter. Michel knew just from playing with his father's phone time and time again how to reject a call.

The thing Dante forgot?

Rejecting or accepting a call automatically unlocked his phone—a stupid glitch, he always thought, which was why he needed to suck it up and get a new one even if he hated changing phones.

It took all of a half of a second for Michel to hit the home screen button twice, which brought up all the apps that were running on the background of the device. His son just happened to hit the right app—the one with the recording.

Softly, the sound of galloping hooves whispered down the pew as his baby's heartbeat came out of the phone's speakers. All eyes turned on him again. Catrina was already reaching for the phone, but Dante?

He just *laughed*.

Because ... of course.

Of course, it would happen like this.

He didn't doubt anyone in his family was unaware of what that sound was. His brothers had their own children—his mother had two biological children.

Yes, they knew what that damn sound was.

It was his mother who spoke first. Always quiet in church. Always respectful of Mass, and the service they had come to watch. Always making sure her children understood to sit down and shut up until it was over.

"Was that what I thought it was. Antony, was that what I thought—"

"I don't know. Dante?"

"Yes, Ma," Dante murmured. "That's what you thought it was."

He expected the rest of his family to at least keep quiet for the last two minutes or so of mass. They didn't. His brothers started first—standing from the pew with loud congratulations and strong hugs coming his way. His parents followed right after.

A whole church watched as the Marcellos celebrated.

They probably didn't understand.

He really didn't give a damn.

WINNING

"You're sure?" Lucian asked.

Dante nodded.

Gio smirked. "And you're pissed off like nothing else."

Dante nodded again.

"How'd you find out?" Lucian asked.

"Gaetano is in town," Dante informed.

Even his tone came off as cold and detached. It was easier this way. Easier to take his emotions out of the equation and just handle the situation. He could deal with his anger and Catrina later. Right now, he just needed to focus on finding his wife and putting her ridiculous need to hide things from him to bed.

"That tells me nothing," Lucian said.

Dante took a corner sharply, sending his unbuckled brothers swinging in their seats.

"Slow the hell down," Lucian grumbled. "I have a toddler, a newborn and a wife to go home to, Dante. Fucking hell."

"Jesus, are you trying to get us killed?" Gio barked.

"You do remember the time you drove Dad's Mercedes into the telephone pole while Lucian and me were sleeping in the backseat, right?" Dante asked. "Let's go to a party, you said, it'll be fun. Oh, waking up with a bloody mouth and a broken rib was all kinds of fun, asshole. Sober driver for once in your goddamn life, Gio, and you nearly killed all three of us in the process."

Gio quieted.

"That's what I thought," Dante muttered.

"I swerved to miss a raccoon!"

"There was no raccoon dead on the road," Lucian argued.

"Because I swerved to miss it, dumbass," Gio growled.

"Oh, shut up, the both of you."

"Still no raccoon," Lucian said under his breath.

Dante barely caught the sight of Gio's fist slamming into the shoulder of his oldest brother before the youngest Marcello brother was back in his seat like nothing had even happened. Lucian rubbed at his shoulder with a scowl that could rival the devil.

This was why he called his brothers tonight.

Because they were grown ass men.

Because they were best friends.

And sometimes it still felt like they were teenagers tearing up pavement together. Even with kids, wives, mortgages, and Cosa Nostra chasing their asses daily.

Sometimes ...

"Anyway, I found out Gaetano is in town," Dante said again.

"So?" Lucian asked.

"So, he only comes in from LA when he's got business to discuss. Now, I don't mind Catrina doing her thing, or discussing ventures. She's safe with Gae, he'll take care of her."

"They're close, right?" Gio asked as he lit up a cigarette in the back seat.

"Yeah."

That was a bit of an understatement.

Catrina and Gaetano might as well have been best friends, as far as Dante was concerned. The closeness between the two could rival the closeness he shared with his wife.

Dante didn't mention that to his brothers, though.

Fact was simple—he wasn't jealous of Gaetano or the relationship the man had with Cat. Why would he be jealous? It wasn't like Gaetano had any interest in what was going on between Catrina's legs or getting up under her dress what with his preference for men. Besides, Cat didn't have a lot of friends as it was. The ones she did have, she kept close. Like Gaetano. Dante wasn't about to take that away from his wife.

His brothers might not understand.

That's all.

"So what's the problem?" Lucian asked.

Dante sighed, pulling his car into the parking lot of a club his wife owned. She'd bought the property and shoddy building a few months ago, spent a good four-hundred-grand getting it up to par and on the legal side of things, and then opened it for business.

By the looks of the parking lot, the place was packed.

"The problem," Dante said, "is that my wife didn't tell me Gaetano was in town."

"I don't get it," Gio admitted.

Lucian shrugged. "Me, either."

"She didn't want me to know," Dante explained quietly. "Which is why I said I found out he was in town. That means, Cat is doing business. Some kind of business she knows I wouldn't approve of right now."

Lucian frowned. "Dante—"

"Shut up. My wife, my house, my rules. You manage yours, Lucian."

Gio leaned between the seats, his cigarette dangling between his lips as he said, "You know, millions of women have gone through this before Catrina, man. It's nature. It happens. It's what their bodies are made to do."

"Those women aren't Queen Pins working in a very dangerous environment with a mob boss for a husband, Gio."

"Fair enough," Gio muttered.

"And not all of those women struggled to have a child," Dante added quieter, his anger rising again. "We're not going to get another shot after this, okay. This is it for us. So forgive me if it pisses me off that my wife is knowingly putting herself and her pregnancy in danger simply because she's crazy."

Gio coughed. "You said that, not me."

Lucian agreed.

"What if she had asked you to go with her tonight for whatever she's going?" Gio asked.

"I told her no business."

"But—"

"No business means no fucking business," Dante interrupted sharply.

"Yeah, well you go tell her that." Lucian smiled in that cocky way of his. "I'm sure it'll be one hell of a fun show."

Anxiousness slipped through Dante's veins. His brother had a point, which was why he brought Lucian and Giovanni along for the ride.

"That's why you two are here," Dante informed as he turned off the engine.

Gio smacked the middle divider with his hand. "Right, you're funny tonight, man. Hilarious."

"I'm serious."

Lucian glared at Dante. "Coward."

Dante smiled. "Hey, if your wife was Catrina Marcello and you were about to break up her little schemes, what would you do?"

Lucian still glared. "Coward."

"My point exactly."

"You're ridiculous," Gio muttered. "For one thing, she isn't that bad. It's only when she's in a mood that you kind of have to steer clear."

Yep.

And at the moment, Catrina was ten weeks pregnant, hormonal as fuck, and apparently doing business after her husband had explicitly forbid her from doing so.

It was going to be one hell of a fun night.

"She's working, so she's in a mood," Dante informed. "And I'm the boss, so you two just stay quiet, do whatever I ask, and stay out of the range of her claws."

"Coward," Lucian repeated.

Dante smirked at his brother. "Oh?"

"Yes."

"Then go in there and get my wife, Lucian. What the boss wants, the boss gets. Right?"

Lucian's cheek twitched.

"Go get her," Dante continued unfazed, "and you can bring her home to me. I don't mind going to pick up my son early from Ma. Maybe I'll take Michel out for some gelato if you think it'll take a while to get Cat out of here."

"You're an asshole," Lucian said.

"You don't get to pick your family, brother."

"Lucky for you," Gio mumbled as he got out of the car. "We'd have kicked your ass out long ago."

*

"Dante."

Cat's eyes burned with a fire as she glanced up at her husband from the booth she was sitting in. Dante offered Cat a smile he knew was cold.

She started this, after all.

"What are you doing here?" Cat asked, lifting her glass of sparkling water to take a sip.

"Evening, wife," Dante murmured. "I could ask you the same thing."

"Working. I own this place, remember? The owner has to stop in every once in a while."

Cat's excuses were lies.

Dante knew it.

He could fucking smell the bullshit from feet away.

Several men sat around the booth, surrounding his wife. What Dante didn't want to do was cause a major fuss and make Catrina look unworthy or bad in front of her men, if that's what they were. Dante didn't have an all-access pass to Catrina's inside business. He knew the few faces she had at on the front lines, like Gaetano and Pao, but that was it.

It would do neither of them any good to get into one of their battles in front of people.

No good at all.

Gaetano waved from the seat across from Cat. "Boss."

"Gae," Dante greeted.

Quietly, Lucian and Gio stepped to either side of Dante.

Catrina sighed heavily. "You brought your brothers?"

"Boys night out," Dante lied. "Apparently, you're enjoying the same thing. I thought we talked about this Cat—no business. There was a reason we agreed on it. Gaetano was handling things, wasn't he? Or have you fallen short, Gae? Is she pissed about something you did, is that it?"

Gaetano chuckled. "No, of course not. But you know how she is."

"Has she told you that she's expect—"

"Shut up," Cat warned.

There it was.

One claw.

Dante smiled. "You haven't told him?"

Catrina eyed her husband from the side, the fire burning brighter. "I was going to before I left. We had things to discuss first."

"It's kind of important, Catrina. I think Gaetano would understand and maybe, he'd even get why I showed up tonight."

Catrina tapped her jeweled, manicured fingernails to the table and with a jerk of her head, the booth cleared of men except for Gaetano. Dante watched the men go and his brothers followed behind to keep them from returning.

"What am I missing?" Gaetano asked.

Catrina frowned. "Dante—"

"We agreed, Cat."

"No, you demanded," she argued hotly.

"And you agreed," he said simply.

"I did not!" Cat scowled and added, "I am not fucking disabled, Dante. I'm not doing anything wrong. There's nothing problematic that might cause me harm, bello. We're having a conversation about an issue that came up between a few men and a couple of the girls. That was all. I need to handle these things."

"Gaetano handles those things. That's why he's situated in LA. Isn't that what you told me?"

Cat smacked her hand to the table. "You don't understand, Dante. It isn't like Cosa Nostra—they take advantage when someone they're frightened of isn't around. There aren't rules to this. You know all of this, so why you're fighting with me, I don't understand."

"We're not fighting. You're fighting. There's a difference."

As he spoke, Dante kept his tone level, quiet, and calm.

No doubt, that just pissed his wife off more.

While Catrina knew how to push every button Dante had, he knew how to push hers even more.

"You could have called," Catrina muttered.

"I did. Check your phone."

"It's turned off."

Of course, it was.

That was also why he couldn't get a decent location on her GPS.

In a blink, Catrina smiled and turned on the charm.

She should have known better.

Dante never fell for that shit like every other man in her life did.

"Dante, give me a few and we'll go home."

"No," Dante murmured.

"Bello—"

"No."

Cat sucked in a breath, a heat pinking her cheeks.

Dante didn't take his eyes off his wife for a second as he said, "Gaetano, could you leave, please? I need a moment with my wife. Clearly she's more interested in acting like the Queen instead of Catrina Marcello tonight, so you'll need to step out."

Gaetano looked all kinds of uncomfortable. "All right, regina, give me a call tomorrow or something."

"Sit down and shut up," Cat ordered.

The man sat back down in the booth, shooting Dante with a wary look.

It wasn't the first time that Dante had pulled rank between the two and forced Gaetano out of a situation so that he could have a proper discussion with his wife on something, be it life, family or business related.

"Are you going to make this hard, donna?" Dante asked.

Cat sneered. "No bella this time?"

"We both know you're beautiful as sin, Cat. But right now, you're just a woman who is seriously pushing your fucking luck tonight."

"I am fine, Dante," Cat said. "You're being ridiculous."

"Protective," he corrected.

"Over-protective," she shot back.

Maybe so.

Maybe he was.

"I get that right, Catrina," Dante said. "You know I do. Right now, I have every damned right to protect you however I see fit."

"I am not disabled," she repeated.

"Were one of the problem men here tonight? You said there was an issue with a few men and a couple of the girls. Were any of the men here at this table?" Dante asked.

Cat shot Gaetano with a look that kept him quiet.

Dante didn't need an answer with that.

"One of them was, huh?" Dante's anger edged higher, sharpening like the blade of a knife. "Fantastic."

"It was important, Dante," Cat said softly.

"Then you could have asked me to come along."

"I needed to be here as me, not as your wife."

"That is exactly who you are!" Dante practically roared the words. Anyone in their vicinity would have heard it. Quieter, he growled, "My wife, Catrina. A mother, too, and an expecting one, for that matter. You even had the nerve to lose the enforcers trailing you tonight because you knew we'd discussed you taking a step back from this for the next few months."

"Expecting?" Gaetano asked.

Catrina waved her fingers in the air nervously. "Yes, but—"

"Cat," Gaetano hissed, "this was fucking serious tonight. Mick was pissed off and you were poking at him like you were trying to make him react."

"I would have handled him," Cat replied blithely. "That was the entire point, Gae."

Gaetano nodded, standing from the booth. He gave Dante a clap on the shoulder as he passed. "I get it, really. Good luck."

"Gaetano," Cat snapped, standing as well.

"Sit," Dante demanded.

Cat glared.

Dante didn't budge.

"Sit back in that both, Catrina, or I will pick you up and carry you out of here with your pretty ass high in the air for anyone to look at while we walk away. Sit down right now."

Catrina didn't move an inch. "I can't believe you."

"Then we're in very similar boats, sweetheart."

"You're impossible. I was fine."

"Sit down," Dante said, his tone darkening.

Catrina did as she was told, thankfully.

"Where is Michel?" she asked.

"With my mother."

"Your brothers are coming back."

"Good," Dante said, "then they've done their jobs and escorted your men off the property for the evening without trouble. Now, I just have to get you home as well."

If stares could kill, Dante would be dead.

"I have work to do," Cat said, frustration thick in her voice.

"I ended that when I had your men escorted out, or did you miss that? You've always been a quick woman. It's one of the things I love about you."

"Sometimes, you make it difficult to return the favor."

So be it.

"Easy or hard, Cat, it's your choice."

She made it easy ...

When he picked her up and carried her out.

*

Dante stood in the doorway of the master bath, watching his wife draw a bath. "Are you still angry with me?"

It'd been a week since the club incident. Catrina didn't say more than two words to Dante the entire week.

Those words?

Fuck and you.

Dante also slept on the couch.

Worth it.

"Catrina," Dante said, still waiting for his little queen to even grace him with her attention.

Despite feeling justified in his actions, the silence and anger was starting to eat away at him. He adored his wife—she was everything to him. He didn't like to fight with her, especially because fighting with Catrina was so emotionally taxing, it could rival just about anything, including death.

"Yes," Catrina said quietly, "I'm angry with you, bello. Still."

"I'm not going to apologize."

Catrina dropped the silk robe she wore, exposing her nakedness beneath. Dante's mouth went dry at the sight of his wife's skin and curves. Her body was a living piece of art. Fucking perfection right there in flesh and bones.

Problem was, with no talking came no fucking.

Not even angry fucking.

That was the best kind, too.

"Cat," Dante said, her name coming out heady and thick.

Catrina didn't say a thing as she climbed in the tub and sunk beneath the bubbles. "Si?"

Goddamn it.

"Why are you angry?" he asked, trying to tamper down his lust. It didn't help that his cock was hardening under his slacks as his wife lifted her bare legs from the water to rest them on the edge of the tub, criss-crossed. Catrina's legs were one of her best features. She knew it, too. "We agreed on no business during the pregnancy, Catrina."

"No one else knows about the pregnancy outside of our close family."

"Your point?"

She ignored his question.

"Or rather, they didn't until the other night," Catrina continued, frowning. "It's hard enough that I have a husband and a child, Dante. Do you realize how they look at me sometimes?"

"No," he admitted.

"It's not like your business. Being a Queen Pin isn't like being a

Don, bello. It's difficult. My ability to keep people under control depends on their level of respect and fear of the person holding the highest position. And while being a wife and mother is a wonderful and amazing thing, it's also a weakness. Lesser—that's how they feel about me. Like I am the lesser of them. I have—"

"You know that isn't true," he interjected quietly.

"—never felt like the lesser person in those situations, bello."

Dante understood, but his feelings remained the same. "We agreed, Cat. No business."

"But—"

"This isn't negotiable, Cat. This isn't one of those things we'll fight and fuck out, okay. It isn't. I don't ask you for very goddamn much, but I am telling you this. No business."

With that, he left his beautiful as sin wife, her painted red lips and her sexy legs alone in the bathroom. Even though it practically fucking killed him to do it.

*

Dante closed the door to Michel's bedroom with a sigh. Fifteen books about trains later and the toddler was finally asleep. Dante loved his son, no doubt about it, but the boy was terribly particular about his naptime routine.

He got that from his type-A mother.

Dante didn't complain, really.

The smell of something warm and rich floated up from the stairwell. Dante followed the deliciousness to find his wife in the kitchen, sitting at the table. One of Cat's best dishes happened to be a homemade spaghetti and meatballs with a concoction of spices that could make a person's mouth water.

Dante's was no exception.

"This is a surprise," Dante said from the entryway.

Cat shrugged. "A peace offering."

"Oh?"

"Mmhmm."

Dante took note of the fact his wife wore a dress that happened to be one of his very favorites. She must have changed while he was putting their son to bed, because she had been wearing skinny jeans and a blouse earlier. The silver studded heels she wore sent sparkles casting over her ankles and calves.

Sex.

Dante could practically taste it on his tongue.

"Peace offering, huh?" he asked.

"I thought we could talk."

Just the demure sound of her voice told him that his wife was out for blood. His, to be exact. But if she wanted to play those games, Dante was up for that. He sat at the table across from Catrina and ate the meal in silence.

"Talk," he said quietly.

"I will talk to Gaetano."

"Absolutely not, Catrina."

"You didn't let me finish."

Standing from the table, Dante wiped his mouth with the napkin before washing back the taste of the spices with a half of a glass of wine his wife had set out for him. Then, he moved around the table, keeping Catrina in his sights all the while. When he stood in front of her, he dropped to his knees. Catrina didn't say a word as his hands traveled over her thighs under her dress.

"Talk," Dante said.

Sighing, Catrina murmured, "If you're willing, you could fly out to LA with me, settle some things, and all will be well. But I have to do it. Me, not someone else."

"No."

"Dante ..."

He let his hands travel higher under her dress until silk and lace edged around his fingers. Catrina's gaze darkened as Dante ghosted the tips of his fingers along the seam of her sex over top of her panties.

"No," he repeated. "No business. We agreed."

"You demanded," she said weakly.

"And you agreed."

"It's not the same thing, bello ... God."

Cat let out a shaky breath when two of his fingers slipped under the silk of her panties to graze her sex. Clearly, it wasn't just Dante who had been frustrated and wanting something for the last week. Catrina seemed all too pleased to have her husband's hands between her thighs, touching her. Dante didn't mind a bit.

He found her wet, hot, and tight as two of his fingers slipped into her core. Nothing was more beautiful than Catrina when Dante was fucking her. It didn't matter if it was his fingers, mouth or cock, she was sexy as hell.

Her sex clamped down on his fingers, wetness soaking his palm when he curled the digits hard into her G-spot. Catrina's quiet cry was high and broken, like she'd been needing that, wanting that. Dante didn't mind providing it.

"There," he murmured.

Catrina shifted her hips with every thrust, meeting his hand. "There."

"So sensitive," he noted, flicking his thumb up to graze her clit.

Her body jerked at the touch.

"Merda," she breathed. "You're killing me."

"Mmm," he agreed, pushing the skirt of her dress higher around her hips to see the sight of his fingers working her sex under her panties. "Fucking perfect. Come, Cat. I want you soaking me even more. I need a fucking taste of this pussy. It's been a goddamn week, kitten. That's too long."

"Harder," she demanded.

He obliged, stroking her sex faster and deeper until her thighs shook and she was crying his name. When her snug, wet walls started to flutter around his fingers, Dante stood, keeping the rhythm between her thighs going, and kissed his wife bruisingly hard. His tongue claimed her mouth as she came undone around his hand.

"Hmm," Dante hummed, grinning as he kissed the apple of her cheek.

Cat shuddered. "Talking, Dante, we were supposed to be—"

"It's still not up for discussion, bella."

"Fine."

Dante removed his hand and placed it to her still trembling thigh. "What was that?"

"Fine," Cat muttered. "You win."

"It's not about winning."

"Liar. It's always about winning with you."

Dante smirked. "Well, as long as I get what I want, then yes."

"No business."

"No business," he agreed.

"Until the baby is born."

Half-winning, then. Dante would take it.

THE NEWBORN

Catrina Marcello had never been more terrified of anything in her life than the moment when she needed to leave the hospital after her daughter's birth. She had come to learn several things in her cozy, comfortable stay in the Labor and Delivery ward with the nurses close by.

One, she didn't know fucking anything about babies.

Nothing.

Two, having to do all of this alone—take care of a newborn, and keep the baby alive—was going to be everything but easy.

Her birth and hospital stay had been rather easy, all things considered. No interventions needed, other than being induced, and nothing to be concerned about. The pain had been terrible, as she expected it to be, but it wasn't anything she couldn't handle when it came right down to it.

Honestly, she had been so excited to meet her baby girl—this beautiful creature she had only gotten glimpses of during ultrasounds, and listened to her heartbeat week after week—that the pain became a distant memory to Catrina the moment little Catherine was put into her arms.

Nothing mattered after that.

Nothing ever would.

Oh, she loved her daughter instantly. Completely and entirely. She fell in love once—on sight—with the boy her sister birthed, who had subsequently became Catrina's son. And then she fell in love a second time with her husband—a man she had never thought she would find for herself.

So, yes, she knew love. She knew how powerful it could be, and how instantly life-changing it was when it came along to strike her back to her knees, and remind her why faith was good, God was real, and life was beautiful.

She had loved Catherine before she was ever even born. But then she was born, and in a blink, it all changed for Catrina again. In a single breath, her life and heart was upended all over again by nothing more than love.

A love so fierce, uncontainable, and unbelievable that Catrina barely even understood how to handle it. Her heart felt too full—too big. How was it supposed to handle all of this? How could she feel all of this?

But she did.

So, she let it reign.

And then as quickly as that amazing feeling had come, it was replaced slowly over the following few days with a deep-seated fear and insecurity that Catrina just couldn't seem to shake no matter how hard she tried. She was not the kind of woman to feel like the lesser—to find herself put down by silly things like insecurities.

But as she watched the nurses easily bathe, change, and feed Catherine while the very actions felt so foreign and strange to Catrina when she tried to do it, those ugly monstrous feelings made themselves known time and time again. She could take care of her daughter, of course, but not without being shown how first.

And not without feeling as though she were doing it wrong every single time. She always just assumed during her pregnancy that the natural maternal instincts would kick in for her, and she would know what to do. She would already know how to take care of her child, and how to keep this precious little girl alive.

After all, she had a son, now. A toddler, sure, but he was still practically a baby, wasn't he? Did he need similar things to Catherine?

Catrina figured so.

She was wrong.

A newborn was not the same at all.

And that just created a bigger, and more awful, feeling for Catrina.

Those doubts grew.

They were burrowed into her heart now.

Could she even be a mother?

Was she supposed to be one?

"Cat?"

Catrina glanced up at Dante's call of her name. Sitting in the hospital issued wheelchair—as she was not allowed to leave the hospital walking due to their policies—she kept a firm grip on the swaddled bundle of pink in her arms.

Catherine's green eyes—like her father's—were opened, and staring up at her mother. An innocent stare, yet still seemingly mesmerized all the same, too. It made Cat's heart hurt a bit. This beautiful little thing was depending on her. Catherine already looked for her. She needed her mother, and very little else.

So why did Catrina feel like a fraud?

"You okay?" Dante asked.

Catrina offered her husband a smile, and nodded. "Yeah."

It wasn't entirely the truth. She didn't know what she was. Dante was a little too busy stroking his palm over the top of Catherine's mop of dark hair to notice Catrina's off tone. "Car is all pulled up and ready whenever you are, bella."

That did make her smile. Even in sweats, and an oversized sweater, no makeup, her hair in a messy bun, and probably looking like she was still a few months pregnant, he called her beautiful.

And she knew he meant it.

"I'm ready," she said.

She wasn't.

Dante scooped the baby up anyway to move Catherine into her car seat in the backseat. Catrina finally got up out of her wheelchair, and moved further away from the hospital. Further away from the safety it provided, and the comfort it had allowed. Further away from where she was just starting to learn how to be a mother to a newborn, and closer to something else entirely.

Insecurities.

Wariness.

Fear.

*

"Cat?"

At the slightest whisper of Dante's voice, little Catherine's tiny limbs spasmed, and her eyelids fluttered. It was the threat of the baby possibly waking up after Cat had just spent two hours to get her to finally go to sleep that sent her hissing at her husband.

"Shut up!"

So, maybe that was a bad idea.

Instantly, Catherine's eyes popped open, and the wailing started. Nothing was getting this child to sleep well, or rather, nothing that Cat did was getting Catherine to do anything well. She failed at breastfeeding, the baby had gone through four different types of bottles to no avail, and little else seemed to make the girl happy.

One week after leaving the hospital, and Catrina was still just as lost as the day she had walked out of it. Fucking wonderful.

"Sorry," Dante murmured. "Didn't mean to wake her up."

It wasn't even him.

It was Cat.

But he took the blame because he was wonderful like that, while she was fucking awful.

Dante quickly crossed the living room, and scooped baby Catherine out of her wicker Moses basket. All it took was a few whispered hums from him, his arms rocking her to and fro, and the baby girl was back to sleep like she had never even been awake to begin with.

"Why is that so easy for you?" Catrina asked.

Dante passed her a look that she couldn't decipher. "Pardon?"

"The baby—everything is easy for you with her. She'll sleep for you, and eat for you. She doesn't cry for you, and when she does, you soothe her like it's nothing. I try everything you do, and everything everybody else does, and she just … it doesn't take. It's like I don't fucking know how to take care of her or something."

Dante just stared.

Catrina swallowed hard, and glanced down at her clenched hands mumbling, "I don't know."

She had never felt so entirely out of place with something in her life before. Never so entirely useless at the one thing she should be good at. This was her baby. She made her, and birthed her. And she didn't even seem to know how to keep her alive, for Christ's sake.

"Cat," Dante said softly, "why don't you go relax for a minute. Lucian called to let me know he came to pick up Michel earlier, so I know he's not going to be back for the night. And I'm home now, so I've got Catherine. Just … go have one of your salt baths, and take five minutes to breathe."

"I—"

"Go."

His tone offered no room for argument. Usually, that would be the cue for Catrina to stand up, and do exactly that. Their entire relationship was built on the fact he loved her because she was a challenging woman who liked to challenge him.

They wouldn't be them, otherwise.

And still, she hesitated.

Still, she was too exhausted for even that.

So, she didn't.
She just did what he said.

*

Catrina came out of the bath to find her house was ... strangely quiet. She knew it was just about the time Catherine would need to feed, and so, the baby's cries should have been filling up the house until she finally got a bottle.

And even then, she still cried sometimes.

What a strange thing ...

"Oh, you're out, Cat."

Catrina tightened her silk robe a little more at her waist at the sound of her mother-in-law's cheery voice. Leaning out of the nursery, Cecelia wore her usual sweet smile.

"Dante didn't say you were coming over," Cat said.

Cecelia shrugged. "He called me to come over a little while ago, actually."

Oh.

"Why?"

"Because he thought ... well, he thought maybe I could help," Cecelia said.

Catrina's throat tightened a little bit, and her chest ached. She had the strangest urge to be pissed at her husband, and yet grateful at the same time. She wanted to refuse and deny any help or the idea that she needed it because of foolish pride, and the need to make everyone believe she was entirely in control of every single aspect of her life.

And yet, she couldn't do that at all.

"I thought this would be easy," Catrina said quietly. "Not ... taking care of a baby, but just ... I don't know."

"I do," Cecelia said, stepping out of the nursery and closing the door behind her. "Suddenly, you get this baby shoved into your arms, and the first thing you think is, Oh, I love them. And then the second thing is, What the hell am I supposed to do?"

Cat laughed. "Even you?"

"We all have moments when we feel out of our element, Cat. There's nothing wrong with you, either, just because you're feeling that way. Not every woman is born knowing how to be a mother, and that's okay, too. Some have to learn it, but as long as you love your baby with all of your heart, then the rest will work itself out."

"You think?"

Cecelia smiled in that way of hers again. "Oh, I know. And since you have me here, I would love to show you all the things that helped me with fussy little Dante. Did he ever tell you about the night he was born?"

"No. What happened?"

"He cried loud enough to keep his entire wing up for hours on end. They released me early just to get him out of the hospital, I swear. And he kept crying, and crying. I swore he only stopped crying when Antony held him during that first week, or if I swaddled him tight enough that he didn't know if he was still in the womb, or out in the world."

"Huh," Cat said.

Cecelia nodded. "But it passed. All of this passes, Catrina. Eventually."

"I do, though."

"What is that?"

"Love her entirely," Catrina said. "I just wish I didn't feel so fucking bad at it."

"That is the very last thing you are bad at, I promise you." Cecelia waved a finger. "And that feeling? Yeah, that will pass, too."

Her mother-in-law was right.

Cat just needed someone else to tell her it.

Sometimes, that was just how life worked.

THE BIRTH

Dante peeled open his eyes, and knew without turning over that his very pregnant wife was not in bed with him. So was Catrina's ways, lately. Her moods, and sleep—or lack of it—determined whether or not he woke up alone, or warm with her beside him.

He didn't blame her, really.

Especially lately.

Being nine days overdue to deliver could make any woman restless, and a little snappy. But if that woman was Catrina Marcello?

It could make her downright terrible.

He meant that with love.

Good God.

Dante meant that with all the love in the world because he did. He did adore and love his wife more than anything else in his life. The truth was still the truth no matter which way he tried to spin it, and the truth was that Catrina was ready to have their child.

She had probably been ready a month ago when she accidentally left their home with two entirely different pairs of heels on. Or even when the fake contractions kept her up for hours on end, but every call she made to the doctor about coming in to see if it was real labor usually ended with—call us when you see a show, water, or both. Not the response his wife was looking for, at all.

Or maybe she was entirely over being pregnant and overdue when she suddenly decided that her very expensive maternity dresses no longer looked cute.

He thought they looked fine.

Damn.

She always looked fine.

Even more so now, really. Now when she was carrying his child, and more perfect because of it. It drove him crazy; his need and want for his wife kicked up a notch or two simply because she was pregnant, and entirely his. He told her that—remembered to tell her that as much as he possibly could, but sometimes more often than not, she just didn't hear it.

Or maybe she didn't want to hear it.

Normal, his brothers told him.

The end is always the hardest, his mother said.

Get out of her line of fire, his father warned.

Antony had probably been the one that was the most right with his advice. And like Dante when he thought how difficult his wife could be, Antony meant no harm in his words. Not to Dante, or even to Catrina.

It just was what it was.

Rolling over, Dante pushed out of bed, and grabbed the sleep pants he had discarded the night before. Pulling the pants on, he made his way out of the bedroom to find the upstairs portion of his home was quiet and peaceful.

Not unusual for a Saturday morning.

But the downstairs?

It was quiet, too.

That was entirely unusual.

Usually Michel would be tearing up a storm while making his mother laugh. Typically, it was his son who woke him up if Catrina was already awake and getting ready for the day. It was Catrina's sly way of waking Dante up without her actually being the one to do the deed.

Yeah.

He caught onto that trick.

Not that he minded.

"Where's Michel?"

Catrina looked up from the cup of tea she was nursing when Dante leaned in the entryway of the kitchen. Her bare face—free of makeup—was fresh, and flushed. She rarely came downstairs in the morning if she wasn't already entirely done up for the day. Makeup and hair included.

"Lucian came and grabbed him," Catrina said. "I called and asked."

"I was supposed to take him for gelato today. I promised."

Catrina smiled. "Other plans, Dante."

"Like what?"

"The hospital called—there's an opening today."

Oh.

Oh.

They had been waiting for that call for Catrina to go in and be induced now that she had made it past one week beyond her due date. He figured his wife's lack of makeup, and her messy bun made a hell of a lot more sense, now.

"She's coming," Catrina told him.

He grinned.

His principessa was almost here.

*

"They're checking her again right now," Dante said.

Giovanni grumbled on the other end of the phone. "Jesus, how long has she been laboring now?"

"Twenty-five hours."

"Shit, that woman is probably—"

"You want me to what?" Dante heard his wife snarl.

"Okay, I gotta go," Dante told his brother. "Update people for me. I probably won't be on the phone for a while. At least until she's here, you know?"

"Yeah, sure, man."

Dante hung up from his brother, and headed into the hospital room. Catrina was sitting up on the bed with her hospital gown back over her legs as she glared at the doctor standing at the end of the bed.

"You have chosen against Pitocin," the doctor said.

"Because the risk of it turning into one long contraction is not something I want to deal with," Catrina told the man.

"The Cervadil—"

Catrina looked to her husband. "I'm only at three."

Three centimeters.

Too many more to go.

"It's a suggestion," the doctor said. "A little painful, too, but not as much as the recovery from surgery would be. I know you don't want to have a cesarean, Catrina. If anything, this could help to open you up a little more."

"What are we talking about?"

"Using a balloon-like device to open my cervix," Catrina said.

"No," Dante said.

The doctor looked at him.

So did his wife.

Only Catrina smiled, though.

He knew what his wife wanted being that she had to be induced, and as little intervention as possible was the way she wanted to go. It was her body. Her choice. If something went wrong, or the baby became distressed, then Catrina was fully fine with stepping back and letting the doctor do whatever was needed.

But right now?

Right now it was all on her.

"At twenty-four hours after the onset of labor, we typically start to consider cesarean," the doctor said.

"As long as the water has broken," Dante put in. "And her water has not."

"But she has been laboring—"

"We're not discussing surgery."

"And the baby's heartbeat is still fine," Catrina added.

The doctor sighed. "Okay, I will be back in an hour to check you again."

And have this same useless conversation again.

Dante didn't bother to tell the man that, though. Soon, the doctor was gone, and they were once again left alone in the hospital room.

"Climb the stairs—I climbed the fucking stairs," Catrina muttered under her breath.

"Come here," Dante said, remembering something from their birthing classes. "Here, amore, we'll do something different instead of walking the halls, and climbing stairs."

Catrina gave him a look, but held out her hand. He helped her down from the bed, and then pulled his phone from inside his pocket. A couple of swipes on the screen, and soon, he had music filtering into the room.

A fun, fast beat that his wife loved. One that made her dance, and smile.

Birth was painful, yes.

Long, sure.

Difficult and hard, absolutely.

But it was also memorable. And he wanted Catrina to have good memories of the day their daughter was born.

Plus, if it helped her along … well, win-win.

"What are you—"

"Dance with me, regina."

Catrina cocked a brow. "Calling me Queen right now, bello,

really?"

"My Queen is amazing—unstoppable, and she knows it. My Queen likes to dance, Cat. So dance for me."

She took his outstretched hand, and soon, the two were dancing. It was an hour later when the doctor came in before they took a break.

She was at four, then.

Progress.

Catrina didn't notice the time crawling by when Dante was making her dance, and keeping her happy. The contractions barely slowed her down, too.

*

It took:

One deep breath.

One hard exhale.

One more push.

One long cry.

One single tear.

One second of silence.

One wail from a baby.

One amazing woman.

One perfect baby girl.

And everything changed for Dante in the blink of an eye. His life had already been changed once by Catrina, and then again by Michel.

But all of the impossibilities in his life were made possible when a blood-stained, pink-cheeked, dark-haired baby with his coloring, his wife's features, and their shared life was put into his arms.

Everything that wasn't ...

Everything that couldn't be ...

Everything that shouldn't ...

Suddenly was.

And she was perfect.

Her little button nose, and puffy cheeks. Her eyes that weren't quite opened fully, and her soft whimpering cries that soothed as soon as he started rocking her. Her little pink lips puckered into a bow, and those tiny little fingers ...

All wrapped around his thumb.

Dante fell into a corner chair with his daughter tightly swaddled in his arms, and he didn't know what to say. He looked up to find his wife was looking over at him with that soft smile of hers—always knowing, but never speaking her thoughts out loud unless she needed to.

"She's perfect," Dante said.

Little Catherine.

Beautiful, and full of grace.

A life just beginning.

A soul as old as time.

Perfect, like her mother.

Stubborn, like her father.

Dante's impossibility.

Catrina's gift.

And he didn't know what to say to her.

He waited so long …

He was not supposed to have her at all.

And he didn't know what to say.

"Say hello," Catrina whispered.

Dante did just that.

"Hi, sweet girl …"

Catherine's eyelids fluttered at his voice, but her eyes didn't open completely.

That was okay, too.

"I'm your daddy."

Catherine's eyes opened.

And for a moment, time stood still.

THE SILENCE

The thing about silence that people didn't realize until they were stuck in the midst of it?

Silence echoed.

It filled spaces.

It was uncomfortable, and cold.

Unwelcome, and yet right at home.

Silence was an unknown killer.

For the last day, Dante's home—a place that had been his haven for years when the outside world had never felt *safe*—became filled with that silence. His wife was still there, and he was drawn to her side more often than not, but she didn't speak. Neither did he.

Because what could he say?

What *should* he say?

Silence was always an option.

It was another thing people didn't realize about it. When someone wasn't ready to talk, when they didn't know how to handle things around the, silence was an easy option because it graced someone with *time*.

Silence was also an *answer*.

And right now, it was the only one he had.

Because what else did he say?

What did a father say when his daughter tells him that she was raped?

Oh, he was fucking angry—not at her—but he was. So angry. *Violently* angry, and yet there was nothing he could do to subdue the emotion. The rapist was gone, his daughter was alive and well—years later—and his chance to fix the situation, not that it could be, was long gone.

Instead, what he was left with was time, and silence. Time to think, and a quiet mind to do it with, even if everything else around him seemed to be screaming. He couldn't *do* anything except consider and wonder and *think* ... think far too much, so that's what he did. He absorbed the information, and what had transpired after. He hurt for his child, and he wished he had known. *God* ... he wished he had known.

Would it have made a difference?

Might he have helped?

What if it made it worse?

These were things he didn't know.

Not knowing *killed* Dante.

Sitting behind his large oak desk, Dante listened to the voice yammering on through the speak of his phone. He didn't reply back with more than a grunt, or the occasional agreement, but he certainly wasn't *all in* with the conversation. And yet, he continued picking up that phone to call someone else each time another conversation ended.

His mother.

Father.

Lucian.

And now, *Gio.*

They knew, of course, what happened because he told them. Because he needed *someone* to talk to lest the silence become too much, and swallow him entirely.

"Man, go talk to your wife," he heard his brother say.

Dante's gaze shifted away from the window to the phone on the desk that he had on speaker. "What?"

"I've been singing *Twinkle Twinkle Little Star* for thirty seconds, and you just stayed quiet the entire time."

Had he?

Jesus.

"I have talked to Cat," Dante said.

"*Have you?*"

Well, not really.

Not because he didn't want to, either.

He just ... hadn't figured out what to say. Or even, how to say it.

"What do I say?" Dante asked.

"To who?"

"Catherine. Catrina."

"You say *sorry* to Catty," Gio murmured, "because that's probably all she needs and wants to hear, and if she, by chance, needs something else, trust that she'll let you know. You don't push—not for details, or answers, or anything else because it wasn't *your* rape, Dante. It's her trauma, and she is allowed to deal with it in whatever way best suits her."

"Yes, and for years that was in destructive ways."

Partying.

Drugs.

Self-harm.

Dante could list more, but he didn't. And *God* ... he felt so fucking stupid because it all seemed clear now. People said hindsight was twenty-twenty, and they were *right*. Looking back, it all made sense, and he was punishing himself for missing it.

Except this wasn't about him.

And he wouldn't make it that way.

"But not *now*."

He had a point.

"Anyway," Gio said quickly, "what I mean is ... I just never understood why society felt like when a woman was raped, she needs to *justify*. Explain *why* she was a victim, or why it happened. Why do they have to work to explain why we should understand and sympathize? What happened, *happened*—that should always be enough. Full stop. Someone hurt them? *I'm sorry*, that's it, *let me help to fix it*, if they want that, and it's never their fault, no matter how many times they or someone else says otherwise. It's never their fault, and sometimes, just the way people say things can make it seem like it is. Just be careful with your words, you know? Don't ask her for more."

"Okay."

"As for your wife ..."

"Hmm?"

"I don't think you owe her shit except to ask her how she is. Silence is deafening, man, and it's louder than even the screams."

He wasn't wrong.

*

Dante found his wife later. Given the time of night—a surprise to him, considering the time that seemed to come before he realized it—he was unsurprised to find Catrina sitting at her makeup vanity. A normal nightly routine for her.

She sat there.

Washed away the makeup.

Cared for her skin.

Waited for him.

Tonight wasn't any different, it seemed.

Well, it *was*.

He felt the difference in his bones as he stepped into their massive bedroom, and her gaze drifted to him as she pulled the pins keeping her striking red hair in a chignon at the nape of her neck. She said nothing, but that had basically been their life in a nutshell for the last couple of days, and he still wasn't sure if he was ready to ... handle all of this.

She didn't say anything.

Didn't ask questions.

Dante crossed the bedroom, and while he would usually ready for the night while she finished up her business at the vanity, he went to her instead. Sitting down beside the bench she used to rest upon while she cleaned away the evidence of the day, the side of his face found his wife's thigh, and that's where he stayed.

While she worked.

While he *hurt*.

But she hurt, too—he knew that better than anyone in their life ever would. Because it was him Catrina came to when she spilled her secrets. *Him* that she told things that gave her nightmares, and truths she didn't share with the rest of the world from a time in her life before she found him, and he had her.

"Is an apology really good enough?"

Catrina said nothing.

He was grateful.

After Catherine had been there ... they had a moment. All that anger he felt came spilling out, and Catrina let him rage. And then when that rage left, all that was left was the silence. And a part of him knew that he was handling this differently than his wife because he couldn't share the experience his daughter had.

But his wife *could*.

Catrina's fingers found Dante's hairline, drifting through the strands, and for the first time, he dared to ask his wife, "How many times?"

She hesitated.

"Four," she replied quietly.

Four.

Fucking four.

Four times his wife had been assaulted.

Twice for his child.

He knew the statistics—one in four women. The thing was, nobody ever thinks they're going to line the women up in their lives, and find out one of them is *one in fucking four.*

"I'm sorry," he said, tone strained.

It didn't seem good enough.

It just didn't seem like it was *enough.*

Catrina's hand left his hair to lift higher so that she could wipe away the wetness that slipped down her cheek, and just like that, her tears were gone. But only on the outside, he knew. Because he didn't think that pain like that ever really left.

It didn't matter her status.

Her wealth.

This life they had.

Pain was still pain.

And she got to relive hers through the trauma of her child.

His silence had come from a place of ignorance.

Hers had come from a place of *knowing.*

It wasn't the same.

He wished it didn't have to *be* at all.

"I'm sorry."

THE SECRET

Dante POV

Dante smirked down at the screen of his phone with a glee even he couldn't contain at the sight of his brother's text.

Just arrived, it read.

"Why does your face look like that?"

Dante *attempted* to fix his face when he glanced up to find that his wife had come to stand on the other side of their kitchen island, but even the sight of her cocked eyebrow wasn't enough to shake the smugness he felt.

"Well?" she asked when he didn't answer right away.

"Gio's here. The bookie called a half hour ago with the final numbers on the run we went in on. I won. Which means I get to tell him he was wrong, I was right, and—"

"Stop gloating."

Dante grinned. "I'm not."

Yet.

But he would.

As soon as Gio came inside.

Catrina shook her head. "That's a level of petty even *I* can't manage to reach, Dante."

"Listen," he said, pointing a finger at his wife even though he knew that came with its own set of risks, quite frankly, "you can't just come in here with your *better than me* attitude and tell me not to have my moment, Catrina."

"I didn't tell you not to have it. I said it was *petty*."

"And?"

Because he didn't see the problem.

Now that Gio, Lucian and Dante were all grown men, had kids and grandkids of their own, their life phased out of the mafia and its suffocating rules that had completely surrounded their entire lives ... well, the three of them had a chance to act like real brothers in a way they hadn't since their younger teen years.

Before they'd chosen to follow their father, and everything that came along with that. Sometimes, it felt like they were making up for lost time with their late Friday nights, and closer to lunch breakfasts on Saturdays. All the running jokes between them couldn't be contained, even if it had every single one of their wives rolling their eyes on a regular basis. None of the brothers cared, honestly.

They were having *fun*.

Dante had only now realized how long it'd been since they were really able to sit back, and have fun with each other without some sort of undercurrent running between them because of the family and the goddamn mafia.

"Keep your pettiness," Catrina told him with a small smile as though she could read his mind, "but you know he'll get you back for it the first chance he could."

"Likely," Dante returned, "but shit, that's half the fun, Cat."

"Right."

"What's fun, now?"

Dante found Gio had finally come inside, and was now standing in the entryway of the kitchen. He grinned his brother's way, ignoring how he could see his wife rolling her eyes out of the corner of his eye. "How I just soaked you for twenty-k on the last game—"

"*Fuck sakes*," Gio groaned, tipping his head back and letting out a sour laugh. "Did you seriously make me drive all the way over here for *that*? You made it seem like something was fucking wrong, Dante."

"Yes, the fact you owe me twenty-k is *very* wrong because it's not in my bank account."

"*Twenty-k?*"

Gio grinned.

Dante made a face. "Cat, now—"

"You're betting tens of thousands of dollars with your brothers through a bookie, Dante? *Really?*"

"I'm bored," he said defensively.

"*Bored?*"

"Maybe it's a mid-life crisis, I don't know!"

Catrina dead-stared him from the other side of the island. "Dante, you are *well* past mid-life."

"Oh, shit," Gio crowed.

"Shut your face and transfer me the money, Gio." And then to his wife, Dante said, "Just had to twist that knife in deeper, huh?"

"Dante, most people don't even have twenty-k in savings, and you're just throwing it around—"

"How much did that limited edition Louis Vuitton bag cost, Cat?"

That quieted his wife *really* fast.

"You know," he added, "the one that came *hand-delivered* by the company last week in a fucking *armored truck*? Only what, two made in the world? More than twenty-k, I bet."

"This isn't about me, this is … shut up, Dante."

*

Gio POV

"Well," Catrina said from the other side of the kitchen as she leaned over the island to pat her husband on the cheek, "at least you don't look *well past* middle-age, oh, and my bag collection gains in value which is ten percent of our wealth."

She then smacked his cheek before adding, "Bet less, Dante."

"Fine," he muttered.

Gio managed to keep his smirk in check just long enough for Catrina to leave the kitchen, but that was only because he knew better than to make his sister-in-law think he was trying to make fun of her warnings.

Her claws were less sharp.

The bark didn't come as often.

All that was true, sure.

It also meant when it did come, no one was prepared for it because Catrina let everyone get just comfortable enough *not* to walk on eggshells before she reminded them exactly who she was. You'd have thought life and kids and time would have softened the woman a bit—and maybe it did, in some ways—but she was still Catrina fucking Marcello even on her good days.

"Are you transferring me the money?"

"Shut up, Dante, you'll get your money," Gio said, walking further into the kitchen. "The least you could have done was have a coffee waiting for me since you got me all the way over here just to gloat, though."

His brother laughed.

The *ass*.

"Did you hear from Lucian this morning?" Gio asked, making his way to the electric kettle to turn it on. "Doesn't that mean *he* owes you twenty-k, too?"

"His phone is off. I called Jordyn—she said he had a thing. I don't know. I will gloat over him later, too, no worries."

"I bet, you fucking prick."

"Dante?"

Gio went about pulling a coffee cup from the cupboard as Catrina came back to the kitchen entry.

"Yeah?" Dante asked.

"There's a man at the door."

"Pardon?"

"An enforcer. He's at the door."

"One of ours?" Dante asked.

"No, he's one of Lucian's, I think."

Gio forgot his cup on the counter as he turned to look Dante's way. Sure, they all had a man or two that looked after them or their wives when they were out and about. But with Dante not being the boss anymore, they didn't have a revolving door of made men coming in and out to answer to the boss.

After all, Dante wasn't the boss now.

"You coming?" Dante asked Gio.

He nodded. "Why not?"

They kept a calm demeanor for Catrina—not that the woman would have cared either way, and she could handle any situation—but that was just how they did their business. Even now, after all these years, and no longer being active in the family. Inside, though, Gio was concerned about what might have happened to cause the enforcer to come visit Dante.

They found the man—he was one who looked after Lucian, or the man's wife or kids when needed—standing on Dante's front stoop. None of the three spoke until the front door of the house was closed and they had privacy. And even then, it took Dante talking first to make the nervous enforcer meet the brothers' stares.

"Something wrong, Grayson?"

"Uh, boss—"

"Not the boss," Dante was quick to say.

"Right, right. You know I do a lot of the driving for Lucian's daughter—the one who's in town from Cali, right?"

"Lucia," Gio said.

"Yeah, that one. I've been taking her to the hospital once a week. Wasn't really given a reason why."

"Lucia's going to the hospital?"

Dante passed Gio a look.

He shrugged, not knowing anything about *that*.

"No, I guess it's for Lucian," the enforcer said, "and I don't think I'm supposed to say anything. I mean, he didn't even tell me, and I'm not sure any of the other guys know but—"

"Spit it out," Gio snapped.

"He's sick—cancer."

What?

Surely, Gio hadn't heard that right.

"Are you—"

"Positive," the enforcer was quick to say, "and we all know how you three are, so I thought … maybe I shouldn't have said anything."

Gio's chest hurt.

Dante's expression had blanked.

"No," Gio said, "you did exactly right."

"He's there now?" Dante asked. "At the hospital?"

"I believe so."

"Call Jordyn," Dante murmured.

"Man—"

Gio didn't even get to finish his statement.

"*Call Jordyn.*"

BYGONES – A DIRTY POOL ERA SHORT

Dante POV

Dante stayed as still as a statue, staring at the landline phone on the corner of his desk, while his wife flew back in forth outside the office doorway. It was like for the moment, with the news she had learned, Dante didn't exist to her. She had other things to worry about right then, and he really didn't take offense to it.

He had things on his mind, too.

Things like that phone.

And a call he should probably make.

"Yes, yes, he's coming!" A pause came from his wife and he looked up to see her pass by his office again, but this time with a phone at her ear. Was she talking to someone in their family? Maybe a friend of hers? Catherine, even? *Someone.* Someone that she cared enough about to let them know she was excited. "I'm grabbing our bags now, and we're heading over to the hospital to be there with her … no, Dante called Michel; he's got a situation to handle with a bad accident that happened—a bridge collapsed? Yeah, it's not good but of course, that's Michel and you can't talk him out of that hospital if he thinks he's needed. Not that it's a bad thing, you know."

His wife's voice faded the further she went down the hall. Once again, he couldn't see her through the office doorway. Another door clicked shut, and her voice cut off entirely, letting him know that she had disappeared into their master bedroom to finish grabbing their things and probably end her conversation.

It meant he had to hurry up here.

Make a choice.

Soon, his wife would be back and he would have to leave this space. Not only would he not have the number then that he needed to call, but he also didn't think that was the sort of phone conversation that should happen while they raced into the city to wait for the birth of their first grandchild.

Not just your first grandchild, his mind reminded.

Right.

Like he needed the extra memo.

Dante knew.

Which was exactly why he was still sitting there at his desk like a fucking idiot after being told his first grandchild ever—his *grandson*—would finally be making his way into the world. Because despite something being the *right* choice, that didn't always mean that it was also the easy choice. Those two things were not always mutually exclusive.

Not that it changed what Dante needed to do.

Nothing made a difference to that.

Instead, he pulled on the wisdom his father had shared with him time and time again throughout his long life. He thought about Antony, and what he would have done in a situation like this, and while the answer he already knew didn't change ... it strengthened his resolve to do what had to be done.

Dante had just reached for the phone after pulling out a drawer in his desk when the voice of his wife echoed from the office doorway. He didn't even look up from where he searched for the black book with every phone number he might ever need hidden safely beneath its leatherbound cover.

"What are you doing?" Catrina asked.

Dante let out a slow breath, flipping page after page. The name and number would be near the end, he knew. A favor from a friend—that's how he got it in the first place, even if that meant Dante owed somebody else a favor now and he hated being in anyone's debt. He'd just the number just once before. Made a single call to the man the number belonged to so that he could be *sure* ...

"Calling Charles Casey," Dante said.

Catrina quieted in the doorway.

Dante let her have those few seconds while he finally found the number. His fingers hovered over the keypad but didn't press down. Instead, he looked to his wife.

"Do you think you should do that?" she asked.

"It's been ten years. He's not had more children—the man is never going to remarry, Catrina. He lost a woman once ... it would be like me losing you. There's no moving on. He didn't replace the things he lost, including his daughter. This baby isn't just our first grandchild, and I think the offer should be put out. If you think differently, please let me know why now."

"I just ... maybe you should tell Michel, let him decide."

158

"It's not about Michel, and he will understand that."

Catrina chewed on her inner cheek. "You're going to do it one way or another, won't you?"

"I would appreciate your support, though."

"Right." Catrina nodded. "Of course. And I'll be downstairs when you're ready to leave."

"I love you, Cat."

She smiled. "Oh, you know how much I love you, *bello*."

He did.

Always and forever.

Once his wife had gone, Dante punched the numbers into the phone and picked up the receiver to put it against his ear. He thought about that first call he'd made to this number, how his hands had shaken more than they should because he had been pissed and *nervous*—two things he didn't want to be.

But it had been his *son*.

His kid.

"*Are you going to come here—are you coming after him?*" was all Dante had asked Charles Casey after he explained who he was. "*Give me the respect of telling me at least. Let me protect my boy when I have the chance to because he won't let me otherwise.*"

Charles had simply replied, "*No, I'm not coming for the lad.*"

"Casey here," came a jovial accent on the other end.

Dante drew in a quick breath, coming back to the present and his reality and straight out of the past in a blink. "Charles—it's been a long time, Irishman."

It took the man a second.

Then, *two*.

"You feckin' Italians."

Dante almost smiled.

"What do ye want, Marcello?"

"It's been ten years hasn't it—a long time. Gabbie's a lawyer now, yeah? Probably one of the top five defense attorneys in this state, and she's not even been part of the bar more than a handful of years. You should be proud, Charles."

The man on the other end cleared his throat. "Is she?"

"Took that dream from her Ma, I heard."

"She did. That doesn't tell me what you want."

"I appreciate you never made trouble for me and mine here. I never got the chance to tell you that."

"And I'm sure," Charles replied drily, "that you didn't call today to do it, either."

"You're right. I called to tell you Gabbie is giving birth. Her first child. A boy. I thought you might like to come to New York and say hello. Catch up."

The man on the end went quiet.

Dante gave him a moment before he added, "The longer you take to apologize, the harder it will be for her to forgive you. Oh, I'm sure she's forgiven you for *herself* ... but that's not you, is it? You've not heard her forgiveness given to you. I bet it's a lonely life you live. Most of your family's gone now—lucky bastard you are to have lived through all of this, but for what ... for *what*, Charles, when you're living alone. I am extending you the chance to no longer do that. Please, accept."

"And what's the strings, Marcello?"

"The past."

"What about it?"

"It stays there, Charles."

It took the man all of a half of a second to reply.

"I give me word, Marcello."

"You can call me Dante. All my family does."

THE CHICAGO WAR

DAMIAN | LILY

HITS AND KISSES

Damian pulled the leather driving gloves on one at a time, tugging them firmly to make sure they were in place. It was almost like a ritual for him before a killing—something that he found put him into a different headspace.

There was no husband here.

No expectant father.

No forgotten child.

No Capo.

No Damian.

Just an Outfit man doing business.

A business he was rather good at.

Killing.

His thoughts drifted back to an earlier time, a time when he was living in even more seclusions and without outside influence than he did now. He remembered that call from the boss all too well—his first order for the Outfit, his first kill.

Terrance had a guard that had been caught spying on his granddaughters during private moments. He wanted the man to understand the depth of his wrong doings and sins.

Damian did it all with a fucking smile.

After, however, when he was back home alone, Damian found himself restless and overthinking. More so than he had ever been before.

That lessened over time.

The kills got easier.

The jobs became simpler.

Just another blank face.

Stepping out of his Porsche, Damian sent off a text message to his wife.

I'll be home soon, his read.

Lily answered back a few minutes later. *Just leaving Abriella's place.*

Don't wait up for me, he texted back.

Damian knew her response before it even came through.

You know I will anyway.

Yeah, he did.

And that was exactly why he loved his wife.

Damian slid his phone back into his jacket pocket, and began his stroll across the street toward the apartment building on the other side.

Another enforcer for the Outfit would lose his life tonight.

It wasn't all that much of a loss.

Darryl, as Tommas had said, had been far too close to Joel to allow the man to live. Loose ends were only good for one thing: fucking shit up.

Damian didn't leave loose ends.

No man's soul was worth twenty-five to life.

None.

*

Damian put his ear to the apartment door, and listened for any sounds of movement within. He heard nothing but the buzz of a television set. Sliding a small compact case from his pocket, he flipped open the side and chose the tool he wanted to use. Keeping an eye on the long, dark hall of the third floor, he checked for people that might come out of their apartment and see him as he slid the long, tapered end of the tool into the lock.

A few quick jiggles of the tool, and Damian felt the spikes drive into the proper position for the tumbles of the deadbolt. He turned it slowly, not wanting to make any noise. Once the lock was open, he turned the knob and pushed on the door. Inside, the apartment was dark except for a flicker on the far wall that gave away where the television was positioned in the next room.

Quietly, Damian closed the door and put the tool back into his pocket. He'd made a few calls after he'd spoken with Tommas, and he knew that Darryl wasn't running the streets at his usual haunts. Damian assumed the enforcer must have gone home.

Pulling the gun out from the waistband of his slacks, Damian grabbed the long silencer from the inside of his jacket. He spun the silencer into the barrel, making sure it was tight and good.

No one needed to interrupt his business because of the sound of a gunshot, after all.

Damian learned a long time ago how to walk without making a sound. It was useful in his business, and it allowed him to come and go without being seen. He made his way down the hallway, and checked around the corner where the television was playing a rerun of a comedy sitcom.

Darryl sat on the couch with his back turned to Damian. The man was probably asleep, but guessing by the half empty liquor bottle on the television stand, he had some help getting that way.

Easy.

Too easy, even.

Damian flicked the safety off his gun, cocked back the hammer, lifted, aimed, and pulled the trigger.

He didn't even think about it.

Darryl's body flew forward with a quiet gasp and blood splattered on the wall next to the couch when the bulleted entered the back of his head.

A rattling, hard last breath.

It didn't matter who you were.

You could be rich or poor.

Famous or unknown.

Dirty as shit or as clean as an angel.

The death gasp was always the same.

Killing was a messy business, Damian thought.

He could hear the telltale *drip, splat, drip* as blood hit the carpet just a few feet away.

Damian let out a sigh, unscrewed the silencer from his gun, and then looked around the apartment quickly.

Tommas believed that Darryl and Joel had been planning something. While Damian was taking care of the Darryl problem, Tommas was going through Joel's office, electronics, and whatever else he could find to see if there was anything. Damian would be the one digging through Darryl's place for any clues.

Damian didn't know if anything would come up.

He supposed that didn't matter.

Time to get to work.

*

Damian pulled off his driving gloves, jacket, pants, and shoes. He opened the garbage bag and stuffed the items inside. Tying the bag up tight, he hoisted it over his shoulder and turned on his heel to go inside his house from the connecting garage.

Lily stood in the doorway, watching him in that way of hers.

Shit.

"You should be asleep," he told his wife.

Lily cocked a brow. "I told you that I would wait up."

Damian shook his head, and took a couple of steps closer to his wife. "I would have woken you up when I came to bed, Lily."

"I worried about you tonight."

"I'm fine," he promised.

"Are you?"

"Yes, sweetheart."

Lily flicked a look at the bag he held. "I take it you don't want me to wash those clothes."

Damian was always honest whenever Lily asked. "No, I'm going to burn them."

"Bloodstains?"

"Not likely, but I don't want to take chances."

Lily frowned. "Who?"

Now, Damian was a little surprised to hear that coming out of his wife's mouth. Lily was never so brazenly open about asking the exact details of Damian's business. Sometimes a simple, *I took care of something,* sufficed her curiosity.

"That enforcer of Abriella's," Damian admitted.

Lily's expression turned to stone—blank and unreadable. "I didn't like him—I heard things he said to her."

"We all have." Damian tossed the garbage bag to the side as he came to stand in front of his wife. "You still should be sleeping, Lily."

She smiled. "I told you—"

"I know, you were worried. I'm fine."

"Liar. You won't sleep tonight."

She knew him too well.

It was the after part of his job, see.

And he overthought that every time.

Maybe being Tommas' underboss wouldn't be such a bad thing. There was less killing in his current position, after all. Less killing meant less overthinking.

"Do you want a coffee or something?" Lily asked.

Damian snagged her wrist and pulled her closer. His palm rested on the swell of her stomach, feeling his baby boy move within.

"No," he said.

"You sure?"

"Positive. I'd like a kiss, though."

Lily gave him a tiny smile. "Yeah?"

"Right now"

She stood on her tiptoes and pressed a soft kiss to his mouth.

Damian instantly stopped overthinking.

FATHERS AND SONS

It took one tiny breath to change a man.

One blink.

One second.

One last push.

One gasp.

One cry.

One soul.

One life.

One little boy swaddled tightly in blue, and staring up at his father with hazy blue eyes, and silence all around.

Just the one.

"Damian?"

He thought ... months ago ... he had been changed forever. That it had been his one moment for his life to turn on its side and be irrevocably different.

And it had been a good thing.

This was not the same.

This was not the same at all.

"Damian," Lily said again.

He didn't blink.

He didn't breathe, or move, or make a sound.

Damian just kept holding his son all swaddled in blue, watching him with familiar eyes and pouting lips.

"Hello, sweet boy," Damian said.

I've been waiting to meet you.

You look just like your mother.

I'm terrified.

Do you know who I am?

All of those questions ran through Damian's mind. He thought about saying them all, or even saying nothing at all.

Instead, he murmured, "Everything's going to change now that you're here."

Damian just didn't know how much.

"Damian," Lily said one more time.

He turned to his wife, stepping close enough to her hospital bed that she could reach out and run her palm over their son's soft, misshapen head. The baby's dark hair was one of the only features he had taken from his father, Damian mused.

From the baby boy's little lips, to the shape of his eyes and his jaw, he took after his mother. Damian didn't mind—his wife was beautiful.

Leaning down, Damian pressed a kiss to Lily's lips. She smiled against his mouth, her gaze lowering. Covered in scratchy white hospital blankets and tucked into bed, Lily was healing and doing well just hours after her first child was born.

She had done damn well.

Damian was proud of his wife.

And so grateful.

She brought his child into the world with her usual fierceness and stubborn nature, refusing to let the pain overwhelm her or frighten her. His child was healthy, pink, and breathing.

Damian couldn't ask for more.

"Let me see his face again," Lily whispered.

Chuckling, Damian sat on the edge of the bed and placed his son on Lily's lap with care. The baby boy was cradled between her bent knees. Lily ran her fingertips all over the soft, sleeping lines of the baby's face.

"Where did my brother go?"

"Theo just ran out for some grub," Damian told her.

Lily smiled brilliantly. "He was so excited, too."

"I know. He didn't want to leave. Eve convinced him to go get us all food."

"I'm still set on Joseph," Lily said out of the blue.

Damian sighed, staring down at his boy. "Okay."

"No argument this time?"

How could he argue?

"I didn't know if it would fit him, but now that he's here," Damian said, shrugging, "it fits him pretty damn well, sweetheart."

Lily grinned. "Joseph Theo Rossi."

"That's quite a couple of names he has to live up to," Damian noted.

"He can do it."

Damian laughed. "You're so sure of yourself."

Lily poked her husband in the arm. "Of course I am. He's your boy—your son. How can he fail at anything when he's got you for a father, Damian?"

That was the million dollar question, wasn't it?

It still scared Damian a whole hell of a lot.

But he was pretty sure he was ready for it.

"Thank you, Lily," Damian said.

"For what?"

Damian cupped his wife's jaw in his palm, and swept his thumb over her pretty pink lips. "For everything, sweetheart."

She had given him everything, after all.

*

Joseph was a happy baby once he learned to sleep through the night. The first couple of months were a blur of dirty diapers, refilling bottles, and sleepless nights for Damian. Not that he hadn't spent a lot of nights awake before his son was born.

Damian didn't mind taking night duty. He let his wife get extra hours of sleep because she deserved it. He quickly learned to make fast work of changing the baby's diaper to avoid getting pissed on. He laughed his way through the messes and exhaustion, and his wife was there every step of the way.

He didn't know how to be a father.

That was Damian's biggest worry.

He couldn't remember his own father, and the men who raised him hadn't exactly been the best role models. So he did his best—he gave Joseph hours that could have been spent doing something else, he rocked his boy to sleep every single night, and he loved his child.

What else could he do?

He just wanted to be a good father.

"One more bite," Damian said, holding out the spoon full of peas.

Joseph glowered at his father from his high chair. "Nah."

"Joe."

"Nah."

"*Joe*," Damian said again.

Joseph didn't even blink. "MA!"

Damian jerked in surprise at his son's shout, and the peas spilled off the spoon and onto the highchair and floor. Twelve-month-old Joseph broke into a fit of pealing giggles at having bested his father.

For the most part, Joseph was quiet and content to sit in a corner with a handful of toys and be by himself. He didn't need constant entertainment.

It wasn't like him to be so loud.

"Goddammit," Damian mumbled under his breath, rubbing a hand over his face. "Look what you made me do, Joe."

Soft laughter echoed from behind Damian. He turned on the chair to find a very tired, nine-month pregnant Lily standing in the kitchen entryway. She shook her head as she walked further into the kitchen, taking Damian's outstretched hand. She pulled his hand in closer, and pressed it to the side of her rounded stomach. His heart kick-started at the feeling of his child moving under his palm.

Another boy.

Damian couldn't wait, but he knew Lily was tired as hell. Her second pregnancy was not as easy as the first had been. She was sick more often, and it seemed like all she had to do was feel the wind and she would catch a cold. Add in their one year old that kept her running after him while Damian acted as Tommas' underboss for the Outfit, and she was exhausted.

He tried to help as much as he could, whenever he could.

Like today.

After coming home to find Lily going crazy with cleaning, he demanded she go upstairs, have a nap, and he would get Joe something to eat. Thankfully, she went without much argument.

A fun, drunken, child-free night had left the couple with something extra.

Both Damian and Lily had wanted to wait another year or two before having another child. At least until Joseph was potty trained. It obviously hadn't ended up that way. In his drunken foolishness, he'd forgotten that his wife was in the midst of switching birth control. Lily had forgotten, too.

Damian didn't care. He was excited for a second son. But he did wish it was easier on Lily.

"How're you feeling, sweetheart?" Damian asked.

Lily shrugged, smiling when he leaned forward and placed a kiss to the crown of her rounded stomach. "Still tired."

"Go back upstairs for a while. I'm good here."

"Yes, Damian, I can see just how good you are down here."

Joe smacked his hands to the highchair over and over.

"Mamamama."

"He made a little mess," Damian said, chuckling.

"I saw who made the mess," Lily teased.

Damian caught his wife's gaze, noting how she winced a little but tried to hide it. His hand, still resting on her stomach, felt her muscles tense all over. He knew that look on his wife's face.

Was it finally time?

"Lily?"

She sighed. "I would love some more sleep."

Damian cocked a brow. "Why did you get up?"

"Contractions. What else?"

She laughed, and it was filled with relief.

Damian smiled, but a hint of anxiety simmered in his blood. He kissed her stomach again. "Go sit in the living room. I'll give Tommy a call and finish feeding Joe. Don't worry about the bags, I'll grab them, too."

Lily's fingertips danced over Damian's cheek and up into his hair. "You're too good to me."

"I love you, Lily."

Damian wasn't the kind of man who expressed affection openly. His wife always understood, and never asked him for more than he could give her. But he did love her—entirely.

"Love you," she echoed sweetly.

He rubbed her stomach, hoping it soothed whatever worries she might have. No doubt, Lily would do great once again. She was a champion like that.

Joe started babbling again, taking Damian's attention away from his wife for the moment.

"I guess supper time is done, huh?" Damian asked his son. Joe threw a pea at him, and he barely dodged it. "Joe, no throwing food."

"Dadada," Joe babbled, grinning widely.

Damian forgave his son instantly. "Almost time to meet your little brother, buddy."

Joe threw another pea.

*

Cory Dino Rossi made his way into the world in a quick few hours. Once Lily's contractions really started, the baby boy didn't take long at all.

Damian balanced his one-year-old on his hip to show Joe his new baby brother being washed and dressed by a nurse behind a glass window. Tommas had brought Joe to the hospital the very second Damian called to say that Cory was born.

"Look," Damian said, pointing at a kicking, crying Cory. "That's baby Cory."

Joe's brow puckered. "Bay-beeee."

"That's right. Baby Cory."

"Bay-beee."

Damian held his oldest son a little tighter, wanting to keep him close. His most important goal in life had been surviving, keeping out of people's way, and staying alive. Then he married Lily, and she became his focus.

Now, he had his boys, too.

He wanted them to be happy.

To be safe.

To succeed.

He thought about his wife, and her pleased, proud smile as he left her behind in her hospital room to follow the nurse who was washing Cory up after yet another failed attempt at breastfeeding.

He wanted his sons to find love, too.

One like he had.

Strong, soul-deep, and so beautiful.

But he knew that had to start with him. Growing up, Damian hadn't exactly had the best models of love surrounding him. He didn't even know how to love someone properly. Lily came along, and that somehow melted away.

His sons would always see a father that loved their mother. A man who respected his wife, treated her like she was so precious, and adored her like she was the most important thing.

Because she was.

Fathers taught their sons how to be men.

So yeah, that started with him.

Damian still hoped his boys knew that he tried to be good for them—a good man.

*

Twenty Years Later …

"Joe, stop that goddamn fidgeting," Damian said sharply.

Joe scowled at his father. "I'm nervous, all right."

"Be nervous, but stop the jittery bullshit."

"Easy for you to say, Dad," Joe muttered.

Damian smirked, but hid it by turning his head to look out at the tress passing their car by. Unfamiliar streets of New York colored his vision and he relaxed in the backseat. Once or twice a year, Damian took a trip to New York to sit down with old friends, talk business, and make sure there was no trouble between families.

It was just one of his jobs as Tommas' underboss.

He had learned over the years to appreciate the spotlight.

Or as much of it as he could.

"Dad?" Joe asked.

"Yeah?"

"Cory would have been better for this, not me."

Damian sighed quietly, and turned back to look at his oldest son. Joseph and Cory, despite being only a year apart in age, couldn't have been more different. Cory was outgoing and had a big personality. He loved people, and he liked attention. He was charming as hell, and the twenty-year-old knew it. He had women coming and going all the time.

Joe, on the other hand, was quiet. He preferred his own company. He didn't like the limelight, and his business in the Outfit ended up being a lot like his father's first job had been. Joe was Damian's right-hand, doing whatever his father needed in the shadows without ever batting an eye about it. He was fearless in that way, and Damian loved his boy for it.

Cory had chosen to work under Adriano Conti as a Capo.

Damian was just as proud.

He let his boys grow up to be whatever they wanted—whatever they needed. He didn't push either of his boys toward the family business, or demanded that they join the Outfit when they were old enough. Each of his sons chose that all on their own.

And they were good at it.

But the two were still like night and day standing next to one another.

"I know Cory would have had more fun maybe," Damian said to

Joe.

"Exactly."

"But you're in a position where you could use a bit of education on the rules of other families," Damian said, shrugging. "And as someone once told me, Joe, comfort zones are reserved for weak men who are afraid to try something new. I want you to succeed—you chose this life, son. Don't shy away because you prefer to hide away."

Joe frowned. "I hate it when you do that."

"I know," Damian replied smugly.

"How much longer?"

"Actually, we're almost there."

Another ten minutes later, and the car was pulling up a long, winding driveway. It wasn't Damian's first time visiting the Marcello mansion, but it was Joe's. Manicured grass and tall trees lined the driveway. Before long, the car pulled to a stop.

Damian and Joe were just getting out of the car when the front door of the mansion swung open. Loud, happy laughter echoed out as several girls piled out of the home in a large group. A couple of them, Damian recognized to be Lucian Marcello's daughters. The others must have been their friends.

Damian fixed his jacket, waiting for his son to join his side. Joe didn't come. It was only then that Damian noticed one of the girls was trailing behind the rest of the women.

And Joe was watching her. She was watching him, too.

Well, then …

Damian cleared his throat.

His son acted like he didn't hear a thing.

"Joe," Damian said loudly.

Joe snapped out of it, glancing over his shoulder. "Yeah, Dad?"

The five girls piled into an SUV, and tires squealed on asphalt as they pulled out of the driveway.

"Find something you like?" Damian asked innocently.

"Uh …"

Damian raised a brow, amused. Unlike his youngest son who toted a different female around depending on what month it was, Joe wasn't the type. He'd had only a few girlfriends, and he was never very serious with any of them.

"The last one—you were watching her," Damian said.

Joe spun on his heel, laughing. "So what if I was?"

"Since when do you stare like that?"

"I don't."

Exactly.

Joe wanted to know the girl.

Damian could see it. He didn't need his son to verify his suspicions.

"Leave it alone, Dad," Joe said, trying not to smile.

"I didn't say a thing."

"You're thinking it."

"No, I'm thinking that I should give you a heads up," Damian corrected his son.

"What's that?"

Damian's hand landed on Joe's shoulder, and he turned them both around to face the Marcello mansion. On the doorstep, three men stood side by side, waiting for their guests to come up and greet them.

"That girl, Joe, is Liliana Marcello."

Joe grimaced.

It couldn't be fun to find out that someone who had caught your eye was the daughter of a fellow family's underboss.

"Oh?" Joe asked, sounding far too innocent.

Joe was anything but innocent.

Damian laughed.

"The man on the left end is her father—the other two are her uncles," Damian added. "She's a year younger than you. Lucian is intimidating as hell. Don't let him know you think so, however."

"Thanks?"

"That's a start." Damian patted his son's back hard. "Best way not to fuck this up, Joe, is not to act like a *cafone*. That is something you're incapable of doing. I know because I raised you this way. Do you want to know that girl?"

"Maybe," Joe said.

He did.

And Damian would make it happen for his son.

Damian nodded at the house. "Start with her father."

ADRIANO | ALESSA

CRAZY AND YOUNG

"Ugh," Alessa grumbled, tossing her bag to the chair. She quickly fell into the same spot with a huff, and a glare. "I am so over this now."

Adriano chuckled, toed off his boots, and bent down in front of his wife. He put his hands to her knees, and offered her a smile that wasn't returned. "It's almost over."

"I am nine days overdue, Adriano. This is *never* going to end."

"You're being dramatic."

Alessa pouted. "So? I'm a *whale*."

"Lissa."

"I am!"

Adriano's fingertips tightened on his wife's thighs. "You are not. You're beautiful."

And it constantly drove him crazy.

Adriano was beginning to think he was a little crazy what with the way his wife's pregnancy turned him on like it did. Was that normal? To be hot for your wife just because she was carrying your child?

He didn't know, but he was.

"She's going to come when she comes," Adriano said.

Alessa's mouth popped open and her eyes widened.

He instantly realized his mistake.

She had been adamant about not knowing the baby's gender if she could help it. Adriano, being his usual self, had sneaked a look in the file after an ultrasound when the tech's back was turned. He wanted to know what his first child would be.

He wanted to be prepared.

The baby was a girl.

A pretty little Conti princess.

Alessa didn't want to know, so he had been extra careful not to tell her.

And he just fucked that up in a big way.

"I am so sorry," Adriano said, laughing.

What else could he do but laugh?

Alessa smacked him on the shoulder. "You … you … asshole! I wanted it to be a surprise, Adriano."

"I know, but it just slipped out. And if you don't go over the next couple of days, they're going to induce you anyway. What difference does it make? You're going to find out today or really soon, babe."

"Ugh."

Adriano chuckled, leaned up, and pressed a kiss to Alessa's scowling lips. "Sorry."

"You're forgiven … I guess."

"You guess?"

"Well, now that I know, I just realized how little things we have for a girl."

Adriano cocked a brow. "Is that so?"

"We need to go shopping."

Dammit.

Adriano bent his head down, and let out a sigh. "Any excuse, I swear."

"But she needs little dresses, and headbands, and shoes. Oh, my God, shoes, Adriano. She'll need different pairs for church, and—"

"Tomorrow," he interrupted quickly, chuckling. "We will go shopping tomorrow for twenty pairs of shoes and the dresses to match."

Alessa smiled brilliantly. "Okay."

"So … about the name," Adriano started, wondering how to go about the conversation. "We haven't talked a lot about it."

"I was thinking we could go with Adrianne if the baby was a girl," Alessa said.

Adriano nodded quickly. "Are you dead set on that?"

"Kind of. Why?"

"I was hoping we could name her Corrine, after your grandmother, and Mia as a middle name."

Alessa's gaze widened, and an understanding dawned. "I'm sorry, I didn't even consider—"

"It's okay. I like your choice, too."

"I like yours more," she whispered.

Adriano grinned. "Corrine, then?"

Alessa nodded. "Corrine."

*

"Adriano!"

Adriano bolted up out of bed, eyes wide and his heart racing. He cussed under his breath as his vision cleared. "Yeah?"

Alessa screeched his name from the bathroom again.

He pushed out of bed, ignored the cold floors, and made his way to the bathroom. He tried to push the door open, only to find it was locked.

"Let me in, babe," he mumbled.

"No, go get me new pants," Alessa said quietly.

Adriano's brow furrowed, and he rested his forehead to the door. "Okay. Can you open the door?"

She scared the fuck out of him yelling like that.

The least she could do was open the damn door.

"No," Alessa said, sounding entirely humiliated for whatever reason. "I peed my pants. Go get me new ones. I'll clean up."

Adriano took her words in for a minute, wondering ... "Lissa, did you wake up wet?"

Because the bed hadn't been wet when he crawled over her side.

"No."

"Lissa," Adriano said again, firmer the second time.

"Adriano, leave me alone for a minute. I just want new pants right now."

He was thinking it was more likely her water broke.

She was eleven days overdue, and supposed to be induced the next day in the morning if labor hadn't started on its own. They spent the last three days walking up and down the malls, shopping for girl things that Alessa was sure the baby needed. He spent his nights loving his wife up and down.

Sex was supposed to help, after all.

Adriano didn't mind *helping*.

"Lissa, was it pee, or did your water—"

"Just go get me new pants!"

Jesus.

"Fine," Adriano said, surprised at her anger.

He stumbled back to the bedroom, still half asleep. It didn't take him long at all to find a pair of thick leggings he knew Alessa liked, and to get back to the bathroom. After knocking on the door, he waited for what felt like forever before she finally opened it a crack.

Alessa snatched the leggings from his hand with a mumbled thanks. Then, she slammed the door in his face just as fast.

Adriano waited, quiet and patient, for his wife.

He knew Alessa was scared.

So was he.

This was new.

They were crazy young.

Maybe too young.

So yeah, he waited her nerves out.

"Adriano?" Alessa whispered from behind the door.

"Yeah, babe?"

"It wasn't pee."

He laughed tiredly. "Any pain yet?"

"No."

"That's good, right?"

Alessa opened the door a crack, and peeked out. Her eyes were watery and wide. "I'm scared."

"Me, too. It's going to be great. You'll do fine. I love you, Lissa."

"Don't look down."

Adriano rubbed at his forehead, confused and tired. Far too tired for this. "What?"

"During labor. You're not allowed to look down. Or under the sheet. I said so."

Well then ...

"It's just birth—"

She pointed her finger in his face. "Say it, Adriano."

"Okay, I promise. No looking."

Alessa dropped her finger, and her gaze. "I made a mess on the kitchen floor."

"I'll clean it," he said. "Why don't you get your stuff ready, and it'll be by the door when we have to go. Call your sister and Tommas, too. I'll give Eve and Theo a call after I'm done in the kitchen."

She opened the door a little wider, stepped out, and gave him a sweet kiss. Adriano woke up a little more at her sensual grin.

"I'm not ready for this," she said.

Adriano put his hand to the rounded swell of his wife's stomach. "I know, but she's ready to say hello, Lissa. She wants to meet the world. See her mom. Be held by her dad."

Alessa smiled at him. "You would see it that way."

Only because his wife taught him how to.

Alessa was all the light in Adriano's dark life.

But he supposed his life was about to get a little brighter.

*

Swaddled in pink, sucking on her thumb, and topped off with a too-large, fuzzy pink hat, Corrine Mia Conti slept happily in the plastic bassinet.

So unaware, Adriano thought.

So unknowing, he knew.

The baby girl—his baby girl—didn't have the first clue of the hell that had ensued during her mother's pregnancy. She didn't know how volatile her family had been, how scary the world around them was, and how close she had come to not even existing.

But none of that mattered as Adriano stared at his little girl.

None of those things were important.

Just Corrine.

Ten little bitty fingers.

Ten tiny toes.

She was blue-eyed, but that could change to his green, he knew. She had tufts of dark hair that peeked out from under her pink hat. Her nose sloped like her mothers, but she had his mouth and cheekbones.

Innocence, entirely.

Pure love.

Adriano smiled, scared to move or touch Corrine for fear she might wake up.

If she woke up, then he would have her in his arms again and he wouldn't let her go. As it was, the nurses had needed to pry her from him hours ago for her first bath and her hearing test.

"She's beautiful," Abriella said softly.

Adriano's smile grew bigger. "Yeah, she is."

"Quiet," Tommas said.

"For now," Abriella joked.

"How's Alessa doing?" Evelina asked.

Adriano straightened, and turned to his sister. "Really good, but tired. She was having a shower, so I didn't think she would miss the baby if I brought her out to see you all."

Evelina tugged on Theo's hand, bringing her husband closer to the baby. Adriano stepped back from his child, and watched as four people leaned over the sleeping baby in the bassinet, and fell in love at first sight.

Babies had that effect on people.

Corrine was something special, though.

Something really special.

Adriano knew it.

His daughter was the first principessa of the next generation of their families to be born. She had come into the world just days after the war between all their families had finally come to an end. Corrine was just one little string that added to the strong bonds between the four families.

She helped to make it grow.

That was important.

"We have to do a party," Abriella told Tommas.

"A meet and greet, maybe."

"Yes, I like that," Evelina said.

"What about Lily and Damian?" Theo asked.

Tommas nodded. "We'll have one for their baby boy, too."

Adriano smiled, amused at how no one was thinking to ask him or Alessa what they wanted. "Can we wait a couple of weeks?"

"I guess," Abriella mused, "but you know I'm going to be over there a lot anyway."

Yeah, he knew.

And he was grateful.

"Me, too," Evelina added.

"Thanks," Adriano said. "I'm sure we'll need it."

"You'll do fine," Tommas said, eying the young Capo from the side like he knew Adriano's worries just by looking at him. "Don't fret the small things, Adriano."

He would try not to.

*

"Adriano?"

"Hmm?" he asked, never looking up from Corrine's tiny, sweet features.

"Come here," Alessa demanded.

Adriano strolled across the hospital room, rocking and shushing the baby at the same time. It was the middle of the night—their third night in the hospital. Tomorrow, Alessa and Corrine would be released to go home.

He was scared.

Just a little bit.

He was excited, too.

Sitting down on the edge of the small couch, he leaned over and touched his nose to Alessa. Her smile was wide, honest, and beautiful.

Just like her life.

They were young and stupid.

They'd been so reckless.

For years, really.

But goddamn, it was worth it.

"Love you like crazy," Adriano told Alessa.

His wife smiled bigger, brighter.

"Love you, Adriano."

He glanced down at sleeping Corrine.

"Are you ready for this little girl here?" he asked.

Alessa laughed. "I got through the birth, didn't I?"

She had.

She cried, begged, and screamed more, but she had.

And damn, he was proud of her.

Adriano couldn't have done what Alessa did.

"We can do this, right?" Adriano asked.

Because they were still young.

Still crazy.

Still together.

Alessa nodded, and stroked her daughter's cheek. "Yeah, Adriano. We can do this."

ENDS AND BEGINNINGS

"Wait," Abriella said, her gaze narrowing. "*You* invited her here?"

"Why not?" Alessa asked.

Abriella looked to Tommas for something—Alessa didn't know what. Tommas only shrugged in response. Abriella sighed when she found no help from her fiancé, and turned back to Alessa with a scowl.

"It's not like she's family or something," Abriella said quietly. "I know this was an Outfit gathering to meet and greet Corrine, but she didn't have to be a part of that, Lissa. Just because she was fucking our brother, and playing his little whore—"

"*Abriella.*"

Tommas had spoken softly, but firm enough to silence whatever else Abriella might say. Alessa watched—confused—as a shocking range of emotions flitted over Abriella's features as she stared at Tommas.

"That was wrong of me," Abriella said. "I was out of line."

Tommas passed her an indecipherable look. "You were. She's …"

"Just a woman," Abriella finished softly. "Same as me."

Tommas nodded. "Yeah, babe."

Abriella's brow crumbled and she tipped her head down. "I'm sorry, Lissa. It wasn't my place to tell you who you could or couldn't invite to Corrine's meet and greet."

Alessa had no clue what had passed between Abriella and Tommas, but her sister's fast change in opinion likely meant it was something personal. Alessa wasn't the kind of person to pry, and Abriella probably wouldn't explain it anyway if she did ask.

"I know she was close to Joel," Alessa said.

"Yeah," Abriella agreed. "And that worries me, Lissa. Everyone is happy—safe. I don't want to see that end up changing because we inadvertently invited the trouble right back inside our lives again."

Tommas' hand landed on the back of Abriella's neck like he was reassuring her with his touch. "There was a reason why I didn't go after her, Ella. There was no need. She was harmless, and I knew that from the start. Her deeds only went as far as Joel asked for them to, and with him gone, she is … lost."

Abriella still didn't seem entirely pleased. "If you say so."

"I do."

"I didn't want to be rude," Alessa said. "I invited her mother and father, who are good people, and figured she should be allowed to come to. That was all."

"I'm still going to keep an eye on her," Abriella said.

Alessa didn't doubt it.

Abriella was protective like that.

"Whatever," Alessa said. "But if you expect her to do something terrible, you'll be sorely disappointed. Like Tommas said, she seems kind of lost."

Abriella didn't have much to say after that. Once her sister and Tommas was gone, Alessa went back to piling snacks and treats on her paper plate. She felt Adriano's presence at her side without even hearing or seeing him approach.

Tipping her head to the side, Alessa let her husband kiss her on the top of the head.

It was the little things that made her smile.

Nothing more.

In Adriano's arms, their two-week-old daughter slept swaddled in her yellow blanket. The first week home alone with the baby had been hell. An anxiety induced, sleep deprived hell.

Alessa wouldn't change it for the world.

They learned together.

They stayed awake together.

And Corrine made it all worth it.

"What was all that about?" Adriano asked.

Alessa looked up at him. "Hmm, what?"

"Abriella and Tommas. Seemed like you three were having an intense discussion that you didn't want overheard. I waited until it was done before coming over."

"Oh," Alessa said, sighing.

Her gaze traveled across the room, finding the topic of her earlier conversation with Tommas and Abriella.

The girl was lonely.

She looked lonely.

All by herself, sitting on a chair in the corner, her hands in her lap, and her head down.

So lonely.

Chloe.

"Just my invitation to Chloe today," Alessa said quietly.

Adriano frowned. "She hasn't done anything."

"I know, but Abriella finds it hard to trust people."

"She'll have to learn," Adriano said. "Especially being Tommas' wife, you know."

Alessa didn't respond to that.

"I'm sure Chloe appreciated the invitation, Lissa," Adriano added.

Alessa hoped so, but it was hard to tell. "No one has even said hi to her."

Adriano ticked Alessa under her chin. "Then why don't you go do it, huh?"

Actually, that sounded like a great idea.

*

"Hey, Chloe," Alessa said.

The blonde, blue-eyed woman glanced up from her lap with a furrowed brow. Chloe met Alessa's smiling face, and offered her own back. The smile didn't reach her eyes.

"Hi, Alessa," Chloe said softly.

"Thanks for coming."

Chloe shrugged. "Thanks for inviting me."

Alessa shifted Corrine from one arm, to the other. "Did you get a chance to see Corrine?"

"No, not yet. I didn't want to intrude on someone else's time."

"You're not intruding," Alessa said. "I promise. Do you want to hold her?"

Chloe didn't look entirely comfortable with the idea, but she quickly nodded and held her arms out to take the swaddled baby girl. Once sleeping Corrine had switched from her mother's arms, to Chloe's, Alessa swore the entire room had gone silent.

A pin could have dropped and it would have been louder.

Chloe quickly looked around, like she was taking in the people staring at her holding a Conti baby.

Alessa refused to pay them any mind. "Hey, Chloe?"

"Yeah?"

"It's okay," Alessa said.

Chloe smiled just a little. "Thanks."

Alessa was all too aware how these people looked at Chloe. Like the girl was nothing more than a man's puppet—his whore to do with what he wanted. Joel hadn't helped Chloe's reputation at all in that regard.

But, Alessa would not be someone who fed into that hate and negativity.

It was a different time.

The war and fighting was over.

People needed to move on.

"We named her Corrine Mia Conti," Alessa said.

"That's a very pretty name," Chloe said, watching the baby.

Chloe seemed to be entirely enraptured as she looked at the child. She traced the baby's tiny nose and ran her fingers through Corrine's dark tufts of hair.

It was a sweet sight.

Even Alessa thought so.

"Hello there," Chloe said to the sleeping baby. "You're a very pretty girl, Corrine. I bet your daddy is so proud."

"Adriano is very proud," Alessa agreed, laughing.

Chloe sucked in a shaky breath, smiled again, and then stood. She handed the baby back to Alessa, being careful not to jostle Corrine too much and wake her. Alessa took her daughter back, unsure of why Chloe was handing her over.

"You can keep holding—"

"No, that's okay," Chloe interrupted quickly. "I, uh, just … need to grab a drink of water. Give someone else a turn with her. She's beautiful, Alessa. Congratulations. And really, thank you for inviting me today. I know it couldn't have been easy."

"Actually, it was easy."

Chloe frowned. "Sure."

Confused, Alessa watched as Chloe turned on her heel and left the room without a backward glance. The moment she was gone, the quiet murmurs started.

Alessa ignored them all.

She was more worried about Chloe.

What was wrong with the woman?

Why did it seem like holding Corrine had hurt her?

Not a moment too late, Adriano was back at Alessa's side. His arm snaked around her waist, holding tight and strong.

"You okay?" he asked.

"I am," Alessa said.

"But?"

"But I don't know if she is."

"Sad, you think?"

Alessa didn't know. "Maybe, but it seemed like more than just that, Adriano. What if she misses him or something? Do you think she loved him?"

"Who, babe?" he asked.

"Joel."

Adriano rubbed at the back of his neck. "I don't know. He didn't treat her well."

"Doesn't mean she wouldn't have loved him."

"Yeah, I guess you're right," Adriano said quietly. "Here, let me take the princess. Give your arms a break."

Alessa smiled. "You just want to spoil her."

"So? Stop judging me."

She handed over their daughter with a laugh.

*

Alessa stepped out on the enclosed back deck to take a breather. She didn't mind parties and the people, but sometimes she just needed a break from it all. It could quickly become too much when it got too loud and crowded.

She was grateful for all the love, though.

Her daughter had been shamed so much before she was even born. People whispered about the unborn baby like she was just a giant stain on her mother and father's families for what they had done by sneaking around and getting pregnant.

Corrine was just an innocent child.

She hadn't asked to be made, or born.

So yeah, Alessa was happy.

Overwhelmed, but happy.

Alessa quickly realized she wasn't alone on the back deck. In the far corner, Chloe had sat on the bench, and was staring out at the back property of Alessa and Adriano's new home. They had bought it shortly before the baby was born. And just in the nick of time, too.

Nonetheless, Chloe had pulled her legs up on the bench, and had wrapped her arms around her knees like she was hugging herself. She didn't seem to notice Alessa standing there watching her.

"Chloe?" Alessa asked quietly.

The young woman's head whipped around. Instantly, she was clamoring off the bench like she had done something wrong. "Sorry, Alessa. I didn't mean to hang out back here or anything. I just wanted a few minutes—"

"Away from the party?"

Chloe nodded. "Yeah."

"It's fine. Me, too, really. I love them all, but sometimes they can be a little much."

"I get that."

Alessa took a few more steps closer to Chloe. "You okay? You seem kind of … sad."

"Yeah, I'm okay."

Lies.

Alessa could hear the woman's lies.

"You sure?" she asked.

Chloe shrugged. "Just a lot has happened. Sometimes, a person has to process, you know?"

"Yeah, I do."

More than Chloe could possibly know.

"Is it Joel?" Alessa dared to ask after Chloe had sat back down on the bench.

Chloe's gaze cut to Alessa, widened with shock. "What?"

Alessa waved at Chloe as if to explain what she meant. "You— this—is it about Joel?"

"Maybe. I'm kind of in a bad spot. I don't know what to do."

"Maybe I could help," Alessa said.

Chloe scoffed, but it just sounded sad. "You hated your brother."

"I hated who my brother turned into over the years, but he was still my brother," Alessa corrected gently. "I still remember playing tag with him in the backyard, or having a great game of hide and seek when he was left to watch over us. Joel wasn't always like he was, Chloe. There were times when he was different—happier, nicer, and a better man. He could have been great, but someone ruined him."

"Your grandfather," Chloe muttered under her breath, looking away. "Your mother's father did that to Joel."

Alessa didn't argue the point, because she didn't know for sure.

But she did know that her mother's father hadn't always been nice to Joel. There were stories—rumors—but she didn't know if any of them were true or not.

Joel never talked about it.

He wouldn't give his sisters the chance to ask.

"And he treated everyone else like he had been treated," Chloe added quieter. "Like trash—disposable, unimportant things in his life. Letting someone too close meant he was too close. God, it hurts a person when you care, when you're trying so hard and the one you love just hurts you over and over …"

Alessa flinched at the pain in Chloe's voice.

"I'm sorry," Alessa whispered.

Chloe shrugged. "Don't be. I knew what I was getting myself into. But now, I don't know what to do."

"You can find someone who will love you and care for you like you should be loved and cared for, Chloe."

"Not in the position I'm in now."

Alessa's brow furrowed. "I don't understand."

"Who is going to want someone like me, Alessa? I know what they say about me—the names they call me. A whore, a slut—useless. And that's not even the worst of it."

"What could be worse?"

"That I'm pregnant," Chloe admitted, barely above a whisper.

Alessa froze. "What?"

"Pregnant. About eight weeks along."

Oh, Joel.

Her heart clenched for her brother, and for Chloe.

And for the baby.

Another baby that might be shamed like Alessa's daughter had been just for being conceived. Nothing more.

"You never told him?" Alessa asked.

"I tried," Chloe said, "but he was so angry. And I know what everyone else will think now. They'll talk and say that my child is a bastard, or that the father is unknown. I don't want to do that to myself, or the baby. I know I deserve it, but—"

"Hey," Alessa interrupted sharply. "No one deserves that. Ever, Chloe."

Chloe dropped her gaze. "He wanted me to get rid of the baby. I think he was scared that he couldn't do it—be a father. At least, not a good one. And maybe he was right. Maybe I should because this is impossible to do alone."

"You're not alone," Alessa said. "Abriella and—"

Chloe barked out a laugh. "Your sister hates me."

"She doesn't hate you. She doesn't know you, Chloe."

"I don't want to do this alone."

Alessa quickly crossed the rest of the space separating her and Chloe. She bent down and wrapped the woman in a hug, holding tight.

"You're not," Alessa promised.

"I wanted him to love me," Chloe said, crying.

"Someone else will—someone better."

Chloe didn't say a thing.

Alessa still held tight.

"Who he was isn't reflected on who you are," Alessa told Chloe. "Anyone who thinks differently isn't important enough to have your time or attention. You have people, Chloe. You can have friends, a family if you want. Me, for starters. Please don't feel like you are stuck doing this alone, because you are not. We're here. Just ask. Speak up. *Something*."

Chloe nodded. "Thank you."

"It'll get better. I know it will."

"I just want to be happy," Chloe mumbled.

Sometimes, the end of someone's story wasn't the final moments that others thought it should be. Sometimes, that end was simply just the beginning for someone else.

Alessa hoped this was Chloe's beginning.

For something far better.

THEO | EVE

FOREVER AND EVE

Theo watched the rays of sunlight filter in through the bedroom window, cascade over the floor and bed, and shot straight lines over Evelina's prone form.

He liked her best in the mornings.

Wrapped up in cotton.

Sweet and pretty.

Content and rested.

Yeah, Theo liked this a lot.

It was one of the only times in the day when Theo felt nothing but a soothing calm sweeping his senses. When no noise muddled up his thoughts or feelings or words. He could watch Evelina in his bed, see her so unbothered and unconcerned about the outside world, and he could be happy.

Just … happy.

All of him focused in on her, and that was it for him.

Theo didn't think Evelina even knew what she did for him.

After all, she never asked why he woke up before her every morning. She just assumed he was an early riser, someone whose eyes cracked open at the first sight of light in the windows.

She was wrong.

Theo didn't correct her.

He woke up every morning before Evelina to feel, to see love, to be *alive*.

And nothing more.

If there was ever such a thing as true peace—if being the kind of man he was, he could believe in peace—watching his lover sleep was it.

And that's how Theo knew.

His forever was always going to be Eve.

*

Clink.

Tink.

Clink.

Tink.

The spoon hit the sides of Evelina's cup of steeped tea rhythmically. Over and over. Without saying a word, Theo held out a teaspoon half-filled with sugar.

The *clink-tink* sound stopped as Theo turned the spoon over, dumping the sugar in. Evelina flashed him with one of her sexy smiles and went back to stirring her tea.

Then, Theo held the small box of creamer out, and poured a small amount into Evelina's tea for her. The dark brown melted into a creamy beige as she stirred silently.

Turning on his heel, Theo leaned against the counter, and sipped on his own black coffee. He glanced around his apartment, taking in the changes around the place since Evelina had taken up residence.

Throw cushions on the couch.

A decorative rug.

Bright, colorful artwork on the walls.

Flowers on the table.

Although, to be fair, the flowers were from him to her.

Theo didn't think he would be the kind of man to bring flowers home, but he couldn't resist the pink roses he'd noticed in a flower shop window the day before. Evelina's smile, her quiet thanks, and her hard kiss had made the flowers worth it.

He'd probably bring a few more home.

Once Evelina was finished prepping her tea, and she was satisfied it had steeped long enough, she tucked herself into Theo's side without a word. She sipped on her tea, and put her head to his shoulder.

Theo grinned, glancing down to see the content, pleased smile his girl wore. She didn't say anything, just snuggled in closer, and let him wrap an arm around her shoulders. Theo put his mouth to the top of her head, and gave her a kiss.

Evelina sighed.

Yeah, he still liked mornings the best.

But they were better with Evelina.

It was the quietest time between them. She rarely asked his plans for the day, but Theo always made sure to call her every once in a while to let her know things were fine.

She'd worry otherwise.

He didn't think that would be fair.

It took him a little while to figure it out, but love wasn't all that hard to explain.

People liked to say it was many things entangled into a giant mess of something huge.

It wasn't all that big to Theo.

But it was still everything.

Love was in the little details.

Evelina's smile.

Her happy silence.

His warm apartment touched by her.

Her hands tucked against his chest as she slept.

Silent mornings.

Sugar and milk in her tea.

His love was in the details.

Evelina wasn't the kind of woman who needed words to know.

She just did.

*

"Hey," Evelina said softly.

Theo shrugged on his blazer, and turned on his heel to face his lover. She leaned against the hallway wall, watching him and he stepped into his leather shoes.

"I shouldn't be gone all day," he told her. "Nothing too busy."

Evelina nodded. "Sure."

"Don't worry about me, okay."

"Kind of hard to do."

"But easy to say," Theo said, finishing her unspoken words.

"Yeah, Theo."

He didn't want her fretting and worried all damn day while he was gone. There was still a lot of unhappy people in the Outfit causing trouble, and they weren't mixed up with those people. He refused to take sides—Evelina just wanted to be happy.

He wanted her happy, too.

Still, Theo could plainly see the worry in Evelina's eyes.

"Why don't we do something tonight?" Theo asked. "Dinner, movie, a show. Whatever you want, babe."

He didn't really want to go out.

But if it would make Evelina smile, he would do it.

Evelina made a face. "How about I cook us something, you grab a movie on the way home, and we can make a night in?"

Theo laughed. "You know me well."

"Of course."

Her words had been spoken quietly, but surely.

Almost as if she wanted to say, *Did you expect anything else, Theo?*

He didn't.

She just … knew.

"Night in then," Theo said, smirking.

"Sounds perfect," Evelina replied. "Get going so you can get home faster. And Theo?"

"Hmm?"

"Be careful."

Theo blinked, his smirk melting away. "You know I'll be fine, right? Nobody is coming after me, now, Eve."

Or them.

And that was most important.

Evelina's stare dropped down to the floor. "Seems more bystanders end up being hurt when something happens rather than the people who are intended to be hurt. I just don't want you to be one of them. That's all."

Theo took a step forward, and then another. Before he knew it, he had Evelina wrapped in his arms, a hand holding her back tight, and another wrapped up in her wavy hair. She shuddered against his strong hold, but stayed quiet.

His *girl* …

God, he loved this woman.

"I'm always going to come home," he promised.

Evelina nodded.

"Every night, Eve."

She nodded again.

"To you," he finished firmly.

Finally, she seemed to relax at his words. Theo took that as a battle won. He knew she worried a hell of a lot, but there was only so much he could do to calm her concerns. Which most times, wasn't a whole hell of a lot.

"What can I do, huh?" he asked.

Evelina glanced up, her brow furrowing. "What do you mean?"

"So that you know I'm always coming home to you, no matter what happens."

"I know you will, Theo."

"Do you?"

"Yes," she whispered.

He still wondered ...

Theo thought about the morning he'd spent with Evelina, from the moment he woke up and watched her sleep, to the tea he helped her make without even being asked.

Every morning was the same.

Each one.

And he loved it.

Theo smiled, cupped Evelina's face in his hands, and swept his thumbs over her cheeks. "I want to keep doing this with you, Eve."

"Do what, Theo?"

"This," he said, waving one hand at the hallway. "Waking you up in the morning, watching you put on one of my shirts to be lazy in, helping you make your tea the way you like, and seeing you at the end of the hall before I leave. Every single morning. I want to keep doing this with you. Don't you know that? Forever, Eve."

Her tongue peeked out to wet her bottom lip. "Forever?"

"Yeah. This makes me ..."

"What, Theo?"

"Happy," he admitted. "You make me so happy."

And alive.

She made him live.

Evelina's smile grew to a brilliant sight. She reached up, and grabbed his wrists, holding tight. "You always know the right things to say."

Theo chuckled. "I know."

"I love you, Theo."

He leaned down and pressed a quick kiss to her mouth.

"That's the only thing that matters," he murmured against her lips.

Evelina's eyes locked on his, and held strong.

He wondered what was going on in her head.

Sometimes, with Eve, it was hard to tell.

"Theo?"

"What?" he asked.

"Forever, right?"

"I just told you that."

"All I have to do is say the word, right?" she asked.

Theo cocked a brow. He'd said that to her weeks earlier as they walked through a church, hand in hand. All she had to do was say the word, and he would give her whatever she wanted—a forever with him, her happily ever after on their own terms.

One that wasn't effected by others.

No one else got a say.

Only Eve.

"Just say it," he told her. "And I'll give it to you."

Evelina pursed her lips and then said, "Don't go out today."

Theo laughed. "What do you want me to do instead?"

"Maybe go downtown with me."

"To do what?" he asked, confused.

Evelina nibbled on her bottom lip. "Marry me."

Theo's hands tightened on her jaw, and his gaze cut to hers. Silently, he watched her, wondering if she had come up with this for some reason other than the obvious.

He didn't find anything.

Just his girl.

Someone who loved him.

Who made him happy.

Theo didn't even think about it.

He didn't have to.

"The courthouse?" he asked.

Evelina shrugged. "It's not like it's the first time you've been there, you know."

Theo laughed, loud and hard.

Damn.

Who wouldn't want this woman as their wife?

Theo bent down and kissed Evelina hard, reveling in the sweet heat of her mouth and the demanding strokes of her tongue.

"Is that a yes?" she asked when he pulled away.

God.

There was so much shit going on.

Someone would be pissed.

Someone else might throw a fit.

Marriages shouldn't happen in the Outfit unless approval was given.

And …

Fuck those rules and those people.

Theo promised Eve.

She could have it her way, on her terms.

He *promised*.

"Go put something white on, Eve."

∗

"Hey, Adriano," Theo said, holding the phone to his ear.

"Morning," Adriano replied on the other end of the call.

Theo caught Evelina's smile out of the corner of his eye as she leaned over the display cabinet and pointing at something silver and gold within. She would pick the right rings, Theo knew. Evelina had damn good taste. He wasn't worried.

"What are you calling for this morning?" Adriano asked.

Theo wasn't nervous. Not even an ounce of anxiety colored up his tone when he said, "I'm going to marry your sister."

Adriano didn't hesitate. "Great, man. She said yes, then?"

"Something like that."

"We could do an engagement party or something."

Theo knew those events were common. He wasn't interested.

"Not needed," he said simply.

Adriano laughed. "Why not?"

"Because I'm going to marry her."

"You already said that."

"This morning, Adriano. I'm going to marry Eve this morning."

Silence filled the phone for a second.

Then, Adriano spluttered like he was coughing on his drink or something. It took him an entire minute to calm down and speak again.

"Where?" Adriano asked.

"The courthouse."

"Don't you think she deserves—"

"I think this is what she asked for," Theo interrupted smoothly. "I think this is the day she wants—peaceful, her way, and us in front of a judge and nothing more. I think she deserves everything that she asks for and wants, Adriano."

"Well …"

"Well, what?"

"Okay then," Adriano said. "What time? I'll drive down with Lissa."

Theo shook his head, knowing Adriano couldn't see it. "She wants to do it on her terms. Just us."

"But—"

"Respect that, Adriano," Theo said quickly.

Adriano sighed. "Get one picture of her for me. Call me right after, Theo. And fuck you for not convincing her to do a proper wedding where I could walk her down the aisle."

Theo chuckled. "She's happy."

"I know, man. But you will let the girls throw a small party for you both tonight. I'm sure we can throw something together on last minute notice. This should be celebrated, Theo."

He didn't even have to think about it.

He wanted Evelina to be celebrated.

"Throw her something," he said quietly. "I'll show her off all night, let her party and smile."

Adriano laughed. "All right then."

Theo hung up the phone, and turned to find Evelina holding out a ring for him to look over. It was a simple gold band with two white gold strips on the outer rims. He tried the male version on, and it fit perfectly.

Like it was always supposed to be there.

Huh.

"Well?" Evelina asked.

"It's perfect," Theo said.

Evelina waved her hand, showing her own off. It matched his. "Mine, too."

He pulled her close, tipped her head back, and kissed her. She instantly parted her lips, letting him into her mouth to kiss her deeper.

Yeah, perfect.

Reluctantly, Theo pulled away.

"Let's get us married," he said.

Evelina grinned. "Let's do that, Theo."

LOST AND FOUND

"Joseph and Cory are down for the count," Evelina said.

Theo looked up from the magazine in his hand, smirking wickedly. "Knocked out enough not to hear—"

"Theo, those kids have ears like I can't even explain. No, we're not having sex while they're sleeping down the hall. Then I'll have to listen to Lily bark at me about how she had to have another sex talk because her husband conveniently left the house while her back was turned."

Her husband scowled. "This is why we didn't have kids. They ruin everything."

Evelina gasped. "That is not why we chose not to have kids, Theo!"

"Well, it could have been a reason."

"It wasn't."

Theo shrugged. "All right, it wasn't. Come to bed, *donna*."

Evelina stripped her clothes off, grabbed one of Theo's T-shirts, and slipped it on. By the time she was under the covers on their bed, Theo had tossed the magazine aside and flicked off the bedside lamp. She felt his hands find her in the dark, stroking, holding, and bringing her closer until she was wrapped up in him, their legs were tangled together, and his lips were pressing to hers.

"I do love those kids," he said, his words whispering against her cheek.

Evelina smiled. "Yeah, I know, Theo."

"But I swear to God, they break everything."

She laughed. "Stop it."

"They do, Eve. Everything. I turned my back for five seconds earlier and Cory flooded the bathroom!"

"You sneaked outside to have a cigarette and left the five-year-old alone in the tub, Theo."

"So?"

"So, you can't do that and expect nothing to happen," Evelina said, muffling her laughter into his chest. "It's like telling him to go to it."

Theo rolled onto his back, taking Evelina with him. She stretched over her husband's form, using her hands as a pillow on his chest.

"I wouldn't be a very good father, anyway," he said quietly.

Evelina frowned. "Don't say that. You'd be a wonderful father, Theo."

"You think?"

He'd posed his question quietly, and Evelina could hear the slight vulnerability that was hiding in his words. Children wasn't a topic that Theo or Eve brought up all too often. They had decided years ago before they married that children wouldn't be a part of their future— at least not their own biological children.

Eve didn't want her past to repeat.

Theo was the same.

"I know you would make a good father, Theo."

She knew a lot of people looked at them and searched for some sign of their unhappiness or loneliness. Like because they didn't have a child of their own, they must be missing something. As if having one another wasn't enough.

Eve had news for those people.

They were perfectly happy.

Sleeping in when they wanted.

No worries.

Spoiling everyone else's kids.

It was perfect for them.

"Theo," Eve said, reaching over to turn the lamp on.

He was staring at the wall, quiet and thinking.

She knew that look.

"Yeah, Eve?"

"What's up?"

"Nothing," he said.

"You're lying."

Theo scowled, and ran a hand over his face. "I just wonder about you, that's all. Sure, years ago you were the one who said that kids wasn't in your long-term goals, but I have to wonder if it's changed since then. I see you with Adriano's girls, and Lily's boys. And even Tommaso when his father lets him out of his sight long enough for us to steal him. You love everybody's kids. You're great with them."

Eve's brow furrowed. "So?"

"So it makes me think maybe you should have some of your own, and I just can't give that to you, babe. I don't want—"

She leaned over him and kissed him quiet, fast and hard. "Stop, Theo."

Theo's lips curved into a sinful grin. "Okay."

"You make me so happy."

"Do I?"

"You know you do."

Theo nodded. "Yeah, I guess I do."

"And for another thing, you love those kids just as much as I do. You're the one who comes home on any given night with yet another niece or nephew in the backseat with an armful of junk food. Don't act like it's just me."

He chuckled. "You're right."

"I am always right."

Again, Theo went quiet and still. "I worried, though."

"My God, about what?"

"That maybe you would wake up one day, look around, and be lonely."

Eve hated that her husband thought that way at all.

"Never, Theo. How can I be lonely when I have you?"

The very next moment after the words left her lips, Evelina found herself turned in the bed and under her husband's weight. Theo hovered above her with his wild, dark gaze and smirking lips. She couldn't help but let her hands wander over his fit, toned form. Theo's cut muscles jumped under her touch.

"I said no sex, remember?" she said weakly. "The boys—"

"I am sure you can keep quiet."

"I can't."

"You can." Theo grinned. "I'll gag you, bend you over, and prove you wrong."

Jesus.

That sounded heavenly.

"Say yes," he demanded.

Evelina could only nod.

She didn't know how to tell him no.

Theo wasted no time proving Eve *entirely* wrong.

*

"You want some food?" Evelina asked.

Theo's head snapped up, and a smile bloomed over his handsome features at the sight of her standing in his office doorway. She regularly came to the strip club just to take five minutes away from the rest of the world and spend it with Theo.

But she liked the dancers, too.

"God, yes," Theo muttered. "You're a lifesaver, babe. I'm starving. Get in here and shut the fucking door."

Evelina stepped in, slammed the door, and pulled a chair up to her husband's desk. She handed him over the bag of Chinese food, and let him paw through it for what he wanted. He grabbed out his usual favorites, pulled off the wrapper for the chopsticks, and handed them to Evelina. Then, he got a pair out for himself.

Theo held the box Beef and Noodles out to Eve for the first bite. She took it with a wink.

"I thought you were going to chill with Lily tonight?" he asked.

Evelina grabbed another box of food off his desk. "I did, but it ended early. Cory broke his wrist, and the ER trip kind of blew that all to hell."

Theo cringed. "Please tell me he didn't break his wrist while on those rollerblades we bought him."

"Okay, I won't tell you that. But when Damian calls you to rage about the rollerblades we bought his kid, make sure you have something ready to say back."

"Jesus." Theo sighed, shaking his head. "That kid has no stealth or grace. He sure as shit didn't take after his father, let me say."

Evelina laughed. "Be nice."

"I am. He reminds me of Lily when she was young. Broken bones, scraped knees, torn clothes from climbing fences."

"She's still clumsy," Evelina noted.

"See, exactly my point. Poor kid is doomed to never be able to walk on two feet properly. It's in his genes."

Evelina's laughter filled the office. "Don't say that, Theo!"

"Didn't say nothing that isn't true," he mumbled around a bite of noodles. "Besides, Joseph took after his father enough that Cory will never have to worry. His big brother will watch out for him, and that's the most important thing."

Theo quieted after he made the admission, and dug into his box of Beef and Noodles with the chopsticks, pushing food around but not taking another bite. Evelina could see by the dimness in her husband's eyes that he was thinking of his own big brother, and how Dino had taken care of him.

Theo's guilt had lessened over the years, but it still lingered sometimes. There wasn't much she could do for Theo when he slipped back into memories except let him have them. After all, they were the only thing he had left of his brother.

Evelina let him eat in peace

After they were done, Evelina gathered all the boxes and garbage, put them in a bag, and gave her husband a kiss.

"I'll go toss these in the garbage bin out back," she said.

Theo nodded, hooked a finger into the collar of her dress, and pulled her closer until their noses touched. "Make it fast, woman."

"And why should I do that?"

"I'm still hungry, and you didn't bring dessert. I expect you to rectify that when your pretty ass is sitting on my desk, your legs are spread wide, and my face is buried between your thighs."

Eve let out a shaky breathe. "You're terrible."

"You like it."

She didn't even bother to deny it.

*

Evelina lifted the top of the garbage can, and tossed the bag of Chinese food boxes inside. She turned on her heel, and promptly froze right where she stood.

She didn't blink.

She didn't even breathe.

All she could see was the shaking barrel of a gun pointed directly at her face.

A click resonated in the alleyway.

The hammer being pulled back.

Eve swallowed hard.

"Where's your fuckin' money?" she heard asked.

The tone of the person was gruff and low, but still somehow sounded young. She was still focused in on the barrel, and that flashing silver circle that could light up at any goddamn second. The hand holding the gun held it in a tight grip, but he was still trembling.

"I said, where's your fuckin'—"

"Inside the club," Evelina interrupted quickly, and quietly. "I don't have any money on me."

"Phones, jewelry, something," the guy barked.

Evelina's brow furrowed the longer she listened to him speak. It was almost like he was purposely trying to make himself sound older. Finally, she looked beyond the gun in the face, taking in the person who was trying to mug her.

He stood at her height, if not a couple of inches shorter. A black hoodie covered his head, shielding his face from her view thanks to the shadows in the alleyway. His free arm hung limp at his side, and the sleeve of his hoodie had been shoved up around his elbow.

Evelina gasped at the many marks on his arm.

Blackened, blue, and yellowish.

Circular, oval, and all around.

Like someone had grabbed and held too tight.

Like someone had hurt him.

"My phone is inside, and so are the rest of my things," Eve said softly.

She wouldn't beg this person not to shoot her.

What good would it do?

"That, there," he said, pointing at her left hand. "Your ring, give it to me."

Instinctively, Eve held her hand behind her back. "That's my wedding ring."

He jerked the gun closer, making Eve back into the garbage bin.

"Give it to me, I said!" he shouted.

Evelina sucked in a ragged breath, willed away her nerves, and tugged her wedding ring off. It was the first time she had ever removed it since Theo had put it on her over a half of a decade earlier.

She held the ring out, silently.

The guy reached to take it, but she held strong to the piece.

"More than anything you could take from me, this means the most," she said in a whisper.

He stuttered, his grip loosening on the ring.

"I ... I need to eat," he mumbled. "I can't go back now. I need to eat. Don't you understand?"

Evelina's heart broke. "I'm sorry. I have food inside, if you'll just drop the gun. And money, too."

He hesitated, but slowly, he lowered the gun.

It was only then that Evelina realized how young this person must be. Any career criminal, someone who had lived on the streets for years making what they could through violence, wouldn't have lowered their weapon.

They wouldn't have been so trusting.

This person needed help.

"Can I take it?" Eve asked, holding her hand out. "The gun, I mean."

She didn't expect him to hand it over, but he did. She looked it over, noting it was too light in the hand.

The guy kept his face down. "It's not real, miss."

Eve let out a relieved sigh. With the way fake guns were made, sometimes it was hard to tell. When young boys were getting shot on the side of the road because they held a fake BB gun that looked like the real thing, a person couldn't be too careful.

Without a word, she reached out and pushed the guy's hood back.

He had tears streaming down his very young face.

A boy—no older than fourteen, maybe fifteen.

Bruises littered his neck and cheek. His eye was blackened, and his bottom lip was split.

Evelina's hands trembled when she tilted his face up to make him look her in the eye.

"My name is Eve," she said, offering him a smile. "What's yours?"

"Tyler."

"How old are you, Tyler?"

"Almost sixteen."

Jesus.

He was too small for that, she thought. Too skinny, even if he was tall for his age.

"Who hurt you?" she asked.

Tyler flinched away from her hands again. "Nobody."

"Someone," she pressed gently.

He didn't respond.

Evelina didn't push for more.

She nodded at the exit door. "Come with me, we'll go in, you can warm up and eat, and we'll talk a bit."

Tyler shook his head. "No, I shouldn't. But thank you. I'm sorry for—"

"You're coming inside," Eve interrupted strongly, "and that's the end of it."

*

Theo's smile faded away when Eve stepped aside, and the tall, but quiet teenager walked in ahead of her. Her husband's gaze asked a million and one questions while also taken in the beaten, silent boy who waited quietly with his head down.

"I found someone out back," Eve said.

Theo's gaze dropped to the plastic BB gun in her hand. "Is that so?"

She handed the toy weapon over to him, and grabbed the left over Chinese boxes on the desk. Waving at Tyler, she made him sit in a corner chair, and gave him the food boxes.

"Thank you," Tyler mumbled.

"Eat," Eve said.

She sat down in her chair, feeling the tension radiating off her husband from just a couple feet away as he looked over the gun.

"Eve," Theo started to say.

"Look at his face, Theo."

Theo did.

"And his arms," she added.

Theo's jaw ticked.

"He needs someone to help him, Theo."

"*Eve ...*"

"You needed someone to help you, too," she said softly. "He just needs help. Look at him."

Theo sighed, discarded the toy weapon into the trash bin, and said, "What's your name, young man?"

"Tyler," the boy mumbled around the food in his mouth.

"You're from Chicago?"

"The Heights."

Theo winced. "What about your mom and dad?"

"Just my dad. Mom left years ago."

Tyler was a wealth of information when his hands and mouth were filled with food.

"He's almost sixteen," Eve said. "Right, Tyler?"

"Yes," the boy said, nodding.

Theo's gaze dropped to the bruises littering the boy's arms. "I bet he doesn't tell you that he's sorry after he's done, does he?"

Tyler's hands froze as they lifted toward his mouth. Very quietly, he said, "No."

"You know it's not your fault, right?" Theo asked.

Eve pressed her lips tightly together, hearing the thickness in her husband's tone.

"Feels like it," Tyler muttered, his head still down.

"Well, it's not," Theo replied. "You're just a kid. I suppose you don't have a place to sleep if you're running around in alleyways at night trying to steal from women like my wife here, huh?"

Tyler flinched. "I'm sorry, sir."

"My name is Theo, not sir."

"Theo, then."

Theo's gaze flicked to Eve, and she could see his past catching up to him all in one blink. Sometimes, that was how it worked for Theo. He could go years and not think of a single thing that hurt him from his past. And other times, it was always present, hurting him terribly.

"He just needs some help," Eve told him.

Theo nodded.

Like he had needed help.

*

Tyler had been the first.

But he wasn't the last.

Evelina and Theo never had children of their own, but over the decades, more children came in and out of their home than they cared to count.

Children with broken bones, and black eyes.

Children with burns, and night terrors.

Children to hit them, who cried in corners, who hid in closets, and some who wouldn't even speak.

Eve had never seen her husband more tender than when he rocked a toddler to sleep after she had woke up screaming for her daddy to stop.

She had never seen him stronger than when he sat on the edge of a tub, bandaging his bleeding arm after stopping a young boy from harming himself.

She had never loved him more than in the moments when he

healed himself by helping others, because he had been so unable to help himself.

Each child broke Eve's heart a little more.

It made her hate people.

It made her cry and wonder.

It shook her beliefs and her faith.

Innocent children.

Broken teenagers.

Abused babies.

But Theo worked to help them every single time.

With every child they took in, helped to mend, and then watched as they went again.

He fixed it.

Why did they need their own children?

There were so many others in the world who needed them more.

"Hey," Eve said, leaning in the doorway of their spare bedroom.

Theo kept the rocking chair moving as he glanced up. "Hey, babe."

In his arms, a baby boy slept.

Just four months old.

Kalen was the youngest child they had ever taken in.

He had been born to an addict mother, high on meth from the moment she was pregnant to the day she gave birth. Sometimes, Kalen screamed until he was red all over, and he shook himself to sleep. Other times, he was failing to grow and catching every little cold there was to catch.

He didn't sleep well.

He was irritable.

He had been born addicted, too.

"Want me to take a turn?" Evelina asked.

Theo shook his head. "No, I got him. He just wants someone to touch him as he sleeps. That's all."

Eve smiled. "Okay."

She watched her husband for a little while longer, soaking in the knowledge that Theo's past had taken him down the wrong path.

He'd been so lost.

It just took him a little while to be found again.

TOMMAS | ABRIELLA

LINES AND GAMES

The lines were clearly drawn in Abriella Trentini's life. Lines she shouldn't toe, and shouldn't cross.

Tommas Rossi, Outfit Capo and a man eight years older than her, was one of those lines.

Yet there she was, for the third weekend in a row, at the man's club, watching him interact with people while she stayed off in the corner of the room, rejecting drinks and advances because her attention was somewhere else entirely.

Like on Tommas.

Tipping up her glass of sour puss and 7Up mix, Abriella took another sip. She wished that she had some kind of good excuse for her sudden obsession with Tommas, but she didn't. Three weekends earlier, he'd saved her from a beating at her brother's hand. Then, he urged her to keep doing her own thing, regardless of the opinions from others.

So, that's why she was there again.

At his club.

Drinking when she shouldn't be.

Dancing if someone asked.

Hoping he might notice.

Abriella took another large pull from her glass, letting the liquor settle heavily in her stomach. The truth was pretty simple.

Tommas was far better than Abriella at following the rules.

Clearly.

He pretended like he didn't notice her at all.

Except ...

Abriella glanced over her shoulder, searching in the direction she knew Tommas had been last. He was still there, chatting with a server about something or other.

Jealousy burned in her gut hot and stinging.

The server was young and pretty.

But Abriella took a little solace in the fact that Tommas might have been talking to the server, but he looking across the room.

At her.

*

"You do realize how much shit I would get in if they found an eighteen year old drinking in my club, right?"

Abriella shivered at the dark voice whispering in her ear. "How much?"

Tommas reached over her shoulder, picked up her nearly empty glass, brought it to his own mouth, and downed the rest of the liquor in one go. Then, he put the glass back to the bar top.

"A lot," he murmured. "Lost liquor license, fines out of my ass. And that's just me. That doesn't include what they'd do to you."

Abriella shrugged, and waved at the bartender before waving at her empty glass for a refill. "I'll take that risk."

Tommas chuckled, and spun Abriella's barstool around. She found his blue gaze to be both curious and heated as he looked her dress and heels over. "I suppose your punishment would be a hell of a lot less than mine, anyway."

"Not from my family."

"Yeah, even from them."

Abriella realized that he was probably right. It wasn't like Tommas could pretend to the Outfit that he didn't know Abriella was coming to his club weekend after weekend to party out her stress.

And to watch Tommas Rossi.

It was his club, after all. He had to know everything that was going on inside of it. And if he didn't, then that wouldn't look very damned good on him.

"I would stop coming if you asked me to, Tommy," Abriella said quietly.

Tommas nodded. "Yeah, I know you would."

So ask, she wanted to say to him.

Tell me to go away.

The man had to know the only reason why she kept taking these stupid kinds of risks was because she was coming here for him. Because she was toying, and testing, him.

If Abriella wanted to drink and party, she could get into any club she wanted for that. Her brand new fake ID looked better than the real thing.

She didn't *need* Tommas' club.

He had to know that.

Tommas flicked her with another one of his silent, heated looks, and then pushed away from her barstool. "Enjoy your evening, Ella."

She smiled on the outside, but hurt everywhere else as he walked away.

What was she doing wrong?

What would push the Capo over the edge?

*

Another week came and went.

A new weekend found Abriella right back in the same goddamn spot.

The difference this weekend was that Abriella had stopped playing her quiet game, and stepped up to practically screaming at Tommas in silence.

She could feel him watching her as he did his rounds.

Seeing her dance—watching her with the man she danced with, and the hands grabbing, roving … touching.

It was just a dance.

Innocent, even.

But she surely hoped Tommas didn't think so.

When Abriella wanted something, she would have it come hell or high water. She wasn't quite sure why, but she wanted Tommas. Maybe it was her fascination with the Capo, or maybe it was the fact that everything about him screamed off-limits to her in a big way.

She always had liked things that were wrong and bad for her.

Tommas sort of, kind of fell under that category.

Abriella sighed into the hands of the man she was dancing with. His erection, digging into her ass as they grinded together on the club's floor, did little for her. He was handsome guy, as far as that went, but she hadn't even bothered to learn his name.

He was simply a means to an end.

Finally taking her focus off her dancing partner for a moment, Abriella looked over the crowd again. She easily found Tommas at the bar. Usually he was doing his rounds, checking on his workers, or chatting with people that must have been regulars to the joint.

Not tonight.

Tonight he stood alone, drink in hand …

Watching her.

Abriella smiled at him.

Tommas didn't return it.

If she had to guess, his end was coming really soon.

*

Abriella fixed her hair in the bathroom mirror, and wiped away a smudge of red lipstick at the corner of her mouth. She gave her appearance one more check, and then left the other women in the club's bathroom to do their thing without her taking up the sink and mirror.

She barely walked out of the bathroom and someone grabbed her arm. It might have frightened her if she didn't recognize the deep woodsy scent of Tommas Rossi's cologne.

He pulled her further down the dark hallway toward his office.

Except they stopped before they got to it.

Abriella's back hit the wall, hard. The impact took her breath away, but she didn't mind. Staring down the burning blue eyes of Tommas, she tipped her chin up, defiant.

"What?" she asked.

Tommas bared is teeth. "You know what."

"I don't, actually."

"You do. I am not a stupid man, Ella, and I know what you've been doing. Weeks, girl. You've been playing a cat and mouse game with me for weeks."

Abriella smirked, unable to hide it. "Have you figured out which of one of us is the mouse and which one is the cat yet?"

Tommas' jaw clenched, and his gaze darkened. "You're going to get yourself in a lot more trouble that you can handle, Abriella."

She didn't respond right away. A group of women left the bathroom, chattering away and laughing just down the hall. They didn't seem to notice Abriella or Tommas in the shadows just fifteen feet or so away.

"You're eighteen," she heard Tommas say low after the people were gone.

"So?"

Age meant little to a person who had been forced to act much older than she was for most of her life.

"I'm not a game," he told her.

Abriella blinked, her gaze cutting back to Tommas. "What?"

"I'm not a game, Abriella. I won't be treated like a game for nothing more than some woman's amusement when she needs to blow off steam or rebel." Tommas raised a brow, never taking his eyes off of her as he spoke. "Do you understand that?"

She did.

That didn't meant she would listen.

And really, he seemed to like her game.

"Could be fun," she told him.

Tommas groaned. "Ella."

"Innocent fun between two people."

"No."

"Over when it's done," she added softer.

Tommas swallowed audibly. "You're going to get me killed."

"You're a smart man, right? I'm sure you'll figure it all out. I'm not worried."

He leaned down close enough that their noses almost touched. "You should be. Stupid is stupid no matter which way you twist it to your benefit. It will always be stupid."

Abriella grinned. "Then why do you keep coming closer, Tommy?"

Tommas frowned, but he almost looked like he was in pain. Abriella briefly wondered if she had pushed him too hard in all of this.

She didn't think she was wrong in her assumptions about him.

He clearly wanted her.

It was the risk that she wondered about.

Was it worth the reward?

Tommas rested his forehead on the wall directly above Abriella's shoulder. He stayed still and quiet for a long time, but he also kept Abriella pinned in place when his hands found her waist and squeezed tight.

Hard enough to hurt.

She loved it.

"You were out there tonight with that guy, acting like ..."

Abriella stilled. "Like what, a slut?"

Tommas jerked back up instantly. "I wasn't going to say that."

"No?"

"No, I was going to say you were acting like you were trying to push my buttons."

Oh.

Abriella glanced away. "But what if I wanted to be?"

"Be what?"

She let the words slip out, despite how strange they felt for her to say them. "Be someone's little slut."

Tommas groaned in that pained way of his again.

Abriella was quickly learning that she liked it.

A lot.

"Don't do that," he warned.

"Say what I'm thinking?"

Tommas tipped his head to the side. "Always do that."

"That's what I'm thinking, Tommy."

"Stop," he told her.

"I think you like my games," she whispered.

Tommas shook his head. "You're wrong."

"I'm not."

Sure. Simple. Sweet.

Abriella was terribly good at this. "And if you're worried that you're taking something that doesn't belong to you, or that I'm too innocent to be messing around with a man, I hate to disappoint you. That happened three years ago."

She asked a boy to stop once.

He didn't.

The shame from that one encounter left Abriella feeling like it was only her fault. Like the position she had put herself in left her open to be hurt in that way.

Then she met another boy.

She told him to stop.

And he did.

It hadn't been her at all—it was all him.

"I won't be some lamb," Tommas said.

Abriella's brow furrowed. "A lamb?"

"The sacrificial lamb you bleed out in an attempt to hurt your family and push against the boundaries they've set out for you. That's not fair to me. I won't let you do it."

"I just want to have fun," she said.

Tommas wet his lips, finally let go of her waist, and took a step back.

Abriella's shoulders sank when he once again shook his head.

"No," he told her.

She hadn't even been more mad than she was in that one moment.

"Who's playing games now?" she asked.

Tommas smirked, sinful and wicked. "It's not fun, is it?"

Bastard.

Abriella liked it.

He tipped his head back toward the bar. "Go back out on the floor, and enjoy the rest of your evening."

"Tommy—"

"And if you come back next weekend ..."

Abriella swallowed hard. "What about it?"

"Think it over for the week. But if you do come back next weekend, I'll be in my office."

"And?"

Tommas' gaze found hers, steady and strong. "The door will be open."

She pushed past him in the hall, and walked back out to the club.

A week, was that all he wanted?

Abriella gave him his week.

And that following Saturday, she was right where he told her to be.

In his office.

On his desk.

Dirty, but awfully good, too.

And a whole new game started to be played.

THEY CAME TO BE

"We should do something," Tommas murmured.

Abriella couldn't help but shiver at the way his words whispered over her skin like the softest kiss. His lips grazed the back of her neck as he spoke, and she could feel his breath pulsing against her nerves. It spoke to just how close she truly was to him even if his hands were resting behind his head at the moment, and she was sitting cross-legged in his lap.

Naked.

In the back seat of a Mercedes Benz.

Abriella glanced out the window at the darkened parking lot of a hotel that was famous for its two-year waitlist when it came to holding events.

Oh, did she forget to mention they were supposed to be inside at someone's wedding?

Because, *yeah.*

That was the thing about Tommas, and her. Ever since they started playing this game with each other a couple of months ago, they couldn't seem to stop. Things like this—sneaking off when they shouldn't even be *talking* to one another—were risky. And yet, they continued to do it every single chance they could.

Abriella hadn't found a reason to regret it, yet.

"Do what?" she asked.

"Something," he said. "We should do something else."

Abriella's brow furrowed. "Something else? Are you purposely being vague, or …?"

Tommas shifted beneath her, making his still semi-hard erection press against her tender ass. He'd spanked her ass hard enough to make sitting down a difficult and careful task, but she wasn't about to lie and say she didn't like it.

Because she had.

Too damn much.

That was another thing about Tommas that kept Abriella coming back for more. It went beyond the sex—because that alone was fucking amazing—and into something deeper. This man had the strangest ability to make Abriella feel the *most* free she had ever felt in her life when she was on her knees, and begging for more.

Yet, outside of sex, they became something else entirely. He treated her with care, and respect, and nothing less would do.

She'd never known a man who understood the difference between the things woman chose to do in the privacy of a sexual encounter, and the woman outside of a bedroom … or a car … and alley … *wherever.*

"You're not even listening to me, are you?" Tommas asked.

Abriella giggled when his fingertips grazed over a ticklish spot on her side. He'd found that fucking spot once, and used it against her every chance he could. Especially when he wanted her attention to focus on him, and nothing else.

Smart man.

Abriella liked those.

"Stop," she gasped when his tickling intensified. "Tell me what you said!"

That was another thing about Tommas—he understood the words *no, don't,* and *stop.* He didn't even need a fucking verbal cue for him to know he needed to back off, and quit whatever it was that Abriella didn't like.

She trusted him.

Far more than anyone else …

"I said," he murmured in her ear, "that we should do something else."

"I heard you say *that.* You're not telling me *what,* though."

He kissed the spot right behind her ear. "I was thinking something other than *fucking,* Ella."

She stiffened in his lap. Tommas didn't miss it if the way his fingers tightened on her waist was any indication.

"What, like … friends?" she asked quietly.

Tommas made a harsh noise in the back of his throat—something dark, lovely, and deep. It heated her insides up instantly, and had her aching between her thighs. Why? Because that sound made her think he was *jealous.* Even if he didn't say it, that's what it sounded like. She had no reason to think he was, and he had no reason to be jealous. They didn't put labels on this thing they were doing together.

They weren't *something.*

That was the deal.

Or … it was supposed to be.

"I was thinking ... a date, actually," Tommas said.

"We're not doing—"

"But we could be," he interjected. "I would like to. Would you?"

Abriella swallowed the thickness building in her throat. Her first thought was to say yes, and agree. Whatever he wanted, whenever he wanted it. Why not? Tommas Rossi was literally everything Abriella hadn't even known she wanted in a man until he was standing in front of her, and smiling in that sexy way of his.

Her life, lessons, and future kept her quiet.

Tommas sighed after a second passed. "Leave me hanging, then."

"It's just ..." Abriella glanced down at her hands in her naked lap. "We can't really *be* anything, Tommas. It'll never be anything ... or come to anything. It can't."

She was Trentini *principessa*.

The oldest girl.

She knew what her life was going to be once the decision was made. A husband would be chosen, and she would be given away. That's how it worked for girls like her. She didn't expect anything different.

This was her fucking *life*.

It was all she knew.

"So?" Tommas asked.

Abriella let out a short laugh. "*So?* Really, is that all you have to say? So?"

Tommas shrugged behind her. "I mean ... yeah, baby. So what?"

"Tommas—"

His hands tightened on her waist again, and hushed her words from slipping out. He kept her argument silent while he spoke again.

"I don't like to *share*," Tommas said. "And while we're doing *this* ... I want to make sure I'm not sharing you."

Abriella glanced over her shoulder to find his stormy blue eyes locked on her. The intensity of his stare made her chest tight. "You're not sharing anything—promise."

"Good, then this shouldn't be a big deal. Let me take you out—dinner, a club. A show, if you want. Whatever you want to do, let me know, give me some time, and we'll do it."

Abriella abused her bottom lip with her teeth. "No one can ever—"

"No one will know anything. I'll make sure of it."

He sounded so sure.

Confident.

How could she tell him no?

"So, a *real* date, then, huh?" Abriella asked.

Tommas gave her one of his sinful grins. "A first date. And hey, you got to try the ride before the show ... so, you don't even have to worry about a bad fuck at the end of the night. You know what you're getting."

Jesus Christ.

This man was something else.

And she kind of loved it.

THREE LITTLE WORDS

"Ella."

Wearing nothing but one of his t-shirts, and a pair of black cotton panties, she spun on her heels with a wet whisk dangling precariously from one hand. He thought, possibly, she might splatter the egg mess still coating the wires of the whisk all over the island counter as she stared across at him, but he didn't really care about that.

It was hard to care about anything else but her when she stared at him. All he needed was her attention, and just like that, the rest of the world disappeared. Did it make sense? Did it constantly drive him fucking crazy?

Did he always wonder *why?*

Yes to all.

And then he figured it out.

All at once.

Staring at her while she cooked them scrambled eggs in an apartment that wasn't even technically *his* or hers. At least, not on paper. Their names couldn't be on the apartment he rented in the city for them to sometimes sneak away because otherwise, someone might find out their little secret.

The fact they did this together at all.

It wouldn't end well.

Couldn't.

Instead, he used a fake name and matching IDs to get the place. That way, if someone looked into his business, this wasn't one of the things that would come up. The two of them could remain like this in their private, secret bubble that no one could touch.

For now.

"Yeah?" Abriella asked.

Always sweet.

And yet, with a touch of slyness, too.

Sexiness.

Her smile curved at the edges, drawing those pretty lips of hers into a shape he had come to adore. Her eyes crinkled a bit at the corners, too. And the apples of her cheeks popped with a touch of pink.

That's how he knew her smiles were real.

Other people seemed content to ignore the fake ones she plastered on for the sake of politeness and what was expected of her. Tommas was not the same. He decided it would be a *much* better pay off for him if he took the time to peel back all the layers of what made Abriella Trentini tick; find every single one of her secrets that made her *her*. And once he learned all those things, Tommas just didn't know what to do with it.

Because it only taught him one thing.

He loved her.

Wholly.

Entirely.

Stupidly.

"Do you have something to say, or are you going to just keep looking at me?" Abriella asked.

"I love you, Ella."

There.

He said it.

Couldn't take it back now.

Definitely couldn't change it.

Abriella's loose stance stiffened up a bit. "We said we weren't going to do that, Tommy. Why would you do that?"

She was right. Months ago, lying in bed together after managing to finally sneak her away from the rest of her family for a night, she'd whispered in the darkness that *I can't fall in love with you—don't fall in love with me, Tommy.* It made sense, of course, because this was only supposed to be fun.

Nothing more.

Nothing less.

Except when she whispered those words in the darkness, still sweaty from the way he'd held her against the mattress and made her come again and again, he heard the shake in her voice. Felt that right to his bones. *And what it meant for his own heart.*

He heard and felt it all.

She loved him then.

He loved her, too.

"And if we do love each other," she had added that night after her first statement, "then we won't say it out loud—it won't hurt."

Again ... that made sense.

And then he watched her dance, and cook.

Smile at him over her shoulder.

He wished he could give her the world.

That felt like it started with three little words.

"I love you," he said.

He didn't miss the way her hand shook, still holding that whisk. Or how a line of water dampened her eyes. That smile of hers faded away slowly because he broke the rules she'd made, and *fuck* …

Fuck.

He wished he was sorry for it.

Wished it wouldn't be hard for her.

But he still wanted to give her the world.

Maybe not today.

Or tomorrow.

Or next year.

Someday, he'd figure out a way.

And he'd give her the world.

Their world.

Together.

"Not supposed to say that," she whispered. "We said we weren't going to—"

"We break rules all the time."

Abriella sucked in a breath. "Tommy—"

"Still going to love you. Whether or not you say it back, or if you need to run. Today, tomorrow … whenever, still going to love you, Ella."

"*Killing me here.*"

He shrugged one shoulder, grinning. "Just wanted you to know."

"I just wanted to make you *eggs*."

"And?"

"And then you had to change *everything*."

Tommas shook his head. "Changes nothing. I only stated the obvious."

That made her pause.

Why?

Because he didn't lie.

Tommas did a lot of things.

Lying wasn't one of them.

It was her that found comfort in lies.

She lied to the people closest to her.

To everyone else.

Even to herself.

Never to him, though.

She never lied to him.

"I wanted to pretend for a little while longer," she said.

Tommas arched a brow. "Pretend what?"

"That this wasn't going to end with my heart broken."

"It'll never end, if you don't want it to."

Abriella shook her head. "You can be the optimist, Tommas, but I'll forever be the pessimist."

"As long as you're the pessimist that loves me."

"You know I do. I think I've always loved you."

Yeah.

The world.

How did one give the world to someone who had become your world, anyway? He should probably figure that out.

BLOODY AND BROKEN

Tommas tossed a piece of popcorn high, tipped his head back, and caught the bite easily when it dropped back down. He relaxed into the chair at the sound of Abriella's laughter.

"You fucking showoff," she teased.

Tommas winked. "Don't be jealous of my skills, Ella."

She laughed more. "Skills, right."

"Hey, you know my skills."

Abriella sobered with a deep grin. "Think you could get away with showing me just how skilled you are—"

Her words stopped up short when a nurse entered the room. The young woman gave Tommas a smile that he returned, but only for show. He'd needed to charm and flirt his ass off enough as it was just to get inside Abriella's room after hours, plus make sure no one reported his visits to Abriella's family.

Knowing all that didn't stop Abriella from glowering at the nurse or Tommas.

She was so jealous.

Tommas loved it.

"Nighttime meds," the nurse said.

Abriella sighed, took the little paper cup, and tossed back her pills without much fuss. He knew the nurses had started putting a sleep aid in her night meds because Abriella wasn't sleeping well. In fact, she woke up on and off throughout the night from nightmares that she refused to admit she was even having.

It bothered Tommas to no end.

He worried about her constantly.

Especially when Abriella tried brushing things off that he knew had to be bothering her. Things like getting shot in the back, needing emergency surgery, and almost losing her life.

But his girl was strong as hell.

A goddamn fighter.

She didn't like to be weak.

Tommas waited out the nurse's check of Abriella's surgery scar to her back where they had dug the bullet out of her body, plus stitched up the back of her lung where it had punctured the organ. It was just luck that the goddamn bullet missed her ribcage or spine like it did.

Both would have had disastrous consequences.

Finally, the nurse left.

"Well, there's your answer," Tommas said.

Abriella pursed her lips. "She only comes in here to look at you and flirt."

Tommas chuckled. "She does not. She didn't say a damn word to me and you know it. She brought your meds in, thank you very much. Stop being jealous."

"I'm not—"

"You are green all over, Ella."

Abriella snapped her mouth closed. "Yeah, well, shut up."

Tommas hid his smirk by shoving another handful of popcorn in his mouth. His girl turned the television on, and put the channel on one of the comedy networks she liked so much. Before long, Tommas had discarded his bag of popcorn and shrugged of his suit jacket. He climbed into the small hospital bed with Abriella, careful to avoid her IV snagging on him somehow.

Once he had her snuggled into his side, Tommas ran his fingers through Abriella's soft waves of hair. She watched her sitcom, giggling to herself every so often when something was funny. Tommas was far too preoccupied with watching her to even care about what was playing on the television.

Abriella was far more entertaining, anyway.

He also kept an eye on the clock.

At twelve, the nurses would ask him to leave. He was pushing his luck and the good graces of others just by coming and going like he did after hours. Tommas wasn't about to push it anymore and demand they let him stay.

He hated leaving Abriella.

She despised the hospital, the nighttime noises, and the beep of machines. She complained about the sterile smell, the scratchy sheets, and the lack of sunlight coming in from the small window.

Tommas knew what her problem really was. Abriella wasn't a brat complaining about every little thing she could. The girl just didn't want to be stuck in a hospital bed. She didn't want to be … helpless.

He could relate to Abriella's feelings, so he sympathized with her hatred for the four, white walls currently keeping her locked up tight. It probably didn't help that Abriella was in pain, and of course, all the bullshit going on around them.

It didn't take long before Abriella's eyes drifted closed. Tommas kept stroking her hair, watching her fall asleep beside him. He didn't think the nurses had told her about the sleep aide, but she didn't need to know.

Abriella needed rest.

To heal, her body demanded sleep.

Tommas stayed with Abriella until his time was cutting terribly close to the end. At ten to twelve, he carefully pushed out of the bed, mindful of Abriella's back and the tenderness she felt when jostled too much. Lifting her hand from where she had tucked it in under her chin, Tommas pressed a quick kiss to her palm.

He grabbed her notebook off her stand, and scribbled a quick note for her to wake up to. She never said a thing about him leaving her night after night, but he knew it had to bother her just a little.

Abriella didn't want to be alone.

Tommas didn't want to leave.

It might as well have been the story of their goddamn lives. Or rather, their relationship. He was always leaving. She was always being left behind.

Tommas wished that wasn't the case.

But it was.

He gave Abriella's hand one more kiss, and slipped out of her hospital room without looking back.

That only hurt.

*

Tommas sipped on his coffee, waiting. It wasn't long before Nate slid onto the stool beside his Capo.

"Hey, boss," Nate said.

"Evening. What do you have for me?"

Nate shrugged. "Exactly what we suspected. Nothing."

Tommas blew out a heavy breath, frustrated and irritated. "You didn't get anything out of Joel's men on what he might do?"

"Yeah, nothing, Tommy."

Goddammit.

Running a hand over his face, Tommas tried to tamper is anger. He'd been waiting Joel out ever since the restaurant shooting. He hoped the man would do the right thing and take out the issue that had caused Abriella to take a bullet to the back.

That issue being Laurent.

Tommas' own father.

Sure, it was likely that the bullet that hit Abriella hadn't actually come from Laurent's gun, but the entire shootout shouldn't have happened at all. It wouldn't have happened had Laurent not been such a fucking fool, following after Joel Trentini like the man knew what he was doing.

Joel didn't know a fucking thing.

Laurent should have known better.

Taking out Joel was too troublesome for Tommas at that moment. It would probably cause him more issues than he could handle, so that was an option he couldn't take. His father, however, would be simple.

Easy, even.

And God knew Tommas was pissed off enough to do it.

Years.

So many years of abuse, neglect, and hatred had piled up on Tommas toward his parents. They had hurt him over and over, time and time again. Their alcoholism became his parents' first priority, and they never thought twice about the children they brought into the world and were supposed to care for and love.

Laurent didn't know about Abriella and Tommas' relationship. He couldn't possibly understand how badly he had hurt Tommas by putting Abriella in danger like he had.

But it was done.

It still happened.

Tommas couldn't forgive that.

Not for a second.

"What are you going to do now?" Nate asked.

Tommas took another sip of coffee as he mulled over his very limited options. He also considered Abriella because she was always on his mind. She had finally been let out of the hospital and was allowed to go back home.

Unfortunately, her brother had her on an even tighter leash now that she was put on bedrest for healing.

Who knew when he would see her again?

Hold her?

Kiss her?

Love her?

Damn.

Yeah, Tommas was pissed.

"I don't know," Tommas finally said quietly.

Nate frowned. "Sorry, boss."

"No worries. You got me what I wanted, even if it's not what I want to hear. If Joel isn't planning on taking care of my fuck up of a father, then that leaves me to the job."

It's not like he couldn't do it. Tommas could do it without blinking. The abused could only be stuck so many times before the chain finally broke and they struck back. Laurent should have known this.

Tommas wasn't the compliant child that he once was, hiding away and not making any noise as to not disturb his drunk parents. He was an adult now.

"I could take care of it for you," Nate suggested. "Make it fast, you know."

Tommas pushed his empty coffee cup across the counter. "No, I'll do it."

He just had to pick a time.

*

Tommas spun the quarter on the table, watching it spin wildly until it fell with a clang onto its side. Picking up the coin, he repeated the motion. The noise of the spinning and falling coin echoed in the quiet, dingy smelling kitchen of his parents' home.

More often than not, he tried not to come here. Whenever his sisters came home from Toronto for a visit, he would make his way over, but he tried not to stay for very long.

He hated this house.

Loathed the people within.

Despised the memories that wouldn't leave no matter how hard he willed them away.

Despite being a thirty year old man, he often found himself feeling like a young boy again whenever he was inside the home. The young boy who had needed to take care of his even younger twin sisters, who cleaned their crying faces, bandaged their scraped knees, and fed their mouths when there was food in the house.

Those were the kind of memories that Tommas wanted to let go of. He didn't want them mudding up his mind, or affecting his future.

He wasn't that boy anymore.

His sisters were long gone—one dead.

Wasn't that enough?

Tommas sure thought it was.

Shaking off those depressing thoughts, Tommas picked up the quarter again. He flicked it between his pointer finger and thumb, making it spin across the table. The whirl of the coin drew his gaze in, allowing him to focus on his current task and not his past.

Tomorrow, he would start making plans to steal Abriella away for the day. She deserved it after the hellish month she had. He wasn't all too worried about his plans being spoiled—it wasn't the first time he had pulled something like that off with his girl.

And, of course, Abriella was smart as hell.

She didn't mind playing those games.

A throat cleared from the kitchen entryway, making Tommas look up from the spinning coin. He snatched the coin in his palm as his father stumbled into the kitchen a little further. The sluggish movements of Laurent's steps and the hazy eyes told Tommas that his father was likely still drunk—or he'd been drinking quite a bit and was still feeling the effects.

Tommas wasn't even surprised.

"Tommas?" Laurent asked, blinking at his son. "What are you doing here?"

"Laurent," Tommas greeted.

"How did you get in?"

"My key."

Obviously.

Laurent's brow furrowed and he stumbled to the sink. He didn't ask Tommas any more questions as he searched for a clean glass, and poured himself a small drink of water. Then, Laurent moved to the fridge, opened it up, and searched for what he wanted within.

Tommas wasn't the least bit surprised when his father fell down into a kitchen chair with two beers in hand. Laurent popped off the top on his before sliding a bottle down the table for his son.

"Have a drink," Laurent mumbled sleepily.

Tommas eyed the bottle of beer with as much distaste as he could manage. He rarely drank, and when he did, it was mostly for show. He could walk around all night with the same drink in his hand, taking a sip here and there, but mostly dumping it out when someone wasn't looking.

He didn't even like the taste of alcohol unless it was bourbon.

And even then, Tommas was careful about how much he drank.

Addiction ran rampant in his family. He wasn't going to be the next addict Rossi falling down that familiar rabbit hole.

No way in hell.

"No, I—"

"Don't refuse a drink from a man inside his home, Tommy boy," his father said.

Tommas clenched his teeth, swallowing back his anger. For one, because his father knew he didn't like to drink. And for two, because his father called him by a nickname that he used to use when Tommas was young.

Tommy boy.

Like he was still a kid.

His little Tommy gun, Tommy boy, his father used to say.

And then he was forgotten about. Just like his sisters.

"What brought you over here tonight?" Laurent asked. His father blinked at the clock on the wall, like he was trying to discern the time. "Jesus, it's two in the morning."

Tommas flipped the coin in his hand, refusing to even touch the beer in front of him. "Thought we should talk about some things."

"Like what? It couldn't wait until there was daylight and—"

"You were sober?" Tommas interrupted.

Laurent swallowed hard. "Been a long day."

Excuses.

Addicts were famous for them.

"Where's Ma?" Tommas asked.

"Passed out upstairs. Probably won't wake up until noon. What does it matter?"

Tommas was just getting his ducks in a row.

"Just wondering," Tommas murmured. "About the restaurant ..."

Laurent sighed, cringing. He took another long pull from his beer. Tommas couldn't help but notice the shake in his father's hand as he lifted the bottle a little higher.

Tremors were a bitch.

The only way to get rid of them was to drink.

The next day, it started all over again.

Vicious fucking cycles.

"You had no business playing puppet to Joel and going after Riley like that," Tommas said.

Laurent scowled at his son. "No business? Tommy, listen to yourself. It's like you don't even hear what you say. This family—the Rossis—will never go anywhere with Riley Conti as the fucking Outfit's boss. Don't you realize that?"

No, Tommas didn't.

He didn't think that at all.

Riley Conti was one of the few men that Tommas could actually stand to work with when it came to the Outfit and the families. The guy was shady as fuck, he could be a mean motherfucker, and he wasn't all that great of a human being to begin with. But at the same time, Riley didn't hide those things about himself.

Everyone who was anyone knew that Riley was a bastard.

But he was a bastard that liked Tommas.

Tommas couldn't help that Riley didn't like Laurent.

"You're wrong," Tommas said.

"With Riley as the boss, and Joel gone, you'll still be right where you are in ten, fifteen years, Tommas," Laurent said, sneering. "Same as me. I want you going somewhere in this fucking thing, son. Up, you know. You should be going up. And I don't give a shit who has to be buried so that I can get you there. After all this family put me through, after everything I did for you, I deserve that, Tommas."

Tommas tipped his head to the side, taking in his father's words. "Was that why you did it?"

"What?"

"The shooting at the restaurant. Messing around with Joel Trentini even knowing he's a damn snake that you can't trust if your damned life depended on it. Was that why you did it? To further yourself by furthering me?"

Laurent shrugged, smirked, and took another drink.

Like it didn't even matter.

His father couldn't possibly know what he had done. That by trying to help Tommas for his own selfish fucking reasons, Laurent had almost taken away the very thing that Tommas wanted, needed, and loved more than anything.

Because Abriella was his heart.

His breath.

His life.

His fucking *soul*.

And Laurent didn't understand.

He wasn't a good enough father to understand. He wasn't someone Tommas loved or trusted enough to be able to tell his father exactly what he had done wrong, and how badly it hurt Tommas. He had never given his son—his own blood—a good enough reason to trust him.

Laurent was nothing while Abriella was …

Everything.

Fucking *hell*.

Tommas' anger exploded in that moment.

It wasn't even anger.

It was fucking rage.

Pure, unaltered fury.

Tommas had only felt that maybe twice in his thirty years. But this one was the worst—it had to be. It soaked through his body like a tsunami of heat and blinding, blistering emotion that he could barely stand to feel.

He reacted before he could stop himself.

Tommas grabbed the dishcloth that had been discarded to the table, and used it as a buffer between his fingers and the beer bottle when he wrapped it around the neck and picked it up, too. His fingerprints wouldn't be left behind. He swung without thinking, feeling a sickening sensation of satisfaction rush through his bloodstream when he smashed the beer bottle across his father's face.

Laurent fell back from his chair, toppling to the floor, with a loud shout of pain. Tommas enjoyed the sound of that, too.

Moving from his chair faster than he could blink, Tommas kicked another chair out of the way so he could move down above his father. He grabbed Laurent's shirt, ignoring that it was damp with sweat and smelled awful as he pulled Laurent up a little from the floor.

"For me?" Tommas growled.

Laurent sucked in a hard breath, his glassy eyes wide. "Tommas—"

"You think you did that for me?" Tommas shook his father. "You

231

selfish fucking bastard, you've done nothing for me except hurt me!"

"That's not true, Tommy."

"It is," Tommas growled. "You know it is. You're a fucking drunk, Laurent. You and Serena both. A goddamn shame. You couldn't give two fucks about me or what I want, only what I could do for you. Some father you are."

Laurent blinked up at Tommas, still seeming confused. "I don't—"

"Understand?" Tommas asked. "I'm not surprised. You don't know anything about me. You don't have the first clue about what matters to me, or what I might want. You almost fucking killed me, Laurent. Do you understand that? You almost killed me when you caused her to be caught in the crossfire of your goddamn mess! And for what, to move me higher for *your* benefit?"

Silence saturated the kitchen.

Tommas had roared each and every single one of his words. His shouts bounced off the kitchen walls, echoing back to him. Laurent had stilled on the floor, bleeding from his mouth and nose. The bottle must have cut him, and broke his nose. Tommas didn't know.

He didn't care.

"Her?" Laurent asked quietly.

Tommas stiffened. "Shut up."

"Her."

It wasn't even a question that time.

"Shut the fuck up," Tommas repeated, growing the words.

He didn't want Laurent to know about Tommas' relationship with Abriella. He didn't want his father to know because the man didn't deserve to know those kinds of things about Tommas. He hadn't earned the right.

"Are you talking about that Trentini—"

Tommas slammed his father into the floor, soaking up the shout of pain Laurent let loose when his head cracked against hardwood. "Shut your stupid mouth, Laurent."

His father laughed—bleak and weak.

"What are you going to do, Tommy boy, kill me?"

Tommas had thought about it a lot.

He blamed his father for a lot of things.

Laurent would deserve it.

"I didn't want to," Tommas admitted, "but you did this when you hurt me."

"A piece of pussy—is that it? You're mad over a fucking useless piece of ass you could find anywhere?"

That was that.

It was all Tommas needed to hear to lose what little control he maintained. He pulled the gun he always kept safely tucked into a holster at his back. When he brought it around front and pointed it at his father's face, Laurent's eyes flew wide again.

Bloody mouthed and glassy eyed, Laurent stared down the barrel of the gun.

Tommas slammed the gun into his father's mouth hard enough to break teeth. Laurent choked on blood and bone, spitting when Tommas pulled the gun back. He only let his father breathe for a second before he was slamming it into Laurent's face again.

"S-stop, Tommas," Laurent begged.

Tommas didn't hear a word.

He hit his father again.

And again.

He couldn't seem to soothe the rage no matter how hard he hit Laurent. And he tried—God he fucking tried. He couldn't get the gun to hit his father hard enough, couldn't break enough teeth, or make enough blood spill.

Breaking the man wasn't satisfying enough.

Tommas wanted him *gone*.

Laurent might have loved him once.

He might have cared.

He'd been his father's little Tommy gun, after all.

But that was a long, long time ago.

Laurent's face was a bloody, battered mess when Tommas finally stopped hitting him with the gun. His father spit blood and saliva out, choking on his own fluids. He mumbled on the floor, begging for Tommas to let him live—begging for his wife.

Because Serena was so important to Laurent.

Much more than his own children were.

"Don't hurt her, Tommas," Laurent said.

Tommas barely heard a word. He was still caught up in that red hot, white-fueled fury rushing through his bloodstream. It was so much better than the pain and betrayal he felt whenever he thought about his father.

Laurent kept mumbling, begging, and then he was gagging on his own bloody vomit. That was the one and only time that Tommas let his father go.

He didn't want the man's sickness on him.

He lived with Laurent's sickness every single day of his life.

Tommas was terrified of becoming this man. A man who drank his days away and neglected the lives he brought into the world. A man who only cared about what people could do for him, and never gave a shit about anyone else.

"Fucking bastard," Tommas hissed. "That's all you are. So fucking useless, Laurent. You can't hurt a man over and over and expect to get away unscathed. You really messed up this time."

Laurent wasn't hearing Tommas.

He was too busy begging for the life of a woman Tommas also didn't care about.

Laurent only stopped mumbling when Tommas cocked the hammer back and shoved the barrel against his father's mouth.

"I hate you," Tommas said quietly.

Laurent swallowed audibly.

Tommas was glad the truth was the final words his father would ever hear.

He pulled the trigger back.

Smooth.

Easy.

True.

Like breathing.

Tommas didn't look away, either.

THE TRUTH

"Gian," Tommas greeted.

Standing in the entryway of the Trentini mansion, Gian kept his back to Tommas while he stared out the side window next to the grand doors. "Tommas—we made it up the driveway this time, at least."

"A feat, was it?"

Gian let out a slow, but *hard*, breath. "Painful, I think."

"I'm sorry."

"Don't apologize. You're not the one who created those memories for her, you know. And she's so determined to … get over it. I think she's given herself a complex about it, really. She helps everyone else, and yet, hasn't been able to help herself in the same ways."

Tommas understood.

Well enough, anyway.

"Where'd the boys go?"

"Ran off with Tommaso. Abriella said she would call when lunch was finished. You were busy on the phone—I told her not to bother you. The same for them."

"You're not a bother. Besides, I was waiting for you to arrive. Next time, get her to call me down."

"To watch my wife with me?"

Tommas chuckled. "I can do that, too, of course."

"She said to just … let her work through it. She'll come in when she's ready. It took her ten minutes to get out of the car after we arrived. Now, she's just out there sitting on the curb staring at the marble steps."

"Oh."

At the simple statement—but not with any surprise—Gian turned to give Tommas a raised brow. "What was that—that *oh*. What does that mean?"

"The steps—it's where Lea died."

"I know that. What I don't understand is why she wants to stare at them. It's been years since she's even been back to this house, Tommas."

"Or maybe … she's trying to see something else, Gian. Something

235

other than what she sees now when she looks at them."

Because even Tommas couldn't forget those steps.

That day.

His sister's blood.

None of it.

He knew it was worse for Cara—it had to be. She'd been standing right beside Lea when their sister was shot. It had been *her* twin. Because even when Tommas hadn't been able to be there for Cara in her life, Lea always was.

"Could I go out and speak to her?" he asked.

Gian cleared his throat. "I try to follow her wishes—she asked to be left alone."

"Well, *you* married her. I did not."

"True." Gian hummed under his breath. "How about I leave the decision up to you while I go find my monsters and round them up for lunch?"

Tommas smiled. "I can work with that. Plausible deniability."

"Exactly."

They were different men, him and Gian.

In a lot of ways, they were also the same.

*

"Do you remember the sounds she made?" Cara asked suddenly.

Tommas drew in a sharp breath as he came to stand beside his younger sister where she sat on the curb of his long driveway. "I do—gasping and gurgles. She asked for help. It sounded like pain; I remember that the most."

"Do you remember how it took a week for them to get the bloodstains out of the marble grain?"

"I do."

"And—"

"Cara," Tommas murmured quietly.

For the first time since he exited the house—because she hadn't even looked away from the steps then despite the fact he stepped down them—his sister glanced up at met his stare. There, he found the tears ready to fall staring back at him. One blink, and they'd be tracking lines down her cheeks.

"Why didn't anybody pay for that?" she asked. "Everything you all stand for—*an eye for an eye*. And nobody answered for her, Tommas."

"Would you even want them to?"

Because even if he could make someone answer for the death of Cara's twin—his own blood—he wasn't sure that's what she really wanted. Cara had long since settled her role in this life; obviously, because she'd married a made man who eventually took over his own family. That didn't mean she wanted to ask for someone else's blood to be spilled because of her own pain, did it?

It took Cara a moment to respond. Her answer was exactly as he thought it would be. "I don't know, Tommy."

Yeah.

Him, either.

"I have questions, though," she added, "but I don't think they're ever going to get answered."

"Depends on the question."

Cara turned back to stare at the steps again. "Who pulled the trigger—*why?*"

"I have those answers."

In a flash, her head turned back to him. Fast enough to make him stand a little straighter. Her eyes widened, nailing him to the spot. He could hear the answers that wanted to rapid fire right out of her mouth.

Who.

Tell me who.

Why.

Tell me all the whys.

Before she could say anything at all, Tommas said, "I know who killed her. Who *really* did it—not all the rumors or assumptions that people in the Outfit have. No, I know the truth. Every last fucking detail. All the whys and hows and anything in between that probably didn't even matter. I know it all. I only know it because people who love me felt they needed to share that secret because they couldn't stand the guilt of knowing otherwise."

Cara's chin quivered. "Is the person—"

"Gone."

She didn't ask *how.*

Instead, she asked, "Was it even supposed to be her that day?"

"No, but it doesn't matter because it was."

Cara turned back at stared at the steps again.

She didn't ask who.
She didn't ask anything else.
Instead, she said, "Sit with me for a bit?"
"Absolutely. You don't ever have to ask."

GIAN AND CARA | GUZZI LEGACY

TWINS

The thing about toddlers?

They never stopped *moving*.

Cara thought the sight of Marcus darting around the living room like he was a speeding bullet was *not* helping her morning sickness. At all. She didn't remember being this sick with Marcus when she was pregnant, but as everyone liked to point out to her, each pregnancy was different and she couldn't expect this one to be the same as her first.

Shame, really.

She would much rather go back to puking once a day than five times a day. Hell, she hadn't even gained very much weight in her first ten weeks of pregnancy. She thought maybe a pound or two ... but nothing. The constant sickness meant it was hard to keep anything down so she could gain a bit of weight.

"Ma!"

Cara stared at the ceiling in an attempt to soothe the way her vision swam. She seriously didn't think she would be able to make it in time to hit the bathroom if the little bit of bagel she had been able to swallow down decided to make its appearance known when it came back out. Laying back on the couch, she *prayed* Gian got home sooner rather than later because *Jesus* ... she just needed to sleep, or something.

Just keeping her eyes open made her want to vomit.

"Ma!"

"Marcus, Ma is sick."

She turned her head, keeping a hand on the cool cloth currently covering her forehead to find Marcus was standing *right next to her*. She jerked a bit, surprised the toddler had managed to move that quietly. He wasn't exactly known for being a quiet kid, after all.

Marcus frowned, and put a hand out to touch his mother's cheek. Cara smiled, the action as sweet as could be, and ignored the stickiness on her son's hand. Probably from that arrowroot cookie he'd been toting around for half of the morning. "Ma sick?"

"Yeah, baby."

"Sorry, Ma."

"It's okay."

"Doctor?"

Cara laughed a bit, and nodded. "Yeah, Ma is going to see the doctor later. And you're coming too."

Gian had decided that, actually. Cara had been more than willing to tough out these first twelve weeks because the sickness should have waned a bit, and got better toward the end of her first trimester. That's even what that doctor said, too. But here she was, nearing the eleventh week, and it hadn't gotten better at all. If anything, it just got a hell of a lot worse as each day passed.

Gian was worried—that was the problem. It wasn't something he was willing to say out loud because the last thing that man ever did was say something that might upset her. But he was worried that Cara wasn't getting enough to eat because she couldn't keep anything down for longer than twenty minutes. And when she wasn't throwing up what she was eating, she wasn't very interested in food at all.

And if she wasn't eating … then the baby wasn't getting nutrition, either.

So, the doctor it was.

"See baby?" Marcus asked, his eyes lighting up.

She didn't think her son really understood the whole process of the baby, and what was happening. All he knew was that he was getting a baby brother or sister. And to him, a baby meant something that was already small and tangible. Like his friend's mother who had a one-year-old son that was still crawling, and not really babbling just yet other than the usual one syllable words. He didn't understand that his baby brother or sister wouldn't already be crawling and babbling at all when they were first born.

Cara didn't want to ruin his excitement by trying to explain something a kid his age didn't understand, anyway.

Cara grinned, too. "I don't know if we're going to see the baby today. Maybe, though."

"Still not better, then?"

At the sound of her husband's voice coming from the living room doorway, Cara let out a sigh of relief. Not that she couldn't handle Marcus because she could … but when she felt like any second, she was about to spew vomit all over the floor, having Gian around as a backup for their son really helped.

She glanced her husband's way, and offered him a tiny smile. "Not really, no."

Gian did his best to smile back, but it didn't matter, really. Cara could still see the worry in his eyes. He was quick to cross the room, and kneel down beside where she was resting on the couch. One of his hands came up to stroke her hairline as he leaned in, and pressed a quick kiss to her forehead. For the moment, she was content to just sit there and enjoy the feeling of him close. No matter what, *that* always made her feel better.

And then just as fast as she was feeling good again, the need to vomit rose up faster than she could even take in a breath. Cara barely managed to sit up in time on the couch, but Gian already had the garbage can from underneath the side table sat down in front of her, ready to be used.

He was good that way.

Quick that way.

And while some men might have picked up the toddler and headed out of the room to leave their wife to handle her own business, he stayed right there. Stroking her back, her hair, and then her face, too, when she finally finished spilling her bit of breakfast into the trashcan.

God.

"I'm fine," she mumbled.

"You're really not," he returned.

"I feel like *trash*."

Gian chuckled. "And yet, you look like anything but, *mia cara bella.*"

Yes, his beautiful daring. Even when she was throwing up, looked like hell, and could barely manage to get off the couch. Even at her worst, she was still beautiful to him.

God, she loved this man.

*

"Marcus, come see Papa," Gian murmured, kneeling down to take his son's attention away from the row of pamphlets someone had left on the desk inside the doctor's office. Happily, their toddler left the items alone to do as his father wanted. Once Gian had Marcus in his arms, he stood and turned to Cara. "Feeling any better?"

She let out a slow breath, and nodded. "That medication helped."

The doctor finally agreed that clearly, her morning sickness was not waning. And it was very possible she was dealing with a rare type of morning sickness that wouldn't wane, either, and would only continue to get worse. To avoid possible hospitalization when her body wasn't getting enough nutrients, the doctor settled on an anti-nausea medication that was safe to use during pregnancy.

Thirty minutes after taking the meds, and Cara could watch her son dart around the room without feeling like she was going to puke all over the place. Small miracles were everywhere, apparently.

"Good."

Before they could say anything else, the door opened, and Dr. Candel strolled in with his gaze drifting over the paperwork he held in his hands. "Cara, we're sure of your conception date, aren't we?"

Cara glanced at Gian. "I know when I got pregnant."

This pregnancy was planned as much as any fucking pregnancy could be planned. She'd tracked her cycles, knew when she was fertile, and somehow, they managed to get pregnant that first month trying.

"But you're sure—"

"I know when I got pregnant," Cara repeated dully.

"Your hormone levels for pregnancy are ... five times higher than they should be," the doctor said quietly, glancing up to meet her confused gaze. "I can tell you don't know what that means."

"Not particularly."

The man nodded. "Well, there could be a few different reasons for the higher levels, but I think *one* reason might be far more likely than the others, considering—"

"Is something wrong with her or the baby?" Gian asked sharply.

"Uh, I don't think it's just one baby," the doctor replied just as calm as ever. "Given the fact Cara is an identical twin, and there are twins further back in her family's history, genetics say she is more likely to have a set of twins in her lifetime. The other reasons that could be causing this high level don't really apply to her, and there would be a lot of unnecessary tests to see if that was the cause. Whereas, I can tell if she's carrying twins with a simple—"

"Wouldn't we have heard two heartbeats last week when I came in for a normal checkup?" Cara asked.

"You're still early. The babies are still quite low in your pelvis. It's possible one is behind the other, and that is masking the heartbeat."

Cara glanced at the small ultrasound machine in the corner of the room. "Can we find out today?"

"Absolutely. Let's just get you settled on the bed, and we'll find out if my theory is correct."

Gian kept a tight hold on Marcus as Cara slipped back into the hospital gown, and rested back on the bed. Soon, cold gel was smoothed over her midsection, and the doctor rolled the wand lower on her belly before the grainy images on the machine started to take shape. Not that any of them were discernable, but there was one thing that was mistakable on the screen when Cara looked as he stopped moving to capture an image.

"And there they are," the doctor said. "Two sacs, two babies."

"Two," Gian said on the other side of Cara.

She smiled back at him. "*Twins.*"

Marcus blinked at the screen. "Baby?"

Gian laughed, shifting his son so he could get a better look. "Babies, Marcus. Two babies."

"I suppose that explains the extreme sickness," the doctor said, glancing back at Cara. "We'll keep you on the meds. Congrats."

Yeah.

Wow.

"Twins," she said again.

A WEDDING

Cara stared into the mirror, smoothing her hands down the tightened corset of her gown, the sparkling crystals glimmering with every shift of her body as she admired the dress. The last time she had tried the gown on, there were still a lot of missing details. She hadn't been able to put it all on—not the whole get up, until this day. Veil, shoes, and a handcrafted white-gold headpiece encrusted with diamonds that matched the choker at her throat, and the line of bracelets on her wrist, along with the dangling earrings hanging from her lobes.

A bit much, she'd thought when the designer first pitched her idea to Cara. After all, she'd told the woman, why on earth would a mother of three—more kids would come, but for now, she was settled with her three wild boys—wear something that looked suited to be put on a queen for the day of her wedding.

Because you are a queen.

And well… that settled that.

Didn't it?

God.

She loved this dress, though.

It, however, had been just one piece to a much larger day and production that had become her wedding to Gian. Not that Cara was really sure how that happened. Somehow, between talks of a small, intimate wedding with close family and friends turned into a four-hundred guest affair that would last two days.

Two days.

And suddenly, she liked that, too.

As excessive as it was.

She wanted this day.

What goes into a Guzzi wedding?

The biggest church in Toronto. Silk drapes in every corner. Enough flowers to donate a vase to every room to the hospital down the street when the day was done. Stretch limos, and chauffeurs for the guests. Brunch and dinner served by specialty chefs. A dress made to spec by a top designer and paid a price that cost more than most homes. Diamonds in guest gifts, and three-hundred-dollar bottles of champagne on every single table.

What makes a Guzzi wedding different?

Guests from all over the world. Criminals sitting in the front pew, but just far enough away from who they might consider an enemy that no problems would get started during the service. Table seating arrangements that promised the same peaceful outcome. A secret entrance into the church to stop paps, media, and cops from taking pictures of guests. Enforcers taking phones and weapons at the doors, and snipers posted at the tops of buildings, just in fucking case.

What makes it worth it?

"MA!"

Cara turned, grabbing the heavy skirt of her gown to get it out of the way just in time to turn for her oldest boy to come running her way into the private dressing room. Celeste rolled her eyes, and laughed, saying, "I tried to keep them busy, but ... "

"I wants to see yous," Marcus said.

Still just a toddler.

And she loved him to death.

Right along with his twin brothers who at a little over a year old, were just starting to walk, and would scream if *anyone* tried to carry them anywhere. Which was why it took little Corrado and Chris, with their matching grins and dimples in each cheek, twice as long to cross the room to come to their mother.

Corrado had walked first.

Chris decided he *had* to follow along, even though he hadn't been very interested at all walking in the first place.

Cara swiped her thumb along Marcus's cheek, wiping away the crumbs from whatever snack he'd been eating before she pressed a soft kiss to his cheek. She didn't linger, lest the liquid lipstick the makeup artist put on transferred, and stained his little cheek. His dark eyes watched her with a widened awe.

"Do I look pretty?" she asked.

He nodded. "Like a *queen*, Mama."

Cara smiled. "Thank you."

"Ma!"

"Mamama!"

The babbling twins finally arrived to their mother, and she took a moment to greet each of them, too. There was something painfully bittersweet about seeing all three of her boys in their little tuxes. A few years ago, she thought this day would never come.

And here they were.

She didn't have flower girls.

Didn't have bridesmaids.

The wedding was a production, sure.

But only those that mattered took part in the ceremony.

her husband.

His best man.

Her.

Her boys.

And her brother, who would act as her witness.

That was all Cara needed.

So what made this day worth it?

"Love you, Ma," Marcus said.

These people she loved.

That's what.

"Love you, baby."

*

"You still want to do it this way?" Tommas asked at her side.

It was just them waiting behind the large oak doors leading into the church now. The song changed, and she swore the floor vibrated with the sounds of four-hundred pairs of feet standing to wait for the bride.

Cara grinned up at her brother. "Little late to change it now, isn't it?"

"Well ... "

Her laughter rung out in the quite space. "This is how I want to do it, Tommy."

He nodded. "That's all that matters, then."

Her brother always said that.

He never lied, either.

The heavy doors were pushed open by the men waiting behind it for their cue. There were a lot of things she could have took a moment to appreciate. The decorations. Her sons being allowed to freely play at the front of the altar. All of it.

Any of it.

But what she enjoyed the most was the sight of the man waiting for her at the end. In his three-piece tailored to fit tux, looking like her whole life, and a future they had already started living together before rings and vows and a piece of official paper said it was so …

There he waited.

Smiling at her.

Cara smiled back.

And there Cara stood, hand tucked into her brother's arm, and facing a whole church of people who perhaps some, didn't think she was worthy to be where she was in that moment.

Not the wife of a boss.

Not wearing this dress.

Not marrying in a church of this prominence.

She thought, probably, that was one of the reasons why Gian had done this the way he did. When they talked about something smaller, he wanted to go *bigger*. When simple options were placed in front of them, he asked for more.

And Cara agreed.

She'd told him once, hadn't she?

When forever was finally staring them in the face, and all the impossibilities about them finally became possible and true, she'd told him.

You're the boss. You can do whatever you want.

And so he had.

What he wanted was her.

"Our turn," Tommas said.

Cara nodded. "Our turn."

Her brother walked her the twenty feet to the end of the aisle.

She walked the forty feet it took to get halfway down the church's aisle.

And Gian met her in the middle to walk her the rest of the way.

A statement, if she ever made one.

Although, not everything needed to be *said*, to be.

"Love you forever, *mia cara bella*," Gian told her when they reached the end of the aisle.

Yeah, she knew.

So much so, that he had to tell the whole world, too.

And wasn't that beautiful?

THE FATHER

Gian rested comfortably on the bench, and peered over the gravestones just a few steps up the path. He was grateful that he had paid the money to have this bench put in. While he liked the last one that was here just fine, he wanted something … different.

Something personal.

And so, a marble bench with his grandparents' initials carved into the back suited his purposes just fine. Sure, he imagined other people used the bench when they came to visit the graveyard, and probably with a bit of morbid curiosity about just who the initials belonged to, but he didn't care to think about that very much.

It had special meaning to him, and that's what mattered the most.

Or, so he was coming to learn about his life.

Gian was taking the time to … be selfish, in ways. Something he had never really been before because he had been far too caught up in being what everyone else wanted him to be, and doing what *they* needed for him to do.

It had never—or rarely—been about him.

Except for now.

And today.

Well … that was debatable. Today wasn't necessarily about him, but rather, for his mother. And maybe even a little for his wife, too. His mother, he could deny if the situation called for it. When Cara asked for something, Gian found it downright impossible to reject her anything she asked for. Some might call him pussy whipped for that, but frankly, those people hadn't gotten a taste of his wife's pussy.

So what the fuck did they know?

"*Père.*"

Gian glanced down at his oldest son, Marcus. "*Oui, mon fils?*"

"Do you think great-grandpapa Corrado sees you when you come here?"

Gian smiled a bit. "I hope he does."

"What was he like, *Père?* Like *you?*"

He laughed at that. "Some might say we were more alike than we ever knew until it was too late, Marcus."

248

"Huh. Why?"

This kid.

This damn kid of his who Gian loved more than the sun and the moon and the air and the sea combined. This *kid* ...

He asked all the right questions, and usually at the right times. But just because they were the right questions didn't mean they were *easy* ones to answer, either. Because they usually weren't. But so was a child who had not yet learned things like privacy, and shame.

Maybe Gian was grateful for that.

Marcus could be a boy for just a little while longer. Soon, he was going to wake up one day, and leave all of his child-like emotions and attributes behind. Gian remembered when it happened to him— when he suddenly found that playing child games and acting young was not what the men around him seemed to do.

And oh, how he had wanted to emulate them.

Like nothing else.

Hopefully, Marcus had a couple of more years yet to go before that would happen to him as well. At only nine, his boy was already up to his mother's chin when standing tall. He was growing like a bad weed, and it showed. Already needed a new wardrobe this year when he had a growth spurt, and went up two shoe sizes.

And yet, every time Gian looked at his son, he felt two things most prominently.

Love, of course.

His love for his sons was fierce and strong and undeniable. Like the waves of the ocean coming in to crash against the shore, and take pieces of him away with it every time it left. His love for them was bright and burning and dangerous, too. Like the sun when someone dared to stare straight at the burning ball of fire with a reckless sort of regard.

Oh, he would kill for his boys.

He would *die* for his boys.

And he also felt nostalgia when he looked at Marcus. As though for a moment, the world had stopped turning, and he was getting a glimpse into the past. As though he were seeing himself as a younger man—a young boy again.

In ways, it made him miss things.

Miss his life before ... everything else came along.

Made him wish for simpler times, if only for a few moments so that he could remember how innocent he had once been. Before family betrayed him, when he and Dominic had still been young enough to run down their private street and jump in the mud puddles together.

Those times were not his to have again.

They were already gone.

He lived them once.

They were tainted now, too.

Tainted with the heavy, clinging taste of betrayal—the smell of resolution in him knowing that all the things that had been done could never, *ever* be undone again.

And there were days when Gian was fine with that. To this day, he had never once felt regret for the choices he had made all those years ago—the choice that took away his only brother, and thus, shoved a wedge so deep between he and his father that it now felt rather permanent.

Even though—

"Gian," came the gruff voice to his left.

Gian didn't even glance up to greet his father. "Frederic."

"Early as usual, I see."

All he offered his father was a nod.

Yes, he came early for these weekly meetings. Meetings that his wife had convinced him to do when his mother pestered Cara enough to bother Gian with it. The women wanted the two men to mend their bridges, but for Gian, he knew his father.

Frederic burned bridges.

He did not mend them.

And every meeting always ended the same way between the two. This week would not be any different. Gian was sure of it.

"How are you, Marcus?"

Gian's son peered up at his grandfather. Gian could count on both hands the amount of times Marcus had been in the presence of his grandfather for more than fifteen to twenty minutes. It was sad, really. Sickening, even.

Their long-standing feud hurt more than just their foolish prides.

Respectfully, and with a smile because that's how Marcus was raised by his mother and father, the boy replied in French with, "*Je vais bien, Grand-père.*"

"His French is excellent."

His English and Italian were just as good, too.

Gian smiled a little. "He's nine, and knows how to accept a compliment."

Frederic scowled. "I suppose he does. Give us a few minutes, Marcus?"

Marcus looked to his father, and Gian simply nodded. "Okay."

"Not too far, though," Gian added.

Marcus pushed off the bench, and waved a hand over his shoulder. *"Compris, Père."*

Frederic took the seat that Marcus vacated. "Does he prefer French, or something?"

It irked at Gian that his father even had to ask that question. If the man made a little more effort to spend time with any of Gian's boys, he would know damn well the answer to the question he just posed. An answer he should already *know*.

"Depends on the day," Gian settled on saying.

Better to be nice.

Polite.

That was his way of trying.

He couldn't do much more.

The silence stretched on for a while before Frederic broke it with the question he typically used to break the ice during these meetings. It never failed. Gian had gotten accustomed to preparing for it, really.

"Are you going to apologize this week?"

For killing Dom, he meant.

For choosing a woman over family.

For being *him*.

Gian shook his head. "No."

"Shame," his father murmured.

For a long while, the two stared at Marcus up the walkway where he carefully cleaned off his great-grandparents' graves with careful, respectful hands. Every time they came to the graveyard, Marcus did exactly that as though it was his one job to maintain the stones, and clear away any debris.

He had never even met the people buried there.

Never heard their voices.

Didn't know their love.

And yet, he loved them.

"He's a good boy," Frederic murmured, "and in too many ways, he reminds me of you."

Gian swallowed hard. "Is that why you keep your distance from him—and my other boys, too?"

"Partially."

The sting of that admittance was *strong*.

And damn hard to ignore.

Somehow, Gian did it.

He would not lash out; certainly not with his son there.

"But you should know," Frederic continued, "that I pray for him and for you every day, and every night, Gian. I pray that he never does to you what you did to me. I pray that he never takes from you the way you took from me. I *pray* that you never have to know how it feels to feel the way I do every time I look at you—as though I both love you and hate you equally, and it's become impossible to change."

"Too late for that," Gian replied quietly.

"Pardon?"

"Dom made me know that feeling. It didn't have to be my son. My brother did it, but I don't suppose you'll ever understand, Frederic. You've never tried to."

THE GUZZI BOYS

Everything was going to soon change, although Gian didn't know exactly *how much*. As he watched his sons from his position on the marble stairs while they shared barbs and swam in their mansion's indoor pool, he wanted to remember them exactly like this.

Marcus, the oldest. A few months away from his high school graduation. Already responsible. Gian's mini-me, really. Ready for the world, and his place in *la famiglia*. Looking ahead at his destiny, and rarely concerned with his past.

Corrado and Christopher ... one more outgoing than the other, a good ying and yang, if there ever was one, he thought. One pushed the other, they bettered each other. And, in some ways, they reminded each other it was okay to be unique. And *protective* ... good God, were those two so fucking protective of one another.

Finally, his youngest ones.

The *wild* ones.

The two boys of his five that regularly made Gian think he was going to go all the way gray before his time.

Beni and Bene. What else could he say for those two except *twin hurricanes*. They mirrored one another in more ways than people understood. Inseparable, really. Trouble could find them, or they could make it, as long as they were doing it together.

Oh, and the protectiveness Chris and Corrado showed toward one another? It didn't come close to the bond Beni and Bene shared.

So, as he watched his boys, one set of twins sitting along the edge of the pool to tease the younger twins throwing threats from the deep end, while Marcus sat on the diving board, laughing at the antics of his brothers ... Gian wanted to keep them like this.

Not quite men yet.

Still his boys.

The world hadn't touched them in a real way, not yet. He didn't have to worry about being their boss alongside their father. His life revolved around his wife, and their children, while everything else came second.

Soon, it would change. He simply knew, within the year, things inside their large mansion would be a lot different than it currently was.

Marcus would leave home.

Corrado and Chris would become closer to their own graduation.

Beni and Bene would ... well, become more difficult than they already were without their older brothers around to keep them under control. He doubted that he would see all five of them together as often as he did right now.

It was the natural progression of life, though, and he knew that, too. That didn't make it any easier to come to terms with, either.

What Gian didn't know ... was that things would change even more than he was aware. And faster than he realized. Things he hadn't planned for, and never expected, would change the face of his sons' lives in more ways than he counted on.

Some, they were ready for.

Others ... not so much.

He gave Chris a look, unsurprised to find his son hadn't even taken his clothes off to sit along the edge of the pool. He certainly wouldn't do that alone—his deep seated fear of water too much for him to contain—but with his twin at his side, it made the terror a bit more bearable. That, and he liked to do what his brothers did. He liked to be with them, even if that meant sitting alongside the pool while the rest of them swam.

"What are you doing hiding on the stairs?"

The sweet voice of his wife had Gian turning a bit to watch Cara come down the stairs. In her hands, she carried a tray of ready drinks for the boys. Pink lemonade, it looked like, in glasses filled with ice. She was always thinking of their kids, and he loved that.

"Here, let me carry it," he said.

Cara happily handed the tray over. "Are you spying?"

"Appreciating, actually."

"Oh?"

Gian shrugged as the two of them turned on the stairs to watch their boys down below. Bene was now threatening to pull Marcus into the water by his ankles, and Beni was promising to help his twin in whatever way necessary.

Marcus was simply smirking.

A silent *try it*.

"I was thinking, soon ... they're going to be gone," he murmured. "I mean, within the next few years, anyway. And what are we going to do with this big house, then, *mia cara bella*? When it's quiet, and we don't have to worry about waking up to an empty fridge because they all decided to clean it out overnight? What do we do when they're not here?"

Cara smiled, and leaned in close enough to bump her shoulder with Gian's before she leaned up to kiss him sweetly. "We wait to let them fill the house again, of course."

"Pardon?"

"With grandbabies."

Well, he hadn't really thought of that.

"Still different," he said.

"But a *good* different, Gian. And like you said, we still have a few years with them like this. So, while we have it, wouldn't it be better to be down *there*, you know, with them, instead of up here watching them have fun? Participate, and all that."

"I planned on doing that."

Cara grinned, murmuring, "But only after you appreciated, hmm?"

"Exactly."

A king made an army of princes.

Given to him by a queen.

Surely, he was allowed to watch his kingdom grow.

"Yes, something to drink!"

Beni's shout before water splashed drew Gian's attention to his kids. Now, the youngest twins were cutting through the water at a fast speed to make it to the other side of the pool where they would simply be able to take their drinks from their father. Chris and Corrado stood from the edge of the pool to walk over, and Marcus decided to dive down from the diving board and also swim across the length of the pool.

"Best water them," Cara said, "or they don't grow, Gian."

Right.

Cara distributed the drinks to their boys while Gian was happy to hold the tray for her. He listened as their conversations changed from threats of drowning to a game of baseball. All eyes turned on him, expectantly.

"You'll play with us, won't you, Papa?" Corrado asked.

"Yeah," Beni added.

"Make it an even team for both sides," Marcus said, pulling himself out of the water after his mother took the glass from him.

Right.
Because he had his whole baseball team in these boys.
As long as he agreed to play, too.
"Why not," Gian murmured.
Story of his life with these kids.
Why the hell not.

REGRETS

"Where is Chris?"

Gian hadn't even closed the front door to the mansion before his wife managed to notice something was wrong after her husband returned back from his trip to Vegas where he had business to do with The League.

Not surprising, though.

Cara always knew when something was wrong between her husband or with her boys. It was simply who she was—he never bothered to attempt to hide anything from her.

"He …" Gian stopped himself from saying more, and lifted his head to find Cara standing at the bottom of the left staircase rounding their home's gran entry. If he had allowed for this to happen, he thought he should at least stare his wife in the face and tell her at the same time. Wasn't that only fair? "He decided to stay— to join The League. Alongside Corrado."

The Corrado bit wouldn't be a surprise to his wife. The entire reason for this trip to Vegas had been to give teenaged Corrado something … *different*. Or rather, the chance to see something different that the options he had laid out in front of him now.

Chris came along.

He usually did when it came to his twin.

"*What?*"

The word cut through the room.

They almost cut him off at the knees.

"You knew it was a possibility," Gian was quick to say, "and that if the opportunity was offered, I should not offer my input. I thought you worked out how you felt about this before I even took them to Vegas—it's no different *except* that Chris will join his twin with training, *bella*. Can't you look at it like that?"

"Absolutely not."

Gian straightened. "Cara—"

"A *possibility*, Gian. Not a real thing. Not reality for either of them. Just a *possibility* because Corrado would be there—you only even mentioned the suggestion of it for *him*. You barely even mentioned Christopher for this. You made it seem like this wasn't for him at all.

Did you know the possibility was good for both of them to join?"

"I couldn't be sure, but—"

"Yes or no."

Jesus.

"Chris often follows Corrado—*yes*, it was a possibility. Obviously. I didn't think he would in this case so I didn't bother to bring it up into our conversations."

His wife scoffed, echoing him at the same time, "*Obviously*, like I should have known. And what, you couldn't tell him *no*?"

"Would you just—"

"Are you going to apologize?"

"No," Gian said without thinking about it. He didn't need to think about it. "If the boys find something they want or need from The League, then that's *good*. I'm sorry that it hurts you, though."

"What about *them*?"

"They will be fine."

They had to be.

"It'll be the same for both of them, then? The same *everything*?"

A lump formed in Gian's throat, yet he still said, "Yes."

"Are you saying they'll train Christopher like Corrado?" Cara asked, her voice turning shriller with every word because yes, now she understood.

And good *God*, the absolute wreck that became his wife in those moments slammed into him like a Mack truck going straight through his heart. *That*, he would always regret. Hurting her. Until he died— every single moment he'd done something to make his wife feel pain would play on repeat in his mind; every memory a reminder that he had never been worthy of this woman.

And yet, she loved him anyway.

"The same way," he found himself saying. It was nothing more than an echo. "The same training for both, Cara. It's The League's policy."

"The training Cree developed as the best way to break a mind quickly and without lasting *physical* damage—the training that involves repeated *drowning* ... *that* one, Gian? The training I told you made me sick to my stomach knowing anyone would be put through it—that training?"

Every word that came out of her mouth stabbed into him like a knife. He bet he could bleed out every apology on the floor and yet it still wouldn't be enough.

"We talked about this when it came to Corrado and—"

"*And Corrado is not Christopher!*"

Silence followed her scream.

She was right.

Nothing she said was a lie.

He breathed deep.

So did she.

Across the great entry, Cara turned and grabbed the railing, taking the steps two at a time until she came to a stop in the middle. Looking over her shoulder at him, she said, "They only look the same, but inside ... they're two different people. How many times did we tell *them* that very thing—why are you making me tell you? Chris should have come back with you."

"Cara—"

"Find a couch to sleep on, Gian. You will not be joining me."

*

Four long days.

That was how long he'd slept alone on a couch in his wife's library. Oh, they talked a lot over the four days. Talked until the last thing he wanted to do was say another word. Cara didn't ignore him, and she loved dissecting everything she could down to the base emotions of *why*.

They talked. They fought.

She raged.

He let her.

So, on the fifth day when Gian woke up on the same couch, he stared at the wall and wondered if today would be the day something finally changed.

"How long are you going to sleep in here?" came a soft voice from the doorway.

Still staring at the wall of the library, Gian sighed. "Well, I suppose until you ask me back to your bed, *cara mia*."

Cara made a gentle noise and the squeak of her feet taking a few steps into the large space said she'd come closer to him. Not close enough, though. He had to admit that. "It's also *your* bed—our bed, even."

"Mmm, *no*. It's always been yours. Everything that becomes mine doesn't stay that way for long—I give it all to you. So, the bedroom is yours, *oui*? And until you invite me back, I will sleep in here because you've not told me to do otherwise."

"Are you going to apologize now?"

Gian barely had to think about that.

"I will apologize for hurting you—not for what I did. The same way I did when I came home and told you, Cara."

"Do you even regret it?"

He didn't have to think about that, either. He couldn't find regret in giving his boys something that may very well define the rest of their lives—and *God*, he wanted each of his children to find themselves and not just reflect him. He did, however, regret what came after that choice. And every reason for that was tied into the woman who wouldn't come close enough to let him touch her.

Because he knew ...

And so did she ...

If he touched her, if she let him *close*, Cara would forget all of it. She'd let him apologize until his tongue bled and his throat ached. She would forgive him.

She still would like this, too.

Eventually.

But this way allowed her to be angry—for as long as she damn well pleased—and after, to work through it in a healthy way. Gian would let her, too. He always would. As he said, everything that became his, well, he quickly gave it back to her.

Even herself.

"All of my regrets always boil down to what I've done to you. Does that tell you enough or do you need me to say more?"

It took Cara a second. Then, two.

"You can come back to our bed, Gian."

"Are you still angry?"

"*Very*," she whispered.

"I'm sorry."

"I know, Gian. That's what makes this worse."

THE TWINS, A SHORT STORY

CHAPTER 1 - GIAN POV

Gian Guzzi thought his wife had her most beautiful moments when she didn't realize people were watching her. Like in that very moment. Tired because she was seven and a half months pregnant with twins and already a mother to three young and rowdy boys who kept her running from one end of their mansion to the other, she had every reason to want to sit alone in the corner of their private physician's office and enjoy the silence.

Wasn't she owed a bit of quiet time?

He thought so.

Tried to give it to her often, in fact.

But the little girl across the waiting room in her yellow dress, sad about something her father wouldn't give her, gained his wife's attention and that was that. Suddenly, she entertained the little girl, making her smile and happy, while giving the exhausted-looking dad across the room a break. By the time the child's mother came out of the back hallway where they kept the private patient rooms, also looking about as pregnant as his wife, the girl had stopped throwing her tantrum, the father was smiling again, and Cara flipped through a magazine as though she hadn't done a thing.

All the while, Gian just … watched her.

Very little fazed Cara Guzzi anymore. He couldn't remember the last time she had gotten really angry about something—but especially regarding him or their boys. He liked to think that was partly because of him and how much effort he put into ensuring her *constant* happiness—as he'd once promised to do—but he wasn't that selfish.

A lot of this, and their life …

Well, Cara did all that herself.

Queens did what queens did.

Even if that just happened to be calming down someone else's child while waiting for your own doctor's appointment. Considering their own hoard of children, it was safe to say they had their fair share of public meltdown moments. Some of which came with judgment from others, and both he and Cara made a great effort not to do that same thing to other parents.

Five minutes in public with a child wasn't very telling about anything except for the fact that children would always be children.

"Mrs. and Mr. Guzzi?" Gian's attention drifted away from his softly smiling wife at the call of their name. The receptionist who also acted as a nurse in the office greeted them with a warm wave as she said, "Your room is ready if you'd like to come back and wait while Dr. Belled finishes up his report."

Gian was up out of his seat before the woman could even finish her statement with a hand waiting for his wife. Cara's palm slid into his as she tossed her magazine aside. With his bit of support—she never had to ask for it; he was always ready with it—allowed her to lift from her seat with the same grace she'd used to sit in it.

One wouldn't guess she was having any trouble in her final months of pregnancy in that second, she carried all of it so incredibly well.

Yes, she was beautifully swollen with his children. Twins, *again.* Their last children, also, because they'd decided and he had already gone in to have the vasectomy. He didn't say a word—just made the appointment the day after she asked and had that shit done.

She gave him three children—another two were on the way.

How could he tell her no?

"Thank you," she murmured before leaning in to press a quick kiss to his lips.

Gian followed behind her as she headed, smiling to himself. "Always, *cara mia.*"

*

"Still the same?" Cara asked softly.

The doctor raised thick, dark brows and chuckled. He passed Cara a nod before giving Gian a look over his shoulder. "Stubborn boys—you better watch that if they're already showing it this early, hmm, Gian?"

He would have laughed, but ...

"I mean, we came into this knowing she'd be having a second cesarean this time around—a natural birth was a pipe dream, Cara."

She sighed. "I only wanted to dream."

A dangerous dream.

He opted not to point that out.

Dr. Belled shrugged one shoulder, and then hit a button on the keyboard to freeze the frame. "And yes, they're still exactly the same in there. Twin A on the left, head up and facing his brother. And Twin B in the on the right doing the same, little knees tucked right up. Look at their hands. I've never seen another pair of twins *always* be holding hands like that before."

That was what he'd taken a picture of.

Given this pregnancy was Cara's *second* multiples pregnancy and they'd had the usual issues that came along with pregnancy concerning multiples, their checkups and tests were always doubled. They had more than a dozen photos of the twins throughout the progression of months and they were always holding the same hands.

"I think it's sweet," Cara said.

"It is," Gian noted, his gaze taking in the grainy image on the screen. It was much harder to see anything discernible in the ultrasound photos now that the twins were far larger.

"Have we picked names, yet?" the doctor asked, giving them a smile.

Cara laughed, returning just as fast, "Have you decided which one will be born first yet?"

Gian chuckled under his breath but put his hands up in mock surrender when the doctor's and his wife's gaze turned on him like one of them wanted him to pick a side. A long-running joke between the two, he knew better than to get between it. Given the positions of the babies and the fact they would be having a caesarean, the doctor could choose either Twin A or Twin B to be born first and he wouldn't tell Cara which one it was.

So, she wouldn't tell him the names.

"Don't look at me. This is between the two of you," Gian said. "And it'll finish between you two, as well."

"You're not fun, Gian."

"Plenty fun, actually."

The doctor didn't look like he believed it.

Cara laughed. "Oh, it doesn't matter. We decided Benito and Benedetto for names .... but I just can't decide which is which."

That quieted Dr. Belled.

Gian wasn't surprised at all—his wife told him this very thing *many* times. He didn't know how to help, unfortunately.

"Well," the doctor said, "I suppose once you see them ... you'll know."

This time, it was Cara's turn to grow quiet.

Belled nodded, adding, "Mothers always know."

"Except about which twin will be born first, apparently," Cara said, giving the man a look.

The doctor laughed under his breath, turning fast in his chair to face the screen once more. "I'd hoped you had forgotten about that."

"Of course, not!"

Their noise had the nurse knocking on the door to check if everything was okay. Check-ups were always fun with these twins.

CHAPTER 2 – VANNA POV

In the middle of the Guzzi mansion's large grand entry, the photographer's assistants moved with light shields catching the reflection of the beauty lights and brightening the space even more than it already was. In a way, Vanna was grateful to be on the *back* side of those lights because after several rounds of photos between standing and sitting on the ornate red and gold loveseat they were using as a prop for their family photos, her head started to ache.

All the *tip your chin up a little more*s and the *head to the right—to the RIGHT, oh I meant your left, my right*. Anybody could appreciate the production and work that went into the art of photography but sometimes the subjects just needed a break. Vanna wasn't going to complain, as far as that went, because she was grateful for all of this. Somehow, she hadn't even thought about it.

Not the newborn photos.

The family shots.

None of it.

Somehow, in the midst of becoming pregnant, giving birth, and then learning how to take care of a newborn, Vanna's brain disappeared. Okay, maybe that was a little … *rude*. It didn't disappear, it just sometimes took a fucking break.

Cara called it *Mommy Brain*.

Apparently, so did everyone else.

Nonetheless, where her attention wasn't … well, her wonderful mother-in-law stepped up to handle everything. All Vanna and Bene needed to do for this shoot was show up with a few different outfits for the photographer to look through and their baby boy. Cara handled the rest, and the photographer made everything else relatively simple. There had even been a woman there to do Vanna's hair, and another that did a set of nails for her before she beat her face to the fucking Gods.

What dark circles under her eyes?

Her skin looked like a *doll's*.

Marcus had barely even made a sound all morning. He didn't care when they changed him from outfit to outfit or patted his little bottom until his eyes drifted close and he was back to sleeping happily in someone else's arms or on yet another prop.

Then again, as long as that kid had a boob in his mouth, he was pretty happy to begin with. Also, newborn shoots were ... very involved. More went into those than she had realized before today, but she had a new respect for the photogs doing it.

Even if they kept getting their rights and lefts mixed up.

Bene, on the other hand ...

Complained a lot.

He wasn't the only one considering when August showed up—Cara wanted updated pictures of the twins, and family photos from both men as well with their wives—she let everybody know how Beni sulked from the hotel to the house about taking pictures.

Bene did about the same.

Apparently, the twins had never been big on professional photos. Candids were a whole other story, and the mansion was *full* of those. But actual professional shots or even portraits for the paintings? There weren't nearly as many.

"Well, *this* should be amusing," Cara noted, coming to stand on Vanna's left where a servant had brought in a chair for her to use while she fed little Marcus. With his head safely tucked under a thin, cashmere blanket, he fed while she palmed the back of his head and let her thumb stroke the side of his head the way he liked the best.

Her sweet boy.

He was absolutely *perfect.*

"What's that?" Vanna asked.

Cara nodded her head toward the middle of the room. August stepped out of the shot when the photog waved her away and came in their direction.

"Bene, get in there on the left, if you wouldn't mind, and we'll take a couple of shots with just the two of you—"

"I'm not getting on the left."

Cara made a noise under her breath when the man looked away from his camera.

Beni piped up real quick, too, saying, "I don't stand on the right."

August had finally come to stand on the other side of Vanna. Cara, on the other hand, sighed when two voices rang out in the middle of the room to say, "*Ma, it's not right.*"

"Just like when they were kids. Nothing changes, they just get bigger," Cara muttered before saying louder for the rest of the room,

"Beni is always on the left—Bene on the right. That's ... just the way it is."

Ah.

Vanna finally understood. "When did they start that, anyway?"

One of the many things the twins did together that were unique to their bond and that she never understood.

The boys and photographer were back to doing their thing. Baby Marcus continued to feed happily and unaware, warm and soft against his mother's chest.

Cara laughed weakly, giving Vanna a look from the side. "*Well ...*"

*

Cara POV

"What are you doing?"

At her husband's voice, Cara glanced up from the crib that they kept set up in their master bedroom. That way, their babies could sleep with them close but still being safe. It was also a lot easier to just wake and feed and change and then put their twins back down to sleep when they were all in one room together.

Cara nodded at the sight in front of her, never looking up to greet Gian. "Come look."

His soft approach belied the fact that their wood floods sometimes creaked to the heavens. She swore he taught himself to walk quietly because he didn't want her to tell him to be quiet one more time in their home.

The joys of babies and toddlers.

Everything woke them up.

It was only when Gian had come to stand next to het, and his arm found its usual spot tight around her waist, that she looked up at him.

"This is how they want to be," she told him. "Otherwise, they just cry."

Gian smiled.

It still took her breath away.

After all these years.

"I didn't notice," he admitted.

Cara nodded, her gaze drifting back to the twin babies wrapped in blue muslin inside their crib. The two boys, *Beni* and *Bene* had to sleep or play or even be held on the same sides that they had rested inside her womb.

Left and right.

Twin A and Twin B.

Beni and Bene.

CHAPTER 3 – BENE POV

"Tell me something I don't know."

Beni's question had Bene laughing under his breath. The thick sense of nostalgia that wrapped around his chest as he stared at the roof of their parents' indoor pool only added to the light buzz in his mind. Compliments of the bud that Alessio brought back from a job in a country he wasn't allowed to talk about. Which was fine because the guy brought them something better anyway.

"That's not how we play this game," Bene replied.

"How long has it been since we played the game?"

Bene had to really think about that. "I don't … maybe fourteen?"

Beni's chuckles reached his spot and he turned his head to the side to find his twin rested in the same position as him with one leg stretched out on a pool floaties and his other knee drawn up to rest his arm on. He couldn't see Beni's eyes behind the sunglasses but he really didn't need to. Other than the *drip drip drip* of the fountain at the far end of the room, the mansion was quiet.

Funny.

Considering last night for their eighteenth birthday, the mansion had been wall to wall with people. For once, their parents actually let them throw a party at the house. With whatever they wanted because they left for the weekend. Halls were closed off, yeah. An entire wing was off-limits. Guards were posted all over the fucking property *and* the cameras stayed on.

But shit …

They raged.

Hard.

Getting all their brothers there—and Les tagged along from Nevada with Corrado, like he usually did; something they never asked about—had just been the icing on the cake.

"Are we playing, or not?" Beni asked.

"I lost my train of thought," Bene admitted.

"*Focus.*"

His laughter skipped over the pool.

He was just a little high.

Right, right.

The game.

"Tell you something you don't know," Bene mused to himself. His mind flashed with memories of many years past where they had done something similar to this very thing. With quiet all around, the twins would close their eyes, and Bene always asked his brother to, *"Tell me something I don't know."*

Bene always asked.

Beni always answered.

It had been a running joke—something they had been doing for longer than Bene could remember. Like when they were little and used to talk in babbles that no one else but them could understand. They *always* did it … until they didn't.

His first real memory of playing the game, even though he knew they'd been doing it for longer, was their fifth birthday party. A neighborhood kid who must have been feeling like a little shit that day decided to make fun of the twins for being … well, the same. He said they weren't real—*robots*. Called them creepy because when they weren't paying attention, their movements often mirrored each other. They never liked having it pointed out. It wasn't something they could help or even noticed … and they certainly didn't care to change it.

It was a part of them.

Whatever *they* were.

Nonetheless, they were five and *kids*. Someone picking on them didn't make anything easier. Bene went through a whole phase of wanting to look *exactly* like his brother. Beni had a moment where every time someone mixed the two of them up, he flipped out.

They came back to steady ground.

It all worked out.

"This is harder than I thought," Bene said more to himself than his twin.

A few feet away, floating in the pool, Beni hummed his agreement. "See, and that's how I always felt trying to come up with something."

"So, why did you keep answering?" Bene asked.

His brother shrugged. "You kept asking."

Oh.

Then, Bene had a thought.

He did know something.

"You're seven seconds older," Bene said, grinning.

Beni's head turned in his direction, but he couldn't see his brother's eyes under the dark sunglasses. "You asked Ma and Dad— and *never* told me?"

Well … it wasn't that big of a deal. The twins never cared. Their parents never offered the information except when Bene and Beni would tease each other about it. Sometimes, people lied about which one was older just to use it as an excuse for one thing or another.

"I really thought it was me," Bene admitted.

That had his twin laughing.

Bene cracked up, too.

Best birthday morning ever.

CHAPTER 4 – AUGUST POV

"Oh, *that one*," Cara said, her finger tapping the screen while she gestured at the photog's assistant. On the computer screen—where the photog's team had their entire set up ready for them to easily look over the pictures and do any surface editing during and after the shoot—a particular shot of Beni and Bene sitting on the floor with baby Marcus between them was blown wide on the large frame. "Mark it down? I know the perfect spot for it."

August grinned, never unamused with her mother-in-law's passions. Because they never ended. The woman found as much creative energy in reading and writing as she did photography and even gardening. Just to add to it, Cara also managed to raise four sons, maintain a career, as well as being a wife and her own woman. And since most of her sons had married now, Cara still didn't stop.

In fact, she brought her son's wives into the family folds as though they had always belonged there. She made time for each of the girls whether it was coming over to chat over coffee and sweets or reading a book together and chatting about it every night on the phone.

People liked to say that family was everything.

Cara Rossi was the definition of it.

That was … *inspiring*.

Pretty fucking bomb, too.

"Where did Vanna go?" Cara asked absently, her finger swiping across the screen to go from one picture to the next without barely a second between each one. And then all at once, she would stop on an image, the assistant behind them would mark the number down, and off she would go again.

"Somebody got poopy."

And not that August would say anything about it, but that was one *big* reason why she didn't plan on having kids any time soon because the thought of changing a diaper kind of made her want to gag. *So …*

"Ah," Cara murmured. "Did you have a preference for which ones you might have prints of for your place in Chicago?"

"A couple—you know he wants candids."

"Both of them. They *barely* indulge me." Then, Cara laughed. "That's a lie—they indulge me too much, but never tell any of them that."

August grinned. "Promise. Cross my heart."

Cara went back to scanning through the photos while August's attention drifted to where Bene and Beni were now standing next to the bay windows of the grand entry. With the family photoshoot done and the photographer and his team packing up their lighting equipment while Cara went through the photo files to pick out her favorites, the twins were free to do what they wanted.

Good thing.

They hadn't stopped complaining all day.

Mostly, it was amusing. One could tell how much Bene and Beni were loved and spoiled by their parents. Maybe because they were just … special. Or because they had been the babies of the family. It didn't matter … somedays, like today, their privilege showed a little more than on other days.

Lucky for her husband that she loved him.

But she was lucky too.

Look at all Beni gave to her.

At the moment, however, the twins took advantage of the fact that nobody's attention was currently on them. Beni scrolled down his phone while Bene used one hand to text on his own. Side by side, it was impossible to find a difference between the two when they both wore nearly identical outfits with black slacks and similarly colored dress shirts. Of course, if one *knew* … they knew.

Beni was always on the left.

Bene on the right.

Distracted, the two didn't seem to realize how much of their little actions mimicked the other. Like the way Beni tapped his index finger against the side of his thigh—Bene did the same, yet he wasn't even looking at his twin. One started shifting their foot backward on the spot, and the other soon followed until they matched postures again.

"How long have Beni and Bene done that?" she asked. "The … *mirroring?*"

Cara peered away from the screen and eyed her sons as she took in what August had noticed. "Oh, that?"

She'd noticed it before.

Never asked, though.

"Yeah."

"Since they were brand new," Cara said.

"Really?"

"I always told Gian it was muscle memory."

*

Cara POV

"*Look*," Gian murmured.

Sleepy, Cara rolled a bit more to her side to see what had her husband so fascinated. At five in the morning, they *should* have put the freshly fed twins—Beni and Bene—back into their own crib so that maybe they could get another hour of sleep before the rest of their hoard of boys woke up. Instead, they liked this time.

These quiet moments.

Just them and the babies.

They tried to soak them up.

"What—"

"Shh, watch," Gian said.

Between them, the twins had fallen asleep side by side. Beni on the left, of course. Bene slept on the right with his hand pressed against his lips so he could suckle the way he liked after a feeding.

"Watch their little toes and fingers," her husband said.

She did.

When one twitched, the others did, too.

The same spot.

Just the opposite.

Soon, Beni had brought his hand up to suckle like his brother was doing. They looked like perfect little mirrors of one another.

"They do that a lot," she said. "Muscle memory, maybe."

"I doubt it's *that*."

"Well ..."

She did think the mirroring was a little odd. Only because she didn't understand *why*. But it was also quite wonderful. Would it stay the same when they got older?

CHAPTER 5 - BENI POV

"Bene, wait up!"

All he heard was his twin's laughter twisting through the trails in the forest. Just over his shoulder, he could still see part of their parents' property and the mansion just beyond the tree line. Their parents' rules were pretty clear about the woods and the twins.

If they could still see the house, then it was okay. If they couldn't see the house, then they went too far and it was time to come back. Mostly, they tried to follow the rules because people bothered the brothers a lot less.

Sometimes, they also didn't care.

Today seemed like one of those days.

Besides, they had been playing in these trails for longer than Beni could even remember. It's where they learned to ride bikes, and where they played tag or hide-and-seek with their older brothers. And it was also where the twins liked to disappear to when there was just too much going on in the mansion.

Like parties.

Or *birthdays*.

Today was their party.

They probably shouldn't have snuck out.

Oh, well.

There was a lot about eight-year-old twins, Bene and Beni, that was exactly the same. Like the way they looked—*obviously*. But also the way they dressed. How they talked. The expressions their faces made. Or that's what everyone else always told them whenever somebody said they had *bad attitudes*.

Something Beni noticed about other people? When *they* noticed how similar the twins were, then they started treating them as though they were exactly the same, too. Gifts came doubled. Outfits that matched right down to the socks. People just referred to them as *the twins* or *those Guzzi twins*.

As though they didn't have their own names.

Nothing bothered Beni more than when someone started treating him and his twin like they were the same person. Because they weren't. Even if they looked and did things the same, it didn't mean they were. Bene didn't have as much trouble with that as he did.

See, sometimes they *were* different.

Beni learned to swim first. Bene could still run faster. He *always* woke up at the crack of dawn and his brother never did. Bene thought poached eggs were good and Beni thought they were puke on a plate.

But it was a lot easier to just let people think and do whatever they wanted when it came to the twins than it was to constantly correct others. Besides, he didn't *mind*. And Bene really didn't care. So just because it was a little annoying didn't mean it affected Beni enough to make it stop. Plus, their parents and brothers *never* treated them like they were anything other than Beni and Bene.

Wasn't that what counted?

"Wait up, Bene!" Beni shouted, still trying to catch up with his twin.

He couldn't see beyond the bushy bend in the trail. Maybe he should have known better than to come around it so fast, but especially when Bene *loved* to just jump out of anywhere and scare the crap out of him.

Like he did this time.

"Beni!"

His twin jumping out of the bushes with his hands going wild and his voice loud enough that even the people at the party would hear him was enough to send Beni flying back on the trail. Of course, he stumbled over his shoes and fell right on his ass.

Bene's laughter surrounded him, but just as fast, his twin was in front of him and pulling him up from the ground with a strong grip. Once the two were standing face to face again, Beni shook his head while Bene laughed.

"Got you again, bro," Bene said.

"Screw you."

His brother hadn't let his hand go. He squeezed tight, and so did Bene. Their hands locked around each other reminded him of something else that was different between them.

The scars on the side of their hands.

So faint, and thin.

Two red lines.

But Bene's was shorter than his.

They couldn't even remember how they got them.

"Beni, Bene!"

Bene let out a dramatic sigh and gave his twin a grin. "Busted."

"Get back to the house!" came their father's call, faint as it was in the woods.

Beni shrugged and his twin dropped his hand. "Well, we tried."

That would, undoubtedly, be the story of their life.

CHAPTER 6 - CARA POV

Every night, Cara took her time to remove the stress of the day away. It started in her closet where she shed the clothes of the day for something more comfortable in bed. Then, she moved to her vanity where she wiped away her makeup and prepped her skin for the evening. Eventually, she made her way to her library.

Her *favorite* space.

The one room in the entire mansion that had been designed entirely for her. Yes, her husband and boys used it. When she had a patient that came to the house for a session, they often found themselves sitting in the leather couches that faced each other in front of the bay windows. Sometimes, after dinner parties, she brought a few friends up to her library to continue drinking because Gian kept the wet bar well-stocked.

Nonetheless, party or not … patient or none, night after night, Cara found herself back in her library where she ended her evenings with two fingers of her favorite cognac and just *one more chapter* of whatever book she had picked to read for that week. She didn't get to do that as much as she wanted to anymore, either.

Read, that was.

Yet, she made time for it.

Even if it was only a chapter at a time.

"The house is quiet, hmm?" came a familiar drawl from the doorway.

Gian rarely interrupted Cara when she was reading seeing as how he knew it wasn't often she could sit down for longer than thirty minutes at a time to read. When he did, however, she never got annoyed about it. She found him leaning in the doorway—both oak doors to the library stayed wide open unless she had a patient in the library with her. Otherwise, she *wanted* the space to seem open and inviting to others.

Wasn't that the point of a library?

Even if it was a personal one.

"It is quiet," she said.

Despite the *very* busy day they'd had at the Guzzi mansion with the photographer, his team, and photoshoot that lasted well over four hours. Somehow, though, it went off without a hitch. Their newborn grandson, Marcus, even went along with everyone else's plans. Truly a miracle in and of itself.

Cara was going to have beautiful photos to show for it. And that was really what she wanted, which she got. She usually did get what she wanted, anyway.

His sexy smile had her own growing. "And imagine, we have *two* of the loudest ones under our roof and their wives."

Cara laughed. "Plus a newborn."

"I told you, didn't I?"

Well, her husband told her a lot of things. Most times, Cara tried to listen even when she thought Gian was just blowing smoke out of his ass to appease her. It wasn't like it would be the first time he did it.

Shaking her head, Cara went back to her book, asking, "What did you tell me?"

"That you were worrying for nothing about those two—Bene and Beni, I mean."

Her gaze focused on the words at the top of the page in the book. She read the same sentence over and over again, deciding how to respond to her husband. He wasn't wrong, but sometimes in her heart, she still felt heavy about what had transpired between their youngest twins over the past year and a half.

"They'd never been apart and then all of the sudden, they were in two entirely different countries," she said quietly. Sure, over the years the twins had given her many reasons to worry about the two of them. Their wild ways and constant partying when she wished they would focus more followed them for most of their teenage years and even into their adulthood until they both settled down. Still, they were her youngest, too. Her *babies*. It wouldn't feel right to not worry about them when they had always seemed to need her a little more for different things than the rest of her kids did. "How could I not worry?"

"Because it needed to happen. At least this time, they separated themselves. They couldn't live like that, could they?"

It wasn't the first time they had needed to ask that question.

*

The day the twins cried ...

One couldn't properly describe how it felt to be awake and aware of your surroundings, but unable to *move* or do anything more than talk. Having been through a c-section before, Cara knew what to expect and that made going into it easier. She didn't tremble in the paper gown while they inserted the needle into her spine for the spinal, and she didn't shake or chatter her teeth nearly as bad when the anesthesia started to flood her body.

Beside her, Gian sat on a stool holding her hand. In his own hospital gown, booties, and a cap and mask, his gaze continued to drift between her and the curtain ahead of them. The one keeping their doctor and his team hidden from view.

They'd told her when they began.

Explained what would happen next.

It was strange to feel your body being *moved* ... the pressure that she couldn't explain and how heavy it felt in her throat when the whispers behind the curtain started to get a little more excitable and loud.

"Almost," they heard the doctor call over. "Twin A—"

"Benito," Gian spoke up.

"Beni," Cara said softly.

Gian spoke a little louder, agreeing. "Beni."

"Beni will be here in less than ten seconds."

Those ten seconds passed quickly. Beni's cry was as immediate as the doctor's sharp, "*Wait, wait a second!*"

Maybe it was the panic in the person's voice. Or even the *confusion*. Either way, it had Gian moving from his stool despite the warnings from the nurse on Cara's other side that was tasked with monitoring the machines alongside the anesthesiologist.

"Gian," Cara called.

He'd already moved beyond the curtain. His hand didn't let go of hers, though. She counted the seconds. The hushed murmurs between her husband and the doctor followed the same pulling and pressure and then ... *more perfect, beautiful cries.* There was seven seconds between the first cry and the second that sounded distinctly different. They hadn't even announced Benedetto—little Bene—the same way they had his brother.

Everything moved faster, then. The nurse said nothing as she came to separate Cara's hand from her husband, the woman's face clouding Cara's vision as she promised everything was fine and she would meet her babies soon. She also explained that the other nurses were taking the twins to the warming bassinets on the other side of the room.

Gian would follow.

She didn't know how long she waited.

Occasionally, the doctor explained what he was doing at that point.

Cara just didn't care to hear.

Soon enough, though, while the surgeon continued his work behind the curtain, Gian retook his position on the stool next to Cara's prone form. Only now, he had the twins wrapped in white cotton towels with matching blue caps pulled over their tufts of dark hair.

"Say hello really quick," he said, "but then they have to take them again."

Her gaze darted to his.

He stayed happy and smiling the whole time.

"Why?" she asked.

Gian's gaze darted to somewhere behind her—she didn't bother to try and turn her head. She really couldn't, anyway.

Instead of answering her, he pulled the towel away from the twins where they laid side by side in his left arm. Still messy from their birth, with gel swiped across their eyes and little arms twitching, they were wrinkly and *pink* and hers. That was all she noticed at first. And then she understood what must have made everyone pause when Beni was pulled from her womb. Finally, Cara understood exactly why her boys were always holding hands in every single ultrasound.

The sides of their hands were attached with a thin strip of flesh.

Conjoined.

"It just looks like some skin," Gian was quick to explain. "No bone or veins or … it'd make sense why they wouldn't have noticed it if there was nothing to *see* there, Cara."

She understood why he wanted to explain.

She just … it didn't matter.

"They're perfect," she whispered.

Gian smiled again, covering the boys with the towel. His palm found the side of her face, and his thumb stroked her cheek, making her realize how much colder she felt because of the anesthesia and

IV. But his touch was just enough to make it all better for a second. "They're more than perfect. I'll let the nurses clean them up and we'll get them with you."

Right.

Skin to skin.

It's what all her babies had after birth.

"Hurry," was all she said.

The rest, they could deal with later.

*** There are some interesting statistics about how many identical twin births are born conjoined in some way. Sometimes, it is not always picked up on ultrasounds because, like in Bene and Beni's case, there is nothing "wrong" to be noticeable with what you're given to see. This was also the case with my youngest son, who was born with Polydactyly. But because the extra additions were so small, had no bones or major veins, we couldn't see it until he was out in the world and said hello to us. And all he will have to remember that by is one video of me and him when he was a few days old and laying on my couch - I showed him his little steri-strips on both sides of his hands were his extra pinkies had been removed shortly after his birth. Why weren't the twins told?

I came up with this idea later as a fun way to play around with some of the twin-things they did, and where would it have fit in for their books? This was mostly me writing an idea in fun and seeing what came of it for the blog. Also, it wouldn't have really mattered. I hope you enjoyed this little tale about *The Twins*.

XO,
BK.

DID IT EVER

CORRADO | GINNY | LES

Corrado POV

Late at night, or *very* early in the morning depending on how one wanted to look at it, was Corrado's favorite time of day. When everyone else was sleeping, he could be free to walk the halls, let his thoughts wander, and process anything without minding anyone else into the mix as well. Despite how he lived his life, filled with people and family and those that he loved, there was still a part of him that very much enjoyed being alone.

His twin said it was because Corrado just was who he was.

Gian liked to say maybe Corrado needed it.

Everybody had a different opinion.

They usually did.

Les and Ginny, though?

They never said a thing.

No, they simply let him have his nights of walking the halls far too late and alone. Except lately, he hadn't been the one doing any of that at all.

It was Les.

Corrado noticed the further into Ginevra's pregnancy they got, the more Les ... well, *paced*. The thing was, he wasn't like Corrado. Alessio didn't make it known that he had shit going on in his head and needed a moment away to figure it out. His demeanor told them one thing; his behavior at night when he thought the rest of the house was asleep told Corrado something entirely different.

And he didn't like it.

Oh, Les had his moods. So did Corrado. Hell, even Ginny went through spells but Corrado blamed that more on the hormones than anything else because usually, she went about her life as pleased as could be. Nonetheless, when Les went into a mood—everybody could tell.

Not lately.

He'd rather hide it.

That was the problem.

The floorboard down the hall from their master bedroom creaked, and Corrado let out a quiet sigh into the darkness. A few seconds later, the creak happened again. It was almost rhythmic in nature, and he could guess exactly where Alessio was standing based on the amount of time it took for the creak to echo once more.

The next time, Ginevra shifted on the bed beside Corrado, drawing his attention to her. Her hand had come to rest of the top of her twenty-three week swell and the over-sized T-shirt she'd thrown on for her had ridden up just enough that he figured she would soon be stealing a blanket because even though she pretended to enjoy sleeping without one … more often than not now, she woke up *with* one.

And didn't complain about it.

Reaching over, his hand found the spot overtop hers. His thumb stroked the curve of her midsection, slowing just enough to appreciate the firmness of their child growing. Another one of his favorite things—though new, it still seemed as though it had always been.

Or maybe it was just always meant to be.

"Is he pacing again?"

The soft question had Corrado dragging in another heavy breath as his gaze found Ginerva's. Had he not touched her, he bet she would have stayed sleeping. As she should. If pregnancy taught him anything besides what it felt like to sometimes walk on eggshells, it was that a woman needed her rest. Growing a baby was exhausting.

In the darkness of the bedroom, she watched him.

Waiting.

Eventually, Corrado nodded, saying only, "Yeah, babe."

"Why?"

"I don't know."

It's what bothered him the most.

Everything was *good.*

Better.

Always getting better.

After everything, all that they shared could have been changed in ways that would have ruined all they worked for. Instead, despite his selfishness and the hurt between the three of them, they came on top. Even Les had told him—more than once—this had never been better.

More complicated, sure.

But *better.*

"Go," Ginevra whispered against the pillow.

As though she just knew ...

Corrado *made* himself stay put—Les didn't suggest he should do otherwise. Then again, how could he when he was doing his best to hide that anything was wrong in the first place?

She did know them best, though.

Lifting his hand from her swell, Ginevra wove their fingers, squeezed, and repeated, "Go."

How could he tell her no?

He learned that wasn't his job.

With either of them.

By the time Corrado managed to pull on a pair of sleep pants and get down to the office, he found Alessio was no longer pacing. Instead, the man had found a seat in the window bench while he overlooked the small rear property of their brownstone.

Les passed him a look over his shoulder—there was no surprise about his arrival, and frankly, Corrado hadn't bothered to even try. He also didn't make an attempt to ease into the fact that something was clear wrong and he wanted to know what it was.

"Something you need to say?" he asked Les.

Stormy eyes watched him from across the room.

Corrado waited his lover out.

"It snowballed," Les muttered.

Corrado arched a brow. "What did?"

"These thoughts. The doubts. Every little answer to every question I might have about this baby or being a father or—it just ... one after another, you know?"

The choppy, confusing statement might have made someone else scratch their head, but Corrado got it. He understood exactly what Alessio was trying to say without really *saying* it. He took a moment to consider how he wanted to respond—Alessio wasn't known for his doubts and fears; not when he was constantly the most fearless of them all, it seemed.

Sad how their baby—something that would only bring them love—was the thing that scared him the most.

"Have you talked to anybody about it?" he decided to ask.

Because that was the thing he'd come to learn about Les although there had been a time, before Ginevra, when Corrado thought he knew everything there was to know about the man across the room. And one of those things was that, while he wasn't always aware of it, Alessio had more people than Corrado realized who he used as a support system and network.

People he trusted.

People that weren't Corrado.

Which was fine.

It was the *familial* aspect of the people Les surrounded himself with in his life that made Corrado think it was worth something deeper to Les. Those he called when he needed a laugh, or just a too-late chat about fucking life or whatever else it was that put him into a spell every now and then. He found fathers in the generation that came before him. A mother in Corrado's own. Siblings that doubled as friends. Those people weren't his blood, and he really had no family to speak of, but he'd managed to create his own.

Corrado wasn't even sure Les realized it.

"Well?" Corrado asked when Les stayed quiet for too long. "Did you talk to somebody—or were we not the only people you were trying to hide it from?"

"Hey."

The word was sharp.

It *almost* stung, but not quite.

From across the room, Les tipped his chin a fraction higher, his gaze never leaving Corrado's when he said, "I want this—*more than anything*. I just didn't want you—or her—to think differently because I had stupid shit in my head. That's it, that's all."

Of course.

That was just so very *Les*.

"And I did talk to people," Alessio muttered. "Too many people. Cree said shit was normal—Dare told me I was being ridiculous. He's like a goddamn emotionless *rock* anyway, so the whole conversation just went to total shit. Fucking *shocker*."

A chuckle escaped him.

He couldn't help it.

Les grinned at the sound.

Corrado didn't think to ask what those doubts were that Les was feeling—maybe his worth as a father when he'd not really had one; maybe something else entirely. Who was Corrado to say?

Things like this were complicated.

Trauma stayed close to the surface.

God knew Les had a lot of trauma surrounding things like family, parents, abandonment, self-worth, and even *love*. As sad as it fucking was. It still *was*. Corrado would spend the rest of his life making sure he never added to Les's trauma for those things.

He'd already done enough.

"Your father told me it would be great," Les added quieter.

Corrado's shoulder found the doorjamb while he leaned there, replying, "And what do you think?"

"I think they're all right."

"Does the rest matter, then?" he asked.

Did it ever?

"I'm terrified, Corrado."

He nodded in the doorway.

"Me, too, Les."

"It's slightly *less* terrifying with you and her, though."

"Good to know."

He wouldn't soon forget it.

JOHN | SIENA

THE THERAPIST

"Siena is pregnant," John blurted out.

Leonard's next step hesitated, but like with anything John threw at his therapist—even after all these years of them chatting together—he kept on going. He rolled with John's punches no matter what the situation called for. He was good that way.

John didn't know what he was going to do when Leonard retired—officially, anyway.

"Well, congratulations are in order, then," Leonard said, giving John a smile.

"Is it?"

Leonard peered up at the bright sky overhead. "Are you not happy about the pregnancy?"

"Very happy."

"Was it planned?"

"Not particularly."

Leonard chuckled. "Ah, I see."

"What?"

"After all these years, and you still ask me *what*, John? Really?"

"Habit, I guess."

"Mmhmm."

His therapist knew him too damn well, really. It wasn't so much a problem for John as it was ... well, he couldn't fucking hide anything or pretend when it came to Leonard. He had seen John through some of his toughest cycles in his life, and pulled him out of the hell that was depression, mania, and more.

Yeah.

What would he do without this man helping him?

Supporting him?

"It's not the *baby* that frightens me," John admitted. "It's everything else around the baby."

"The *change*."

"Yeah."

"The inevitable," Leonard continued.

"Exactly."

Leonard kept walking, and John kept an easy stride beside his therapist. The sky was bright and blue with not a cloud in sight, and the smell of someone's barbeque clung in the air as they walked the block. It wasn't often they walked during a session, but it really just depended on certain factors, too.

The weather.

His mood.

Leonard's restless legs.

Whatever.

John also suspected his therapist didn't like to allow him to get too comfortable in any one routine with him. Everything else in his life was so carefully planned and structured as to not worsen his mood swings that even his twice weekly—or more, if it was needed— therapy could sometimes become just another thing John *did*.

Not something he wanted to do.

Leonard changed it up, and kept it new. A coffee shop this week, and the couch at his father's place the next. A walk around the block today, and on Friday they were supposed to take Andino's kid to the park for their chat.

It was always something new.

He didn't mind.

"Are you going to give me some mind-blowing advice that takes all my anxiety about this away, or what?" John asked. "I could really use it right about now, and Siena might appreciate me being a tad less ..."

"Snappy?"

"I was going to say *touchy*."

Leonard scoffed. "I know how you behave when you get anxious."

"Yeah, yeah. Advice, or what?"

"I don't have anything, actually," Leonard replied, sighing. "Nothing that's going to make you do a complete three-sixty and look at this in a whole new way with a different perspective. That's not how this works, John."

"And what is *this*?"

Leonard shrugged. "Becoming a father, I suppose."

"Oh."

That was not the answer he expected to get, and by the look on his therapist's face, he suspected Leonard knew that as well. They walked in silence for a bit longer before John had finally come up with something else to say.

Dumb as it was.

"Why not?"

"Because, John, this is fucking terrifying," Leonard said.

John was the one to miss a step, then, shocked out of his mind that Leonard had actually *swore.* He was pretty sure he could count on one hand the amount of times he heard a cuss leave the man's lips, and it wasn't very damn often.

Leonard continued on like John hadn't missed a step, and nothing had happened. "Becoming a parent isn't something anyone can prepare for, really. Oh, sure, you can read those stupid books—you can learn the mechanics of this whole deal, but … it's not the same."

"No?"

"No." Leonard tipped his water bottle up for a sip, and then asked, "Let me pose it to you this way—when do *you* think you would have been ready to have a child?"

That was not an easy question.

Then again, very few questions Leonard asked him were easy to answer.

"I don't know," John settled on saying.

"The answer is probably never," Leonard said. "If you think about it long enough, and allow yourself time to consider everything that you might want to have or do differently or whatever the case may be before you bring a child into the world, then yes, it will probably be never. Fact remains, even once you had all those things, and did all those things, there would be *something else* that would come up to hold you back."

"You think I never would have wanted kids?"

"You want children—I know you do. You told me. Wanting them and being ready for them is not the same, John. Lots of people plan to have kids. Lots more struggle to have children, and pay thousands upon thousands of dollars to finally have their child. And then once they do have that baby—it is a whole different ballgame because life is not what we expect it to be, nor is it what we think it should be."

Leonard smiled in that way of his again, adding, "No one is ever truly *ready.* Like I said, you can attempt something akin to preparing for that kind of change, and yet it'll never be enough, John. Nothing is ever going to be enough to prepare you for the way a child will change you as a human, as a man, and as a husband. I know that's not the answer you want from me, but it's the best and only one I have to give."

"So, you're saying—"

"It's not you, and it's not being bipolar that makes you anxious and worried and … not ready." Leonard chuckled quietly. "It's called being human."

"Well, then."

"Surprise," the man murmured.

"Yeah."

"For what it's worth, and I know you've probably been told this by all the people who matter the very most to you, but you're going to be an amazing father, John. Don't let the *changes* scare you—they're not all bad, I promise."

"No?"

Leonard shook his head. "No, of course not."

"How does it change you, then—why does it change you?"

"Because you'll hold a piece of you, and you'll learn how to help them grow and *live*, and always love. You'll learn that it is absolutely possible to fall in love at first sight, and it will *stun you* at how much love you have for them in that very instant. You don't know them at all—when they're new and pink and squalling—and yet you *do* know them. Your heart and your soul, it knows them. It knows every single part of them. They will amaze you, terrify you, and captivate you from the first time they open their eyes, until the day you finally let them walk away. And they will teach you, too."

Leonard stopped walking, and so did John. Glancing over at the older man, Leonard smiled back.

"They will teach you to look for things that may have seemed insignificant before, but are so amazing when you see it through their eyes. They will teach you to appreciate time, and how it passes. They will teach you innocence and grace and beauty and *life*. They will teach you how to be a better man, and how to be the best father. They will teach you how to forgive more easily, and to love more freely. They will teach you *everything* you need to know, and everything you didn't know existed."

Leonard nodded as though to himself before continuing with, "And they will do it without you ever having realized it until one day someone is looking at you and asking you how becoming a father changes you. And then you will know, John. You, too, will know."

BABY NUMBER 2

Luciano hid behind his father's legs as the retching from the bathroom became impossibly louder. Even John cringed a little at the noise.

"Ma okays?" three-year-old Luciano asked.

John reached back and patted his son on the top of his head. "Yeah, Ma's fine."

"Ma sound sick."

Yep.

She sure did.

"Siena?"

"Don't fucking come in here," his wife snapped.

John cringed again. "You got it, sweetheart."

Whatever she wanted.

You know ...

"Go see Ma," Luciano demanded, pushing at the back of his father's legs with all his little might. "Go, Da."

"No, I don't think so."

Luciano glared up at his father. "*Da.*"

John sighed.

On one hand, he was grateful his son was so protective of his mother. And on the other hand, he didn't know how to explain to Luciano that no matter what John did in that moment, Siena was not going to be happy about it.

The last thing she wanted was him in that bathroom to hold her hair back while she barfed her fucking guts out. She had to hold onto a little bit of dignity, after all. There was very little dignified about being on your knees bent over a toilet while you upchucked your breakfast.

For the fifth day in a row ...

Yeah, John had been counting.

He knew what that meant.

Siena's little *flu* spiel was no longer the case.

It couldn't be.

"Da—"

"Hey," John murmured, spinning around and dropping to his

293

knees. He held his son by his shoulders, and gave him a smile. "Do you want to make Ma happy?"

Luciano nodded. "Yeah."

"How about you go get her one of her special waters from the fridge, okay?"

"Okay, Da!"

"Don't drop it on your way back up here."

"I *won'ts*," his son said fiercely. "I'm Lucky."

John grinned. "You know it."

It was just the idea that he could please his mother—who he loved with all of his tiny little heart—that sent Luciano out of his father's hair for at most, ten minutes. After all, he would have to be careful and slow not to drop the water just to prove to his father he could in fact do it without dropping the bottle.

The kid was predictable that way.

Luciano's footsteps had just started to fade when the bathroom door opened, and John turned to face his wife in the doorway. Pale skin. Darkness under her eyes. Frowning. Messy hair. Siena looked like hell—God, he loved her, but this particular morning had been rough on her in every way.

"You okay?" he asked.

She glanced up at the ceiling and said, "I am starting to think this might not be—"

"The flu?"

Her gaze darted back to him. "Yeah, probably not."

"How late are you?"

"Two weeks."

John nodded. "You didn't think to mention it, or …?"

"Never even thought about it at all until this morning. I never stop going, John. I'm lucky to remember when it *might* be coming up let alone know that I missed my damn period."

Ouch.

Her tone was biting.

"Sorry—I deserved that."

Siena frowned. "No, you didn't. I'm just …"

"Not feeling well. I know, babe."

Not up to par.

Not herself.

John *knew*.

Siena twisted her fingers together, and glanced away. "Would you mind going to the store for me to get a test? Just in case—to know for sure?"

John laughed, and crossed the small bit of distance between him and his wife. He grabbed hold of her face, and tipped her head back so he could stare her right in the eyes. "You don't even have to ask."

"Yeah, I know."

He bent down to kiss her mouth, and then hesitated at the last minute. "You brushed your teeth, did—"

"Yes."

Good.

He kissed her twice, and then pulled away when little feet came pattering down the hall as fast as Luciano's legs could carry him. He bound in between his mother and father, and held up the pink-colored vitamin water that Siena loved so very much. A wide smile stretched from cheek to cheek, and Luciano looked so fucking proud of himself.

"Here, Ma!"

Siena *melted.*

Lucky was her boy.

Her *Ace.*

And his Ace, too.

Lucky did no wrong.

Oh, she loved him.

"Thank you," Siena said, taking the water and bending down to kiss Lucky on the top of his head. "You're my good boy, huh?"

"I luff you, Ma."

"I love you, too."

"You sick?" Luciano asked.

Siena shook her head. "I don't think so."

The boy's brow dipped in confusion. "Then why you *get* sick, Ma?"

Siena glanced up at John, but he was already backing away and shaking his head.

"Nope, that's on you," he said, "I have things to go buy."

"*John.*"

"You walked him into it!"

And she could walk him right out of it, too.

They agreed on that long ago—awkward conversations got passed onto whoever brought it up in the first place. Siena owned this.

*

"Okay, let's let Daddy see if he can tell us what the sex of the baby will be," the ultrasound technician said with a wink in Siena's direction.

John's gaze was already glued to the screen—it hadn't left from the moment she had swung it around so they were able to get their first glimpse of their baby.

In grainy black swishes and swirls, the tech had counted ten fingers, and ten toes. She'd showed them the baby's spine, the profile of their features, and the little beat-beat-beat of the heart working just as it should.

It was all … amazing, really.

Fascinating.

John couldn't look away.

"Right here," the tech said, using her finger to draw a circle on the screen. "This is a leg, and this is a leg, and *this* is a bum. So, what do you see in between those legs and above the bum?"

John's gaze narrowed in on the black spot of nothingness.

Nothingness.

"Nothing," John murmured.

It took a beat, and then *two*. He realized what he had said, and what it meant. He understood why his wife gave a little excited squeal, and why the tech was grinning in a sly sort of way like she had just played a trick on them.

Oh, he *knew*.

Still, it took him a second.

The air sucked from the room.

Siena smiled wide.

"Exactly," the tech said. "You see nothing. So, what does that tell you?"

"It's a girl."

Siena tipped her head back, and pulled John down for a kiss with one trembling hand fisted into his shirt. "It's a *girl*, John."

And finally, he thought, they were almost complete.

Once *she* was here, of course.

They were all just waiting on her.

*

Lina Siena Marcello did not come as easily into the world like her brother had—she refused to turn, and wouldn't be moved. And with every intervention that was tried to make the girl move into the correct position for birth, the more determined she seemed to be to simply stay right in her place.

And maybe that should have been John's first clue.

Maybe he should have known, then …

His daughter was going to be stubborn, and difficult.

And entirely *wonderful*.

"Lina Siena Marcello, you *did not* put sparkly nail polish on Daddy's shoes," John said, holding the shoe in question between his fingertips like it was a fucking cat that might come alive and bite him or something. "*Again*."

"Theys pretty now," his daughter said.

She looked just like her mother.

All caramel curls framing her delicate face.

Big, blue eyes.

Innocence and life.

"They don't need to be pretty," he told his daughter. "They are *my* shoes, Lina. Just like the walls don't need to be pretty, and like Lucky's trucks don't need to be pretty. They are fine the way they are."

His three-year-old girl pushed up from the floor with a loud sigh like he was testing every bit of patience she had left today, and she just didn't have time for it. Yeah, just like her mother. And every other woman in his family that had come before her.

No doubt about it.

Her pretty pink, sparkly dress matched the polish she had used to paint his damn shoes. That had probably been an intentional choice, knowing her.

Once she got close enough to him, John bent down so he was at eye-level with his girl. "*Bambina*, you don't need to make Daddy's shoes pretty. Thank you, but they just don't need to be pretty, okay?"

Her sticky palm came up to pat him on his cheek, and he swore it felt condescending.

Her next words confirmed it. "Daddy, *everything* needs to be pretty."

His daughter.

Was.

Well, everything.

The muffled laughter from the next room had John's gaze narrowing. "I can hear you, Siena!"

"I can't help it!"

So was his life.

He didn't mind.

Much.

THE CYCLES

"That's a whole sleeve of cookies," Andino muttered.

"Shut up," John grumbled around the half-eaten Oreo. "Don't need or want your opinion."

"That's enough sugar to kill a horse, man."

"Said shut up. What part of shut up don't you understand?"

"Yeah, *shut up*, Zio Andino."

John patted his three-year-old son on the top of his head, and passed the boy a cookie for his good work. Some might call it rewarding bad behavior—he didn't much give a shit what people thought about how he raised his kid.

Andino mock glared as he dropped onto the couch in John's living room, and used his two fingers to point between his eyes, and Lucky. "Got my eyes on you, kiddo."

Lucky glowered right back, and mocked Andino with the finger motions.

All three years of him.

Already thought he was ten feet tall, and bulletproof.

John *loved it*.

Siena worried.

What could you do?

"Can'ts watch me," Lucky told Andino, "when I is already watching *you*, Zio."

John almost choked on a fucking cookie he tried to keep from laughing so goddamn hard. His son was damn serious, and he didn't want to downplay the kid's efforts by laughing at him. That did fuck all for somebody's self-esteem.

Andino gave Lucky an appreciative nod. "You're gonna do great things, kid."

Lucky smiled. "I know—Da tells me so."

John gave his son another cookie for that one.

"You don't even like mint," Andino nodded, gesturing at the chocolate mint flavored cookies in John's lap.

It really was a whole sleeve of the cookies.

The *last* sleeve.

They were his wife's. He probably should have made a run to the store, but *fuck* … he just needed sugar, and he needed it in his mouth right *now*. He didn't care if it was fucking cookies that he didn't like.

"Med changes," John said in explanation to his cousin with a shrug. "Leonard wanted to test a drop in dose considering how calm shit's been for two years. It's fucking driving me crazy—not *literally*," he was quick to add when Andino gave him a look. "Just with food, and energy. I want to eat and be on the move and fuc—"

John's gaze quickly dropped to his son who was staring up at him with big eyes before he said, "And the other four letter thing with my wife that we don't say around this one because he repeats *everything*."

Andino laughed. "Yeah, I got it."

"Anyway—that's why. The new meds."

Andino lifted a brow. "And you were good with that—the change, I mean?"

"I trust my doctor."

That trust didn't come easily by any means, but Leonard was always careful with John, his disorder, and how he went about treating it. He let John have a voice, and that made a hell of a lot of difference at the end of the day.

Lucky climbed up on the couch and sat beside his father, fat palm already overturned and waiting for another cookie.

"You had two already," John said.

Lucky gave a pointed look at the whole *pile* of cookies in his lap. He didn't say *anything*. Just stared at the fucking things.

Andino cleared his throat, and looked away to hide his smile.

Then, very quietly, Lucky said, "Ma likes those cookies, Da. They Ma's."

Yes, they were.

Three, and he already understood blackmail.

John handed his kid another cookie.

Lucky jumped down from the couch, and headed out of the living room without as much as a look over his shoulder. Having got what he wanted, he was now moving onto bigger and better things.

Typical Lucky.

John sighed.

"Raising him right, man." Andino smirked at his cousin. "He really is going to do great things."

"I know. That's what terrifies me."

And excited him.

Yeah, that, too.

*

Siena POV

Siena opened the pantry to find … *nothing.*

Well, not nothing.

But a hell of a lot of nothing!

"John!"

"What?"

"Where is my Moon Pie?"

She didn't get a response.

Siena's gaze narrowed on the empty shelf where her pack of chocolate mint flavored Oreo cookies should be. "And my cookies, too?"

Silence still answered her back.

She bet that if she looked in the fridge, the rest of the cheesecake she had left from the night before would also be gone. Along with whatever ice cream was in the freezer, and whatever else John had found to satisfy his sweet tooth in the meantime.

It always happened.

Med changes were hard. Sometimes, it was mood swings that seemed unstoppable, and other times he just wanted to sleep for days. And then there were times like this when he was just fucking *hungry.* Something he couldn't satisfy at all, and he would eat anything as long as it was sweet.

It was most difficult when it was a mixture of several things— hunger, tiredness, or the moods. After being married this long, she was used to it.

Never failed.

"John!"

Her husband's sheepish face popped in the kitchen entryway just as Siena came out of the panty. "Sorry."

"I was saving that Moon Pie," Siena said sadly.

"Want me to go get you some? The store down the block has them in singles."

She shrugged. "Well, maybe I'll just make Whoopie Pies now, anyway."

301

John's eyes lit up. "I'm game for that."

Of course, he was.

It made her smile.

"You're lucky you spend most of the day on your feet, and half of your morning on a fucking treadmill," she half-heartedly grumbled. "Diabetes is still a real thing, though, John."

"I am as healthy as I am ever going to be."

"So you say."

She was just pulling things out of the cupboards when John came up behind her. It was only his lips ghosting over the back of her neck that made her sigh a little, and melt into his hands grabbing her around the waist.

"To be fair, Lucky stole three of the cookies," John murmured against her skin.

"That you stole from me?"

"Plausible deniability."

"Or you use our son because I can't get mad at him."

"And that," John agreed.

"I don't get mad at you, either."

She felt his lips curve into a gentle smile at the base of her neck. "No, you don't."

"Did you sedate it?" she asked. "The sweet tooth?"

John grumbled a bit under his breath. "Not particularly."

"Maybe the Whoopie Pies will help."

"Doubtful, but I am not complaining."

Siena laughed, and he pressed another kiss to the back of her neck. Med changes sometimes also meant unpredictability—they really didn't know how it was going to hit John, or what effect it might have on him from day to day until he regulated and settled in with the new dose of whatever.

This time, instead of sleep, it was eating and energy.

He wanted all the food, all the time.

And he didn't stop moving.

Ever.

Except to sleep—he was sleeping a moderate amount every night, but not nearly enough. It wasn't at a worrying point just yet, but Siena had to keep her eye on it. John had gotten better at being *honest*, too. He knew—like they had known—that hiding things or making something appear better than it actually was only ended badly in almost every situation for John.

This was what came with being *them*, though.

She didn't want John any other way.

After all, he didn't come any other way.

"So, tell me what to do for these Whoopie Pies, and I will—"

"You can get out of my kitchen until I'm done."

It was just easier that way.

John leaned around Siena's side, and pressed a fast, but fleeting kiss to her lips. "Done."

He was gone from the room before she could even pull out her mixer. All it took was the promise of more sugar.

THE SURPRISE

John sat on the end of the bed, and stared at the item Siena had shoved into his hand just before she rushed out of the room to make sure their kids were ready for school. Eight-year-old Luciano pretty much handled himself in the morning, but their four-year-old daughter, Lina, was a whole other breed of monster.

Lina could go through five outfits before she had finally settled on the one she wanted to wear, and even then, she could change the bow in her hair four times, and her shoes a half of a dozen times because they didn't *match* well enough.

And none of that mattered right then.

He could hear his wife talking to Lucky.

Hear Lina calling for Siena from the bathroom.

Knew he should move and get up to help her ready the kids for school and pre-K.

And yet, there he sat, staring like a fucking idiot at this *thing* in his hands. Because he couldn't do anything else but stare at it. He didn't know what in the hell *to do* but sit here and stare at it like the *cafone* he apparently was.

This wasn't the first time.

Not the second.

And still, he was *stunned.*

Hadn't they said they were done?

Hadn't they been *careful?*

Hadn't they—

"John?"

He glanced up at his wife's quiet call of his name. Siena leaned in the bedroom doorway with a small, knowing smile as her gaze drifted from the piece of plastic in his hands to the shocked expression on his face. He'd been wearing that same expression ever since she came out of their bathroom that morning, and put this goddamn test in his hands.

A *pregnancy* test.

"Lucky is ready," she said.

John nodded. "All right."

"You're taking him this morning."

"I know, Siena."

"It happened, in case you're curious, because apparently were just that lucky point-zero-zero-one percent of people who a IUD fails for, John."

"I didn't really wonder ..."

"You're wondering a little," she said.

John let out a heavy breath. "A little, yeah. I just ..."

"What?"

"Christ, aren't we too old for another kid?"

Siena lifted a single brow high. "Well, *I* am not too old."

John heard her teasing, and he chuckled. "Low blow, babe."

"You're not too old, John."

"Forty-two is—"

"Not too old," she said simply. "It's just a shock because it seems like we've never planned for any of our kids, they just come into our lives, and make themselves at home here. And you know what? It's always felt like they were exactly where they belonged, John."

They had.

Forever.

A shouting match started out in the hallway behind Siena between Luciano and Lina. The two kids were like cats and dogs—and surprisingly, *not* because the little one irritated the older one like most siblings would do. No, it was because Lina was a little too particular about her things, and Lucky just didn't give a shit.

World.

War.

Three.

Regularly.

Kids were great.

And he meant that in all honesty.

Siena didn't even pay attention to their kids—as usual, the two would work it out or Lina would get her way. Just like her mother.

His wife came in the bedroom, and closed the space between them. Siena's hands came to land on John's thighs overtop his slacks at the same time she bent down and pressed a hard kiss to his lips. Everything was always so fast for them in their mornings—their house was always on some kind of go, non-stop.

He liked it that way.

Thrived in their chaos.

And yet, with a kiss, she slowed his whole world down for a few seconds. Every stroke of her lips against his calmed his racing heart, and reminded him of why his life was good and perfect and *great*. Why she was good and perfect … and oh, so great.

And them, too.

Yeah, they were all of those things, too.

All too soon for his liking, Siena pulled away, but she didn't go far. Her hands were still resting on his thighs, and she was still close enough to make all of his focus zone in on only her. Next to the moments he got with his kids, Siena was always the best part of his days.

All these years …

All this time …

It was still only ever going to be her for him. There could never be anyone else when his whole life had just been *this* woman—and even before she had come into his life and turned him entirely upside down to make him into this far better version of himself, he didn't think about that time. He rarely ever acknowledged it.

Didn't want to, really.

His life didn't matter until her.

It couldn't.

"I know I put you through some shit sometimes," he murmured.

Siena grinned in that way of hers. "I wouldn't have you any other way, John."

He nodded. "I know—but I think I don't tell you nearly enough and if *you* think that I do, then I don't think that I do."

"You do."

Yeah, but still …

"I love you, Siena."

She kissed him again, whispering against his lips, "I love you more, John."

Not possible.

He'd let her believe it, anyway.

*

"Forty-two," John murmured against the rim of his beer bottle.

His father glanced over at him, and asked, "What are you going on about?"

"I'm forty-two years old."

"You're just realizing this … or?" Lucian glanced at the beer. "I know you don't drink anything harder than beer, but do you think maybe you should lay off that today if you're confused or something?"

John shook his head, and laughed. "You're something else."

Lucian shrugged, and relaxed in his wicker chair. "Who else is going to keep you on your toes?"

"My wife or kids, for one."

"Yeah, but—"

"Andino regularly tests my patience."

"He tests *everyone's* patience."

"Fair," John returned.

Because it was true.

"What's all this age shit about?"

John sighed. "I'm just … realizing that's where I am at in my life."

"And?"

"And I'm going to be forty-two with another baby."

Lucian choked on his next sip of beer. And had John not still been caught in his thoughts, he would have laughed. It took a few seconds before his father cleared his throat, and glanced over at his son with a smile.

"Congrats, then."

"Yeah, it's great."

"And you're wondering how you're supposed to do this child-later-in-life thing, right?"

"I mean …"

"I was not a young man when Lucia came around," Lucian noted, "and it didn't feel any different. There was no change between when you were born, and her. More baby things to buy, maybe. That market soaks you for every dollar they can."

John laughed. "Truth."

Lucian grinned. "One more grandbaby to add to the pile. It's early, but … any names?"

"I was thinking of one, maybe."

"Don't leave me in suspense."

"Jonny or Jonnie depending on the sex—Siena shouted it at me before I left the house. For me, she said."

Lucian nodded. "I like it."

John did, too.

*

Jonny Marcello.
Eight pounds, two ounces.
Born *loudly*.
Born at four-twenty-three AM on a cold December morning.
He was the baby.
The spoiled one.
John made sure of it.
And he was perfect.

NEW FRIENDS

"You sure this is what you want to do?" Cross asked.

Catherine glanced over at him from her spot in the passenger seat. "Why not?"

"I just figure ... well, you've got a good thing going on your own, don't you? I mean, it might not be *you* doing the numbers when they need done, but you've got it handled."

Laughing Catherine muttered, "And I am still hiding far too much money under my bed, Cross. I have no concept of how to hide large sums of money. Every time you pull something out from under the bed, do you want to worry about if there's money inside, or what you're actually looking to find?"

He quieted. "Yeah, you should get somebody on that, babe."

Exactly.

"Plus," she added quieter, "John and Siena have been married for like months now. You know I haven't really tried to get to know her, and stuff."

"That's not because of her, Catherine. That's because we're busy as hell. You're barely even home before you have to take off again."

"Yeah, but I'm home right now. So ... "

Cross pulled the car to a smooth stop on the side of the street. Across from them sat a familiar restaurant. Catherine had passed the place a ton of times, but she had never gone in to eat. Mostly because the business was owned by the Calabrese family—or it had been before her family removed their problem—and the Marcellos simply didn't mix with that bunch. That's what she had always been told, anyhow.

Except now, it seemed.

And really, Siena wasn't actually a Calabrese anymore.

Details were important.

"Did you ever consider," Cross started to say, "that Siena might also have her hands full handling John's side of the business, and she might not have the time to take you on, too?"

Catherine raised a brow. "I think, if that's the case, then Siena probably also knows names of people, Cross."

"So do I."

"Yes, people who want nothing to do with the business of a queen pin at the moment."

"Your mom—"

Catherine rolled her eyes.

Her man just laughed.

"Yeah, yeah. I know. You're trying to do this on your own, babe. Figure all this shit out, and handle your own business. I don't need the lecture again."

"Not a lecture if it's true," Catherine pointed out.

Cross scowled. "You're hanging around my sister too much. Stop it."

"Mmhmm."

Catherine leaned over the middle of the seats, and pressed a fast kiss to Cross's lips. She pulled away far sooner than she actually wanted to—before the kiss could really get good, actually—but she had to. If she didn't, all she would do was blink, and boom, there she would have been in that car with him for hours.

Siena was expecting her.

It was rude to make people wait.

Cross's disappointed groan followed Catherine out of the car, but she simply shot him a wink over her shoulder before closing the door. He'd be fine to amuse himself without her for a couple of hours, surely. She waved two fingers at him from outside the car, and then turned to head for the entrance to the restaurant. She glanced back at the car just as she slipped inside the business to find Cross waiting for her to disappear out of his sights. It was only once the door closed, and she was gone from his view that he finally pulled away from the curb.

The woman at the podium turned to greet Catherine with a wide, friendly smile. "Hello, Catherine, right?"

Catherine blinked. "Uh, yeah."

"Your cousin let me know who to look for," the woman said in explanation. "Siena is back in the offices, unless you would prefer to wait for her at a table, then—"

"The offices are fine."

"Great, follow me."

The woman directed them through the main floor of the dining room, and then past a private section. They bypassed the bar and the doors leading into the kitchen before cutting through a back hallway that housed bathrooms and storage rooms. Siena's office—which actually wasn't big, but wasn't cramped, either—sat at the very back of the hallway.

Behind the desk, Siena glared at the screen on her desktop while John sat across from her desk looking like he was two seconds away from taking the computer away from her altogether.

"First of all," Siena said, "there is nothing wong with my computer, John."

"It's five years old, Siena."

"And it works *fine*."

"Last week, it froze, you panicked, and—"

"We don't talk about that!"

John pressed his lips together to keep from smirking, but it was still clear to Catherine all the same. "Okay, but the fact still remains that it is older, and it should be replaced, love. That's all I am saying."

"Do you know how much work that is going to be for me to move everything over from this to another computer?"

"I think we could hire someone to do it and then you won't have to worry about it at all. See, simple."

Siena stared at John like he was a small child who didn't comprehend large words. "Excuse you?"

"What?"

"Hire someone?"

"Siena—"

"John, literally *no one* but me can be on this computer. What if they accessed the wrong file? What if all the business I have handled for the last several years was right in front of their faces—"

"They probably wouldn't know what the fuck they are looking at. They fix computers, they don't do *accounting*."

Siena sighed.

John looked unmoved. "So, that's settled then?"

"No, it's not settled. I am not—"

"New computer will be delivered tomorrow."

"You're impossible!"

"You need new electronics, that's the end of it."

"I know someone, actually," Catherine spoke up from the doorway. Two heads turned in her direction. John smiled as if to silently greet his cousin, and Siena too offered a little wave as if to invite Catherine further into the office.

"Well, if you're settled, then," the woman said behind Catherine, "I will get back to my work."

"Thank you."

Once the woman was gone, Catherine entered the office, and closed the door behind her. She took the seat John vacated, sitting across from Siena at her desk. The two women stared at one another for a moment before Siena broke the silence first.

"What kind of *someone*?"

"A guy," Catherine said. "I mean, call him a hacker or whatever, but that's kind of like his side hustle. Mostly, he just does whatever with electronics, and if you need a little extra ... or something specific, he can basically hack into whatever you need him to hack into. Which means, he's kind of willing to turn his cheek to any extra business he might find on your stuff for a little extra money."

Siena nodded like she was contemplating that. "I have computers across ten business that need to be upgraded."

"And entire programs that need—or could afford to be—redone for business sake," John put in.

"He could handle all of that," Catherine said, shrugging. "And I promise he's safe to use."

Siena was quiet for a moment before she gave John a look. Nodding her head to the side as if to silently ask him to leave. John didn't need to be told again. He was quick to drift out of the office, and close the door behind him, but not without a wave over his shoulder at his wife and cousin.

That just left the two women alone.

"Sorry I haven't been around much since ... you two got married," Catherine said. "Life is crazy."

Siena smiled—sweet and brilliant. "That's okay. I hear you're doing big things in Cali with your mom."

Catherine nodded. "We can call it that."

"Still making money?"

"Too much for me to handle."

Siena rubbed her hands together. "Too much money is exactly what I specialize in, Catherine."

"That's why I'm here, right?" Then, Catherine glanced at Siena, adding, "Well, not the only reason. Should make friends, too, you know? We woman in this family have to stick together, or all the men railroad right over us."

"Is that so?"

"Not really. They're smart enough to know better. I wasn't lying about the friends thing, though. Do you wanna grab lunch, and maybe do something later—a club, or whatever? Without the guys, I think. They're distracting."

The woman across from her laughed. "*Very* distracting, I think."

"Is that a yes, then?"

Siena nodded. "Yeah, Catherine, sure. I feel like we have a ton to get to know about each other."

To say the least.

Catherine didn't doubt, by the end of it, they would be the best of friends, though. Because despite her joke about the men in her family, she hadn't lied about the other bit.

The women in their family needed to stick together.

That's just how it worked.

ANDINO | HAVEN

DIRECTION

"Andino, be serious."

"I am being serious."

Haven gave him the *most* exasperated look over her shoulder as she slipped her feet into heels that would make her legs look fantastic, but made his feet ache just thinking about her walking around in them all damn day. She never complained, though, so he figured she liked it.

"Really?" she asked quietly.

He stayed leaning in the walk-in closet of their master bedroom—they finally moved into that mansion on the hills, as John would say, and Andino fucking loved it. He bought the place the week after they married, closed within thirty days, and walked his wife over the threshold the day after the ink dried. It took a couple of months for the interior designer to do her work on the inside, but the place was all theirs.

Every fucking inch.

And now he wanted to start filling it.

With babies.

"Really," he said.

Haven gave him another one of *those* looks. It said she thought he was acting fucking crazy, and shit, maybe he was. Before Haven, kids had never crossed Andino's mind except when his mother felt like she needed to point out that, you know, she didn't have any goddamn grandbabies.

Then, he met Haven.

He got her down the fucking aisle.

All he thought about now were kids—like a switch had gone off inside his head, and his focus in life changed entirely. Andino wasn't complaining about it, that was for sure.

"I just …"

"What?" Haven asked, standing straight.

He was right.

Those heels did make her legs look great.

314

Damn.

"I don't think you should switch your shot to an IUD," he said, shrugging. "I think you should just … do nothing."

"I am a month away from the bar opening."

Andino tried not to scowl.

He *really* did.

And failed like a motherfucker.

Haven raised her brow at him.

Andino fixed his face *and* his attitude.

The bar was hers—she bought it. And not with his money, no, with *hers*. He was not allowed to touch the bar. He was not allowed to *ask* about the bar. He was not allowed to look in the direction of the paperwork for the bar.

Nothing.

It was a line in the sand, Haven drew it, and she promised to paint it with his motherfucking blood if he thought to mess with it.

So, maybe she was a little touchy.

You know, 'cause he fucked up her other one.

Andino deserved that, though, so he shut the fuck up, and let his wife do whatever she wanted. And if that meant opening a bar that he wasn't allowed to have any hand in, then that's what it meant. It made her happy, and God knew Andino had enough work and business of his own that he didn't need to be playing in Haven's.

"So, we can't have a family because we work?" he asked quietly.

"That's not what I said."

"Then what are you saying?"

"I've never held a baby, Andino," she said, laughing. "Not one *that* young, and—"

"Do you want kids?"

"Yes."

Her answer was so sure that he didn't feel the need to question her on it, not that he would have even if she said no. Just because his mind was made up on something didn't mean that Haven's would always be in the same zone. And it took two people to make this thing called marriage work, right?

That's what everybody kept telling him.

If she didn't want the same things, then fine.

He wanted her.

That's what mattered.

"Do you want kids *now*?" he asked.

Haven's bottom lip caught under her teeth, and she took a beat to reply with, "I never really thought about it, you know?"

Okay.

"So, think about it now," he murmured.

"Right now?"

"Why not?"

"*Right now*," she repeated, "when you know I am heading out to finalize things for the bar, I have a lunch with your mom, and an appointment with my doctor to put in this fucking IUD."

"Right now," he returned, "because of that appointment. *Think about it now.*"

"And if I say no?"

"Then the answer is no, Haven."

What else did she expect?

"Well, if I was going to get the IUD put in, then don't you think—"

"You told me why you wanted that. Because you won't have to go in as often for your shot. It's not about anything else, it's for that."

"I thought ..."

"What?" he asked when she hesitated.

"That you would want to wait because we haven't even been married a year yet."

"Is that what you want?"

"I thought it was because I thought it was what you wanted, too. And now you want something different, and I'm just thinking about it."

Andino grinned. "Oh?"

"Don't get arrogant."

"Oh, you think this is arrogance, huh?"

"You're arrogant about *everything*, Andino."

Well, she wasn't entirely wrong.

But in this case, she was.

"Actually, it makes me *very* happy to think about you being the mother of my child," he said, shrugging one shoulder, and holding her stare. "I just figured out the reason why I never really thought about having kids was because I never found the right woman to raise them with me, and I finally found you—now, it's all I want."

A sweet smile curved his wife's lips. "You really do have a way with words when you want to."

"My mother says I'm charming."

"Yeah, well, you're also her only child, and she spoiled you fucking rotten, too. I know, I deal with it everyday, now."

God, he loved this woman.

More than she would ever know.

He didn't deserve her.

She could both put him in his place, and make his heart race with love all in the same goddamn breath. He was a lucky fuck because he'd done terrible things—some might say to her, and to others, too—and somehow, he was still able to wake up to this woman every single morning of his life.

"I love you, Haven," Andino said, "and if what you want is to wait, then that's we'll do."

"And if I don't want to wait?"

"Then you best cancel those fucking meetings today. *All of them.*"

She glanced away from him, her tongue snaking out to wet the seam of her lips before she replied, "Even dinner with your mom?"

"Where's your phone?"

She laughed.

Andino wasn't joking. "Where's the phone, Haven?"

"In my bag on the bed."

Andino supposed he had his answer, then. And they wouldn't be leaving this bedroom today because of it. After all, he did like to keep his promises to his wife. That had been his vow, and he intended to keep it.

SURPRISE

"Oh, my God," Haven laughed, stretching across the bed to try and grab the ringing phone on the nightstand. "Come on, Andino!"

"No, I made a promise, and I intend to keep it."

His hands landed firmly to her naked hips before he yanked her back. Just like that, the phone was out of her reach, and the call stopped ringing. She might have been annoyed any other time, but all she could do was smile when Andino's lips skimmed her spine, and traveled higher until he was kissing the curve of her shoulder.

Just like that, her body was singing.

Her mind, *sky high*.

Skin, *so fucking hot*.

He had kept his promise, and hadn't let her leave the bedroom from the moment she agreed to what he wanted—and really, what *she* wanted. Not that Haven was complaining, but she had never been very good at ignoring her phone when it rang.

"Just … let me check who it was, okay?" she said.

Andino let out a heavy sigh, and his forehead touched her shoulder before he shook his head with a chuckle. "You're impossible, woman."

"It might be important!"

"Anyone who wants to take time away from me loving you is *not* important."

"Oh?"

"Yes."

"Even if it was your ma?"

He stiffened behind her. "You *swore*."

Haven grinned against the pillow. "I have no idea what you're talking about."

"*Haven*."

"Still in the dark, Andino."

He grumbled under his breath, rolling away from her to fall onto his back on his side of the bed. Tipping her head up, she peeked over at him, trying her very damnedest to hide her smirk, and failing like nothing else.

Andino rolled his eyes. "Keep laughing."

"I'm *not*."

"You want to."

"But only a little," Haven teased.

They had a deal, him and her. It was one that worked well for them considering how much of a presence Andino's family constantly had in their lives. But especially his parents, and more importantly, his mother. The man would never deny he was a momma's boy through and through, and for the most part, Haven loved it.

He adored his ma.

Loved her entirely too much.

But they did not bring up family in bed.

For whatever reason, that took away any desire Andino had to fuck in an instant. And since Haven preferred Andino's attention to be focused on her in bed, she didn't mind following the rule of no talking about family in bed.

Unless, of course, it got her what she wanted.

Like now.

"Check the damn phone," Andino grunted.

"Stop whining."

She tossed him a cheeky smile over her shoulder as she rolled over to reach for the phone. She didn't get the chance to see how he responded to her teasing because she was more concerned with why the doctor's office for her GYNO would be calling back when she'd texted the line to cancel her appointment later that day.

"What is it?" Andino asked.

"The doctor."

"Probably just wants to confirm—"

"No," Haven said, sliding her thumb across the screen to unlock the phone so she could read the rest of the message. She it read it out loud so Andino could hear it, too. "Mrs. Marcello, the doctor has requested you come to your appointment as expected to discuss something that came up in your bloodwork, if at all possible. If not, please call the clinic back as soon as possible."

She blinked.

What did that mean?

Across the bed, Andino reached for her, his palm sliding up her naked side as he said, "I'm sure it's nothing, huh?"

But it could be.

Her appointment had been for the insertion of an IUD, nothing more. At her last appointment, a couple of months ago, instead of getting the shot like she normally would, they discussed changing the birth control. To be safe, the doctor told her to stop the shot immediately, allow her cycle to return before they went ahead with the IUD, and in the meantime, she had bloodwork done just to make sure everything was fine.

The bloodwork had been a couple of weeks ago.

"Haven," Andino murmured, "just call—they said you could."

"Yeah, but—"

"Babe, *call.*"

Haven nodded, because he wasn't wrong, and she was probably overthinking this whole thing. She was *healthy*, right? She still jogged every day, she ate well, and took care of her body. But she had to think about how her mother battled cancer *twice*, and she had seemed healthy before that happened, too.

"Call," Andino said again, letting her go so he could roll out of the bed to stand. "And I will go make us a coffee, hmm?"

"Sure."

"Unless you want me to stay," he added quieter.

"No, I'm sure it's fine. I'll be right now."

"All right." Andino leaned down, using his hands against the sheets to keep him steady before he pressed a quick kiss to the side of Haven's mouth. "Love you, huh?"

"Love you, too."

She waited until his footsteps could no longer be heard outside of their bedroom before she called the doctor's office back. Andino might be the rational one between them a lot of the time, but Haven wondered if sometimes, he only did that to keep her calm.

Like right then.

The receptionist at the clinic picked up first, but was quick to switch Haven over to the doctor's direct line once she explained that she wouldn't be able to make that appointment. *She* promised Andino, after all, and really ... she could have made it, but she didn't want to wait another five hours before someone would tell her if there was something wrong with her.

She'd rather know *now*.

"Haven," her GYNO said when she finally came on the line.

"Hi, sorry to call back, I know you were probably with a patient or—"

"It's fine. I was finishing up paperwork, actually. You're calling about the bloodwork, right?"

"Uh, yeah. Something came up, the woman said in her message? It kind of worried me, that's all."

"Sorry about that," the doctor replied, "but she's only allowed to tell you what I can tell her, and I can't give patient details out. I figured this was something you would want to know right away, and since your appointment was supposed to be today for the IUD, well … now would be the time to share."

"I'm sorry?"

"You can't have the IUD put in, Haven."

"I decided this morning not to put it in, anyway."

"Well, good, but even if you had decided to continue with the procedure, we couldn't do it."

"I'm not following."

"You're pregnant," the doctor said quietly. "Congratulations."

THE GRANDBABY

"Ah, shit, yeah, we can meet up in like ..." Andino's words trailed off as he glanced at the watch on his wrist. "A half hour, or so? I need to pull some clothes on and—*no*, it's none of your fucking business why I'm not dressed at noon, John, thank you."

He hung up the phone, and turned only to stop at the sight of Haven standing in the entryway of the kitchen. "I was coming back up."

"I know," she said faintly.

Andino's brow arched high. "What did the doctor say?"

"Nothing bad. Standard things."

It wasn't a total lie.

Right?

Haven was still trying to process what she just learned. Hours ago, she had been settled on the choice to have an IUD placed to prevent her from having children for several years, if that's what she so chose. And then, within minutes, with a mere conversation with Andino, she had decided that no, she would rather attempt to begin their family *now*. Once again, everything changed in a few short minutes from a simple phone call from her doctor.

There would be no *trying*.

She was already pregnant.

Haven knew exactly how this happened. Before the IUD could be placed, the doctor had wanted her to go off the shot, and resume her normal cycle. That happened, but in the process, she was supposed to use a backup—condoms. They did ... *usually*.

Sometimes, they forgot.

Clearly, that's how this happened.

She just had to *process*.

Everything was about to change.

"And everything is good?" he pressed.

Haven nodded. "Perfect."

Because it was.

Really.

Even if everything was changing, and her whole life would be different from this day forward, it truly was perfect. Andino would be excited—Haven was ecstatic. She just needed a few moments to absorb it alone before she could bring his excitement into the equation, too.

Fair was fair.

"All right," Andino said. "I know I said we would stay in bed all day, but—"

"Something came up?"

"Something with John's side of things. I should head over so we can figure it out, and clean it up before it becomes a problem."

"All right."

"You don't mind? I did make you cancel that lunch date with my mom, and all."

Haven shrugged. "I'm sure I could get her to go out to lunch with me still."

"Good." He crossed the space between them, his hand landing on the curve at her waist before he dropped a lingering kiss to her lips that had Haven's heart picking up speed. In their soft moments, and the silence, she always found happiness. "I better get dressed, and head out. I will see you tonight to finish what we started, huh?"

Heat shot through her body.

His *promises* ...

"Definitely," she whispered.

Andino kissed her again.

Harder this time.

"Love you, Haven."

More than he possibly knew.

*

"A little late for a lunch," Kim said when Haven approached the private table, "but that's okay, I am sure we can make—"

"I'm pregnant."

Haven had not at *all* planned to just blurt that information out to her mother-in-law. In fact, she hadn't planned on telling Kim at all during their late lunch. She fully intended on figuring out a way to tell Andino first—she hadn't decided yet whether or not a surprise was the right way to go, or simply telling him the news.

Instead, she saw her mother-in-law, and as though she had been holding in some huge secret that she could no longer contain, it just came spilling out.

Wow.

Well done, Haven.

Kim had already been standing, her arms reaching to bring Haven in for a comforting, familiar hug—all normal—when she blurted out the news. In that second, her mother-in-law froze, eyes widening as her hands found Haven's arms, and tightened. Not painfully, but just … as though she were trying to rehear what she heard, and make sense of it.

Like she needed to convince herself it was true.

Kim's gaze watered before she whispered, "*What?*"

"I'm pregnant."

It took her a second.

And then *two.*

"Really?"

Haven nodded.

Kim's hands squeezed her again. "Really, *really?*"

"Yeah, really."

"Oh, my God!"

Kim's scream was loud enough to break glass, Haven was sure of it. And yet, she didn't even have the chance to consider how embarrassing that was because Kim might as well have launched herself around the table to take Haven in her embrace. Her mother-in-law decided to squeeze the life and love right out of her, and replace it with her own. Her muted screeching continued even as she pulled away, cupped Haven's cheeks, and pressed a kiss against her forehead.

"I'm gonna have a grandbaby!"

Haven could only laugh.

She was well aware that for years, Kim hounded on her son for children. Andino had been an only child, and it was only later in life, when he didn't settle down and produce grandchildren for Kim to love and spoil, that she started becoming vocal in her desires. She stopped when Andino married Haven, but she figured that was only because Kim assumed she was finally going to get what she wanted.

Well, she was.

Now.

"Have you told anyone?"

Haven shook her head. "I just found out before I called you to go out for lunch. We only decided *today* to work on having children, and then I got a phone call from my doctor saying—"

"Calm down."

Okay, so maybe she was rambling a little.

Kim let out a exhale. "What about Andi?"

"Not yet."

"You're not serious?"

She shrugged.

What else could she do?

"I didn't really ... plan to tell you, it just came out."

Kim grinned. "Sometimes, we just need to tell someone else."

"But how do I tell him?"

"Any way you want. That's the beauty of it. It doesn't matter how you do it, because he's going to be happy."

Yeah, she knew that was true.

Absolutely.

"But," Kim said, "we can deal with Andino later ... it's *me* who has waited forever for this, so let's sit down, eat, and talk about my grandbaby."

Haven laughed again. "That sounds perfect."

PLUS ONE

"How did you tell Giovanni you were pregnant?"

Walking through the park with her mother-in-law, Haven enjoyed the lush greenery of the trees that provided a canopy over the pathways. She still came here at least once a week to run like she used to every single morning, but mostly, she was able to enjoy the gym they had at home. Which you know, meant she didn't have to worry about enforcers trying to keep up with her as she jogged.

"I didn't."

Haven gave Kim a look from the side. "Pardon?"

Kim shrugged, fixing her sweater that had just been draped over her shoulders. "We figured it out together … a joke, sort of. It had been a bad week for me, I was in a mood I couldn't shake, a headache that wouldn't leave me alone, I was snapping at him every time he turned around."

"That doesn't sound like you at all."

The nicest woman in the world.

Sweet as could be.

That was her mother-in-law.

Kim laughed under her breath. "Right? And especially *not* to Gio—he definitely knows how to get on my nerves quicker than anybody else, but he doesn't purposely do it just to make me mad. In fact, he does everything to avoid that, really."

"So, how did you both figure it out?"

"He brought me home my favorite dish from Lucian's restaurant, trying to … well, soften me up, I think. Put me in a better mood. One sniff of it, and it sent me running to the bathroom. I was mad again, not at him, but just in general. Mad at *everything*. And poor Gio," Kim said, trailing off with a shake of her head, "well, he meant it well, but he told me maybe my period was coming because I was kind of feeling off."

"*Ouch.*"

Kim nodded. "Yeah, that was my first reaction, too, and then I stopped to think about it. So you imagine the scene, me on my knees in the bathroom, and Gio in the doorway staring at me. His eyes started to get wider as I realized he was wrong, but only in the sense

326

that my period would be *coming* …"

"And that's how you figured it out?"

"Pretty much," Kim replied, "but of course, I sent him to the store to get me *a* pregnancy test. He came back with ten. We had decided before that to wait a while because I wanted to finish school, and everything else. Andino was not planned, but to be honest, he came at the perfect time for me and Gio."

"Do you regret not having more?"

"Not for one second."

Kim's confident statement had Haven nodding her agreement. She didn't need to repeat the question, because her mother-in-law put it to rest just like that.

"There were times," Kim said quieter, "where I wondered if it was what *Andino* wanted, though. If maybe he was lonely without a little brother or sister to look after. I was not an only child, and neither was Gio, so we had those questions … but we were never serious on having more after Andino."

"You know, it *really* shows that he's an only child."

Kim grinned. "I know. He had everything … all of our attention all the time. If there was something he wanted to obsess over for months, we fed into it every step of the way. There was nothing he couldn't do, and Gio made it clear from the beginning that we would not be the type of parents who held Andino back."

"I can see how that's translated to his adulthood."

To say the least …

"No one tells him no, hmm?"

Well, people *tried*.

Andino didn't accept it, however.

"You'll know how you want to tell him, Haven," Kim said, "and it doesn't have to be a huge production, if that's not what you want. It just has to be right for the two of you."

Right.

Sure.

*

"How did that go with John?"

Andino milled between the bedroom, and his walk-in closet on the other side of their *massive* master bedroom. Really, this room, the double closets, and bathroom that was big enough to be a small apartment by New York standards, had been what sold the mansion for Andino. For Haven, she was just struck at the *price*, and the fact Andino chuckled when the realtor asked about a mortgage.

We won't need a mortgage, he had said.

The realtor quickly stopped asking questions.

"Went fine," Andino said, coming out of the bathroom with a furrowed brow. "Did you pick up the watch I left in the bathroom?"

"Yes, and put it away."

"Oh."

He headed straight into the walk-in closet, already tugging his tie loose. She could have pressed for more information on John, but frankly, she wasn't interested in knowing what was going on that took Andino away to handle business. She had quickly learned since marrying this man that if she asked, he had *zero* problem with telling her the truth.

Somethings were better left unknown.

Simple as that.

Haven went back to her reflection in her makeup vanity mirror, wiping away the day's makeup with a green, cucumber infused facial wipe. She was just patting a water-based night cream into her face when Andino came out of the closet in nothing but boxer-briefs. He eyed the bed like it was going to be his best friend for the next several hours, and that's how she knew his day had been more stressful than he was willing to admit.

"Hey," she murmured.

His attention instantly came to her.

That was the thing with them …

It didn't matter if he was tired. It didn't make a difference to him that the only thing he really wanted in that moment was a long, deep sleep. As soon as Haven spoke, he forget everything he needed, and his focus turned onto whatever *she* wanted.

"Hmm?" he asked.

She tipped her head to the side, silently asking him to come closer. He did just that, his fingers crazing over the column of her throat while he waited for her to finish rubbing in the last of her cream on her throat.

"Remember this morning when I had to call the doctor back?"

"What about it?"

He bent down, lips pressing to the crown of her head with a soft kiss.

"She wanted to let me know I couldn't have the IUD put in, anyway."

"You canceled it, so what does that matter?"

Right.

That's what she said, too.

"That's not the question you should be asking, Andino."

"No?"

"Nope."

"Then what is?"

She met his gaze in the vanity mirror, her smile growing. "Think more *why can't you have it put in, Haven?*"

His hands that had come to rest on her shoulders stilled, fingers flexing around the curves with a gentle pressure as he took a second, and then two. Still, their gazes held tight in the mirror, and she was able to watch every second of that realization wash over his features.

And *no* ...

She wouldn't have given that up for the world.

That sight?

Him *knowing?*

She wouldn't give that up for anything.

"I'm pregnant."

"Yeah?"

Haven nodded.

"Seriously?"

She nodded again.

"Holy shit."

He took a second to have his moment, grinning wildly like the proud father-to-be that he now was. Then, he simply let his arms snake around her chest where he hugged tight as he leaned down to bury his face in the crook of her neck. She wasn't sure how long they stayed like that—too many minutes to count.

It almost felt like, for a second, they were soaking up being just *them* ... because soon, it would be them, plus one. And that was great, too.

"Thank you," she heard him say, "for everything, Haven."

BABY LYNN

"Clara?"

"No."

"Christina?"

Andino hesitated on that one. It kind of screamed *drama queen, baby of the family, total princess* and he liked that, but maybe not for a first child. "Save it."

The scratch of a pencil against paper resounded in his office, telling him she was scratching of yet another name on her list, before Haven asked, "Marissa?"

"I can't even pass that one off as Italian to my parents. And could you imagine *Dante* when I told him that name? *Fuck*, he would never shut up about it."

"You're impossible."

"I am not, I am simply—"

"*I'm* not Italian," Haven pointed out, "and they all know it, so does it really matter if our daughter's first name is Italian?"

"Matters to *me*."

And to his family.

He kept that quiet, though.

Somehow, they ended up at his wife's due date—today, although the doctor suspected she was going to go a few more days before they became serious about inducing—and still hadn't picked a name for their daughter. A middle name was simple—he agreed on his wife's mother's name. Not Italian, but that didn't matter so much.

The first name?

That was trickier.

It had to be perfect.

This little girl?

His first child?

Blood from his veins?

Yeah, that name had to be perfect, and he didn't give a shit what anybody thought about it. Haven might be annoyed that he was being as picky as he was, but oh, well. His daughter was going to have a name that represented her, their legacy, and whatever else he wanted.

Simple as that.

"Rose," Haven said.

"Save it."

"What are we *saving* all these names for?"

"Other babies," Andino muttered, opening a new tab on the computer to bring up his email. This had been their last two weeks in a nutshell. His wife scouring the internet for baby names, and then incessantly following him around to list them off while he veto'd, said *maybe*, or asked to save the name for a later date. All the while, she loudly and repeatedly let him know how ridiculous he was being about picking a *name*. "We might need them."

"*Other babies.*"

"That's what I said, Haven."

He peered at her over the top edge of the monitor, but he quickly realized that was a fucking mistake. She glared right back at him like if it were possible, he might be dead where he sat. God, he loved that about his wife. She took no shit, and when everyone else around him was willing to bend to him like he was a king, this woman was the first to remind him a king always bowed for his queen, too.

"What?" he asked.

Stupidly.

Did people know that?

Men were stupid anyway, but when their wife became pregnant, hormonal, and in Haven's case, *very much ready* to have this baby out of her body ... men became impossibly dumber. They said and did stupid things with the intention to make their wife happy or just get a smile out of her, but really ... no, it never worked.

Like now.

"You can at least wait," Haven said, every word measured, "for this child to get out of my body before you start harping on more."

"I don't *harp*."

Haven pursed her lips before glancing back down at the notepad in her hands. How many pages had she filled with lists after lists after *lists* of names for him? None of them seemed to fit, and he wished this was easier. Not just for himself, but for her, too.

Everything else about this pregnancy had been rather easy. All things considered. Her morning sickness went away after the second trimester. They didn't have any problems. All the checkups went well.

Picking a name?

Not so much.

"Andino ..."

"Maybe we'll just know when she's here," he said.

Haven peeked back up, smiling a little. "You think? Because you are seriously driving me crazy. You are the most stressful part of this pregnancy, Andino, and even though I love you ... if you don't pick a name for this kid ... just pick a goddamn name."

He knew this whole process was difficult for Haven, if only because she was a planner. As soon as they knew the baby was a girl, the room she picked for a nursery across the hall from their master bedroom was turned into a pastel *wonderland.* And that huge canopy crowning a circular crib that cost more than the four-poster bed in his room?

Yeah.

Silk and chiffon.

The baby's closet was full of clothes, dresses, and shoes. More than he had, and God knew he liked to spend money. That child was going to need and want for nothing for the first three or so years of her life because between Haven getting everything ready, and his family constantly buying shit they would probably never use, their house was full.

Ready for the baby.

She just had to make her appearance.

Without a name.

He could wait until the baby was here, and go through those lists again, but a name lingered on the back of his mind, and occasionally, he kept coming back to it. It was one of the first Haven had suggested because she thought it was nice to match her mother's name with his for their baby girl. He'd only veto'd it back then because, well ... he felt like it was too early.

"I do like Lynn," he said.

Haven raised a brow. "Oh, *now* you like it?"

"No, I liked it then, too. I just thought ... what if we settled on Lynn, and something else came up? Nothing's come up, and it seems kind of perfect."

"Your mom would love that."

Yeah, even though his mother had always gone by *Kim*, she loved the *Lynn* to the end of her name. And he liked the idea of carrying it on, too.

"So, is that *firm* on Lynn?" Haven asked.

Andino grinned. "*Well* ... maybe, we'll just keep looking—"

"Oh, my God, Andino. Stop it."

His laughter colored up the office.

"It's firm, if you like it, too."

"I loved it. That's why it was first on my list."

"So, Lynn?"

Haven nodded. "Lynn Marcello."

GIRLS, GIRLS, GIRLS

"How," Haven asked as the two women sat down at the table, "did I manage to get here before the two of you, *and* I'm three days over my due date?"

Siena laughed. "Come on, you *know* traffic sucks. And you pick the worst time of day for us to have to meet up."

"Lies. I can't help it that I never run into traffic like you do."

"And," Catherine added, "some of us—*me*—just got back in from Cali last night, so …"

Haven rolled her eyes playfully. "Excuses, excuses."

Their laughter drew the attention of the other patrons at the restaurant, but Haven didn't really care. Let them look, she hoped they enjoyed their gawking.

The one thing she worried about the most after marrying Andino? That she wouldn't be able to *make friends*. In his family, mostly. She felt like an outsider coming in, not that anyone had gone out of their way to make her feel as such, but she still did. The Marcellos had lived an entire life within the mafia, and keeping people *out* … Haven had been normal up until the day she met Andino, and she worried that might make it a little difficult to fit in.

And then there was these two.

Siena and Catherine.

Close to her age, also newly married, *fun* … and just her kind of people. They didn't care about the details, or rules.

They just liked her.

And she liked them.

"When are they going to induce you so I can meet my cousin?" Catherine asked. "But she's calling me Auntie C, and that's decided."

Haven sighed, and rubbed a hand over her swell, remembering how Andino had taken the time to do the exact same thing that morning before he headed out to work. In fact, he did that very thing *every* morning for her entire pregnancy, taking the time to stop and say hello to his unborn daughter, not to mention, tell her how much he loved her and couldn't wait to meet her. It was sweet, really … a moment of his loving nature underneath his calm, controlled exterior. Nobody else but her was able to see those parts of him, and she

334

loved it.

"This weekend," Haven said, "if I don't go into labor naturally."

"Worried?" Catherine asked.

Haven shrugged as the server approached their table. "Not really—more about *how* they plan to induce me, and less about the birth itself. I mean, I have kind of came to the conclusion that I won't be able to control anything about the birth. I say I'll do it all naturally, and then I have false contractions for like five hours, and I seriously start to consider an epidural. So, let's just wait and see how it goes."

"I get that."

Siena made a face. "I hear the drip is … rough."

"Right? Anyway, I am trying *everything* to get this girl to come out on her own before the weekend so I don't have to worry about it."

"The usual, ladies?"

The server hadn't even bothered to pull the pad and pen out of her apron. All the employees at Andino's restaurant were used to seeing Haven come in and out, not for the last few months … Catherine, Siena, *and* Haven all made an effort to come each Wednesday to have breakfast, a late brunch, or lunch depending on their schedules. Sometimes, it was just Siena and Haven, if Catherine was out the state for work, too.

Nonetheless, they were used to them.

"Yeah, that sounds good," Catherine said, "oh, and that raspberry tea for Haven."

"That sounds *disgusting.*"

"I heard it's good for dilation."

Haven considered that. "Fine, I'll suck it up."

"So, you're really trying *everything?*" Siena asked, grinning just a bit.

"Pretty much."

"I mean … *everything?*"

Even Catherine snickered at that.

Haven blamed it on mommy brain, even if her baby wasn't born yet—wait, was *pregnancy* brain a thing, too?—why she couldn't figure out what Siena was trying to say. "Why are you both snickering like teenage girls?"

"Sex," Catherine said, reaching across the table to snag a packet of sugar for the coffee the server had poured into her mug. "She's asking if you're having a lot of sex, and if so, we hope it's been *good* sex."

Just like that, Haven understood.

Her cheeks pinked.

The easy answer?

And the obvious one?

Yes.

Actually, she swore from the *moment* Andino knew she was pregnant, it was like his desire to fuck jumped up a notch or two. Not like he didn't already try to get her horizontal on whatever flat surface that he could whenever he had the chance, but add pregnancy to it, and the man was fucking insatiable.

It didn't matter how big she got, or the fact that with being bigger came difficulties which made them need to figure out more interesting ways to get the deed done ... he still loved it, and frankly, so did she.

Sex was great when pregnant.

Nerves for *days.*

And that man found every single one of them.

"Well?" Siena asked.

Haven grinned. "Yeah, that, too."

"Get it as much as you can now," Catherine said, winking, "because once the princess is here, you know what they say ... at least for a little while, there'll be none of that."

"Shame, that is."

She meant that, too. In every sense of the word.

Their laughter drew attention again.

Haven didn't care.

Women should draw attention.

Girls made the world go round.

She rubbed her stomach again, feeling the baby shift under her palm, reminding her that soon ... she would be adding another girl to their little crew. She couldn't wait.

WOMEN

"Are you going back inside?" Lucian asked.

"Yeah," Dante added, shooting Andino a smirk, "isn't that where you're supposed to be?"

Andino ignored his uncles' teasing. His father, leaning against the railing of the back porch while they enjoyed the sun just beginning to set and the comfortable weather, tipped his beer up for a long swig, shaking his head all the while.

"He was told to stay the fuck out of the kitchen for a while."

Dante arched a brow. "Why?"

"She's in pain."

"*And?* That's—"

"I figure when she threatens to cut off my balls, and considering they set her up in the middle of the kitchen in that pool, so she's closer to the knife drawer ..." Andino trailed off, shrugging his broad shoulders. "I'm not stupid, that's all."

Lucian chuckled. "Never thought we'd be doing a willing home birth in the family."

Yeah.

Andino, neither.

He didn't say that out loud, however.

Yes, he would much prefer putting his wife in a damn hospital while she birthed their first baby girl. With doctors and nurses and pain medication and whatever else she needed right at her fingertips whenever she was ready to demand it.

She wanted that, too, at first.

Hell, right up until this past week, she wanted that. And then the doctors kept saying *inducing*. Shit like *medical intervention*. She looked at him one night in their bed and just asked, "*Why won't they let my body do what it's supposed to do? Why are they trying to make it do what they want it to do?*"

And just like that, with only a few days to plan, their birth plan changed.

So, here they were with a midwife, a doula, her mother, and the other women of their family with her for the birth. Something that would never be possible in a hospital considering they only seemed to allow two people maximum in the birthing suites. So, a home birth it was with all the bells and whistles Haven wanted.

Andino's anxiety was through the roof.

What if something went wrong?

What if they needed help?

What if—

"Everything is looking fine in there," said a familiar man as he stepped out the back door, and took the vacant chair next to Lucian.

Next to the midwife Haven wanted, Andino also got the doctor *he* wanted. However, the man was only allowed in the kitchen occasionally to check on the progression of things and make sure everything was fine. If something seemed off, or Haven changed her mind about this whole birth plan at any point in time, then they would take her to a hospital with the doctor en route.

Although, this was Haven's first birth. According to the midwife, and the doctor, everything seemed fine. Haven wasn't high risk—her pregnancy progressed entirely normal, and so did her labor thus far. Nothing screamed dangerous except for the fact that this wasn't the norm … or what he always considered the norm for a birth being they weren't in the usual hospital setting. But lots of women gave birth at home, so it should be perfectly fine. Or, that's what everyone kept telling him whenever he voiced his concerns.

That helped his anxiety.

Slightly.

"And she's asked for you," the man added. "You should hurry, she's getting ready to push."

Andino nodded. "Thanks."

Pushing away from the banister, Andino felt his father's hand land to his shoulder with a supportive pat. Inside the house, he followed the back hallway to the front, and then he lingered just beyond the doorway of the kitchen to appreciate the scene inside.

The women surrounding his wife.

The *silence.*

Leaning over the edge of the pool that had been set up in the middle of the kitchen floor where their island usually rested—it was now pushed to the far end of the kitchen, entirely out of the way— Haven's doula nodded to whatever his wife had just said. The midwife, bent down to peer into the water grinned when she straightened up.

His mother smiled wide.

His cousins ... *happy.*

His aunts, waiting.

All these women ... all of them who had been through this very thing. Or experienced it in one way or another. And he kind of understood then, in Haven's pain as she let out a hard breath, and reached for her mother's outstretched hand, why she wanted *this* energy here.

Instead of a hospital, with beeping monitors, and doctors and nurses coming in and out whom she didn't know and wouldn't understand *her* ... he finally truly understood why this had been the energy in the room that she wanted when their daughter was born. The women in this room were—by far—some of the strongest he had ever known.

His mother, shamed and shunned by her own family, still came out on top.

His aunts—one who came from nothing, disabused and who had every reason to fail, *survived* and thrived; and his other aunt, who also came from nothing, was the definition of self-made, and who could rival her own husband for the most dangerous person in the room.

His cousins ... women who battled their own demons.

Haven's mother, a cancer survivor.

These women were everything that strength encompassed. It was powerful. Women were powerful. And men were nothing without them.

Including him.

"There you are," the midwife said, waving a hand to encourage Andino into the kitchen, "come look, and see how close we are."

We.

Not just Haven.

Because she wasn't doing it alone.

Birth was a process.

An experience.

And it was better *shared.*

For some.

Andino came into Haven's view, and she was already reaching for him. Hair damp, and pushed back, gaze hazy from pain but still so clear with what was close and coming faster with every passing second. His hand found hers, and the two of them suddenly became the only people in the room when their stares met.

"Love you," he told her.

Haven nodded, her throat jumping with a swallow. "So much, Andino."

Lynn Marcello made her way into the world—into her father's waiting hands—at three-oh-four in the afternoon on a Saturday. She was perfect. Her father cried.

And a whole army of women greeted her.

A whole legacy of women *loved her.*

SNAPS THE REINDEER

Clicking between the photos on the screen of his laptop, Andino surveyed the damage that had been bound to happen. The raid on Chinatown, an effort put forth by a task force meant to keep the sale of counterfeit goods at a minimum in New York, ended up putting a major dent into a good portion of John's business on his side of the city. Of course, Andino had a guy with a crew in Chinatown distributing fake—and stolen, real goods—for sale but the main Marcello operation hadn't taken nearly as bad of a hit as John had.

"What are you thinking—total, I mean," Andino clarified.

On the speaker of the call, John cleared his throat. "A third of a million. There's a shipment coming in off a boat next month, so long as it clears customs, that'll get business there back up and running like nothing."

"The only good part of counterfeiting, really."

John chuckled. "Hmm, tell me about it. A low-grade crime."

"Still frustrating."

"And a handful of people spending their Christmas in a jail cell, too," John added.

Yes, that couldn't be forgotten.

Except Andino didn't really care.

After all, it wasn't him in jail. And honestly, that was really the only thing he cared about at the end of the day. Selfish? Oh, certainly.

And?

Because he didn't see the problem with it.

Maybe that wast he bigger issue. Andino wasn't really interested in looking too deep into his psyche or what made him … well, him. He'd learned long ago that he was fine with the way he was—it was everyone else who had the issue.

That seemed like a them problem. And they should probably deal with it.

"Well," John started to say on the call, "Nature of the business, isn't it?"

"Unfortunately."

The giggling from the hallway had Andino looking away from his laptop. John said something else in reply, but Andino was a little distracted by the sight of his blonde-haired daughter peeking her head into the doorway of his office.

All of five-years-old and little Lynn Marcello was the entire light of Andino's fucking life. The only thing he ever needed to do to smile was look at his children or wife. In an instant, they could turn a shitty day around or make his bad moods disappear in a blink.

Lynn's curly head bobbed and her big eyes twinkled with mischief. Marcello mischief, he liked to say.

"Go," he heard her say to something—or someone—out in the hallway.

"I'll call you back," Andino told John.

"Okay, man. Have a good night. We doing Christmas Eve again this year together? Siena wanted to know so she could get everything ready. You know how she is."

"Of course."

"All right, good to know. See you then."

"You, too."

"Come on, Snappy."

Snappy.

It didn't matter how many times they told Lynn the dog's name was Snaps, she called him Snappy from the moment she could say his name. And he answered to it.

Her Snappy.

"Baby Lynn," Andino said, grinning when she popped her head into the doorway again, "what are you up to out there?"

"Nothing, Daddy." Then, lower, she said to the dog in the hallway, "*Pleaseeeeee*, Snappy?"

Andino swore he heard the dog sigh. It was a real thing Snaps did, but especially when he was just about done with his human counterparts. The click-click of the dog's fingernails hitting hardwood announced his presence before he even showed himself in Andino's doorway.

It took everything—every single ounce of patience and self-control—he had inside not to laugh when his dog strolled into the office wearing a pair of antlers that lit up like Christmas lights, with a little Santa hat right in the middle. His big, muscular head tipped side to side as he walked across the office, the antlers following the action. Baby Lynn's giggles followed him the whole way.

"It's Snappy the Reindeer!" his daughter introduced the pup.

Andino pressed his lips together to keep from laughing as Snaps came to sit beside his master's desk. The dog looked up at him, half amused and entirely over it at the same time.

"You look ridiculous," Andino told him under his breath.

Snaps blew out a snort.

Like he was saying, *I know.*

In the hallway, Baby Lynn's peeling laughter followed her as she ran away from her father's office. "*Snappy the Reindeer says Merry Christmas!*"

LITTLE G.

"Hey."

Haven's head lifted from her work at the kitchen's island. Those blue eyes of hers nailed into Andino where he stood in the arched entryway of the room, half in the process of shrugging on his favorite navy blazer.

"Are you seriously going to sneak out of here without even a proper good morning?" his wife asked.

He at least had the decency to look ashamed of himself, but Andino couldn't say much more about it. "I'm already running late, babe."

Haven arched a brow. "*Seriously?*"

"You let me sleep in—didn't even get me up to get the girls off to school."

Not that he didn't appreciate it, because he did—as many kids as they had, every morning could be a goddamn nightmare. Somehow, though, Haven managed to wrangle all their daughters off to school without waking him up. Instead, the small knee of his son that landed a little too close to the family jewels became his alarm clock. Probably not long after Haven got back from getting the girls off to school.

That also meant he was late.

Well ...

A boss was never late.

Everyone else was always early.

Except Andino had a lot of business happening in the city—an uptick in certain areas of *la famiglias* dealings that required more of his immediate attention. The shit had been dragging him away from home earlier and earlier, and keeping him away later and later.

Haven knew it was part of their life, yeah. She rarely complained, although she never hid when she was unhappy with something, either. It at least allowed Andino the chance to correct whatever his wife felt was wrong before it got worse. He still made it his first and last effort every day to keep the mafia's business from affecting what went on within the four walls of his family's home.

She liked it that way.

What more could he say?

"I let you sleep in," Haven shot back, the tiny smile curving her lips telling him the truth. She wasn't all that mad that he was slipping out of the house without as much as a good morning—or a thank you—after the night before. "And I even fucked you last night, too. And you can't take three seconds to kiss me good morning before you leave? *Asshole.*"

Andino laughed.

He couldn't help it.

Except his laugh came out dark and husky because if she thought he forgot last night for a second—his wife was deadass *wrong.* Andino took a few quick steps into the large kitchen—they'd renovated it six months ago, going from a country-style to something more clean and modern now that their kids were getting a bit older and understood to leave shit alone.

Mostly.

He was still working with little G.

The boy was wild. Fearless to an extreme, and he respected the free soul his son was too much to try and tamper the kid's behaviors and moods.

Andino loved it.

"You know how much I like when you wait up for me, babe," Andino said, still crossing the kitchen.

Haven had turned a bit to the side, now watching him approach the island from the corner of her eye. That grin of hers curved a little more—sweet to sexy in a damn blink. "Even when you say not to."

"And wear *lace.*"

She flashed her teeth in a smile that time, replying, "Under silk."

Andino couldn't help his grunt of approval when his hands landed to the edge of the marble countertop on the island. Leaving over the pristine white, he found the side of his wife's soft cheek while his hair swept her hair out of the way of her throat. Then, his thumb had better access to sweep over the tattoo behind her ear. The shiver that answered his action back only had him smirking when she turned her head just enough to catch his mouth with her own.

That quick kiss turned into something far more sinful before he had time to consider it. Her tongue teased his mouth open before daring to flick inside and back out before his could tangle with hers.

"*Mean,*" he muttered when she pulled away.

"Or giving you something to get back faster for," she shot back.

He didn't need reminders.

Andino *knew.*

Very well.

"Good morning," he added, winking as he took a step back from the island. "See, I didn't sneak out without doing it."

"You considered it."

Only a little.

He had catching up to do.

Haven still needed to come first, though.

"Promise I won't," he said, her narrowing gaze making him add quickly, "try again."

That had Haven's grin growing all over again. She stuck her tongue out at him, before handing over a jam and cream cheese bagel half wrapped in wax paper. He hadn't even noticed the food sitting on a plate on the counter.

Haven had a way of distracting him.

Constantly.

"Eat something on your way," she said, "that actually came from your house."

"Will do."

One more kiss to his wife's lips, and Andino headed back out of the kitchen. He was just rounding the entry stairs to exit through the front door where he'd left his Bentley parked the night before when the familiar whoops of his son echoed from the upstairs.

Then, a loud, "*Wait for me, Papa! I'm coming, too!*"

He didn't have to wait long to find out what Giovanni Andino was up to. Little G came down the staircase as fast as his legs could take him, already dressed in a pair of black jeans and the white t-shirt his mother had dressed him in that morning. The same outfit he'd woken his father up wearing. But now, he was pulling on one of his newest suit jackets that Haven had gotten Andino's tailor to make for the boy for church.

Growing spurts didn't stop.

Gio went through clothes like *crazy.*

"I'm coming, too!" little G said, his hand sliding down the banister as his two feet managed to sound like a whole herd of elephants coming down the stairs. "I do business with you, too, Papa. Right?"

Bemusement colored up Andino—the sight of his only son dressed up like his father, wanting to *do business* like he had any clue about that shit. He didn't—wouldn't for a while, yet. Hopefully for as long as Andino could reasonably manage to keep it that way. Forever wasn't an option, but he distinctly remembered the weird lines that had been drawn around the fathers and sons he knew when Cosa Nostra came into their lives as a permanent pillar.

Fuck him for not wanting his relationship with his own son to change, yet.

Even if Gio was only four.

"I can come with you, Papa, right?" little G asked, coming to a stop at the bottom of the stairs.

Just beyond, where he had come from the kitchen, Haven came to stand in the entry, watching him. Waiting, he knew, to see what he would say.

The problem was hard.

The answer was still easy.

"Get your shoes, little man," Andino told his son, his large hand reaching out to snag little G at the scruff of his neck to pull him closer to his father. Instantly, a happy Gio smiled up at him, hugging his hip and wrapping his legs around his father's left one like a fucking monkey.

"*Yes!*" Gio shouted.

"Andi—"

He glanced Haven's way even as he headed for the line of shoes stacked neatly on their shelves by the coatroom. "Can't tell him no, can I? Then, he's already going to be sad about it."

And shit.

He just couldn't take that.

People could call Andino a lot of things, but a monster wasn't one of them. All it took was the simple sadness of his kids to turn him into a groveling *mat* of a human being.

Fuck it.

He was fine with that.

PRESENT WRAPPING – ANDINO STYLE

John POV

"You're not going to tell me what's in those duffle bags, are you?" Siena asked.

On the doorstep of his cousin's home, John angled his body—*and* the bags holding all of his wife's *unwrapped* Christmas presents— further out of her view and reach. "How about you just stay over there and mind your business?"

"You seriously brought my gifts for Andino to wrap, didn't you?"

John kept his face a mask of calm. "No."

"*Lies,*" came a call from behind them.

Jonny, that was.

Their youngest.

Snickers passed amongst his three kids.

Teenagers were … monsters. A breed all of their own. They were also amazing little humans and he didn't have the first clue how he and Siena managed to raise their three kids to this point but here they were.

Little adults.

Almost.

It scared the fuck out of him.

He liked it, too.

"Hey, anything in there for—"

John yanked the bag away from the reach of Lucky, his oldest. Giving the sixteen-year-old a look, he muttered, "And you keep your slick fingers far away from every Christmas present, kid. Swear to God if I find you opened all your gifts again this year before Christmas morning—"

Lucky sighed and rolled his eyes. "I *won't.*"

Right.

Well …

John didn't believe that for a second.

His daughter thought to open her smartass mouth and join in with her brothers and mother but Andino decided to finally save the fucking day by opening his front door. It wasn't like they hadn't rung the doorbell five damn minutes earlier.

"Come on, get out of the goddamn cold," Andino grumbled, waving his arms to get everybody off the stoop as fast as he could. A warm house with the loudness of life and something sweet lingering in the air greeted John and his broad. "Not paying to heat the outside of this fucking place, am I?"

John chuckled under his breath. He would never tell his cousin, but the older they became, the more Andino reminded him of their uncle Dante, and their grandfather Antony. In little ways, sure, but it was still there all the same.

Siena followed after their kids but not before giving John a kiss to his cheek before she went. The hallway cleared out before John could even tell his kids to behave. However, at the sight of their coats hung up on the rack and their shoes all lined up nicely against the wall with Andino's kids' things, John figured ...

They didn't need to be told today.

They knew.

Andino, however, continued to stare at the two duffles John carried. "Please tell me you didn't bring *more* presents for me to wrap?"

Well ...

John gave his cousin his *you're the best* smile. "So listen—"

"Fuck you, John."

*

Andino POV

"It's just ... listen, you have this way of wrapping presents and—"

Andino sighed louder than was necessary *just* to make John shut up. "Yes, but I also have to wrap all of our presents tonight because guess what? It's *Christmas Eve*. Oh, and Haven can't wrap - and our kids are little snoops so she's just hid everything until last minute."

Spinning on his heel in front of the master bedroom door, Andino faced his grinning cousin. He had the slightest urge to wipe that smirk from John's face but at the same time, he couldn't help but laugh at the absurdity of it all. With their kids downstairs tearing the place up and their wives in the kitchen cooking supper and sweets, it was going to be a quiet Christmas Eve.

"Really?" John asked.

Andino shrugged. "I mean, at least she paid someone to wrap mine. She *really* doesn't like this part of the holidays. I was busy, and let it pile up. It's my fault, too."

John let out a breath, offering one of the duffles to Andino. "I'll help—deal?"

He eyed the bag. "You wrap - I decorate the gifts."

John's grin deepened.

Andino shook his head. "Don't even start. I can't help that I get particular about it."

"You mean, that you need actual ribbon for bows and gift tags that look like Martha Stewart crafted them?"

He did his best not to glare.

Really made an effort.

And failed.

John simply chuffed like he didn't expect anything less from his cousin. "Yeah, I wouldn't start anything at all about that. Why would I?"

Andino snatched the bag out of his cousin's hand. "*You wrap,* I decorate."

"Deal."

JOHN | ANDINO | MICHEL

THE COUSINS

Andino POV

"Black leather was *not* the fucking way to go," Andino grumbled, shifting on the passenger seat again to try and get somewhat comfortable. It really wasn't working. "Seriously, do you have the fucking seat warmers on, or what?"

John laughed, and passed his cousin a look. He got a kick out of the way Andino was trying *not* to put too much weight onto the seat. "No, the seat warmers aren't on. What, did you want me to pick white leather so you can spill shit all over it, or ... ?"

Andino scowled. "I don't—"

"Man, you dropped a burger all over my fucking *seats*. And then made a bigger mess when you tried to clean it up. Oh, and the fucking *slushie*. Do you remember that shit?"

"I was drunk!"

"Yeah, not a good reason to spill electric blue slushie all over my fucking car, Andi."

Andino had a good mind to tell his cousin to go fuck himself, but it would only be because he was trying to save some of his pride. It wasn't like John was lying, or anything. Andino was not a food and car kind of person. Some people could eat in cars and not make a mess, and some people—*him*, mainly—could not.

It was that simple.

"Do you know how much money I had to pay to get the car detailed after that happened?" John asked, still ranting away.

"No."

"A thousand dollars!"

"Bet Uncle Lucian appreciated that."

John's gaze narrowed. "He thought I did it, actually."

Andino snorted. "That's hilarious."

"Shut up, Andi."

Finally, the air conditioner in the new Mercedes really kicked in, and Andino found the leather was slightly easier to stand it. John

351

must have left his car sitting right out in the damn sun because the seats had been hotter than the Devil's ass when he first got in the fucking car.

"So, we going to the city, or elsewhere today?" John asked.

Andino shrugged, and scrolled through his phone. A new text popped up which made him quirk a brow. "Wherever. Hey, Michel wants to meet up."

John drummed his fingers to the steering wheel, and nodded. "Yeah, bet he wants a pickup for the next week."

"He's just getting out of classes."

Michel, their cousin, was in his final year of school. Andino went to a completely different school than Michel—his parents put him in a private establishment, while Andino's parents had him placed in a public school. Not that Andino minded. He didn't give a fuck where he went to school as long as he graduated so he didn't have to *keep* going. John, already graduated, didn't even bother with college before he just went straight into the family business.

Andino figured … that's probably exactly what he was going to do, too. No point in beating around the bush. Andino had zero interest in college, and the mafia was in his blood.

Family business it was.

Right after he got fucking *high school* out of the way.

"Yeah, we'll grab Michel. See if he's got something interesting to do today," John said absently while he merged onto the highway. "Let him know we'll be there in twenty."

"It's a forty minute drive to his school from here."

John hit the gas harder. "Actually, let's see if we can make it in fifteen, then."

Jesus Christ.

Well, at least John was always up for some kind of fun.

*

Michel POV

Michel whistled at the sight of the sleek, black two-door Mercedes that pulled up along the entrance to the Academy. Standing from the steps, he shrugged the messenger bag over his shoulder, and neared the vehicle as Andino stepped out the passenger side. Moving the front seat forward a bit so Michel could get into the back, Andino gestured at his cousin.

"Your ride awaits," Andino joked.

"When did you get this?" Michel asked, sliding into the backseat.

In the front, John passed a look into the rearview mirror. "Finally got in today. Delivered it this morning."

"Where's the old—"

"Dad's gonna sell it."

Michel nodded. "Nice."

It took no time at all for the three cousins to be out on the road, and Michel was glad to have the Academy behind him. Not that he hated school, he didn't. An Ace student for every class, he found school incredibly easy. And boring.

That was half the damn problem.

Michel needed something to really challenge him when it came to education. The fucking Academy was not doing it anymore. It didn't matter—this time next year, he'd be in Detroit getting his shit together to start pre-med. He just had to make it through this last year of shit before he got there.

"Did you skip today?" he asked Andino.

The largest of the three cousins, although he wasn't the oldest, nodded. "Yeah, I got better shit to do than listen to some white guy tell me about the history of America."

Michel laughed. "They never tell it right, anyway."

"Exactly."

"Gonna loose your spot on the football team, won't you?"

That did make Andino scowl. "Yeah, well … whatever. What do you want to do today, anyway? John figured you'd have something for us to do. That's the only reason we drove all the way over here to pick your ass up."

"Right."

His cousins grinned, and even Michel couldn't help but laugh at the sight. Michel didn't have a lot of friends—sure, he knew a lot of people. He supplied his whole school when it came to drugs, for fuck's sake. Some might consider him the most popular person just for that fact. Sure, he had people all around him. He didn't consider a single of them to be an actual friend, though.

No, he reserved that for his family.

His *cousins*.

The only people he let fuck with him, really. Anyone else was liable to get a punch in the damn mouth. God knew Michel had his mother's temper, and his father's lack of patience for bullshit.

Or ... other people's bullshit, anyway.

But that wasn't the case when it came to his cousins. He didn't mind any of their bullshit, and they never meant any harm. Besides, with Andino and John ... Michel didn't have to be anybody else. He wasn't the kid with the drugs in his locker to sell, or the bright student who could always answer every question. His last name didn't meant shit to Andino and John because they had the same one as him, and that just meant they were family.

He could just be Michel.

He liked that a lot.

"Let's get food," Michel said.

"That all?"

"Is that ever all, John?"

His cousin smirked. "What else, man?"

"Food first, then we'll go down to Odessa and walk along the docks. See who we can find down there."

He didn't expect to find anybody at the docks, but that was kind of the point. They'd figure something out once they got there. And if they didn't, fuck it, fun usually found them, anyway.

A day with his cousins sounded better than sitting at home doing homework he already knew he was going to ace. It wasn't like the teachers at the Academy actually gave a shit if he did his work or not, anyway.

God, Michel needed to graduate already.

*

John POV

John caught Andino smirking at a girl walking down below the docks from the corner of his eye. When the girl grinned back, Andino winekd and waved two fingers. Not even thinking about it, John struck out and punched his cousin right in the shoulder to get his head back on task.

"Ow, you stupid fuck," Andino muttered, his attention back on John instead of the pretty piece of ass down below. "She was fuckin' cute."

"You're fucking cute," John replied. "What, are you gonna take a cab home when I leave your ass here because you decided to chase a pretty girl down the beach?"

"Might be better than listening to you the whole way."

Michel snickered on the other side of John, but quickly quieted when he shot his other cousin a look.

"What did I miss?" Andino asked. "Michel and this Detroit shit, right?"

"He needs connections there, that's all I'm saying."

Michel sighed. "I don't need *connections*, man."

"First of all, you're a Marcello."

"You need some kind of connections," Andino said, finishing what John didn't say. "Even if it's just to keep in the know, or have somebody to watch your back."

John jerked a thumb in Andino's direction. "Yeah, that right there. Exactly that, man. Nobody's gonna be looking out for you there like they do here, all right. You need connections."

"There's a faction there. A syndicate of the Marcellos. I'm sure—"

"Somebody's gonna need to make calls," Andino put in.

"What if I don't want connections?" Michel asked suddenly. "What if I just want to go to Detroit, focus on school, and say fuck the family business. It's not like I've really been *in it*, you know what I mean? Not like you two are, anyway."

John cleared his throat, and rested his arms along the railing of the docks. Michel wasn't wrong ... he'd never been as hands-on or involved in business like he and Andino had been for the majority of their lives. It never caused an issue in their trio, but it was a fact. "Like at all?"

Michel shrugged. "I never really thought about what I was gonna do after, I guess."

"Should probably figure that out." Andino glanced over at Michel, and shrugged his broad shoulders. "Not that we're gonna give a fuck either way, you know. But for you ... figure out what you want to do, man. That's all I'm saying."

John agreed. "But you still need connections."

Michel sighed, but silently agreed with a nod of his own.

That was just a fact of their life. Involved, or not. Michel was a Marcello. He might not make the calls to ensure he had some kind of protection when he finally took off for Detriot, but John would. Andino, too.

It'd be strange, he thought … for his cousin to be states away, and not just a drive across the city. It'd suck to have their trio drop down to just him and Andino … but this was what Michel wanted, so it was what he was going to do. They weren't going to say a thing about it either way because why should they?

As for John and Andino, well, they'd still be waiting to pick up where they left off when Michel got back. Because that was another guarantee when it came to being a Marcello.

They always came back home.

It's what family did.

RENZO | LUCIA

WHAT.

"Why are you knocking?" Renzo asked.

Lucia laughed, shrugging. "You'll see."

Reaching up, she knocked on the large double doors of the Marcello mansion again. Renzo was right, though. Rarely did she knock when she visited this place. For another Marcello, it was an open-door policy at this home. They came, and they walked right in, just like that. But things had changed since the last time they came here and had dinner with the entire, very large, Marcello family, and she had seen this scene play out one too many times with her other cousins.

A tradition was a tradition.

Renzo didn't have to understand.

He would soon enough.

Beside her, Renzo shook his head with a little laugh. They'd only moved back to New York a couple of weeks ago, and as they'd still been settling into their new place—a penthouse in the city that allowed Lucia to be close to the gallery she would be working at for her aunt, Kim, until she decided to move onto her own thing.

Renzo still traveled back and forth to Vegas a lot. Every couple of weeks, or so. Next week, he would be heading back for … something. A job, probably, with The League, but she didn't ask for details. It was easier that way, although she knew that if she asked, he would say.

She chose not to ask.

Soon, she could hear muffled movement behind the large, thick doors keeping her and Renzo separated from the rest of her family inside the home. They hadn't been able to make it to Sunday services because moving was fucking exhausting. Usually, there were no excuses, short of illness, that would allow a Marcello to miss Mass on Sundays, but moving across country and still trying to unpack a lot of shit allowed them a little leg room.

And of course, her family missed her.

They wanted her back in New York with them where she

belonged, and this was where Lucia wanted to be here, too, because this had always been and would always be her home. Even when she was mad at the world, her father, brother, and anyone that remotely reminded her of them, she still missed New York like nothing else.

She belonged here.

So, they said nothing about a missed service or two.

When the mansion doors were pulled open, Lucia was already smiling. Renzo reached out to sling an arm around her neck, and drag her closer to his side. His lips pressed down to the top of her head as the cheers from within the house started.

Her mother was the first.

Quickly followed by her cousins, aunts, and literally everyone else.

It took no time at all for them to be pulled inside the mansion, and for the doors to be shut. With the rest of the world out of view, they were able to focus on their family and showing off the engagement ring on Lucia's finger.

"Let me get a good look at that ring!"

"Congratulations!"

"Oh, wow, it looks great," her mother said when Lucia held out her hand for her mother to admire the engagement ring that she had already laid eyes on before. Not that it mattered, because now it was on a new hand, and the family tradition of passing down the engagement rings still held strong in their generation. "Did you suspect a thing?"

"She did not," Renzo said, grinning beside her.

"Not at all?" Catherine asked.

"Did *you?*" her husband asked.

She gave Cross a look. 'Well—"

"You didn't either."

"And it was perfect," Catherine assured.

Cross simply chuckled, shaking his head.

Lucia shrugged, still taking compliments from the rest of her family. Her brother's wife, Siena, smiled wide as she offered her congratulations, and leaned in to give Lucia a kiss on her cheek. John wasn't very far behind.

After everything, all Lucia could do was smile at her brother. They'd been through hell and back, but God knew she loved her brother more than she could ever explain. Despite it all, he was still her very best friend and she wouldn't give him up for the world. Yes, it took a little bit of time to get back to that good place with him, but she didn't mind putting in the effort. It was worth it.

"You look happy," he murmured, leaning in for a hug.

She took it, and squeezed back tightly. "I am."

"Glad to see you back."

"Me, too, John."

"*So* ..." All eyes turned on Catrina who looked Renzo's way. "How did it happen?"

Instantly, Lucia felt the heat rise in her cheeks as her gaze landed on her father who had just come to stand right beside her mother. Lucian's arm hugged her mother's waist as he looked their way expectantly.

"*Well ...*"

She looked to Renzo for help.

He just smirked.

"What is that about?" Lucian asked.

"I mean, there was nothing big or planned about it, I don't think. We were just ... he just asked," Lucia rambled, saying it fast to get them away from *that* subject. "So yeah, and I loved it, that's what counts."

"Why is your face red?" Catherine asked.

"Shut up, Catty."

"Oh." Cross nodded, looking Renzo's way. "You asked like that, huh?"

Renzo chuckled. "Well—"

"Like what?"

"In bed," someone else said.

Just like that, Lucia's father's face suddenly matched her own. Red as could be, and he did his best to avoid everyone's stare.

"What."

Lucian's statement wasn't even a question.

Just a *what*.

"Well, you see," Lucia tried to say, but didn't even get the chance to finish.

"I have told all my kids not to do that in bed, because that is not the story I want to be told. Please tell me you didn't—"

"Technically, we weren't *in* a bed," Renzo interrupted. "And I got her dressed first, so all is good."

"All is *not* good!"

Yep.
Lucia could have died right where she stood.
And still, it was great.

FRAGILITY

"Ren?"

He heard Lucia's call of his name, but couldn't be bothered to even turn his head to answer it. That would take a great deal of effort that he was neither capable of, nor interested in. Since his release from the hospital, the visitors had been nonstop. Apparently, Renzo had more people who cared about them that he thought.

Not that it mattered.

He didn't want to see them.

Or maybe …

He didn't want them to see him like this.

Weak.

Incapable.

Tremors rocking his once steady hands. Scars from surgeries. Burns still healing. Jumbled in his mind. Words that came out wrong.

Everything was wrong.

He hated it.

Which meant he hated himself, too.

Instead, he found solace in sitting near windows watching the day and life outside the apartment where he'd currently holed himself into. More than one person had pointed out he was likely experiencing some depression, and frankly, they weren't wrong. It also didn't make a difference to the fact Renzo had no inspiration or drive to do anything.

Including physical therapy.

Or any of that other shit.

It was tiring.

He hurt.

Why bother?

"Ren," Lucia called again.

"Yeah, in a minute, babe," he answered back quietly.

She just sighed.

She never pushed.

He loved her for that.

"He's like this a lot lately."

"We'll see if I can make a difference with that," came a new, but *familiar* voice.

"Fucking *Cree*," Renzo grumbled.

He didn't even get the chance to turn around on his chair before Cree had come to stand in front of his seat. Without grace or care, the large man dropped down in the couch opposite to Renzo with a leather satchel landing in his lap. Just as quickly, he picked the bag up and tossed it to the coffee table between them.

A few items spilled out.

Bags of beads.

Yellow. White. Red. Black.

Leather cord.

"Is that a stick?" Renzo asked.

"A very flexible stick—I need them when I make medicine wheels."

Renzo's brow furrowed, but Cree didn't seem to mind nor did he apparently have any interest in explaining what he was doing. Leaning forward, he grabbed the satchel and dumped out the remaining contents. The four colored beads came in many sizes. There was quite a bit of brown leather cord. And a few sticks, one of which Cree grabbed along with a leather cord at which he bent into a circle and then began to tie off to keep it that way.

"What are you doing?"

"Making a medicine wheel," Cree said, "although that's what the Europeans and Americans named it—we simply adopted it. And I'm doing it because it relaxes my mind, and reminds me what is most important when I work. My father—he came from a small tribe of Indigenous People located on the eastern shore of a Canadian reserve. Maliseet. My mother—she came from the Cree that settled in Quebec."

"Like your name."

"Was only meant to be a moniker—it ended up sticking. I got used to it, we'll say."

Renzo blinked. "So, what *is* your name?"

Cree continued on from the previous topic like Renzo hadn't asked a *very* important question, "Between my parents, they never let me forget where I came from even when for a long time, I did not know if that was who I wanted to be. Not that it mattered, I came to learn, because I cannot change who I am and I learned I didn't want to."

Renzo had the strangest urge to reach forward and grab one of the sticks. He held off, but then when Cree noticed his gaze, the man nodded in silent encouragement for him to do so. He did, arm trembling because he just couldn't stop it anymore. He fumbled with the sticks in his fingers that no longer seemed to cooperate.

"I can't do *anything*," Renzo said.

"You will," Cree replied simply. "Again, after some time."

"I don't want to hear that. I want—"

"To be who you were, but that isn't who you are, New York. Circumstances change us. Or life. *God*. Women—in my case, a man. And so, we get the opportunity to be a better version of ourselves with a little time, care, and *work*."

Renzo's jaw tightened, but when Cree held out a long length of leather cord for him to take, he did. "I'll never be able to get this tied around mine like you did for yours. My hands don't do what I want them to anymore."

"Maybe not today," Cree agreed, "but on another day you will. See, that's what where the *work* comes in, Ren. And I know you're tired and you're hurting and you feel broken, but none of those things mean you can't work. Be grateful for your body, for your mind and your life, because there are a great many who cannot even hold the stick and the cord like you are right now. You're doing something that a week ago, you might not have been able to do at all. So, next week, what else might you be able to do, hmm?"

Well . . .

No one had said it quite like that before. It was always just *you need to do physical therapy, Ren* or *let's work on your memory.*

"You know, you usually drive me crazy," Renzo said. "I was told by the doctors that you make my blood pressure dangerously high, actually."

"I still will," Cree replied, wrapping the cord around the outer perimeter of his wheel. "Whenever I feel it's needed."

"Why would that be needed?"

Cree looked up from his work and grinned. "Depends on who needs it—you or me?"

That made Renzo laugh.

And shit.

He'd not done that in a while.

"What do the colors mean?" he asked.

"Well, first we start with the circle—it means *life*. The circle of life. Or *all things*. The thing about the colors is that meanings vary between tribes and nations. Some even use blue or green or purple in leu of black. To me, and to my father who taught me how to make my first medicine wheel shortly before he disappeared, the four colors mean many things and represent many elements. Life. Seasons. Medicine. Spirits. Each color must follow the proper direction— white is east, yellow is south, red is west, and black is the north. It is not indicative of tribe or people, but rather, we start in the east like how the sun rises and end up in the north where the sun goes down. Same as life; we start as infants and end up as ancients."

"Did your father ever come back?"

"I eventually found out he had been killed."

Ren flinched. "I'm sorry about your father."

"Circle of life," Cree replied quietly.

"But is it?"

"Sometimes the circle is unfair. Eventually, it also evens out. You should give yours some time to do that for you, and while you wait, *work*."

Renzo considered that. "I will."

"And if you're going to sit here day in and day out, the least you could do is ask that sweet girl in the kitchen to sit with you. She's worried, New York. Although why, I don't know. So, you're wallowing. You always did that."

Yep.

There he was.

"Fuck you, Cree."

"No, thank you. I'm quite good."

"You can leave."

Cree shook his head. "My time is not up—we have at least two hours."

"*For what?*"

"This. Me being here. We'll do it often—what we do will change depending on how much you annoy me and what you're capable of. Also," Cree added quickly when Renzo opened his mouth to refuse, "it wasn't a request. Back to your cord and stick."

Perfect.

Just wonderful.

JOE | LILIANA

HER FIRST SIGHT

"Wait, we're going to watch a movie before dinner, but *nobody* thought to get snacks?" Cella asked, side-eyeing Liliana with a glower that could rival the devil's.

"I can't think of everything!"

Cella nodded. "Mmhmm, sure."

"To be fair," Catherine said, leaning over the counter to grab the piece of apple their mutual friend was slicing, "It was technically my responsibility to get snacks. I was otherwise distracted."

"What does that even—"

"Means she didn't get the fucking snacks," Cella grumbled. "Now we're going to have to drive to the store."

"You pout a lot," Liliana told her sister. "You're going to give yourself wrinkles."

She knew that would do it. Cella's lips pressed together in an effort to keep herself from smiling, or laughing … or both. She failed miserably, which only led the other four girls into a fit of laughter, too.

"And what's wrong with wrinkles, my darlings? Wrinkles tell the story of your *life*."

Liliana spun on her heels to find her grandmother standing in the entryway of the kitchen. Cecelia Marcello, no matter her age, still preferred a pretty dress and heels to something more comfortable. Although lately, Liliana had noticed, her grandmother opted for a shorter, stockier heel to her shoe. Better support, she supposed. Cecelia did not like for it to be pointed out, though.

The girls quieted as Cecelia came further into the kitchen.

"*Your* wrinkles are beautiful, Grandmamma," Liliana said.

Her sister, and cousin, agreed. Their friends only smiled.

Cecelia winked, and bopped Liliana on the nose with the tip of her finger as she passed her by. The same way she always used to do when Liliana was a little girl, and as her grandmother would say, thought she was being *smart*. She wasn't such a little girl anymore— gone were the days of puddle jumping, and instead, were replaced by days in a studio for hours upon hours to be something beautiful and captivating on a stage.

But this weekend was not about being a ballerina. It was her time off. Time to relax, and get back to feeling like a real-life human.

"Your fathers, and uncle are outside on the steps. *Please* do not interrupt their meeting when you head to the store for snacks, ladies."

Just how long had their grandmother been listening to them in the kitchen? Liliana wished she could say she was surprised, but she really wasn't. Cecelia was sneaky—a lot like the rest of them, in their own ways, she supposed.

"You got it, Nan," Catherine said, dropped a quick kiss to Cecelia's cheek as the rest of them headed out of the kitchen in a large group of five.

Liliana hadn't known very much about the meeting her father and uncles were having today, but she knew it was supposed to be important. And that was only because that's literally the only thing her father told her. Well, that and the fact that people were coming in from out of state. Lucian didn't even tell her who it was, or where they were coming from. Simply that they would be having a dinner, and she and her friends should join them for it since they had already planned the movie night at the Marcello mansion.

"Do you know who's coming today?" Liliana asked Catherine.

Her cousin shrugged. "Didn't bother to ask."

Yeah, Catherine was good like that. She didn't stick her nose where she would be told it didn't belong. And God knew their uncle Dante—Catty's father—would be quick to tell anyone who was stepping out of line to mind their own fucking business.

Even if that person was a woman.

"Oh, fresh meat ..."

Cella's words drifted off as Liliana stepped out on the large marble entrance that lead outside the mansion. Her gaze drifted across the huge, circular driveway surrounded by an immaculate, rich green lawn to find exactly what her sister had been talking about.

Or rather, *who*.

An older gentleman stepped out of the back of a black vehicle. A second later, a younger man stepped out of the other side.

Liliana blinked.

One was certainly older, yes, but that didn't change the fact that she could clearly see the similarities—even from a good thirty feet away—between the two men.

Probably related.

Father and son, maybe?

Who knew?

"Hush, you," Lucian said to his second oldest daughter as Cella stuck her tongue out at her father when they passed him by. Their father only winked. "Keep doing that, and it might fall out someday."

The girls were already at the bottom of the steps when their father's retort came from the steps. Probably too quietly for the people across the driveway to hear, not that it really mattered. The girls' laughter colored up the yard, drawing attention their way.

He was staring at her, then.

The younger one.

Liliana stared back as she followed behind her cousin, sister, and friends to where their waiting SUV was parked along the far side of the driveway. He kept staring at her, unblinking and frozen in place. She just kept staring back.

He was handsome, she thought. Strong jaw, sky-blue eyes, and a suit that looked like someone had tailored it perfectly to his form. And what a fucking form it was, really. Broad shoulders, and taller than even her.

She liked a tall man, really.

Liliana realized then that the longer the unknown man stared at her—his gaze didn't even drift to the other four ladies she walked with—the tighter her chest became. And not in a bad way, either.

No, in a really *good* way.

Who was he?

"Front or back?"

Liliana snapped out of her daze to find her sister standing beside the SUV with a hand out to give her the option of which seat she wanted to take. It took her entirely too long to figure that out, and answer.

She slid into the SUV.

"Find something you like?" her cousin asked her, grinning in that way of hers.

Catherine always was like that.

Liliana tried to play it off as the tires of the SUV squealed when they pulled out of the drive. "I have no idea what you're talking about."

"Sure you don't," Catherine murmured.

"Oh, the guy?" Cella asked. "Yeah, fresh meat. I saw that. We *all* saw that."

Liliana gave her a sister a look that screamed for her to shut up. Cella only shrugged.

"What?" she asked. "It wasn't like he was looking at any of us."

"Truth," Catherine murmured. "Who was that, anyway?"

Liliana didn't know.

But she was going to find out.

CORY | JOE

THE LITTLE BROTHER

Joe POV

Joe toyed with the pieces of his dismantled weapon, taking his time to check each and every one over while he had them all apart, and in view. His father had always made sure he understood the weight and respect one should have for a gun whenever he was lucky enough to be holding one. And with that came responsibility.

Really, he liked cleaning and taking care of his weapons—though at the moment, he only had a couple. He found that after doing it for a while, it had become a habit for him. And like most of his habits, that turned into a ritual. So, once a week, he sat down at the desk in his room that he was *supposed* to use to do homework, and cleaned his guns.

And his knife collection.

He liked knives, too.

It was the smack of heavy footsteps coming down the hall that almost made Joe pause in his work. Not that it was anything new, or surprising to him. He rarely got privacy to do his business alone, and frankly, he was just used to his tag along, now.

Well, not so much a tag along as—

"Man, you missed out," Cory said, slipping into his room.

Joe didn't even look up at his younger brother's declaration, or entrance. Cory didn't seem to mind, either. His brother crossed the bedroom, glanced over Joe's work, and then headed for the bed. In a plop, Cory fell backwards onto Joe's bed with a groan.

"I think I'm still drunk," Cory mumbled.

Joe did glance over his shoulder at that with narrowed eyes. "You didn't fucking drive, right?"

"No. Simon brought me home."

Good.

Joe didn't say that out loud, but still.

Sometimes, he worried about Cory, and for good reason. The sixteen-year-old was only a year younger than Joe, but at times, the two brothers felt like they were separated by more than just a year in age. Sometimes, it felt like they were made up of two entirely

369

different things—the truth was far more simple.

They shared blood.

DNA.

A home.

Parents, and a sister.

Family.

But Joe and Cory Rossi weren't at all the same. Similar in height and build, sure. Their strong Rossi features—taken from their dad, Damian—were enough to tell anybody who looked for longer than a glance that they were brothers.

That was about as far as it went, though.

Cory was outgoing.

Joe was introverted.

Cory liked to party.

Joe … didn't.

Cory was out to have the best time.

Joe would much prefer to watch others have fun.

His brother could be the life of *any* party, and he liked the fucking spotlight. Joe just couldn't say the same about himself, really. He didn't like to have other people's attention on him for very long, and he found his greatest solace in the shadows.

"You should have come," Cory mumbled, rolling over to his stomach on the bed so he could eye Joe from his position. "You would have had fun, man."

Joe smiled a little. "No, you would have had fun, and I would have … well, I don't know what I would have done, but I wouldn't have called it *fun.*"

Probably stayed to himself. Maybe tried to hook up with a chick as long as she wasn't young enough to get him into trouble, or too drunk to remember her own name and age. Maybe, if Cory pestered him enough, Joe *might* have made an attempt to talk to someone.

That never really ended well.

Cory always said Joe came off as cold.

Whatever.

"Fine, then you could have come for me," Cory said.

This time, his voice really was muffled. Joe glanced over his shoulder again to find his brother had all but rolled over on Joe's bed, and stuffed his face into the pillow. He was lucky to have even heard him, really.

"Cory?" Joe called.

"Mmm, *wheré?*"

"You're in my bed, bro."

Cory waved a hand, and then it flopped right back down on the bed again. Joe was seriously started to wonder just how much his brother *did* actually drink at the party. Apparently, whatever that number was, it was too fucking much.

"Gonna go get you some water," Joe said, standing from his desk.

Cory didn't say anything that time. Joe moved over to the bed, and checked his brother over. Seemed Cory had passed the fuck out, and wasn't getting back up anytime soon. Joe made sure to listen for steady, even breaths, and once he heard that, he was satisfied enough to move on and get his brother shit to have once he woke up.

Hangovers were a bitch.

Reason number one why Joe hated to drink, honestly.

Leaving the sanctuary of his bedroom, Joe padded through the upstairs, and then made his way down to the bottom level. The darkness of the house comforted him, even though he knew he wasn't alone. His parents were likely sleeping, and his little sister, Monica, always went to bed at seven sharp every single night, no excuses.

Tonight hadn't been any different.

Joe filled a glass full of water, and then dug into the cupboard above the stove to find the meds he was looking for. Tylenol did wonders for a head—

"What are you doing, son?"

Jesus Christ.

People called him the Shadow, but there was goddamn reason why people also called his father the Ghost.

Joe swore a man couldn't even hear Damian Rossi walking on fucking *bubble wrap*.

Spinning on his heel, he faced his father. Damian stood in the entryway of the kitchen with his arms crossed, and his sleep clothes on.

"Well?" Damian asked.

"Nothing," Joe replied, hiding the bottle of Tylenol in his large hand. "Getting some water."

"Mmhmm. Did Cory get home yet? His curfew was thirty minutes ago."

Joe looked at the clock—*shit.*

"Yeah, he got home an hour ago."

"Oh?"

"Came up to my room, and we chatted."

Damian eyed his son. "You know that I know you're lying, right?"

Joe just shrugged.

Plausible deniability.

"You would risk getting yourself in shit just to protect your brother, wouldn't you?"

Joe shrugged again.

Because, yeah, he kind of would.

It didn't matter that he and Cory were two entirely different people. It didn't matter that his brother was always pushing him to do more shit, be sociable, or anything else that Joe hated. It didn't really make a difference that Cory had a knack for pestering the living fuck out of Joe on a daily basis, so much so sometimes that he really just thought about knocking his brother out to shut him up pretty regularly.

He'd done that a couple times, too.

Cory could handle himself.

None of that really mattered to him at the end of the day.

What mattered, was that Cory was his brother.

So yeah, he'd always take shit for him.

Damian nodded when Joe chose to stay silent. "All right—keep looking out for him, huh? You're good like that, Joe."

"Whatever you say, Dad."

"Mmhmm. Take your drunk brother his water and Tylenol, and let him know in the morning that his curfew dropped by an hour."

Oh, damn.

Cory wasn't going to like that.

"Got it, Dad."

"But," Damian added as Joe passed him by, "if you go out with him, he can take an extra hour beyond the old curfew."

Shit.

Well, it wasn't *only* his brother trying to take Joe out of his comfort zones.

So was his life.

JOE AND CORY

"When was the last time you talked to your brother?"

Cory stared at his reflection, and admired the sight looking back at him. There was no point in lying or trying to hide it—he was a vain fucker. He liked the way he looked, and he wanted to keep looking like this too because females loved it.

Vain, selfish, and a little too reckless for his own good. That last one, at least, was what his father liked to tell him.

Nobody said it was a lie, though.

Cory found trouble when boredom found him.

Simple as that.

He ran a fine-tooth comb through his hair to smooth the longer bit of the high fade to the side he wanted it on, and then flattened his palms against the well-groomed facial hair that covered his jaw, and throat. He'd taken more after his mother's side of the family in looks—he got the sharp DeLuca jaw, and that same cocky expression that never left his face even when he wasn't trying to look that way. His blue eyes, though, came from his father.

"Are you listening to me, or staring at yourself in the mirror again?" he heard his father ask.

Cory rolled his eyes upward. "I mean, you called *me*."

"Yes, because I had questions."

"If you have questions about Joe, then you should call Joe."

"Joe doesn't answer my questions. He thinks I'm trying to pry."

"Because you *are*," Cory returned. "That's what you do, Dad. You pry when you think he's shutting himself off from others, and then you irritate him until he leaves his house for a few hours. That's what you do—don't deny it."

"If I don't get him out of his house, who will?"

Fair enough.

Cory didn't argue that point.

That was the thing about his brother, though. Despite the two Rossi brothers only being a year apart in age, they were polar opposites. Cory was wild, and enjoyed attention. Joe was reserved, and preferred his space.

There was nothing wrong with that.

It's just who Joe is.

"Well, are you going to answer me, then?" Damian asked. "When was the last time you talked to your brother?"

"Last night."

"Was he out of his—"

"On the phone," Cory interjected. "He's fine. Let him be alone if that's what he wants to be, okay. He likes the quiet."

"Cory, all he would do is *be* alone if we let him do that. That's a lonely way to be."

"He's not lonely, though," Cory countered. "You just worry that he is."

"So be it. Point remains the same. I want you to go check on your brother, and get him out of his goddamn house. I don't care what you have to do to make it happen, that's on you to figure out. Understood?"

Cory sighed. "Joe isn't going to like this."

"I didn't ask if he would like it. He doesn't like a lot of things— you know, going out in public, making friends ... *talking on a regular basis*—but he always comes out better for it when I force him out of his comfort zone."

"Except you want *me* to do that this time."

His father chuckled. "Yes, well ... he does like you."

Cory scowled at his reflection. "If by like you mean we often bust each other's mouths open, then all right."

He did love his brother, though.

Until the very fucking end.

"That's just how you two show your love," Damian said. "Now, update me when you get him out, and make him do something."

"Fine, whatever."

Cory hung up the phone on his father.

He had things to do now, anyway.

*

"Are you going to tell me where we're going, or what?" Joe grumbled from the passenger seat. "And Jesus Christ, slow down before we get pulled over."

"I drive just fine, thanks."

"Yeah, if you're driving on a closed course."

"Should have left your ass in bed," Cory snapped back.

His brother nodded. "I would have appreciated that."

"I bet."

Joe sighed heavily, and stared out the window. Cory chanced a glance at his brother, but found, as usual, Joe's face was passive, and unreadable. It was only his irritated tone and constantly questioning that let Cory know his brother wasn't happy about being dragged out of bed to do ... well, he hadn't told Joe what they were doing.

That might ruin the surprise.

"What would you have done today had I not come over?" Cory asked.

Joe didn't even look away from the window. "Research, likely."

"For what?"

"Have a job coming up down in Mexico for Tommas."

Cory nodded. "So, nothing, then?"

"Not *nothing*. Work."

"You work all the time."

Joe shrugged. "I like work."

"Is that why you spend just as much time in a confessional as you do taking hit jobs from Tommas because you *like* it?"

His brother finally turned away from the window, then, and gave Cory a look that could have burned a hole straight through his head. "One thing doesn't automatically have to mean something else just because you think you can correlate the others."

"So, you're saying that you don't go to confession every time you kill somebody?"

"No, I do. And your assumptions about it are just that—assumptions. Mind your own business."

"And here we are," Cory said, ignoring his brother's statement altogether as he pulled the sedan to a smooth stop on the side of the quiet city street. "Get out, and let's have a chat."

Joe glanced to the side to take in the street, and where they had stopped. "You realize there's a *For Sale* sign in the window of that restaurant, right? It's closed down, Cory. We can't have breakfast here, or—"

"Get out."

Joe cursed under his breath, but Cory was already out of the car, and slamming the door behind him. He rounded the car just as Joe climbed out of his side, and met his brother by leaning against the back passenger door. He gestured at the run-down restaurant.

"So, what do you think, man?"

Joe arched a brow, and then glanced back at his brother. "That you need a new GPS, or … something."

Cory reached out and punched his brother hard in the arm. Joe scowled, and looked about like he might hit Cory back, but decided not to at the last second.

"I mean, I was thinking of buying this place, and doing something with it."

Joe's attention went back to the restaurant. "It looks like its going to fall in on itself."

"Yeah, it needs some work."

"Some?" Joe scoffed. "*A lot.*"

"Be nice."

Joe sighed. "I mean … do you really want to do something with it?"

"Yeah, maybe a pizza joint, or something."

"Then, go for it."

"Yeah, that's the thing, though," Cory said, finally getting to the bit that was really going to make his father happy. "I don't want to take out a loan for it, and you know I only get to remove so much from my trust fund until I turn twenty, so …"

That was his parents' way of trying to keep his wild, recklessness controlled.

Joe laughed, and gave his brother a look. "So, what, you want *me* to loan you what you need?"

"No, I want you to join me. Like a partnership. Yeah—that works."

"A partnership."

"Are you a fucking parrot now, or …?"

Joe did punch him that time. "Fucker."

Cory rubbed the aching spot on his arm, and grinned. "So, is that a yes?"

"Well … I *won't* be doing all the work," Joe warned.

"Nope—partners."

"All right, then yeah, I'll go in on this."

"Great, man."

Cory patted himself on the back inwardly, and stared at the shitty restaurant that he wouldn't have given a second look to otherwise.

This would make his father happy, and get Joe out of the house to do something that wasn't the mafia.

Win-win.

Now, to keep this up somehow ...

TOMMASO | CAMILLA

THE NEW FRIEND

There was someone sitting in Camilla's spot. Cam had sat in that spot every morning since her first day at the Academy, so she hadn't been expecting this at all. She shifted the bookbag on her shoulder to loosen a bit of the weight of all the new school supplies, but it didn't help very much.

She didn't really notice, either, considering she was wondering who that was sitting in her spot on the high wall. It was the perfect place at The Academy to *people-watch*, as her father liked to say. She could see everything from there. She enjoyed watching people go about their business.

But she didn't want to be weird and go sit down next to the new girl—it might creep her out, even if that was Camilla's spot. Besides, the girl couldn't possibly know it was Camilla's spot, either.

Then again, the girl did look kind of alone, and given it was the first day of school and Camilla hadn't seen this girl around before, she figured the girl probably hadn't made very many friends.

And *that* was sad.

So, creeper or not, Camilla went over.

She dropped her heavy bookbag to the ground, and dropped to sit beside the girl who was currently typing out a text on her phone. She didn't even notice Camilla sitting beside her. Camilla couldn't help but notice how pretty she was with her chestnut skin, and wild, corkscrew curls held up in a silk wrap. She was probably a couple of years younger than Cam's thirteen, but not by much.

"Hey," Cam said.

Finally, the girl looked up from her phone. Dark brown eyes stared back at Cam—and the girl smiled hesitantly. "Hi."

"Transfer, or new altogether?"

"Transferred in from The Saint of Redemption Academy," the girl said with a shrug. "I don't really know anybody, and I miss my old school. But hey ... at least, there's boys here."

Camilla laughed. "Yeah, but most of them suck."

"Probably. One tried to touch my hair earlier—had to hit him for it."

"Really?"

The girl arched a brow. "What, the touching my hair thing, or the hitting thing?"

"Well, both now that I think about it."

The girl shrugged. "People should know better—I don't go around touching their hair. Just because mine looks a little bit different doesn't mean it's purposely like that because I want people to come along and touch it. That's rude as heck. Mom tells me just to tell them to stop, but if that worked, people wouldn't keep trying, you know?"

"It is rude." Camilla nodded. "Your hair is super pretty."

It really was, too.

All wild, and gleaming black.

Natural.

And she loved the bright colors of the wrap keeping the girl's hair held back out of her face. That was probably not a look Camilla could pull off—and she tried *everything* at least once—but this girl pulled it off really well.

"Thanks," the girl said. "My mom did it."

"She should come teach my mom."

"Well," the girl said, eyeing Camilla's high-piled, messy bun, "white girl hair isn't like black girl hair, but she could probably show you a thing or two."

"Hey, I am up to learn. I'm Cam, by the way."

The girl smiled a little wider. "August."

"Did the boy at least apologize for touching your hair?"

August shrugged. "Called me a bitch, actually."

"See—the boys here suck."

"Most boys do."

"I know it's kind of early," Cam said, "but have you made any friends."

August shrugged. "One, now."

"Oh."

"Yeah, well … I tend to stick out around here, if you get what I mean. One of these things is not like the other."

Camilla's brow furrowed, and it took her a minute to get what August was trying to say without actually *saying* it. Then again, all she really needed to do was take a look around The Academy's grounds.

It was a sea of *white*.

The only spot of color at the moment was August.

Sure, their school was kind of small, but it was only then that Camilla realized just how ... *white* the place was. She bet that felt shitty for August—to feel kind of put in a spotlight, and yet alone at the same time. To look around, and find absolutely nobody that looked like her.

Yeah, that would suck.

A lot.

"Give it time," Camilla said a little dumbly. "You'll make more friends."

She didn't know what else to say.

August smiled. "It's okay—sometimes one good friend is better than ten friends that aren't so good."

"That's true." Camilla grinned. "So, is that what we are, now?"

"Hmm, what?"

"Friends."

August nodded. "Yep—that's what we are."

Awesome.

The bell rang through the speakers, and echoed over the grounds. Camilla glanced up with a sigh, and then over at her new friend. No doubt, August was still in the lower Academy which meant their lunch times and other breaks would likely be at different times.

That kinda sucked.

They still had the mornings, though.

"Same time tomorrow?" she asked.

August jumped down from the wall. "Same time tomorrow."

Camilla hadn't known it, then, but sometimes the best and most lasting friendships came in the most unexpected moments. It would be August and her family, who over the years, taught Camilla things that she probably never would have known otherwise. It was the start of not only a friendship between two teenage girls, but between *families*, too.

It would be August who Camilla always had to lean on when things were all going to shit in her life. It would be August who was there—a constant pillar of support. She never found judgement from her friend, and only ever found openness, and love.

She found her best friend sitting in her spot.

It all started with nothing more than hello.

Camilla never regretted choosing to sit down, and say hello. She only wished she had known August longer.

THE SPEECH

A few feet away from their wedding party's main table, Tommaso leaned back in his chair to watch the scene unfolding in front of him. Or rather, the way his new bride's whole face lit up when her brother stepped in to ask her for a dance.

Hell.

Everyone had danced with Cam more than he had during their wedding reception. But frankly, more people had danced with him than she had, too. So was the way of a wedding with large families.

Not to mention, *their* kind of families. It just couldn't be avoided, and since it was all about the respect of the matter, really, they didn't refuse. Besides, as his father reminded him more than once over the last few hours—in fact, every single time Tom dared to complain that he wasn't getting any time with his wife—soon enough, he would have Camilla all to himself.

His father had a point.

Tom was *greatly* looking forward to it.

With every new guest that came up to congratulate him and each task they had to complete—from giving a speech to cutting the cake—the minutes ticked by getting closer and closer to that magical one o'clock in the morning when he would finally be able to sneak his wife away to a hotel suite in the city before they jetted off early in the morning for a week-long honeymoon far, far away.

No mafia business.

No *family*.

Nothing but him and Cam.

Tom wanted that to happen.

Now.

But he had to wait.

So he did.

Forever his father's good son—always the boss's best set example. Tom didn't know how to be anything different now, even when he wanted to be.

Cross stepped back from Cam as the song ended, but gave a quick shake of his head at an approaching man like he was stopping the guy from coming to ask for a dance of his own. Which made sense when

Tommaso heard Camilla mutter, "These shoes are going to make me cut my feet off by the time I'm done tonight."

"Sit," Cross replied. "I'll give you a few minutes to rest them."

"Best brother ever."

Cross grinned wide. "I try, Cam."

Once Cam had stepped around the table and Cross shooed another guest away, the man came to grab the item sitting in front of Tom's glass of whiskey. The microphone. While Cross hadn't been *in* the wedding party—although Tom had been more than willing to make a spot for him, had he asked—he had still expected Cross to make time to ensure Camilla felt as special and loved as she should be on her wedding day.

He was her big brother, after all.

One of her very best friends.

It's what they *should* do.

Cam sat down in the chair next to Tom's with a sigh and a smile as Cross turned to face the rest of the room, one hand high with *Tom's* glass of whiskey in hand. Not that it mattered, a server was already waiting with a replacement.

Like the man knew he would need to.

Had Cross planned something?

It wouldn't surprise Tom at all.

"I regret my choice in shoes," Camilla whined. "I wanted to dance more, but this is killing me."

Tom frowned—he loved the shoes she picked to wear under her dress. All six inches of heel and white satin. They were going to make her legs look fantastic when he had her naked and bent over something later.

For right now, though ...

Well, he might be able to help with that. Who in the hell was going to complain if Camilla danced in her heels or the silk stockings instead?

Nobody.

That's who.

"Here, babe," Tom said, reaching for Cam's legs under the table.

"What are you—"

The tablecloth hid how he pulled her legs into his lap to pull off her shoes. The satin heels hit the floor with a *click-click* that was hidden by Cross taking all of the attention when he spoke into the microphone as the room quieted.

"Fuck the damn shoes," Tom told Cam.

She grinned. "Sounds like a plan."

"Everyone in this room knows how loved my sister is," Tom heard Cross say.

"Only a couple of hours left, and we're out of here."

Cam pursed her lips, the glint in her eye making him think of a million and one dirty, terrible things he'd like to do to her right then and there. One thing in particular that had to do with smudging that ruby red lipstick of hers across her mouth while he made her eyes water.

She always looked so pretty like that.

Loved it, too.

"Dad made me promise," he said quickly.

Cam gave him a look. "*I* can't convince you to break the rules?"

She absolutely could.

And probably would.

"Don't test me," he murmured.

Cam winked.

Tom about lost his control right then and there.

"At least promise me one more dance," he said while Cross continued his speech to the rest of the guests, "because I've been dying here, Cam."

"I can do that."

Good.

"And I'm glad to know," Cross said, turning to face his sister and Tom who had moved closer together until their shoulders touched and their grins were angled toward one another, "that my sister has found someone else to love her the way we do, too." He lifted his glass higher to toast them, smiling with a nod as he added, "Congrats—to your forever and ever, Cam, because it's exactly what you deserve."

It certainly was.

Tom would make sure she had it.

THE JOB

"Shhhh."

Camilla's soothing hush had the small preemie in the domed bassinet settle enough that the heart rate monitor stopped beeping. She took a moment to check over the leads attached to the baby's chest with tiny heart-shaped stickers, and then jotted down a few notes into the file tucked into the shelf at the back of the bassinet.

No changes, really.

Nothing since the start of her twenty-four-hour shift.

In the case of premature babies, but especially one like this baby who was still so small that his cry hadn't even developed yet and he cried without sound, no changes weren't exactly a bad thing. When they did see changes, they *hoped* they would be steps forward in the infant's progress. Thing was, every preemie in this ward came in with a fifty-fifty chance.

And this boy wasn't out of the woods yet.

Sticking her hand back in through the holes of the bassinet that sealed around her arms to keep any air that wasn't carefully controlled away from the baby, she rested her warm, *cleaned* hands against his body. He was so small, they could still see his veins running throughout his body under his paper-thin skin. Her hands covered him almost entirely. And yet, his heart rate continued to lower the longer she held him in the only way she could.

They wanted touch *so badly*.

It was one of the best things for these babies.

The beep of her watch had Cam sighing because as much as she would like to stand right there and keep soothing the baby when he probably wouldn't get it again until the next shift of nurses came in, did all their rounds, and had five seconds to sit down and give the infant personal attention *beyond* his medical needs.

The hospital had a whole team of volunteers that came in to hold or rock the babies, and feed the ones that were capable of taking a bottle. However, that was in the daytime and evenings. And the nighttime hours were left to the nurses on the ward who, as it was, were already overworked in a high-stress job that had them watching fifty percent of their patients dying every goddamn week.

She loved her job.

Adored these babies.

But she absolutely understood why the stay-rate for a nurse on the preemie ward wasn't very high over the course of six months to a year. It was hard on the brain. Hard on the heart, and harder on the soul.

Cam was still here, though.

And she didn't plan on leaving.

However, she did need to take a little break, but not because the job was getting to her in any kind of way. But rather, because her father had traveled all the way to Ireland for surgery to correct an old brain injury that had been affecting him for years, and she wanted to be there to help with his recovery. Since his travel and surgery had been a little last minute, so was her time off that she put in for. But she'd been working here for years, never took time off without lots of notice, and didn't complain if her vacation time wasn't given because it didn't work for the hospital. She simply worked something else out.

This time, she put in for emergency time off due to family. There was absolutely no reason for her boss to refuse the time, but that really depended on the man's moods, to be honest. If she only had to go through the head nurse, then that would be one thing.

This was something else entirely.

Camilla made sure to clean up all her stations, and anything else that needed finishing last minute before she headed down to the spread of lockers where her stuff waited. At least, making sure she cleaned up helped with the shift of nurses just coming in. Less work meant more time one on one with the babies.

And God knew they needed that.

Waiting until she was dressed back in her normal clothes, and the second shift of nurses had come in and were settling into their routine, only then did she head upstairs in the hospital to the office where her boss would be waiting.

He'd said by the end of her shift, he would have an answer for her. So, here she was, ready for that answer, and hoping it would be good news. Because otherwise, she didn't know what in the hell she was going to do for her father.

"Ah, Cam, there you are," her boss said when she came to stand in his open doorway.

He didn't look at her in the eyes.

Bad sign number one.

"So I looked over the request you put in for the emergency time off for your … family thing," her boss started.

"And you refused it."

Finally, the man glanced up from behind his desk. "Well, you have to understand that the hospital is already understaffed, Camilla, and we can't really afford for someone in your ward to take time off right now when there are already two other nurses on their vacation, and Jenny will be starting hers next week when Tania comes back."

"Except this isn't regular vacation time," Camilla said, making sure each one of her words came out careful and measured. *For now.* "This is me putting in an emergency request for time off so I can fly to Ireland where my father just had major brain surgery."

"He's alive, yes?"

She blinked. "What?"

"Your father—he's alive, came out of the surgery fine, didn't he?"

Did not being able to speak, feed himself, or get out of bed mean he was *fine?* Because Cam didn't think so, and those were all things Calisto would need to relearn. She would rather be there for a couple of weeks to be one of the people helping him learn how to use his body again to take care of his most basic needs instead of strangers who would only undoubtedly upset him more *because* they were strangers. Everyone had their pride, after all, but her father even more so.

"Just say you're not giving me the time off," Camilla said calmly, although at this point, she didn't have the first clue how she managed it, "and keep everything else to yourself, if you wouldn't mind."

"Now, there's no need for the attitude."

"This isn't attitude. That's a line you don't need to cross. The fact my father still has a heartbeat doesn't negate the fact that he will spend the next several months of his life in intensive rehab before he will even *walk* again. So, if you could just say you're not giving me the time off, so I can then go ahead and find another route in this hospital to get the time off I need to help care for my father, I would appreciate it."

The man across the room stiffened in his chair. "You won't get the time off, and that's my final decision. If you try to go over my head about it, you won't have a job to come back to at this hospital, Cam.

I hope you understand."

Camilla smiled.

Oh, was that what he thought?

There were a lot of things in her life that Camilla tried not to do. Using her family name, her husband's name and status in Chicago, or even her contacts to get herself further ahead in anything in life was one of them. She just didn't do it.

"So," she said, "I suppose when I ask to speak to the board tomorrow and I casually mention how my husband will be pulling back on his five-million-dollar donation ... then they'll be in line with your .... *position* here, won't they?"

Her boss's jaw ticked.

Camilla shrugged. "Well, we'll find out, won't we?"

She didn't wait for a response.

She really didn't need one.

BAUBLES AND BABIES

Camilla's smile grew the longer she held her brand new nephew. Little Nazio slept happily having just been fed by his mother, and then swaddled tight by his father in what was apparently his favorite blue muslin blanket.

Tom wasn't really sure how newborns could have *favorite* things, but here they were. Who was he to argue with the parents of the boy?

Cam flew back to New York far more often than Tom came to visit her family. Business and family obligations often kept him tied up in Chicago more than he cared to admit. But he was settled with this life, now—knew this was where he was meant to be.

Still, when new babies came around and a birth was to be celebrated, he cleared his schedule. Nothing else mattered but family, after all. Even if that family was a couple of states away from them.

His father—still the boss of the Chicago Outfit, and not quite ready to let the reins go—understood, and never said a word.

Water under the bridge, Tommas liked to say about the Donati boss. His father let bygones be bygones when it came to Cross.

The apology probably helped.

It still took a while.

Cross bent down to grab a discarded toy on the floor, and as he straightened up, he asked, "So when are you going to add to Ma and Dad's growing pile of grandkids, Cam?"

Clearing his throat when his wife's eyes widened to the size of small saucers, Tom knew what was coming next. When someone asked a question like that, his wife's next move was fucking predictable.

Even if it was *him* asking the question.

"Oh, Naz is waking up a bit," Cam said, "so I should go find Catherine."

"He's not—"

"Be right back," Cam called over her shoulder as she darted out of the room.

Tom looked to Cross. "She's not coming back."

Camilla's older brother raised a single brow, and nodded. "Figured. What, she doesn't want kids, or …?"

389

Eh.

Tom made a noise in the back of his throat, and tipped his hand back and forth as if to say, *It's a little iffy.*

"Really?"

He shrugged. "At first," Tom said, "she wanted to finish school."

"Which she has," Cross said, his brow dipping in confusion, "a long fucking time ago, man."

"Yeah, and then it was that she wanted to do things—travel, you know."

"Comes with the territory."

"And now it's that she wants us to enjoy being … us," Tom said.

Cross's stance softened a bit as he glanced at his old friend. "And what do *you* want?"

"Not to discuss our childless life with people."

"My bad."

Tom cleared his throat again—a nervous tic he never could quite get rid of, no matter how hard he tried. A lot like drumming his fingers. His father always liked to point it out whenever he was doing it like that would change it.

Never did.

Story of his life.

"Sorry," Tom said, "maybe that was a little out of line."

Cross shrugged, and dropped onto the end of the couch. "Nah, it's your right to tell me to fuck off where you two are concerned. You don't want me in your personal business, then yeah, say so. I get it. I'm a big boy—I know what back the fuck off means. My wife knows how to say it without even *speaking.*"

Tom chuckled. "Don't they all?"

"Comes with the territory," Cross murmured again.

"I don't know," Tom said, finding a spot on the couch beside his friend. "I never really focused on kids when Cam wasn't interested. I've got Joe and Cory's kids under my feet a couple of times a week. August and Beni, too. My sisters … anyway, I haven't lacked kids being around to *miss* it, if you get my meaning."

"Not your kids, though."

True.

Tom didn't admit that out loud, though.

"You turned thirty-one this year, right?"

"What's that got anything to do with it?" Tom asked.

"Curious."

"Yeah."

"Cam's twenty-nine."

"I know how old my wife is, Cross."

His friend smiled a bit—the kind of smug ass smile that drove Tom insane a lot of the time.

"What?" he asked, irritated.

"It's usually the wife's biological clock ticking down, isn't it?" Cross asked. "Never heard of a man who hears it ticking, too."

Tom scowled. "I don't have—"

Upstairs above their heads, girlish toddler giggles echoed from Cece. A baby's cry soon followed.

It was just those sounds alone that made Tommaso stiffen a bit, but not with an uncomfortable sensation that made him want to leave. No, with a kind of longing he hadn't really felt in a long time.

Not since he first met Cam.

Cross glanced over at his friend. "Life is kind of tough like that, Tom. Sometimes, we get the things we want, and other times, we don't."

"Poetic," he murmured dryly.

"Yeah, it's what I do."

*

A short while later, Tom decided to go in search of his wife when Camilla didn't come back downstairs. Cross figured he had crossed a line, and so, sent Tom to bring Cam back without the awkwardness that might happen if it were him.

Fucking coward.

Soon, Tom found his wife in little Naz's nursery. The upstairs was quiet again—Catherine had urged her toddler daughter downstairs to drive her father crazy while Nazio napped, apparently.

Cam hummed a familiar lullaby as she leaned over the baby's crib. Tom stayed quiet in the doorway as she hadn't noticed his presence, and enjoyed the sight of her drifting her fingertips over Naz's chubby cheeks.

"He looks so much like Cross, it's unreal," she murmured.

Tom tipped his head up—seems she knew he was there, after all. "He does, yeah."

Cam looked over at him. "Came to find me, did you?"

"Your brother caught onto your little disappearing trick, babe. Sorry."

She shrugged, but went back to the baby without saying a thing. It was the look on her face that made Tom step quietly into the room, and close the distance between them. Not sadness, or embarrassment that usually came along whenever someone asked why they were still childless—as though it was anyone's business—but rather, just ... curious.

"What is it?" Tom asked when he was close enough to snake an arm around her waist, and pull her close. "Tell me, Cam."

Cam rested her head on his shoulder. "I was just thinking ..."

"Mmm?"

"Do you know why I've always put having kids off?"

"Because you're not ready," Tom said simply.

Cam made a quiet noise. "That, too, yeah."

"What else?"

She glanced over her shoulder, and peered at the items littering the nursery. Baby things, and whatever else. Nappies, lotions, and more filled the top of a dresser. Perfectly cute, and small outfits hung from an open closer.

Baby toys and knickknacks—baubles in every corner—filled the space.

All the stuff that came along with babies.

"This kind of freaks me out," Cam admitted.

"What?"

She turned, and gestured at the room. "*This*, Tom. All of this. The baby swings, and the swaddling blankets. Rattles and teethers. Do you know how many different kinds of bottles there are—or *Christ*, soothers?"

Tom blinked. "No."

"I do. I *do* because I've looked it up. Hundreds, Tom. There are *hundreds*."

He blinked again. "Okay."

"No, it's not okay. Because which one do you even *choose*? How do you decide? And that's before you get into which beds, or swings, or diapers, or—"

Tom had enough. He kissed his wife hard enough to quiet her, and all her anxieties that he never even knew existed. Because that was

Cam—she kept shit bottled up until she couldn't hold it in anymore and it exploded out of her in verbal vomit.

Not that he minded.

Cam let out a shaky sigh when Tom pulled away.

"Okay," he said.

Her gaze drifted up to his. "Okay?"

"Okay," he repeated.

"But—"

"But nothing. You don't have to justify shit, Cam. You don't have to excuse anything to me. As long as you're happy, then I am happy. That's how this has always worked."

She chewed on her bottom lip. A habit he wished she would break because he hated when she abused her mouth like that for all the wrong reasons.

"I do, though," she whispered.

"What?"

"Want kids."

Tom grinned. "Oh?"

"Just … without all the stuff that freaks me out," she added quickly.

"Easy enough."

Cam gave him a look. "You think?"

"It's called minimalism, babe. You think babies need all this crap? No, they need to be loved, comforted, dry, fed, and happy. That is *it.*"

"But …"

"What, Cam?"

"I don't even know how to be a mom, or … whatever."

Tom dragged his wife close again. "Not everybody does. It's not some bred instinct you have the moment you're born. And some people *are* born mothers, and still don't have kids because that's just not what they want in their life. Look at Theo and Eve, right?"

Two of the most paternal and maternal people he knew, and yet, never had their own biological kids. They fostered for a lot of years—still did, when they found a child that really needed a different kind of safe place to heal—but never their own blood.

"Do you want kids?" Cam asked.

"I want what you want."

And that was—his hand to God—the truth.

Some people just went about their life differently. Cam had always been a little different, anyway. Tom didn't mind this being the same.

THE NEWS

"I'm *starving*, Ella," Tommas grumbled.

From behind the kitchen island, his wife shot him a look that could *kill*. He swore he had become accustomed to this kind of game with his wife over the years, and frankly, Abriella had mastered this shit with him. All it took was one look from her, and Tommy knew whether or not he should keep pushing, or back the hell off.

This time was different.

His daughter-in-law was there.

Abriella was far less likely to throw something at him for his pestering when someone else was around. She was predictable like that. Tommas knew which buttons to push with her, and *when*, for that matter.

Marriage was all about compromise, after all.

"I think what you mean to say is, *you're spoiled*, Tommy," Abriella muttered. "The food is almost done. Surely, you can wait another ten minutes for us to plate everything, and get it set out on the table."

"But it's done *now*."

"And you can wait to eat with everybody else just like you always do."

"Ella—"

"I swear to *God*."

Tommas chuckled under his breath, knowing he had pushed his wife to her limits. Really, it was only when he pestered her inside the kitchen that Abriella got touchy like this. Anywhere else, and she had far more patience for his shit.

But really, this was what made their marriage fun.

She would be *so much more fun* later.

Especially once he got her to bed.

She knew his games.

And his tricks.

"Ignore him," Abriella told their daughter-in-law. "You should try some of that red wine I brought back from Italy, Cam. It's wonderful."

Camilla shook her head. "Maybe next time. Keep a bottle for me."

Abriella shrugged. "Your loss."

Knowing he wasn't going to get much more out of his wife, Tommas sighed heavily.

"Fine," Tommas half-heartedly grumbled. "I'll go ... entertain."

"What else is the boss supposed to do when he invites people to his home for *dinner*, Tommy?"

Tommas grinned, and shot his wife a wink over his shoulder. "Get his wife worked up so she's extra sweet for later."

Next to his wife, Camilla cleared her throat.

Abriella's eyes flew wide, and a red heat climbed up her cheeks. "Oh, my God. Get *out!*"

Tommas's laughter echoed down the hall as he headed for the dining room. He found the majority of the guests already seated, and waiting for dinner to be served. Taking a moment to lean over his only son's shoulder, Tommas squeezed Tom.

"I think I embarrassed your wife," he said, "sorry about that."

Tom groaned. "How?"

"She was in the crossfire."

"Jesus Christ. Can't you at least wait until the house is empty to start your foreplay with Ma?"

"But *why?*" Tommas asked.

"Because nobody else wants to see it."

Tommas shrugged.

He didn't ask if other people wanted to see it.

That wasn't the point.

Giving his son a pat on the back, Tommas realized someone was missing from the table. Damian, his underboss and cousin. Best friend, too. Even after all these years, Damian was still the one person—next to his wife, and now son, of course—that Tommas trusted the very most. He doubted that would ever change.

In this life, loyalty like that was hard to find.

And *keep*.

"Where's Damian?" Tommas asked.

"He got a phone call—took it in the living room."

Tommas nodded, but he still felt like he should probably check up on his underboss. If only because it was unusual for Damian to take a phone call during dinner if he was already there with Tommas. After all, Damian didn't answer to anyone *but* his boss.

And that was Tommas.

Giving his son one more squeeze on his shoulders, Tommas

headed out of the kitchen in search of Damian. He figured if something was going on, he would rather hear about it before dinner rather than ruin his meal with the damn news.

Tommas was halfway down the hallway when Camilla came bursting out of the kitchen. With her hand slapped over her mouth, and her face paler than he'd ever seen it, his daughter-in-law damn near knocked him over in her haste to run into the bathroom across the hall. She tried to slam the door behind her, but it didn't close completely.

Shit.

Tommas leaned in the kitchen only to find his wife was distracted with the punch she was making. Maybe she had her back turned to Camilla when the girl ran out of the kitchen.

Who knew?

All he knew was that the sound of Cam's retching in the bathroom was a little concerning. Subtly, he reached over and closed the bathroom door for her the rest of the way to give her a little bit of privacy.

As he waited for her to come back out of the bathroom, Tommas had a heavy realization settle over him. Something he'd overlooked in the kitchen because he had been too busy pestering his wife in that way of his.

Cam refused wine.

Red wine.

She loved wine.

Especially for dinner.

And now vomiting, too?

Did that mean what he thought it—

"Sorry," Camilla said when she came out of the bathroom. Her gaze wouldn't meet his, and her cheeks were stained with red. "I didn't mean to almost run you over, Tommas."

He chuckled, and shook his head. "No worries."

Camilla brushed her hands over her cheeks. "I probably look like shit, now."

"You look fine."

And she did.

Nothing to say she had just spent two minutes puking her guts out.

"Does anyone know?" he dared to ask.

Camilla's gaze shot up to meet his, and he swore he saw the denial already forming on her mouth. Then, she surprised him with a little shake of her head.

"No one at *all*?"

"Just found out this afternoon," she admitted.

"Not even *Tom*?"

Because shit, Tommas kind of figured that was important news for her to share with her husband. Tommas had always been the first to know—next to a doctor once—that his wife was pregnant with their child.

"We came right over here after he picked me up," Cam said, laughing. "I didn't think it was a very good time to tell him, you know."

"Fair."

Camilla glanced over at him again. "How did your wife tell you?"

Tommas smiled a bit. "I don't think that's appropriate for me to share."

"Huh?" Then, she nodded as she said, "Oh, never mind."

"You know it doesn't matter *how* you tell him, right?"

Camilla cleared her throat. "I don't know—Tommaso has waited for this for a long time. I kind of feel like blurting it out might be … anti-climactic."

"He's not going to care. Trust me."

"Yeah, maybe not."

"Why don't you go to the dining room and relax," Tommas suggested, but not really posing it as a question. He didn't think Camilla being on her feet and serving people food was right, considering. He thought she had more than earned sitting down today, and being served instead. Tommas could help his wife. "And don't worry about anything."

"I promised to help Abriella—"

"Like I said, don't worry."

Camilla, like most people who had spent more than ten minutes around Tommas, knew better than to argue with him. Once she was heading down the long hallway toward the dining room, Tommas moved into the kitchen.

Abriella glanced up instantly. "Where's Cam? She just disappeared."

Tommas said nothing, simply crossed the kitchen, rounded the island, and caught his wife in his embrace. Before she could say anything, he was kissing her.

A happy, loving, long kiss.

A lingering kiss.

A fierce, hot kiss that left nothing unsaid about just how much he loved this woman.

A kiss that spoke of their familiarity, and love. Of their many years together, and all the memories they had made in that time. From their life, to their children. Their home, and their perfection. All their flaws, and their now-fused souls.

Because he didn't have a fucking soul.

Now without this woman.

Pulling away, Tommas still kept Abriella pulled in close to him as he stroked the pad of his thumb over her cheekbone. Her flushed cheeks, and wide smile made him grin, too.

"What was that for?" she asked.

"Because I love you."

"Mmhmm. *And?*"

"What makes you think there's more, Ella?"

She pointed a finger at his face, and wiggled it a little. "I just … *know* you, Tommy. I see when you have secrets to share."

"Only you," he muttered, chuckling.

"Spill."

"I don't know if I sho—"

"Tommas, I *swear* …"

"You always use that threat, but never follow through."

"Do you want me to follow through with it?"

Her kind tone belied the sly gleam in her eye.

Damn.

This was exactly why he loved his wife.

"You can't say a *word*," he said, dotting kisses from her cheek to her ear.

Abriella shivered. "I won't."

"You have to let them tell you when they are ready, Ella."

"I don't know what you're talking about, but—"

"Cam is pregnant."

His wife stilled.

Tommas held her tighter.

Finally, Abriella pulled back just far enough to stare him in the face. "Really?"

"Yeah."

She grabbed his face with her palms. *"Really, really?"*

"Guess you're finally going to get that grandbaby, Ella."

Her quiet, yet still excited squeal somehow managed to echo in the kitchen. Tommas laughed, and then shushed his wife with another kiss.

But really, he wanted to shout it, too.

But it wasn't his news.

He shouldn't even know.

So, he would just ... have to wait.

WHISPERED SURPRISES

Camilla hugged the cup of tea her mother-in-law had brought out from the kitchen for her, and watched from her chair as Tommaso lit up an entire fucking room. Sometimes it still amazed her how this man was capable of doing that—so enigmatic, and electric. He was a lot like his father in that way, she thought.

People tended to gravitate toward them, and paid attention when they spoke. It wasn't like they could exactly help it. Tommaso just ... took over a whole room, and he didn't even have to try. Sometimes, Camilla thought he didn't even realize it.

Like this was just who he was.

Engrained in his *being*.

And Camilla was in no way immune to the daze that everyone else suffered from when Tommaso started doing his thing. In fact, it was a favorite part of her day to simply sit back, and watch her man.

Because he was *her man*.

Entirely hers.

And wasn't that something to be proud of?

Camilla smiled, and tipped her tea up to take a drink of the hot liquid as Tommaso clapped his cousin Joe on the back before reaching over to smack his other cousin, Cory, on the side of his face with a gentle pat. Those two brothers regularly made it their mission to show up at her house at least three times a week, but often times, more. Joe was quiet, while Cory was loud.

Yet, when the three of them got together ... that all went to hell. It was like they couldn't help it. Camilla didn't even mind, really.

She was so caught up in watching her husband that she didn't notice her mother-in-law had come to sit beside her at the table again. Dinner hand long been served, and so had dessert. Now, the families that made up the Chicago Outfit would simply spend their evening catching up, and being a *family*.

It was important to them, she had come to learn. This thing they called *the* family. Some weren't related by blood, but the way they acted toward one another, they might as well be. They protected these moments in their life like nobody on the outside would ever understand. Sure, disagreements happened ... but they were quickly resolved, and without much fanfare to say they had even happened in the first place.

At first, it had taken Camilla a bit to get used to so many people constantly coming and going from her house, and life. Going from one family member's thing to the next—her family wasn't nearly as large as this, after all. But it was hard not to love people when it was people like *these*.

"You're awfully quiet tonight," Abriella said next to Camilla.

She gave her mother-in-law a smile. "Am I?"

"A little. Something on your mind?"

Camilla wanted to laugh.

Was something on her mind?

Other than the fact she lost her entire lunch before supper, and then ended up blurting out the fact she was pregnant to her father in law before she could even tell her husband?

No.

Nothing was wrong at all.

"Not really," Camilla said.

It was the truth … kind of. She didn't care that she had told Tommaso's father first, really. She was more anxious about the fact she didn't know how to tell *him*. He'd been great about the whole *baby* thing. He'd patiently waited for Cam to live her life, and do her thing. He never pressured, or demanded *anything*.

They lived, and loved.

Traveled.

Bought crazy, expensive shit that didn't need to be within *miles* of a walking, curious toddler. They owned a top floor, glass-walled penthouse suite in the middle of the city alongside their suburban mansion.

They didn't even have back seats in three out of their five vehicles.

They did all the things that people who were childless had the ability to do because that's what Camilla had wanted for so long, and Tom was more than happy to go along with whatever made her life perfect.

But didn't he know?

She was *most* happiest with him.

Always would be.

"You are a little out of it tonight, aren't you?" Abriella asked.

Camilla's gaze swung back to find her mother-in-law was smiling in that way of hers. A *sly* way. Abriella was cute like that. Whenever she had a secret, that's exactly how she smiled.

"Sorry?"

Abriella raised an eyebrow. "I just talked to you for two minutes, but you entirely zoned out and stared at Tom instead."

Camilla laughed, and waved that off. "Tired, maybe."

"I don't think so, but that's okay. Big changes in our life means we all need some time to adjust, Cam. Trust me, I understand that better than anyone."

She gave her mother-in-law a look, and wondered ... did she know? Had Tommas told his wife what he knew about the pregnancy?

If that was the case, Abriella didn't say a thing. She simply stood from the table, gave Camilla a wink, and patted her daughter in law's cheek with a soft palm before joining her own sister further down the table.

Camilla decided to just shake off the odd conversation, and put her focus back on Tom and how she was going to tell him the thing he wanted to hear more than anything else in the world. Had she said he'd been waiting for this?

Because *he was*.

"What are you doing over here smiling to yourself, hmm?"

It was Tommaso's dark whisper in Camilla's ear that made her realize her mother-in-law wasn't lying. She was a little out of it— completely zoning in and out for no reason at all. It was noticeable.

Hell, she hadn't even noticed her husband coming across the whole room to stand directly behind her.

Turning in her seat Camilla found Tommaso grinning down at her. There was something about this man that made Camilla's heart speed up in the best way when all he was doing was staring at her.

God.

She loved him for that.

"Thinking about you, actually," she said.

Tommas cocked a brow. "Oh? Good things, I hope."

"When is it ever *bad* things, Tom?"

"That time I ate your candy stash."

She gave him a look. "That was a shitty thing to do."

"And I apologized!"

He did, too. In the *best* way.

His hands came down to cup either side of her face before he dropped a quick kiss to her forehead.

"Love you," he said quietly.

Camilla smiled softly. "Too much, I think."

"*Never.*"

Staring up at him again, Camilla found that time stopped. And the rest of the room disappeared. It was just him and her, and nothing else mattered.

Maybe that was her problem.

She'd been overthinking, and worrying about things that just didn't matter.

"Tom?"

"Yeah, babe?"

Camilla gave him a half smile, whispering, "I have a secret."

His blue gaze lit up with mirth. "Oh? A good one?"

"A *very* good one."

"Care to share, or …?"

Silently, Camilla popped open the clutch that had been resting in her lap for the better portion of the night. She knew what was resting on the very top. She'd opened the bag over and over again just to make sure what was there was still real.

The pregnancy test was very much real.

And still blinking the word *pregnant.*

Tom glanced down, and Camilla could literally feel when his gaze landed on the item she was showing him. How his stance softened, and his hands tightened on her face. The slight jerk that worked its way through his body, and the soft noise that escaped his throat.

She could have waited.

Let it be … them.

Private.

It didn't matter, she knew.

Any way at all would have been perfect for Tom.

"Yeah?"

She peered up to find he was staring at her again. Stormy blue eyes, and love right there. Her whole life was this man.

Camilla nodded, and whispered, "Yeah, Tom, we're—"

She didn't even get to finish her sentence before his lips were on hers, and he was kissing her hard enough to take her breath away. It sent her chair rocking back on two legs, but he was right there to catch it.

Camilla could only laugh.

So was their life.

CROSS AND CATHERINE ERA

THE SCARE

Dante POV

"Go ahead," Dante urged, pushing the shoe-sized gift box across the table. "Open it."

Lucian eyed the simple, white box. "Is something going to jump out at me?"

Gio chuckled in his seat at one end of the table. Antony laughed at the other side. Their noise drew the attention of other patrons around them, but they ignored the diners.

"No, something is not going to pop out at you, Lucian."

Dante's older brother did not particularly look like he believed him.

"You sure?" Lucian asked.

"Yes, I'm sure."

"Why don't you open it for me, then?"

Dante shook his head. "You know what, yeah, man. Something is going to jump out at you—my goddamn fist in your face if you don't open that fucking box!"

"Dante," Antony admonished.

Gio snorted at their father's scolding.

Grown men with adult children, and they were still getting bitched at by their father.

Dante gave Lucian a look. "Open the box, Lucian."

"I don't think I really want to open it now," Lucian said.

"Open the box, Lucian!"

Again, his shout drew attention from the other diners nearby. Neither Dante, nor Lucian, broke their staring contest.

This was a battle of silent wills between them that had been ongoing for months now. Ever since the incident at the restaurant with Cross. All of that was long over, sure, and proper amends had been made.

Things were good.

Except for Lucian and Dante.

Blame it on the fact they were both stubborn fuckers, and too alike for their own good. It made things like this—asking for forgiveness—particularly hard. Or maybe neither one of them wanted to be the one to apologize and say they were an asshole.

Whatever it was, it had officially gone on for long enough.

"You know," Gio said, "I miss when we were younger and used to just beat the shit out of each other when we had a problem. It was a far easier solution."

"Right," Lucian said, passing Dante a look. "This would have been done months ago."

"Because I would have kicked your ass," Dante said.

Lucian smiled coldly. "Keep thinking that."

"First of all," Antony said, once again verbally stepping in between his battling sons. "No one but you three miss when you used to beat the hell out of each other to settle problems. Seriously, what is wrong with all of you? People would think we raised a pack of damn dogs, and not gentlemen."

Dante knew what was coming before Gio even did it. Their father had opened for it with that last statement, after all.

"Woof, woof," Gio said, smirking.

Antony looked upward, saying, "God, save me. Lucian, you better open that box."

The warning was as clear as a summer's day in Antony's old, gravelly voice. His voice had changed a bit over the years to show his age, and yet, the tone remained the same. A good old father's threat if they ever heard one.

It was comforting in ways.

Almost.

Despite the issues the Marcello brothers sometimes had with one another, they still knew better than to push their father. Too much stress on Antony, and they would never hear the end of it from their mother.

None of them wanted that.

At all.

"Fine," Lucian said as he gave Dante another look. "Better be worth it, man."

Dante shrugged.

He had nothing left to say as the item inside the box would say it all for him.

Lucian pulled the gift box closer, flipped open the top, and reached inside to pull out the tissue paper keeping his gift hidden. All the while, he kept his gaze locked on Dante like he didn't trust his brother with an inch.

Dante seriously hoped this would fix shit between them.

A peace offering, of sorts.

Without, of course, either of them actually needing to apologize to the other one. It was what it was, and they were who they were.

Marcellos.

None of them would ever change.

Finally, Lucian pulled out the gift Dante had gotten specially made for him. A rose gold tinted Eagle—his brother's favorite weapon of choice. Big, heavy as hell, expensive, and very dangerous.

His brother had but two weaknesses. Only two things for Dante to use in order to weaken and soften Lucian a little.

His family.

And his love of custom guns.

Lucian whistled low as he plucked out the gun with careful hands. He looked the piece over with the eyes of a man who truly loved guns, and understood the work that must have gone into this particular one.

"Lucky," Lucian said, clearly reading out loud the inscription on the barrel of the gun.

"I thought it was appropriate," Dante said, "even if you never went by that nickname with us."

Lucian cleared his throat, but said nothing.

Lucky was the nickname his bio-father had called him.

"How many of these were made?" Lucian asked.

"Two."

Lucian's brow shot up. "Really?"

"Yeah, man. One for you, and one for the man who designed it."

"Damn."

Both Antony and Gio smiled. Lucian was still toying with, and looking over, the gun in his hands. He probably wouldn't let the thing go for hours.

Dante knew then that he had his older brother caught. Everything between them would be just fine after today.

"When did you have this done?" Lucian asked.

"A while back."

Shortly after their feud started.

He really did hate fighting with his brothers.

Lucian grinned, and his gaze lifted to meet Dante's once again. "You're forgiven."

Dante smirked. "Kind of figured."

"But you're still an asshole."

"That's not new," Gio put in.

Antony shot his youngest son a look that quieted him from saying more.

"Well—"

Dante's ringing phone stopped Lucian from saying more. He held up a finger to ask for a second before answering the call.

"Yeah, Dante here."

"They're going to *Vegas*, Dante!"

His wife's screech damn near burst his eardrums. He almost touched his ear after pulling the phone away just to see if it was bleeding or something. The volume of her words actually made the speakers crackle.

All the men at the table shot him a look—wary and concerned. They had likely heard Catrina loud and clear if the looks on their faces were any indication.

"Jesus Christ, Cat," Dante said as he put the phone back to his ear. "What in the hell is wrong with you yelling at me like that?"

"You ... you ..." His wife spluttered before finally settling on saying, "You call her, Dante, or him! I don't *care*. You call one of them and make sure they're not going to Vegas to do what I think they're going to do! *Right now, Dante!*"

The loudness of her tone didn't decrease a bit. If anything, she could louder.

"Cat—"

"I will absolutely die, Dante," she hissed. "Do you understand that? I will die if she does this to me. I have already had one child elope. I cannot handle another one of my children breaking my heart that way. Call them now!"

Dante blinked. "Are you talking about Catherine and—"

"*Yes!*"

"Cat, I am sure they're not going to elope."

He actually wasn't sure, but he figured calming down his wife was more important at the moment. Catrina sounded like she was two seconds away from breaking down entirely. Well, if she hadn't already fallen down that fucking rabbit hole.

It kind of sounded like she had.

"You don't know that!"

"Catrina, now—"

"Mark my words, Dante, if they elope because you didn't stop them, I will never, ever forgive you!"

"Okay, now you're starting to sound a little psychotic, *donna*."

"I will never forgive you," she repeated, now deathly calm. "You better make sure that's not what they're doing."

Catrina hung up the call.

Silence passed around the men at the table for a second ... or three.

Finally, Lucian spoke first.

"Well, that was interesting."

Gio cleared his throat, and stood from his seat. "I think I'm going to go home to my non-violent, happily pleasant wife, and thank her for never yelling at me loud enough that my nuts ascend back into my body."

Dante looked at his father. "Can I come stay with you and Ma for a couple of days?"

Because given the fit his wife seemed to be in over something as simple as a Vegas trip, it kind of sounded like he might need a different place to sleep. Catrina—despite how she tried to say otherwise—would not be calmed by Dante making a phone call to their daughter or her boyfriend.

Antony chuckled. "Nope."

Damn.

That was that.

THE FIRST MEET

Almost five-year-old Catherine tried again to run up the slide. The same way her older brother and cousin had done it just a minute before. She didn't know if it was because she was too small, or there was too much snow, but she couldn't make it. All over again, she fell down the slide and into the snow at the bottom.

Catherine huffed. Her breath colored the cold air white. "This is stupid."

"Is not just 'cause you can't do it," Andino said.

"You can just use the ladder, Catherine," her brother, Michel, said.

"I don't *want* to use the ladder. I want to go up the slide!"

Michel rolled his eyes. Andino just ignored Catherine altogether. She was far smaller than both of them, and this wasn't fun at all.

Catherine sat down on her backside. The cold snow covered the ground, and seeped through her thick, pink snow pants. The only good thing about this stupid day was that Christmas was almost here.

She loved Christmas.

"Are you gonna come up and play, or what?" Michel asked.

Catherine turned her back to her brother, and refused to answer. She even crossed her arms over her chest. Something her mom would have said made her look like a brat.

Well, her mom wasn't there.

And Catherine *wanted* to be a brat.

"Fine, be like that, Catherine," Michel said from up on the playground equipment.

"I will!"

She still didn't turn around or unfold her arms. It usually got her what she wanted. Eventually, someone would fold and give her what she wanted.

It always happened.

"Ah, just leave her alone, Michel," Andino said. "We can play alone, anyway."

Catherine scowled.

Her cousin was mean.

"Yeah, I guess," Michel said. "She can just use the stupid ladder. It's right there."

"Who cares?" Andino asked. "We're up here, so let's make a fort with the snow."

"Okay."

Catherine stayed right where she was, and refused to budge even an inch. She knew it wasn't really her brother's or cousin's fault that she couldn't get up the slide like they could.

She was still mad that they could do it, and she couldn't.

Sometimes, Catherine hated being so little. It made everything harder for her to do. Everyone else around her was taller, and faster. She could never keep up.

Sniffling, Catherine pushed up from the cold ground. Her boots crunched on the snow as she headed away from the playground. She could see her Uncle Giovanni sitting on a bench beside a man she didn't know. Her uncle had been the one to bring them to the park, but now, she didn't want to play at all.

She just wanted to go home.

It was only when Catherine got closer to her uncle and the unknown man that something else caught her eye. Or ... someone else.

A boy—sitting all alone on a bench nearby. He had no one sitting with him, and there were no other kids playing except her brother and cousin. The boy was probably not as old as her brother—not tall enough, she thought. He had to be older than her, though. Maybe he was the same age as Andino.

Even though the black-haired boy sat all alone and didn't play, he didn't seem like he really minded all that much. He looked fine by himself. She also thought he kind of looked like the man sitting next to her uncle. Maybe the man was his dad.

Catherine wondered what that felt like—to be happy all by yourself with no one else around. She thought that kind of seemed lonely. She didn't like to feel lonely.

She didn't want the boy to be alone, either, even if he didn't look all that lonely.

Catherine changed directions and headed for the unknown boy, instead of going to her uncle to tattle. She was almost standing right in front of the boy before he even noticed she was there. He had brown eyes, and a nice smile. He didn't say a thing to her as she climbed up to sit beside him on the bench.

"Hi," she said eventually.

"Hi."

"I'm Catherine."

"Hi, Catherine."

She gave him a look.

"You're supposed to tell me *your* name," she said.

"Why?"

"Because it's polite."

"What do you know about being polite?"

"My daddy says it."

"But you don't know what it means, huh?"

"Kind of," Catherine said, "but a little bit no, too. He only tells me that when I meet new people, anyway. You're new people. It's polite, so what's your name?"

"Hard to argue with that."

"Huh?"

"Nothing." The boy laughed. "My name is Cross."

Catherine smiled widely.

She liked his name.

It was different, like him.

"Hi, Cross."

I GUESS

"Shit."

Catherine looked away from the television in Cross's apartment to watch him come back through the living room. He grabbed the leather jacket he'd previously discarded to the chair, and shrugged it over his shoulders before he came up behind where she sat on the couch.

"Are we going somewhere?" she asked.

Because *God* ... she just wanted to stay here.

With him.

Hide away from the world.

Do their thing.

Cross's fingers tangled into her hair, and with a gentle tug, she tipped her head back for him. Without warning, he bent down and dropped a kiss to her lips that had Catherine smiling all over again and suddenly not caring at all if he did want her to get up and leave the apartment.

She'd thought being thirteen and with Cross was something else. And the years that followed just got better.

Now she was seventeen ... and it was still good.

Still perfect.

He was still hers.

Far too soon for her liking, Cross straightened back up while Catherine ran the tip of her tongue along her lips to lap up what taste of him remained.

"I have to run across town," he explained, "and you can just stay here. It won't take me too long, I promise."

She sighed. "Promise?"

"Hmm?"

"You can't kiss me like that and then *leave*, Cross, it's rude."

His grin turned sinful in a blink.

She *loved* that.

"I've heard patience is a virtue," he told her.

"Says the man who doesn't have an ounce of his own."

Cross laughed. "Point taken. I won't be long."

Well, what fight could she put up, really?

414

"Fine," she booed.

Cross winked, adding, "And I forgot, but Cam is coming over in a bit. I promised to take her out to a movie tonight, but then you came over, too. I couldn't very well tell you no, and I already promised her, so ..."

"It's fine."

"Yeah?"

Catherine shrugged. "Sure."

"I just ... I mean, you two don't hang out very often together and all."

"She's your sister, Cross. It's fine."

But he also wasn't wrong. It wasn't that Catherine didn't like Camilla Donati. In fact, it was quite the opposite. What she knew about Camilla, she did like quite a bit. The few times they did hang out, usually at Cross's parents' place for dinner or something, she didn't mind it.

But did she have the girl's number?

Did they chat?

Were they *friends*?

Not really.

Camilla was a couple years younger. In an entirely different place in her life. She did her own thing and the two of them never found time to find a middle ground between one another where they could forge a real friendship. Except for maybe Cross, but he was so busy even that he couldn't be used for that, either.

So was life.

It just worked out that way sometimes.

"Listen, I'm fine," she repeated to him, "you just get whatever you need done, and I'll be here when you get back."

"You better."

He dropped another kiss to her lips.

Catherine smiled all over again.

*

The opening of the apartment's front door had Catherine calling out, "Is that you, Camilla?"

It took a second for the girl to answer back.

"Uh, yeah?"

415

Catherine quickly grabbed the bowl of popcorn she'd made and headed for the living room. Camilla was just dropping her bookbag into a chair when Catherine came into the room.

"Cross had to run and do something. He figured—"

"We're supposed to go to a movie tonight," Camilla interjected.

"Yeah, I didn't know about those plans until after I got here. I hope you don't mind me tagging along later?"

Camilla gave Catherine a look from the side, and then shrugged. "Nah, I guess that'd be okay."

She *guessed?*

Catherine really didn't know much about Cross's sister.

At all.

So much so, that other than offering the bowl of popcorn, the two girls barely spoke at all while Catherine started the episode on the television that she had left on pause while she made her snack. Not that Camilla seemed to mind the silence, but Catherine had to wonder if that was nothing more than politeness.

After all, she knew *some* things about this girl.

Cam liked to be loud.

Loved attention.

Or was that just with others?

Was she different in private?

"You know," Camilla said beside Catherine on the couch, "that Cross is my best friend, right?"

"I didn't know, but thanks for telling me."

"You're not close to your brother?"

Catherine considered Michel.

"I love my brother—we're not best friends."

And she was fine with that.

He'd do anything for her if she asked it of him. And she would do the same for him. They weren't, however, the number one contact for each other and she was fine with their occasional conversations rather than being on the phone with him every single night. They'd just never been that type of siblings.

Some weren't.

"Oh, well …" Camilla tossed up a piece of popcorn, and easily caught it into her mouth before chewing, swallowing, then saying, "Cross is mine, anyway. He's the *best* big brother."

Catherine had no doubt.

Then, Camilla looked over at her with an arched brow, saying simply, "So you know, if *you* make him sad, I know you did it."

Oh, did she?

"Yeah, I know it," Camilla repeated, "and I don't *like* it."

"Is that … a warning for me?" Catherine asked.

"Kind of sounds like it, right?"

"A little. Here I was thinking we might actually make friends."

Camilla smiled. "We're friends."

"Are we?"

"Well, we *will* be, maybe."

"Does the warning still apply even then?"

Camilla didn't even hesitate. "I guess so, Catherine."

Noted.

Very much noted.

And the funny thing?

Catherine respected the hell out of that.

BEFORE THE WEDDING

"God, this dress was worth every single penny," Catherine's mother said, making one quicker sweep around her daughter to check for anything else that might need fixed last minute. For Catrina, that could be as simple as a tiny thread sticking out, or a single hair out of place. "Do you love it as much as I do?"

"What do you think?"

Catrina winked. "That you're glad your father paid for it?"

"Cute."

"Well …"

Catherine laughed, and turned a bit to watch how the blush-colored ballgown shimmered as she moved. She had wavered on which style of dress to choose—she was lucky enough to have the body type that would look good in just about any style. And her mother made her try on every single style just to make sure she knew what each one looked like on her body.

In the end, she went back and forth between a form-fitting mermaid style dress that was draped in lace from the plunging neckline to the hem of the long train, and this blush-colored ballgown. During those fittings, her mother had pointed out the lace, mermaid style was very close to the dress Catrina had worn for her wedding. Catherine knew it was true—she saw the pictures of her parents' wedding. That alone was enough to make her consider the mermaid dress a little more.

For whatever reason, though, she kept going back to the ballgown with its pretty color, and *a huge* train. She wasn't the type to go for something like this—she rocked sexier styles and this felt very … *regal*. And royal.

Her mother said exactly what she was thinking, then, reaching out to fix the crown that rested beneath her veil. A gift her father had gotten made by a jeweler overseas—her *something new*, he'd said. God knew it looked good and fit under the veil. It set the whole look off, to say the least.

"You look like a queen about to take her throne," Catrina said, smiling.

Catherine glanced back at the mirror again.

Her mother wasn't wrong.

"Ready to go downstairs and get this show started?" Catherine asked.

Catrina nodded. "Just about. One last thing …"

"What's that?"

Catrina was quick to round the table in the private room and pull out a small gift bag underneath. Inside the bag, she pulled out a tiny velvet box, taking a moment to look it over and hold it in her hands before coming back to stand in front of her daughter. She smiled and shrugged a little bit.

Catherine almost found it funny.

In a way, she thought her Ma looked … *nervous*. That wasn't like Catrina at all.

"It's going to seem a little silly—"

"Nothing you give me is silly, Ma," Catherine said quickly.

She wasn't lying. For a long time, she'd tried her very best to be different from her mother, but the truth was far more obvious. They weren't clones of one another, but they were very similar in a lot of ways. She loved her ma far more than she would ever be able to explain.

Catrina nodded, and then opened the box. Inside, a small ring rested in black velvet. Sitting atop a thin white-gold band was a cluster of blue sapphires. "You know … when I was a young girl, I didn't have very much. We were a poor family, and what little bit of things we did have, well, they were cherished items. And when my mother married the man who would be my half-sister's father, this was the ring he gave her for their engagement."

Catherine blinked. "But you don't like him."

Maybe she had said that a little too bluntly, but honestly, that was putting it mildly. Whenever Catherine *did* get her mother to talk about her family, which wasn't very often, Catrina didn't hide the contempt she felt for the man who essentially forced her out on her own at a young age. The man who hated her, in a lot of ways. Or that's how Catrina always seemed to describe it to her daughter.

"I don't, you're right," Catrina murmured. "And maybe that's why I kept this ring tucked away for so long, even though it had exchanged hands after being given to my mother, and—"

"What do you mean?"

Catrina quieted, and Catherine could tell just by the way her mother's jaw worked, that she was chewing on her inner cheek. More nerves—it just felt strange to see her ma like that.

"My mother gave it to my sister before she headed out on her own to try and find me," Catrina finally said, although her voice barely broke a whisper. "When I found my sister the first time years later, when I came back for her, she still had it. She gave it to me ... asked me to keep it safe, said I could give it back when the time was right."

Catherine felt the telltale prickle behind her eyes, but blinked to keep the tears back. "Oh."

"The time never got to be right," Catrina murmured quickly. "You know what happened to Catherine, and so I have kept it tucked away."

"Ma—"

"Waiting for the right time," Catrina said, smiling and meeting her daughter's gaze. "You are her namesake, and so I thought it would be better in your hands, now. And you need your *something blue*, too."

"Wouldn't Michel be—"

Catrina was quick to shake her head. "No, he has his own piece of his biological mother. Something else I kept tucked away."

Catherine didn't ask her mother for more details in that regard. She didn't have to because they never did. It wasn't something they talked about, really. It was never made to be a big deal in their family, and honestly, the one person who might have made it into a big deal—Michel—never actually saw it as a problem.

Catherine had learned the truth about her brother's paternity shortly after her brother was married. But apparently, Michel had known since he was fourteen, and found some kind of paperwork in their father's desk. While the world and all the legal documents said Catrina was her brother's mother, the truth was that it had always been Catherine—Catrina's sister. And his father, well, their mom and dad didn't talk about that.

Not that it mattered.

Those were the details.

To Michel, and to Catherine, his mom and dad were Catrina and Dante. Nothing ever changed that. Her brother didn't have a complex about a history he really didn't know, and didn't seem to care to know. She didn't know what, if anything, her mother told her brother. That shit wasn't for Catherine to ask. It really wasn't her business.

With careful hands, Catrina passed over the small ring with the beautiful cluster of sapphires. Catherine slipped it down her index finger, happy to find it was a perfect fit, really. And for some reason, it kind of felt like the ring had found a good and proper home on her hand.

Catrina smiled at her daughter. "I know, silly, right?"

Catherine shook her head, stepped forward, and hugged her mother without warning. It took Catrina a half of a second before she was hugging Catherine back. "Not silly, Ma. I love you, and it. Thank you."

Thank you really didn't seem like enough. The way her mother hugged her tighter said it absolutely was.

"Let's get you married, Catty," her mom whispered.

BEFORE THE WEDDING

"Smile, *bello*."

Dante gave his wife a look just as they came to a stop next to the seat where she was meant to sit for the duration of the ceremony. "I am … aren't I?"

Catrina smiled softly, and leaned in to kiss his cheek. "You are. Sometimes, I just like to keep you on your toes."

He chuckled.

She was always good for that, no doubt about it.

"Are you ready for this?" she asked.

Really, Dante hadn't been expecting that question from his wife. Then again, this whole day had seemed like one thing coming at him after another. He really didn't get time to sit and focus on one thing before another was coming for him. From the moment he woke up, he had to move, move, move. He didn't even get the chance to really stop and *think* about what this day meant.

That didn't mean it wasn't on his mind—oh, it very much *was*. He just hadn't given it the time to properly think on it. Maybe that was better, anyway. His daughter was happy; she was marrying the man of her dreams, and Dante knew that. There was no questioning it, not that he wanted to.

"Of course, I'm ready, Cat," Dante said.

Catrina nodded. "Mmhmm, not the least bit sad, then?"

Damn this woman.

"You just sit in your chair and look beautiful like you're meant to. Got it?"

"All right."

She pressed another fast kiss to his lips, and patted his cheeks with her fingertips in that way of hers. It was what he loved most about his wife, he supposed. No matter what, Catrina was still Catrina at the end of the day. Keeping him on his toes at every turn, and making sure he was the best man he could possibly be. He had to be. After all, he was standing beside the best woman.

Once his wife was settled into her seat, Dante went back and walked his mother to her seat, too. He waited while Cross came in with his mother, and walked her to her seat. The theatrics of a wedding—things that annoyed other people—were the same things that Dante enjoyed about a proper service.

As soon as everyone was where they were supposed to be, Dante headed for the back. All that was left now was for the ceremony to really get started. Checking his watch before he slipped through the back doors of the church, Dante lifted his head as they closed behind him to see the line of women in chiffon staring back at him.

All were smiling, some were whispering.

He stepped past the line of his nieces—all being Catherine's bridal party—to find his daughter waiting at the end with her back turned to him. With her attention down on the large bouquet in her hands, she didn't notice him staring. He took that moment, feeling the noise at his back quiet a bit as his attention focused in on her.

His only girl.

His impossibility.

Funny—she was very possible, and she proved that to him time and time again. Stronger than people gave her credit for, and more amazing than anyone would ever possibly know. She was the perfect mixture of her mother and father. God knew she looked just like Catrina, but she had a whole lot of him coloring her up, too.

She made him so fucking proud.

They knocked her down; she got back up ready to *fight*.

Like his kid should.

Thing was—she wasn't just a *girl* anymore, either. Very much a beautiful young woman about to take the biggest steps into a life of her own. And maybe, even up until that moment right then, Dante was still seeing Catherine as his little girl. The one in her pretty clicky shoes and sparkly dresses. The little girl who still held his hand when they walked down the street, and always wanted him to tuck her into bed night after night.

But she wasn't that girl anymore.

She was *this* woman.

Catherine turned then and lifted her head to find her father standing there. He might have been embarrassed to have to catch him staring, but he couldn't even bother to feel that at all. She'd asked him earlier when she revealed her dress to Cross whether or not he was sad about this day.

He'd not really been sure if his answer was honest, then.

He knew, now, though.

No, he wasn't sad at all.

"Ready to get me married, Daddy?" Catherine asked.

Dante nodded. "Yeah, time to get you married, *vita mia.*"

*

Cross POV

Zeke's hand landed firmly on Cross's shoulder as the music changed again. His friend's silent show of support. He knew what that song meant—he and Catherine had gone around and around and around in way too many conversations to count over which song should be the one she walked down the aisle to. Something more traditional, or something altogether different.

All this time ...

He'd waited *all this time.*

And in just a few moments, all the time he waited would mean absolutely nothing. Moments of his past that would feel like they hadn't really been the struggle he thought they were because this moment right here meant it was all worth it, anyway. Every moment spent waiting for Catherine, and this day, would be worth it.

That was surreal.

Not once since he woke up that morning had he really stopped to appreciate how unreal this entire day was. Maybe because a part of him had still believed it couldn't possibly be real even though he knew without a doubt that it was very much real.

The doors at the back of the church opened at all once, and Cross's head snapped up instantly. There were so many familiar faces in the crowd, honestly. People he'd known his whole life. Friends he'd known for decades. People he loved beyond words. And yet, the only thing he really wanted to see was standing at the back of the church with her hand tucked around her father's arm.

Cross smiled, then.

Catherine, all the way at the end of the aisle, smiled back under the blush color of her veil.

He'd seen her dress already—the damn woman knew what he needed without even needing him to tell her a single thing about it either way—and yet, it still kind of struck him to see her standing there again with it. His heart felt the same way it had back at the hotel—like it was about to beat right out of his chest, like he couldn't control it at all. His lungs still ached with every single breath he took. And yeah, his gaze still blurred a bit with the threat of tears, but he blinked them back. He didn't want to miss this, not for *anything*.

He'd waited all this time, after all.

He was not going to miss her walking to him now.

There was no way in hell he was going to miss this woman walking to him—this beautiful, amazing woman who belonged entirely to him. There was no other person on this earth who was made for him. Not like Catherine. He belonged to her, too.

That's kind of how love worked, he supposed.

Cross wasn't entirely sure how long it took for Catherine and her father to come down the aisle. It kind of felt like he was in a daze, like his vision tunneled, and the only thing he could really see was her soft smile getting closer and closer with every passing second. Each step she took had his heard thundering impossibly louder.

And then there she was ...

Right in front of him.

Dante handed her hand over with a nod and a smile before taking his leave to sit beside his wife. All things that seemed to happen in the background of Cross's mind, really. He was still focusing on Catherine.

And her soft smile.

He found his fingers trembled a bit when he reached up to pull her veil back like he was supposed to do. Never once did her gaze leave his, though.

And there she was again ...

God.

"I love you, Catherine."

It wasn't like she needed told again. God knew he told her all the fucking time anyway. He couldn't say it enough, really. She still liked him to say it, and he still needed to tell her. It was his thing.

And she exactly what to say back.

Forever.

Catherine's smile widened a bit. "Promise?"

Cross grinned. "Always, babe."

AFTER THE WEDDING

Catherine POV

Laughter came from the people surrounding them, and hands hit the tables repeatedly. Makeshift drums, maybe, but all Catherine could do was shake her head at the sight of Cross grinning in that arrogant way of his. All the while, he had a piece of cake lifted in his hand for her to get a good look at. Not a big piece, mind you, but it was big enough for him to make a whole mess across her face like she had done to his just a second before.

"Don't you *dare*," she warned.

"You know what you gotta do, Cross!" someone shouted behind him.

"Don't let her get away with that, man!"

Catherine tried to give her new husband a glare that promised certain death if he dared to ruin her makeup, or God forbid, spill some of that cake down her beautiful dress. "Cross, I *swear* ..."

"Swear what, baby?" He arched a brow, that white frosting still smeared a bit to the side of his mouth. If she wasn't entirely terrified that he was going to ruin her makeup, she might have thought this conversation was comical. "That you smooshed a whole handful of cake into my face but now you don't want me to do it to you? How is that a good lesson for you, huh?"

"It wasn't a whole handful!"

"Because I dodged most of it."

Okay, so that wasn't a lie.

"But that's only because I never get anything over on you," Catherine said in a fast rush of words. He was closing in on her, after all. Only a few steps away with his hand still raised and ready to streak that cake all over her face. And he was probably going to do it with a laugh, too. "So I have to take my chances when I can, you know?"

"Right, baby. I'm *sure*."

"*Cross*."

Cross just grinned. "Hope you're ready for the pictures of this to be hanging up on our wall for *years*, Catty."

"Oh, my God, come on!"

"Just do it, Cross!" someone shouted.

Zeke, it sounded like.

Fuck him, too.

Catherine would make sure she got Zeke back at another time. She could hold a grudge like nobody's business. He should have known better, frankly.

Her thoughts scrammed when all of the sudden, Cross came at her when he must have thought she was distracted. Self-preservation kicked in, and she turned as fast as she could in that huge dress to get away from the man coming her way with fingers sticky with icing. Unfortunately, the first thing she almost ran into was the cake table, and by the time she turned around to look for another way out, it was already too late.

Cross's arm wrapped around Catherine's waist, and he tipped her back before she even knew what was happening. Without warning, he dropped his head down, and his lips met hers in a fierce, hungry kiss that took her breath away. Catherine felt high, then. Like she was floating amongst the clouds with this man. The rest of the cheering room disappeared, and nothing else mattered. She wasn't thinking about ruined makeup or icing in her face. The only thing that mattered then was the way Cross's lips felt working against hers as his tongue darted into her mouth for a taste. She could still taste the remnants of the icing she'd smooshed on his face on the edge of his tongue, too.

Her eyes locked on his as he pulled away just a little bit, a sexy grin curving his lips in the sexiest way. Cross brought his icing-covered fingers in front of her face, and wiggled them back and forth. "Open up, babe."

Catherine sighed. "Why do I even try?"

"Trust me."

She parted her lips for him, and he slipped those two fingers in her mouth for her to take the sweetness right from him fingertips. She did just that, too, sucking his digits clean before he righted her back to her feet. Then, he used a napkin someone handed over to wipe the corner of her mouth and her lips with gentle pats that wouldn't smear her lipstick.

All the while, he grinned like the fucking cat who had gotten the *whole* bowl of milk.

Smug bastard.

God, she loved him.

"Had a bit of icing from my kiss on your mouth," he said, winking. "You were never going to smear me, were you?"

Cross shook his head. "You said not to, babe."

Catherine smiled.

She should have known. She made the limits; he always followed them without question. He was just amazing like that. Yet another reason why she loved him, really.

"Give me that napkin, let me wipe you, too."

He handed it over; the crowd went back to clinging their glasses for another kiss.

They got what they wanted, too.

*

Cross POV

"If the couple of the hour would please join in the middle of the dance floor for the next song, please," came a voice over the music. "Please clear the dance floor for Mr. and Mrs. Donati for their first official dance as a married couple, and then we'll join them again a little later."

"Think that's supposed to be you, man," Zeke said.

Cross gave his best friend a look. "You think, smartass?"

Zeke simply grinned, and slapped Cross on the back. Someone else shoved Cross on the shoulder, forcing him away from the group he'd been talking to, and onto the dance floor. The last time he saw Catherine, she'd been helping a little girl fix the bow on the top of her head. Now, he found her parting the crowd on the other side of the dance floor.

Yeah, she still looked every inch a fucking queen.

He met his wife in the middle of the dance floor, and the second he had his arm wrapped around her waist, and her hand cupped in his as the song changed to the one she'd picked for this dance, the rest of the world disappeared. Her glittering green eyes watched him as they moved in a familiar step around the floor.

Cross felt like ... he needed to imprint everything about this moment. He wasn't sure why, but he did. There was so much that happened over the day, really. He'd never stopped moving, going from one thing to the next, and constantly running for this or that. Weddings were exhausting, honestly.

Right then, though …

He just wanted to remember this.

How she looked.

Her smile.

That pink tint to her cheeks.

The way her fingers tightened around his.

All of it.

Cross was so caught up in those thoughts that before he'd realized it, the majority of the song was over, and the Dj was inviting others to join them on the floor, too. He'd not said one word to Catherine the entire time, and she hadn't spoken to him, either. But maybe they really didn't need to.

Sometimes, a silent moment was better.

"How much longer before we're out of here?" he dared to ask.

Catherine laughed. "Patience, Cross."

Yes, because patience was exactly what he was known for.

Not that it mattered.

The end would soon come, and he would get his wife the hell out of here so they could finally start the rest of their lives together. He could deal with a couple more hours pretending like he was going to share this woman with the rest of them.

But the very second he knew they could get out?

That's what he was going to do.

Like Catherine could read his mind, she laughed again and repeated, "Patience."

Sure, sure.

"It is what it is, Catty."

"Mmhmm."

Yep.

And he was what he was.

Never gonna change.

DAD

"Can I? Can I do it, Papa?"

Catherine followed the voice of her four-year-old son, letting it lead her to the rear French doors of their three-level home that took them to the veranda. Standing in the doorway, her gaze scanned the large backyard at the same time she heard Cross reply to Naz, "Yeah, jump. I'll catch you."

Jump?

She didn't have to search for long before she found the source of their conversation and the fucking answer to her question. There stood her husband, fifteen or more feet down on the ground from where their son currently waited. *In this fledgling treehouse.* Right then, it was nothing more than the bones of what would be the treehouse. Likely by the weekend, it would be finished once all the guys came back over to help Cross put in the walls, the roof, and a better way up than the boards nailed into the side of the tree and a plank they walked up like they were currently using.

The better question, though?

Why was Naz up there?

They had already agreed the kid wouldn't be playing in the treehouse until it was fully safe and ready to do so. Hell, the thing didn't even have walls.

He shouldn't be up there.

Never mind talking about *jumping.*

The second the kid let it slip that he and Cece might like a treehouse, Cross had shit planned out before he laid his head down that same night to sleep. Though he held everything in his life in high regard, the one thing he took most serious was being a dad.

Their dad.

Catherine loved him so much for that. Her father had been the same way as she grew up—always willing to put less important things aside so that his kids never felt like they were an afterthought to Dante. It was the same reason why she knew that if today, or on any other day, the only thing she wanted to do was call and talk to her dad, she could do just that. Dante wouldn't make her think anything else.

Their kids would be the same with Cross, she knew. Catherine didn't think he understood how much that would mean to them in the future, but someday he would. *Hopefully.*

"Are you gonna jump, or what?" she heard Cross call.

"Yeah! Like, *fly*, right?"

Cross chuckled, his gaze darting toward the house before snapping right back to where Naz was still hanging dangerously close to the edge of the platform. *Fat too high.* If he noticed his wife standing at the rear doors, she couldn't tell. Not that it mattered. Surely, Cross wasn't really going to let him jump down from there.

"Hurry, before your Ma—"

Catherine opened her mouth to shout out to Cross *and* Naz that nobody was going to be jumping down from that goddamn treehouse. But she didn't get the chance to say anything at all. Naz took three quick steps back in his little Timberland boots, and then he darted forward just as fast. He didn't even *think* about it. Didn't look the least bit scared or worried. In fact, he was nothing more than a blur of a smile with arms stretched wide as he flew off the side of the platform and fell *fast* to his waiting father before.

She felt her heart *drop.*

Swore it jumped right back up into her throat at the same time.

Catherine didn't even get the time to appreciate how thick her anxiety could become before everything was fine and okay again. Because Cross caught Naz and just as fast, the boy had two feet on the ground. His little toque with the furry ball on top bounced the same way he did while his pealing laughter echoed over the backyard.

"*Again!* I wanna do it again!"

Cross looked toward the house once more, but this time, his gaze did land on Catherine. While she felt *something* akin to amusement, she was also sure her face didn't look like it. "Probably not, buddy."

That was that.

Naz headed for his tree swing.

Cross followed right behind.

It was still taking time for her to get used to the fact that their son wasn't *anything* like their daughter, in a lot of ways. Her husband didn't have a problem with that—that morning he snuggled with Cece after breakfast until he heart was content. This afternoon, he was letting their boy jump out of a treehouse like the kid had wings.

Later, he'd probably dangle Naz upside down by his ankles before he played pretend tea with Cece like he usually did in the evenings. When their daughter had been Naz's age, Cross wouldn't even let the girl look at a *street* without looking like he might kill anything and everything that dared to move in her direction.

Naz?

He just let the kid go.

Catherine didn't get it.

That was Cross, though.

And he was just being a dad.

She knew that.

Even if sometimes it scared her to death.

THE TEENS

The front door to Catherine's Newport home slammed shut with a loud bang. Stomping and teen girl screeches soon followed.

"Ma! Ma, where the fuck are you?"

Catherine rolled her eyes as she pulled a casserole from the oven. "In the kitchen, Cece."

All too soon, the seventeen year old tornado that was Cecelia Catherine Donati stormed into the kitchen. She looked every inch like her mother—Catherine's features, her smile, and more stared back at her.

But those eyes?

All brown, and soul-deep.

That hair?

Currently chopped to shoulder-length, and black as night.

And good God …

Her attitude?

Sometimes snarky, and often times, aloof. Occasionally restless, and lately, a touch too much of smartass.

All of that?

Cross Nazio Donati right out of bed.

Catherine saw a younger mirror of herself when she looked at her daughter, but sweet Jesus, she found Cross reflecting back, too.

"Could you not cuss the moment you walk through the front door?" Catherine asked. "Just save it for elsewhere, Cece."

Her daughter clicked her tongue, and rolled her eyes upward. "Like you don't swear all the time, Ma?"

Damn.

She had Catherine there.

Another con to add to the list about having children that might as well have been your little twins.

A person couldn't get away with shit.

"What happened now?" Catherine asked.

Maybe if she moved Cece back onto the issue at hand—whatever it was that sent her storming into the house—then her teen would stop looking like such a smug little shit.

Doubtful.

It was still worth a shot.

"Well?" Catherine asked. "What happened?"

"The same thing that happened last week when I agreed to drive Naz's spoiled ass home, Ma. What else?"

All at once, annoyance and exasperation shot through Catherine. She hadn't known it was possible to feel those two things in such extreme ways at the same time until her kids became teenagers overnight. Teens who seemed hell-bent on driving each other—and thus, their parents—crazy.

"I'm sure Naz didn't—"

"Ma, he dumped a whole can of soda on Frankie's head, and then he threw the can at his face."

Cece stared hard at her mother like she was trying to let that statement sink in. All Catherine could do was press her lips together to keep from smiling. She was ninety-nine percent sure that was not the reaction Cece was looking for at the moment.

"And do you know why he did that, Ma? Do you *know why*?"

"No, but I assume you're going to tell me."

"Because Frankly *may have* looked like he was *possibly* touching my ass with his hand after he hugged me goodbye in the parking lot."

Yep.

That would do it for Naz.

Nazio was terribly protective of his older sister even being four years younger than her. Age didn't make much of difference for Naz—his position was always made clear where his sister was concerned.

Like a giant bloody line in the sand.

Bloody, because he had no problem using the next fool's blood to make the line stand out more when needed.

He didn't like guys messing with his sister. Not all guys, of course. There were a select few boyfriends Cece had in which Naz made an effort to tolerate.

Still, he hated far more of them than he liked. And he had absolutely no problem with letting them know that, too.

"Ma, you have got to tell him to back off," Cece said.

Catherine had.

So did Cross.

Nazio was just … Naz.

Far too much like his father. Difficult to a particular point. Fiercely protective, and beautifully good in his heart.

"I will speak to Nazio," Catherine told her daughter.

"Speak to me about what?"

Nazio leaned in the doorway looking like every inch a thirteen year old tsunami full of piss, vinegar, and hormones. The smug as shit smirk he wore—a mirror of his father in every single way—said he had probably been listening to their conversation in the hallway.

"Ugh." Cece threw her hands high, gave her brother a glare, and then said to her mother, "Deal with him, Ma."

Nazio smiled at his sister as she huffed, and stormed from the kitchen. Catherine gave her teenage son a look for instigating more trouble. Naz only shrugged in response.

"Really?" she asked.

"What?"

"Why do you antagonize her, Naz?"

"Because I can."

Jesus.

Catherine pointed at the table. "Take a seat."

Nazio strolled leisurely into the kitchen, and dropped his too-tall frame into a chair usually reserved for his father. Only thirteen, but puberty had kicked in hard for Naz over the last year. His voice had dropped a couple of octaves, the facial hair was coming in, and he was getting taller by the damn day.

Sometimes, she wished he would slow down a little bit. Just be her baby boy for a while longer.

It wasn't possible.

Catherine headed around the island, and went to the table. She pulled her son's beanie from his head, and dropped it to the table in front of him.

"You know the rules," she said.

Naz smiled over at her. "No hats at the table."

"Mmhmm. Now, why can't you just let your sister and her boyfriend be, huh?"

He cocked a brow. "Frankie is a tool, Ma."

"But you know Cece can handle herself."

And she *could.*

She did.

Catherine and Cross made sure of that.

Naz shrugged. "Cece doesn't even really like Frankie. He's a distraction until Juan gets back into town. I'm not going to pretend to like the asshole until then. That's all I'm saying, Ma."

Catherine sighed. "You don't know what she's waiting on Juan, now."

"Ma, everybody knows she's crazy as fuck over him."

"Stop swearing at the table."

"Whatever—you can't deny I'm right about Cece and Juan, though."

There was something about Miguel's nineteen year old son that Cece couldn't escape from the time she was fifteen. Of course, being Catherine's right hand man meant Miguel's family often mingled with theirs. Juan and Catherine had grown from being children to young adults together, and now ... this.

"Naz, just ..."

"What?"

"Lay off a bit."

Naz *meh'd* under his breath. "I'll try."

"Try what?"

Catherine found her husband leaning in the kitchen entryway. Leave it to Cross to smell food and come looking after all the trouble was finally taken care of. His way of dealing with Naz was to take the boy to a shooting range, or out to work on ... whatever. Cece, on the other hand, Cross simply let the girl do whatever she needed to do to get her spells out of her.

It was their life, though.

Their children were not like other children.

They had and lived a different life.

Catherine sighed as she stood from the table. "Your son poured a can of soda over Cece's boyfriend's head after school."

"And then threw it at his face," Naz added. "You can't forget that part, Ma."

Cross nodded—*appreciatively.*

Ass.

"Frankie?" Cross asked.

"Yep." Naz stood from the table, asking, "Are we good, Ma?"

"As long as you remember what I said."

"I will," her son promised.

And likely not listen to it, either.

"Go find your sister, apologize the best you can so she will be a little bit pleasant when she comes back downstairs, and then tell her supper is ready," Catherine ordered. "Do not antagonize that girl more than you already have, or so help you God, Nazio, you will not like what happens to you when you get back downstairs."

Nazio gave his mother the two finger salute, not even the least bit concerned about her threat. "Got it."

As her son passed Cross in the doorway, Nazio snatched a hundred dollar bill from his father's raised hand. Cross's smirk grew as Catherine gave him a look.

What the hell?

"Well done," Cross murmured, never looking away from Catherine. "I appreciate it."

"Thanks," Naz said, laughing. "I would have done it for nothing, too."

"I bet, son."

"Cross!" Catherine snapped, finally understanding the exchange between father and son. "You did *not* pay him to do that to that boy!"

Her husband didn't even have the fucking decency to look ashamed over what he had done, or that he got caught doing it, either.

"What? I hate that fucking Frankie prick, Catherine."

"Seriously?"

"He's a tool."

And he wondered where Nazio got it from.

Really.

THE LIFE

"Naz, come touch the water," Cece called.

Little Nazio didn't even bother to peer up from the sandcastle he was attempting to build. His focus had been zoned in on that task since they arrived. It was more like a mound of wet sand with his handprints all over it than an actual castle. The two year old didn't really seem to mind all that much.

"No, Cece—castle," Naz muttered.

Cece only rolled her eyes, and went back to splashing at the edge of the water. Her bright yellow polka dotted bathing suit stood out brightly against the backdrop that was Jacob Riis Beach. She was fine with wading about knee-deep into the water, but nothing more than that.

Certainly not deep enough to get her hair wet.

Or even her bathing suit, really.

Cece kicked a foot through the water a bit too hard, and splashed a few droplets onto her legs. The six year old screeched her disdain, and ran backwards out of the water like something was after her.

"Such a diva," Catherine told Cross.

He chuckled. His dark aviator sunglasses hid his eyes from her view. She was tucked tightly into his side on the large blanket. They made it a regular thing to take their kids to one of their favorite spots.

Cross turned his head a bit, and even though she couldn't see his eyes, she knew he was staring at her. Likely in that same intense way he always did—as though she had suddenly become the sun, and he was the world revolving around her.

Nothing else mattered.

"Wouldn't happen to know where she gets that from, would you?" he asked.

Catherine grinned. "Nope."

"So, were going to pretend like you didn't make me walk very carefully to this spot while holding the blanket just so that no one would accidentally kick sand on it?"

"Listen, nobody—"

"And then you made me pick you so up you could kick your flip-flops far enough away from the blanket before I could put you on the blanket without your feet ever having touched the sand?"

Catherine pressed her lips together to keep from smiling.

Nothing he said was a lie.

Goddamn him.

"Nobody wants sand on their blanket, Cross!"

His lips curved wickedly at the edges. "Mmhmm."

"Do you want to clean sand off me when we get home, huh?"

Cross's grin—somehow—turned even more sinful when he said, "You know I love cleaning sand—or whatever—off of you, babe."

Heat shot through Catherine.

Lust quickly followed.

Two kids, and well into their marriage, and the two of them were still just as crazy in love and hot for each other as ever. All it took was a single look from her husband, or a sexy promise whispered into her ear.

This man had been her first everything—kiss, sex, and love. He taught her about all of it, and somehow things were never boring between them.

"Not here, Cross," Catherine told him, ignoring the heat traveling over her cheeks and neck. She gave a pointed look in the direction of their playing children. "It's not like we could sneak off to finish something you start."

"First of all," her husband drawled, "we have two men—*my* men—within thirty feet of us right now. They could absolutely entertain and watch the kids if I needed them to for a few minutes."

"Only a few?"

Cross pulled down his shades just enough for Catherine to get a good look at his eyes. It was enough for her to know she might have hit a nerve.

Poor man.

"More than a few, then," she said quickly, winking.

"Thank you." Cross fixed his glasses once more. "And secondly, you proved my point when you asked if I wanted to have to clean sand off you when we get home."

"Now—"

"Because *regardless*," he interrupted, "you will still make me clean you off twice before you even entertain the idea of getting into our bed. Don't want sand in the sheets—there won't be any on you to begin with. You're a bit of a Primadonna, babe. Own it."

Damn him.

Catherine pouted. "But you love me."

"Lucky I do, too."

She was lucky.

She knew it.

Cross's arm tightened around Catherine, and pulled her in close to his side once more. His lips touched down to her temple with a light kiss as he murmured, "Love you."

Catherine smiled. "Promise?"

"Always, babe."

A screech broke their perfect moment up. They found their two kids ten feet away, and glowering at one another. It wasn't often the two fought. They were actually pretty good playmates, for the most part.

Not at the moment, though.

Cece was lying on her back covered in wet sand—a sure sign the kid was three seconds away from a meltdown just because she was now dirty. Nazio stood over his now ruined sandcastle that Cece had apparently flattened with her back when she tripped.

"Cece!" Nazio howled.

Cece wailed. "I have sand everywhere!"

"Cece—my castle!"

"It was in the way, Naz!"

Little Nazio looked to his father—all exasperated, yet over the whole debacle in a blink. He never looked more like his father than in that moment. His next words made it all the more apparent, too.

"Oh shit, Da, my castle."

Cross cleared his throat.

Catherine pressed her lips together to keep from laughing.

"Okay," Cross said to her, "that boy is all me, though."

Oh, yeah.

Most definitely.

THE FIRST DAY

Cece POV

"Okay, everybody, we have to start clean up, clean up time!"

The kindergarten teacher's voice traveled over the classroom of overly excited children. Cece, at only five, wasn't much for getting messy, or being too loud. Not to mention any of the other things these kids were doing. She would much rather be back at home with her ma, daddy, or Nazio.

But Ma said she had to go to school.

Ma said it would be fun.

Ma lied.

Cece had made friends because that was easy for her to do. And sure, she got to wear her pretty outfit, and do her hair nice. Ma even let her have lip gloss because today was a special day.

But people kept bothering Cece here. She was always having to do this, or that. She couldn't just do what she wanted to do. Cece's Ma and Daddy always told her to listen when the adults were talking, though, so she was trying to be extra good at school.

It was still pretty hard.

But her favorite thing was supposed to happen soon—after lunch, the teacher was going to take them to the library.

The library was the first place she had gotten to see when her ma had taken her to visit the school. That, and the older girls with the pretty dresses were the only reason Cece was excited to attend.

That, and her ma.

Ma seemed excited, too.

Cece didn't want to disappoint her ma.

"Cece," the teacher said, "please go help the other kids pick up the toys."

"But I didn't mess them up or play with them," Cece said.

"You all played with them, sweetheart."

"I didn't."

"Cece."

She hadn't played with the stupid toys. They were the kinds of toys her baby brother, Nazio, might play with. But at the idea that she might not get to go to the library, Cece helped everybody else to pick up the toys.

"Let's line up, everybody, and get ready to go down to the cafeteria."

A little bit closer to the library.

Cece happily skipped to the spot where the rest of the kids had been directed to stand in line. She liked the way the skirt of her dress swished when she moved, so she moved her hips to make it do the sound again.

Not paying much attention to anyone else, Cece felt a sharp tug on her hair. So hard, actually, that it yanked her head back.

And *hurt*.

"Ouch!"

Cece huffed, and turned to face the boy behind her.

"Don't pull my hair," she told him.

The boy—Matthew—only smiled at her. He didn't even say sorry!

"Don't do it again," Cece warned him one last time.

Cece learned from watching Ma, and Grandmamma, that one warning should be more than enough for somebody to get the point, and stop. If one warning didn't seem to work, then the person deserved whatever they got.

She gave the boy one more look she hoped was mean enough to make her point, and then turned around to face the teacher coming down the line of kids.

Then, the boy pulled her hair.

Again.

Okay.

She told him to stop.

He didn't.

Smiling sweetly just like her ma and grandmamma did before they got mad at somebody, Cece turned to face the boy again. He was still smiling in that way of his—a way that her daddy would say was *smug*.

A smile that made Cece want to punch him in the throat. She saw her daddy do that to someone once. It seemed easy enough.

Cece did just that.

She smiled all the while.

The boy dropped to the floor.

"Cece!" the teacher shouted.

Well, crap.

There goes the library.

Oh, well.

*

Cross POV

"Wait," Cross said, "so is the boy also being punished?"

"For what?"

Cross stared at the principal, and hoped to hell the woman could feel his frustration and hatred radiating from his gaze alone. She only stared back silent, and looking stupid behind her too-large desk.

Catherine stepped in to save the day. "I think what my husband is trying to ask, is that will the boy who pulled Cece's hair be spoken to for his behavior as well? Has his parents been called in like we were?"

"He was punched."

Cross scowled. "Quite aware, yeah."

"He is not going to get in trouble because your daughter punched him."

Catherine cocked a brow.

Cross chuckled at the sight.

Hell was coming, and her name was Catherine Donati.

"We've apologized for Cece's outburst, and you can trust that she will be spoken to—thoroughly. However, do explain to that little boy, and his parents as they probably need a fucking memo, too, that when a girl says no, or asks him to stop doing something, he needs to do that. Instantly. No questions asked."

"Mrs.—"

"Make sure he and his parents know that should my daughter make her personal space clear again, and he once again violates it and ignores her request, that she will do exactly what she has been told to do."

The principal gaped.

Catherine tipped her chin up as if to look down on the woman. "I hope I have made myself clear here."

"You cannot advocate for your child to be violent and—"

"People may not put their hands on my child when she has told them *not to*. Just because the way she put her hands on him happened to hurt him more than the way he pulled her hair doesn't negate the fact that he has not yet learned—or not been taught—to keep his fucking hands to himself."

443

Catherine laughed, adding, "Unless you're telling me that I should explain to my daughter that her body and personal space and her ability to be an advocate for those things and herself makes no difference to anyone here at this school. And if that *is* the case, then tell us now so we can make a choice about our daughter's education. We picked this school for a reason—it is progressive, and caters to each child's specific needs. Are you choosing to regress with this nonsense, now?"

"No, no, of course not!"

"Good," Catherine said.

"I will make sure the boy is spoken to. I do also believe that it may be best for you to also explain to Cece that when she becomes violent as a first response, then she loses her voice. It is overtaken by her other actions."

Catherine arched a brow again. "So, I suppose she should simply continue to say no, and let him touch her until someone else steps in to save the day, right?"

The principal's brow furrowed, and for a moment, Catherine's stance softened. Cross figured his wife had made her point, but she drove it home with one last statement.

"If you changed their ages to something a bit older, and replaced hair pulling with something more physical and intimate, then we're moving into dangerous territory. Rape culture does not begin with girls showing off leg and bra straps. It starts with girls who learn their voices do not matter when a boy's is louder, their bodies will not be respected, and young men who have never been taught the word no when they are constantly *excused*."

Clearing her throat, the principal replied, "It will be handled."

"Thank you," Cross said, holding a hand out to his wife. Catherine took it. "And we will speak with our daughter."

To explain that she did exactly right.

Cross held the office door open for his wife, and then followed Catherine out. Cece sat on a chair in the corner. Nazio sat beside his older sister, and played with one of his trucks. As long as Cece was nearby, Naz tended to be very well-behaved.

He hoped that stayed the same once the two were older.

Cece looked up as her parents approached. "Am I in a lot of trouble now?"

"No," Catherine said, "not with us."

Cece looked at the office door. "But here?"

"You really shouldn't hit people at school," Catherine said.

"You didn't say *can't*, Ma," Cece pointed out.

Cross smirked, but hid it by looking away. Their daughter was a smart girl.

"Did you consider telling the teacher before you hit the boy?" Catherine asked.

"No should be enough," Cece said. "I said not to pull my hair, Ma, and even gave him *the look*, too."

"No should always be enough," Catherine agreed.

Nazio looked up from his truck. "No touch. No touch—no, Ma. No touch."

Catherine smiled faintly at Cross. "Why does the eighteen month old get it, but the five year old does not?"

He wished he had the right answer for his wife.

All Cross could say was, "At least we won't be the parents on the other side of this equation someday."

"Small blessings."

Catherine picked up their son, and Cece dropped off the chair when Cross offered his hand to her. The four of them walked out of the office with Catherine and Nazio leading the way.

"Good job," Cross told Cece quietly.

She preened.

The two bumped fists.

"I know what you're doing, Cross!"

Of course, she did.

His wife hadn't even turned around.

THE YEARS

Zeke POV

Sundays were made for *nothing*. Doing absolutely nothing. That was, after church services were over, and you know, he'd apparently showed his face long enough while sitting in a pew to make those around him think he was an appropriate, God-fearing man.

Or so he was told.

But after?

After, Sundays were made for doing fuck all.

Zeke was fifty-five. And because he'd made to this age, he didn't have a lot of fucks to give anymore. Not that he ever had to begin with, as far as that went. His father, God rest Wolf's soul, used to tell him that he was too restless. Always wanting to do something, or be somewhere.

What his father would think now to know Zeke's entire week revolved around getting to this one day where he could sit on his front porch, watch the damn sun pass over the sky, and think about ... well, *life* ... he didn't know what Wolf would say.

Sometimes, he thought he'd give anything to hear his father talk to him again. All those years he spent thinking every word that came out of his father's mouth was nonsensical babble meant to lecture and irritate ... that wasn't the case at all. But it was too late now. So instead of wishing for things that couldn't be, Zeke came out on his porch every Sunday to look at the sky, and talk to his father in his mind. He felt closer to Wolf that way. Even his father's grave didn't make him feel this close.

"You want another coffee, or no?"

Zeke glanced over his shoulder, but kept the porch swing moving back and forth at the same time with the tip of his shined leather loafers. His wife, Katya, stood in the threshold of their front door. She rarely interrupted his time out here. All these years of marriage between them had worked out all the kinks they faced when they were brand new, maybe too fucking young—*even if they hadn't been all that young at all*—and didn't know how to be a couple instead of just one person trying to survive and navigate the world.

She'd been terrified.

Abused by people all around her.

Broken, too.

Maybe that shaped his little Russian wife in certain ways that weren't always to her benefit at first, but it also made her amazing. Resilient, and strong.

Back then, he'd been stubborn, selfish, and not at all aware of what it took to be the best man he could be because he was far too accustomed to being the man he already was.

They worked those kinks out, though.

That was the thing about time. Give it enough space to move on, and it would change everything. The person you might have been twenty or thirty years ago was not the person you were now.

Growth meant change.

Zeke peered down into his empty coffee cup, and then glanced up at his wife again. "No, I think I'm all right, actually."

Katya smiled in her sweet way. "Mmm, okay. You've got a guest coming, by the way. I suspect he'll be here anytime."

He tried hard not to scowl, and failed. His wife only laughed.

"It's only Cross," his wife said, shrugging as she turned to go back in the house. "And even he can't ruin your Sundays, Zeke."

Well, that was true.

Ride or die.

That's what he and Cross had always been. From *babies*. All this time, and that had never changed. Oh, sure, he'd done some shit to test Cross over the years. And to be fair, his best friend could be a special kind of difficult to deal with when he was in one of his moods. But it just wouldn't feel right if his friend wasn't there.

Like missing his left hand, really.

Katya hadn't been exaggerating. Cross pulled into Zeke's driveway less than two minutes later, spinning *very* expensive tires as he did so. Zeke whistled at the car his friend stepped out of appreciatively.

Setting his cup aside, Zeke moved down from the porch as he eyed the black Bugatti with all its chrome, and sleek lines. "When did you take this baby out of storage?"

Cross leaned against the hood—an action he probably would have killed anyone else for doing—and shrugged with one of his arrogant grins. "This morning after church. Figured we could tear up some pavement. Maybe do something other than sit around on your porch all damn day."

Zeke gave his friend a look. "Don't say that like it makes us old, Cross."

His friend grunted under his breath, and looked up at the sky. Salt had started to pepper both their hair, now. They had more lines around their eyes and mouths when they smiled. Time had swept into their life to change the obvious things, but it was what was under the surface that was still the very same.

Two fucking troublemakers.

Two old souls.

Two *friends*.

"Maybe I felt like that when my shoulders ached after waking up."

Zeke laughed. "Like my knee is fucking killing me after chasing Katya's new puppy all day yesterday?"

Cross glanced his way again. "Who the fuck wants to be *old*, Zeke?"

"We're not old. We're fucking *distinguished*."

That earned him another laugh.

"Yeah, keep telling yourself that."

He would. And he'd keep telling his friend that, too, as much as Cross needed to hear it.

"So, driving?" Zeke asked.

Cross nodded, and fixed his leather jacket. "Yeah, let's take a fucking drive, man."

*

Cross POV

This was the fucking *life*.

Seats pushed all the way back, and reclined as far as they could go. Feet up on the dashboard, and the sunroof opened so beach air could come into the Bugatti. People staring at the car as they passed, trying to peer through the dark tint of all the windows to see who was hiding inside.

No Cosa Nostra.

No family worries.

No *nothing*.

"All right," Zeke muttered beside him in the passenger seat, "this was better than the porch."

Cross smirked. "Told you."

Years ago, he might have punched Zeke in the arm along with making his statement just because that's how they once rolled. They weren't that young anymore, though, and nobody needed a sore shoulder for acting like an asshole.

"Remember that *one* street race we entered into with the Camaro?" Cross asked as he pulled out a rolled joint from his inner pocket. He was in his fifties, his kids were grown, and he had all day to sit here and sober up. He was gonna *smoke*. "You were *wasted*."

Zeke chuckled as Cross lit up the joint, and took a hard drag before handing it over while holding all the smoke in to let it do its thing. "It was only because I was wasted that I agreed to be your passenger. Had they known I was out of it, you never could have entered. Almost wrapped us around a fucking *tree*."

Cross sighed as thick gray, heady smoke filled the car, and traveled up through the sunroof to escape. "Good times."

"How was that good? I thought Cal was going to *kill* you."

"Not even a chance."

Zeke smirked a bit, and glanced over at him as he handed the joint back. "I guess not, huh? Wolf wasn't scared at all to put the fear of the devil in me. Cal, on the other hand … *most* soft-handed Cosa Nostra boss I have ever known."

"Soft-handed, but not weak."

"No, not that at all." Zeke coughed on his exhale when he muttered, "Do you think that was because he thought you—"

"I think it was because he spent his whole childhood getting smacked around by a man who told him it was going to make him a better man. And you know, had he tried that with me, Ma probably would have had his balls. Doesn't matter; never even crossed his mind."

"Mmm."

The two men grew silent as they finished their smoke, and then rested back in their seats to stare up at the cloudless sky.

This was his kind of day. No problems, his best friend, good smoke, and all these years between them. All the years of memories and good times and children, their wives, weddings, birthdays, and everything in between.

All the years …

"This is the fucking life," Cross murmured.

Zeke sighed. "Yup."

"You're so high."

"Yup."

"We're probably going to have to call someone."

"As long as it's not one of our wives, we'll be fine."

Yup.

THE NEIGHBOR

Naz POV

"What did I tell you, kid?"

Nazio sighed, and shrugged. "I didn't mean to kick it over there. Sorry, won't do it again."

With his new soccer ball he'd gotten for easter dangling in the neighbor man's hands, way across the street where he wasn't allowed to go because his father told him not to, Nazio would say just about anything to get it back.

He didn't see what the big deal was, though.

It was just a *ball.*

And he really did try not to kick it into the man's yard, mostly.

He wasn't *trying* to be a shit.

He just sometimes *was.*

Or, that's what his grandpapa Calisto said.

"No, I think I'll keep your ball for a couple of days. It'll teach you a lesson about respect."

Naz's brow dipped.

His father talked about respect all the damn time. Like how they had to respect people's positions around them, or even about his ma, too. *She's a wife, Naz, no fucking excuses, you give a wife respect, got it?*

A lot of the times when it came down to something simple, his father would settle the issue with the statement of *it's the respect of the matter.*

Naz was pretty sure he understood respect.

Or the respect that counted for him.

It probably wasn't the same kind of respect that this man meant.

"Aw, come on, please can I have my ball back?"

"So you can kick it right back into my front yard again? Don't think so, kid."

The guy turned to walk away.

Naz glared. "Fine, fuck right off, then."

His dad said that a lot too.

Naz figured out how to say it *right.*

And finally, he had a time to say it.

451

Maybe the *wrong* time, though, if the way the neighbor spun back around on his heels was any indication. "What did you just say to me?"

Well, that was the thing here.

Naz knew it was wrong.

But he'd made a choice, so he kind of had to stick it out.

The pride, and all.

His grandpapa said it was a *Donati* thing.

His other grandpapa said a good doe of it came from the Marcello side of him, too.

Naz just figured he didn't know any better.

Or his brain was wired wrong.

Because he didn't care a bit when he said, "*I said*, fuck right off, then."

And that was how Nazio found himself being marched up his driveway by the neighbor while the man muttered on about disrespectful little shits and *all this Donati trash*. The guy was mad, and Naz just wished he'd stop squeezing his shoulder so hard.

Naz felt the change in atmosphere the moment his father opened the front door. At his young five years, he still knew when his father felt some kind of way. He'd seen in the smallest of ways how his father could change his mask from the same man who tucked him into bed to the man that had pistol-whipped an enforcer that thought to smack Naz in the back of the head for not walking fast enough for his tastes. And with blood still staining his white silk shirt, and dotting his knuckles, Cross then took Naz across the street for his favorite gelato while he watched his men clean up the mess from a city bench.

And apparently, seeing his kid standing on his front porch with the neighbor's grip a little too tight on his shoulder, and his mouth already open to bitch about Naz ... well, that was enough to make his father flip his switch in a blink.

"Your—"

That was all the man got out of his mouth before Cross reached for his wrist, flinging it off Naz at the same time he snapped, "Get your fucking hand off my kid before I rip your shoulder from its socket."

The neighbor held his ground, not showing fear, but smart enough to know he shouldn't put his hand back on Naz again. "Well, I guess

I know where he gets his mouth from, huh?"

Noise came from within the house, but Naz couldn't discern the sound of that when his attention was entirely caught by the sight of his father, who towered over the neighbor by a good three inches, come out of the doorway all at once, his form lining up chest to chest with the man.

And there was Naz.

All three and a half feet of him.

Staring up at the two men *knowing* this wasn't good.

And all it took was the idiot opening the door with a bad expression and his hand on Cross's son.

"*What* did he get from me?"

The neighbor swallowed.

The house turned *quiet*.

"He was throwing that ball again, and I warned him. Your kid—"

"Naz, come here."

The arms of his godfather were quick to grab Naz from the side, drag him in behind his father, and then into the house. Although, Zeke didn't close the door. Down the long hallway, his mother peeked her head around the corner, Catherine's eyebrow lifting a bit as though she were wondering if she was going to have to clean blood up today.

His ma had a look for *everything*.

Got that from her ma, he noticed.

In his short moment of being distracted by the sight of his mother, Naz seemed to miss the fact that the neighbor had rushed to justify his reasoning for being on their front porch.

Zeke didn't seem to notice Naz turning around to see his father cock his head to the side when he muttered, "My kid told you *what?*"

"I shouldn't have to say it again."

"Oh," Cross said, laughing darkly under his breath, "but you *really* should."

The neighbor cleared his throat. "As I *said*, he told me to 'fuck right off, then.'"

Zeke's hands on Naz's shoulders flexed, but not painfully. He heard the choked laugh that came out of his godfather, too.

"And if I understood you right," Cross said, "he told you that because you wouldn't give his ball back. And he's *five*, so you know he's not listening to anything but when someone tells him food is on the table. For whatever reason, that was enough to tell your brain it was okay to put your hands on *my* son—and we know you know who the fuck I am—and march him right to my front fucking door, huh? Like I *said*, if I understood you right."

"Listen, I'll throw the ball back over, but you better keep it on your side of the street. It was just a lesson for him, that's all."

"Oh, you will? And what, I should thank you for that, yeah?"

"You know what," the neighbor muttered, seemingly growing a second set of balls in the span of seconds, "fuck it, no, you're not getting the ball back. You don't *own* this suburb, Donati. I don't care who you are."

Cross turned his head to the side just enough for them to see the way he grinned, and it felt entirely *wicked*. "No, you keep the ball, man."

"What—"

"I said what I fucking said. Keep the ball."

Cross stepped backward with two fast strides, came within the house, grabbed the door, and slammed its shut. Down the hallway, his mother made a high noise under her breath that sounded both amused and anxious at the same time.

"What the fuck was that?" Zeke asked. "The fucking balls on that asshole, I swear. No respect at all."

"Get your jacket."

Naz glanced up at his dad. "What?"

"Get your jacket on, we've got business to do."

Zeke's hands squeezed Naz's shoulders. "What does that mean?"

Cross smirked, his stare darting to Zeke as he shrugged. "Means we're going to have some fun. Naz, get your damn jacket."

He didn't need to be told again, swinging out of his godfather's grip to jump and swipe his jacket off its hook. His father already had the front door and was reaching for Naz's jacket to help him slip it over his arms.

Zeke didn't even ask more questions, simply followed along with a call to Catherine, "Give my wife a ring for me, would you? I'll keep these two out of trouble."

Naz heard his mother's snort before Zeke shut the door.

*

Cross POV

"What in the hell are you doing?"

Cross nodded down at his son, who had stopped himself from picking the next ball out of the mesh bag at the sound of the neighbor's shout. Naz didn't question his father—ever. Anyone else, and he would give them hell when it came right down to it, but not his father.

He pulled the next ball out of the bag, and whipped it across the street just as the neighbor came stomping down the pathway beside his driveway.

Cross rocked back on the swinging bench, half amused by the way Zeke turned his head sideways to hide his smirk at the neighbor's indignant ranting. He lifted the cigar to his lips, and pulled in a thick drag as the man glared at Cross's five-year-old son still whipping balls onto his property across the street.

"What is he doing?"

Still, Cross said nothing.

Beside him, Zeke shook his head. "Gets shriller the madder he gets."

"Cute, huh?"

"Tell him to stop right now, Donati!"

Cross smiled. "That'll be a no."

"What—there's fifteen balls in my yard!"

"Yeah, there's another bag in the SUV, so we've got another forty, at least, to go."

"Are ... are you *serious?*"

"Next time, guess you'll just throw him back his ball and shut your fucking face, right?"

The man across the street huffed.

Naz kept throwing the balls.

Cross just smiled.

"Fuck this," the guy muttered, 'I'm calling the cops."

Now *that?*

That had Cross roaring.

With laughter, that was.

Zeke, too.

God.

This was going to be a good day.

And a good lesson for Naz.
About his father.
Himself.
This life.
And *business*.
He controlled everything.
No one controlled him.

CECE AND JUAN

CHAPTER 1 - MIGGY

Cece POV

2 years old …

Cece bounced through the room, ignoring the calls of her name and the many people surrounding her mother. It wasn't anything unusual, and whenever she accompanied her ma to California for *business*, as her mother liked to say it, there always seemed to be more faces around than Cece cared to keep count.

They all knew her name.

She barely remembered theirs.

Everyone was nice, sure. They never said mean things, or even yelled at her. No one said she was in the way, and they always treated her with what her da liked to say was the *proper respect* a Donati *principessa* deserved. Not that Cece understood what any of that meant, but she did know that she liked it all.

That was enough for her.

Besides, she was more concerned with where her Ma was in the large space. After running through the hallways with one of the hotel's maids chasing after her, she was ready to find her ma, have a snack, and that juice she liked.

No big deal.

She darted around a rather *large* and quite tall man when she heard the sound of her Ma's familiar voice telling a girl that she needed to get with the program, or get the hell out of it. The girl was quick to reply with quiet *yes, Queen.*

Yeah.

Business was always fun.

Even when Cece didn't really understand it.

All she knew was that when her mother came to California for a week, they stayed in their big suite at a hotel that always knew them by first and last name, had Cece's favorite things on hand whenever she wanted to pick up the phone and call down to ask—her Ma taught her how to do that—and people never stopped coming by.

In New York, the only people that visited were men for her da.

In Cali, it was all about her ma.

"Ma!"

"Oh, and Miguel, I need you to stay behind for a moment, if you wouldn't mind."

"Not at all, Catty."

"Hmm."

Her mother's quiet hum was quickly followed by a short, "Catherine, I mean."

"Better, Miguel. *Better.*"

Cece found her mother sitting in the large chair that dominated the sitting space of the living room section of their suite. She tried not to bother her ma when she was doing *business*, if only because well, it was a little strange. So many people listening to her ma when she spoke, and everyone *staring.*

Oh, Cece liked being stared at.

She loved attention.

This was for her ma, though.

It wasn't the same.

She understood well enough that her ma was doing *important work*. Work that shouldn't be interrupted just because Cece wanted attention for one reason or another. Her ma always reminded her every time the private jet landed in Cali to *be a good girl, Cece.* And she did because she promised she would.

And she so loved her ma.

More than *anything.*

Catherine reached for Cece as she came to stand next to her mother's chair. In her ma's lap, a cup was already being passed over. In her pretty pink dress with the white polka dots all over, a cup of juice could be a dangerous thing, so Cece took her time drinking the liquid, making sure not to spill the sticky, red liquid on her dress.

That would make her mad.

She hated ruining her pretty things.

Her ma flattened her palm against the top of Cece's head, smoothing the dark, wildly unruly curls at the crown as people gave their confirmative replies to whatever she had said before they started filtering out of the hotel room. A few stragglers stayed behind, chatting in hushed tones as the tall man from earlier stepped up. He *was* one of the familiar faces to Cece, although she could never quite say his name right. And when Cece couldn't say something right, she simply didn't say it at all.

His golden skin with reddish undertones gleamed in the light, the contrast of his white teeth as he gave her a friendly smile making Cece grin back even with her cup up to drink from. His eyes were a darker brown than even hers, but still *warm*. He constantly followed her ma around when she was in Cali, and sometimes, even in New York or wherever her ma went to do business.

Cece thought they were friends, but she didn't know.

"And what did you want to speak to me about?" he asked.

Catherine glanced down at Cece. "Her, Miguel."

"Pardon?"

"Did you notice she was all over the place today?"

He shrugged. "She's a kid—she's gonna run, Catherine."

"*Right*, but I need to have my eyes on her, either way. Or rather, a pair of eyes that I trust. You get what I am saying?"

"Please tell me you don't mean for me to be a babysi—"

"That's a little juvenile and rude, considering."

"I'm sorry?"

"What is the most important thing in my life, Miguel?"

He cleared his throat, scratching at the back of his neck. "Listen, I don't mean to say that she doesn't need someone looking after her, but do you really think it should be me, Catherine? I've had your back for *years* in this business. I'm not sure putting me on the kid is going to benefit you or this organization in any real way."

"Except it will because she is the future of it."

His gaze darted between her mother, and then Cece.

It took a second.

Then, two.

"I love the kid, you know that."

"Why do you think I asked you, Miguel?"

"She won't even say my name. I don't think she likes me very much."

"She does," her ma assured. "You like Miguel, don't you, Cece?"

She peered up at the big man.

She saw lots of those before.

Most scared her.

Not Miguel, though.

She tried so hard to form his name properly in her mind, to make her mouth say it the right way, but all that came out was, "I likes Miggy."

Catherine grinned. "See, *Miggy*."

"Jesus Christ—don't."

"I think it's cute."

"My Miggy?" Cece asked.

Catherine nodded. "Yeah, he's going to be yours."

She smiled at the man. "*My* Miggy."

Miguel looked Catherine's way with the most exasperated expression he could muster. "If someone else calls me that, I will rip their esophagus out."

Cece frowned.

She didn't know what that was.

Didn't sound good, though.

"Me, too?" she asked him.

Instantly, the man's irritation melted away. "Never you, Cece."

Right.

Because he was her Miggy.

Her ma said so.

CHAPTER 2 - JUAN

Cece POV

Three years old ...

"I can't wait to see you, Cece."

She grinned down at the face of her father staring back at her from the iPad in her lap. The car swayed as it took a turn in downtown Los Angeles, coming out of the roundabout which always made her dizzy after they went around a time or two, but she barely noticed it all while she spoke to her dad.

"Tomorrow?" she asked.

Cross nodded. "Around lunch."

Good.

She missed her da.

"All right, give the tablet back to Ma, and I will call you tonight. Okay?"

Cece nodded. "All right. Loves my daddy, Daddy."

Cross smiled. "Love you, my girl."

Next to her in the back seat, her mother took the tablet from her hands. A quick word passed between her mother and father before the tablet was shut off and put to the side. By then, Cece had already turned to look out the window at the passing buildings. Familiar to her now, really, because she had driven these streets with her mother and a driver in the front countless times before.

Again and again.

To her, California felt like home, too.

Same as New York.

Soon, they came to a familiar restaurant where her mother always liked to eat if they arrived at a good time and weren't exhausted coming into town. Because then, Cece wasn't in any kind of mood and her ma liked to say she *needed a nap*. Even if she didn't want to have a nap. She still had a nap, though.

Her mother only stepped out of the car after the driver—usually it was Miguel, but this week, someone different had picked them up at the private jet strip—came around to open her door. Miguel would usually take *Cece* out of her car seat, if he was driving them, but today it was her mother.

"Where's my Miggy?"

"Inside," her ma said.

Oh.

"Why?"

"His wife had a last-minute thing," Catherine said as though Cece were supposed to just understand what that meant. She really didn't. "And so, we had to make other arrangements. But he's waiting inside, and he'll be with us for the rest of the week."

Well, Cece understood and liked that well enough.

"Okay!"

The driver followed them to the front door of the restaurant, and only turned back to return to his vehicle once they were safely inside. Cece was still looking over her shoulder, watching the man leave, as they headed deeper, her mother walking straight past the woman at the podium as though she were important enough to simply walk in and pick whatever table she wanted to eat at that day.

Who knew?

Maybe her mother could.

Someday, Cece would understand that's *exactly* what it was.

"There's my Cece!"

At the call of her name by a familiar voice, Cece spun her head around fast, finding one of her other most favorite people waiting at the other side of a very busy restaurant. He was already standing from his chair smiling her way, waiting to greet her the same way he always did.

To anyone else, Miguel was *terrifying*. His size, demeanor, the tone of his voice … she knew people were scared of him, saw the way they acted around him. Cece, however, wasn't scared of him at all.

Ever.

From the day he became her personal bodyguard, he also turned into her best friend. A playmate. Someone who made it his first mission to make sure she was safe but having the time of her life doing it.

Catherine let go of her hand, and Cece darted forward, not paying attention to anyone or anything else before she found her way into Miguel's waiting embrace. He hugged her tight, lifting her up to stand her on the seat of the chair next to the table so that she could be a little higher to hug him.

"How was the plane?" he asked.

"*Loud.*"

Miguel laughed loud enough to draw attention. "It always is. So hey, guess what?"

Cece grinned. "What?"

He turned a bit, giving her a better view of someone else sitting at the table that she only then noticed. A young boy, about her age, or maybe a little older. *Definitely* taller, considering he could actually see over the table without needing a booster seat like she did. The young boy smiled her way, eyes so dark she thought they looked like the sky at nighttime, and his features familiar to her in a comforting way. His hair was just long enough to touch his eyelashes, and curl around his ears.

"Cece, this is Juan," Miguel said, "my son. I had to grab him last minute from his preschool today because his little sister got sick, and their ma had to take her to the doctor. So, he had no one to pick him up from preschool. I thought he might like to come along with me today, maybe you two could play while me and your ma talk, huh?"

"Okay," she said.

The little boy—Juan—smiled.

Cece's heart beat faster.

She smiled back.

"Hi," he said, "Cece."

"Hi, Juan."

CHAPTER3 – HER

Juan POV

Five years old …

"Juan, come see this bug!"

Glancing over his shoulder to see one of his neighborhood friends bending over the sandbox at the park near his home, Juan didn't move from his spot on the blanket. In the small patch of grass, he *would* rather be playing over there, but he was also just fine where he was. Mostly because—

"Do you wanna?"

Juan smiled at Cece. "Want to what?"

"Play. With your friend."

He shrugged. "Nah, I'm okay."

Cece didn't look like she believed him, but she went back to flicking her finger against the screen of her tablet, playing some bubble bursting game that she liked. She wasn't a *dirt and bugs* kind of girl. She wore pretty dresses, shoes that clicked when she walked, and he couldn't remember a time when her hair wasn't perfect *all the time*.

It was just who she was.

And yet, when he wanted to go to the park, she was quick to come along. She carried her tablet as they walked the four houses down in the suburb to get to the park, and he carried the blanket she *always* sat on. Juan might play a little while, but then he quickly found himself heading back to wherever she had decided to sit on the blanket.

He didn't know *why*.

Never tried to convince her to play like he did.

This was okay, though.

Juan didn't mind sitting with her. Even if he liked the sun, and she preferred to sit in the shade. Even if he wanted to see what that bug looked like—he bet it was cool—and Cece would rather stay right where she was on her blanket.

Yeah, because he liked being there.

With *her*.

"You shouldn't ignore your friends," Cece said.

Juan hummed under his breath, leaning over to pick a few green blades of grass from the ground. He braided them, a trick his ma, Stephanie, taught him one afternoon when they went for a walk together. "But you're my friend, too, Cece."

She looked up from her tablet. "I know."

"So, I'll stay with you."

"Yeah, but—"

"Who's going to play with you?"

Cece smiled a little. "*Well* ..."

He didn't need her to say the answer when he already knew it. Fact was, Cece could make *a lot* of friends, if she wanted to. Everyone liked her. She smiled, and the whole world smiled back. It was one of the things he liked the most about her. A constant ray of sunshine, she gave him every reason to be happy.

Not everyone was like that.

Another thing about her, though?

People quickly realized she wasn't like them. Or rather, kids their age did. She didn't want to dress like them or play the same way they did. At the large family dinners and parties, they often had, she would be found sitting on her mother or father's lap, listening to every word around her, instead of running through the house with the rest of the kids.

She didn't find fun in the same things they found enjoyable, and she would much rather hang around with the adults who watched them than the kids closer to their age group. Which was fine for Juan, because whatever.

Some people found that weird.

He just didn't care.

He liked Cece the way she was.

Juan was four when he first mentioned to his father that his other friends didn't seem to like to play or hang out with Cece the same way he did. Oh, they liked her, sure ... but they couldn't or wouldn't, sit with her for an hour just to do whatever *she* wanted. They only wanted her to do what they wanted. And when she wouldn't, well, she was left on her own.

What his dad said?

Cece is special, Juan, and you just have to like her the way she is. She doesn't care what the other kids think about her; she's fine either way.

He learned something, then.

And from watching Cece, too.

She would be fine alone.

Sure, she would.

He just didn't want her to be.

Why should she be alone when she had him?

"I'm okay to play alone," she said quieter.

Juan moved from the Indian-style position he had been sitting in to his back on the blanket. Like this, he could stare up at the sky and watch the fluffy white clouds pass by the blue landscape overhead. His second favorite pastime, next to being with Cece.

Because that was the thing.

He'd learned it shortly after meeting her.

As long as he was *with* Cece, whether they were following his father and her mother around, sitting in front of a television to watch the *one* cartoon she actually liked, or sitting on a blanket in the park instead of playing on all the equipment, none of it mattered. They didn't need to talk, and they certainly didn't need to play the same way all the other kids did.

Just being together was *fun.*

And he'd do this forever, he thought.

With her, he'd do it forever.

Because it was her.

Juan just didn't know why.

Not yet.

CHAPTER 4 - THE BEST

Cece POV

Six years old ...

"Well?" Juan asked.

Cece looked over at him, her peripheral vision taking in everything else in her surroundings at the same time. The intricately designed carpet her grandmother had imported from Japan, and the table that rested upon it, acting as their current shelter and hiding spot from the rest of the dinner party.

Well ...

It wasn't like Cece didn't enjoy being out with the rest of her family when they had these *things*. She did, and she certainly enjoyed being the center of attention when it was all the adults in her family giving it to her. And then other times, the parties went on for *hours*. They talked and talked and talked more. About things she didn't understand, or stuff that just didn't interest her. And since this was when she was allowed to stay up later than her normal bedtime, she tried to use that to her advantage as much as she could.

By doing something she liked.

Like hiding under the table and listening.

And tonight, she was extra lucky because Juan had come to New York with his father. Since it was summer break, he didn't have to be at school, neither did she, and he was going to be there for another week before he had to go back to Cali. As far as she knew, because she asked her mother every single day just to make sure plans hadn't changed, she and her ma would be following them to Cali within a couple of days.

Which was good.

Because Cece hated when Juan was gone.

She liked it better when he was near.

"I'll go get it for you," he told her.

Cece smiled because *yeah*, she knew. "But someone might see, and then we'll have to go to bed."

She was pretty sure, despite being allowed to stay up late on their dinner party nights with her family that it was way past the time when she was allowed to stay up. It was almost guaranteed that if she came out from underneath the table, or even Juan because everyone would know wherever Juan was hiding, so was Cece, that they would put her to bed.

She didn't want to go to bed yet.

So, hiding it was.

"It's okay," she said, "there'll be some tomorrow."

Juan scoffed, rolling his dark eyes her way. Despite being seven, and only one year older than her, she sometimes thought they were both—somehow—older than their years. It could be just a passing thing one of them said, or like this, with him and his attitude. Thing was, she liked his attitude too, and he *always* put up with hers.

So, it worked.

"Doubt any will be left tomorrow. They drink, and they eat."

"And laugh a lot."

"Yes, until there's nothing left. So, I will go and get you some, and be right back. Okay?"

"I told you, Juan, they'll see you and—"

"No they won't. Be right back."

"Juan!"

She whisper-hissed at his back as he slipped out from under the tablecloth at a spot where no one's legs were sticking under. Although only a few people still remained in the dining room. Most had moved onto the sitting room, or even the smaller table in the kitchen where they liked to play poker. Juan had to have heard her call to him, but it didn't slow him down in the slightest, and he didn't turn back around.

Because *of course.*

Cece grew silent as she waited for the inevitable to happen. For Juan to get caught crossing the room to grab the treat she had been whining about for the last hour, an adult to ask where she was, and then they'd both get put to bed even though she wasn't even tired.

And Juan would probably just roll his eyes when she said *I told you so* to him again. Because yeah, this wasn't even the third time they tried this trick together.

Then again, she was glad she had him for this.

No one else would bother to try.

Cece was still smiling, and still waiting for one of the adults—

probably her parents—to lift the only thing keeping her hidden and out of view, the tablecloth, when Juan quickly slipped back underneath it with a grin.

One that looked way too sly.

And pleased.

He held out a plate.

A whole *plate*.

Filling the plate was her favorite treats—pink macaroons. Her ma made the *very best*. But she only let Cece have a couple because she might get a stomachache, or because sugar was bad for her teeth.

Psht.

She brushed her teeth.

And who couldn't eat ten macaroons?

Babies.

Cece's eyes went wide. "Nobody saw you?"

Juan shrugged. "Nope. Learned my lesson the last time—was quick and quiet and nobody saw a thing."

Hmm.

She didn't know if she believed that. She heard people still sitting around the table, even if she hadn't gained the courage to peek her head out and check quite yet. But who knew? Maybe he had managed to sneak out and back without anyone seeing him.

And what did it matter?

But hey, she had her macaroons.

Her hiding spot.

A bedtime that didn't exist.

And Juan under the table with her.

All things Cece loved.

Worked for her.

She took a macaroon from the plate and offered another to Juan. He took it with a smile, and even though she knew he didn't like them as much as she did—fudge was his favorite, and she'd make sure her ma made him a whole pan of fudge before he left for Cali— he still ate it with a smile.

"Good?" he asked.

Cece nodded. "The best, Juan."

Just like him.

CHAPTER 5 - A CRUSH

Cece POV

12 years old …

"Yeah. I got it, Catty."

Cece peeked up from the book in her hands with a raised eyebrow. Miguel was already looking her way as well, and she could tell just by the way his lips pursed and he lifted his broad shoulders that plans changed. She was used to that now, though. Whenever she came to Cali with her mom, things were ever-changing. One day she might be expecting to do something, and in the next minute, they'd get a call that something else had happened.

Nothing new.

She didn't mind.

Besides, it meant more time with Miggy.

And also Juan.

She liked that.

A lot.

Given it was summer, it didn't matter if plans had to change. It wasn't like she had to be to school on Monday—thank God—so whatever. During the school year, it felt like the months dragged by. She'd much rather be traveling to Cali with her ma, but instead, she was reminded by *both* her parents that education was important.

And that her family was in New York.

So, why did Cali feel like home, too?

Nobody ever had a good answer for that.

"Well?" she asked Miguel.

"Guess you're staying here for the night. Your ma's meeting is going to run a little late, and she figured you would probably rather stay here than have me drive you back to the hotel after midnight. That gonna be a problem, or …?"

Not really.

"It's cool, Miggy."

Miguel smiled. "Cool, princess."

He was the only person allowed to call her that other than her family. Because they—and Miguel—didn't turn it into a joke. Cece wasn't *anyone's* joke. And she didn't mind reminding people of that fact, either.

"Once Stephanie gets home with the kids, we'll figure out something for dinner," he added, "or shit, maybe we'll go out."

"Either is good."

"All right." Miguel nodded over her shoulder. "How about you go tell Juan to chill out and take a drink of water? He's been out back kicking that damn ball for two hours and I'm sure he's forgotten to hydrate."

"He's practicing, that's all."

Miguel smiled. "Not sure why ... he doesn't really need to. He's going to make the team when school starts back up, and he knows it."

"Doesn't mean he can't be the *best* player, though."

"You sound like him."

Cece only shrugged in response to that. What else could she say? She tended to listen to Juan when he talked—they were best friends. That's what friends were supposed to do for one another. Even when she wasn't spending time in Cali, the two of them still talked about literally everything. On FaceTime, Skype, texts, or whatever else. They were always in contact. It wasn't like she cared about or liked soccer in the same way Juan did, but it mattered to him.

So, it mattered to her.

Simple.

"Well, *whatever*," Miguel said, "go tell him what I said, yeah?"

"Okay."

She pushed off the stool at the kitchen island, still reading her book all the while. In fact, she kept reading all the way to the back of the house, even when she pushed the rear patio doors open and stepped out onto the porch. She only looked away from the words on the page at the sound of a rhythmic *smack smack smacking.*

Cece didn't even see Juan at first, she already had her mouth opened to shout for him to take a break and get a drink. But then her eyes fell on him at the far end of the back lawn where he moved from foot to foot, back and forth, chest bare and glinting with perspiration that dotted his brown skin while he kept a soccer ball up in the air. First bouncing it off his knee, then the top of his right foot, then the left, before it came down to roll off his chest, and then he kicked it high again. Concentration hardened his features, making all those strong lines on his face all the more severe.

So handsome.

Never once did the ball hit the ground.

He moved like water after it.

It wasn't the first time Cece saw him practice. It sure as hell wasn't even the tenth time, she saw him without a shirt on. She was also well aware that Juan was a handsome boy. He certainly had more than enough girls who seemed to watch him wherever he went. Even his father teased him on and off, calling him *pretty boy* just because he could. Before that moment, though, Cece had never really *thought* about it.

Not like she was right then.

She'd never noticed that his chest had become more defined.

Or that his brown skin had a golden sheen.

How his hips narrowed down from a strong back.

Or the way his eyes seemed all the more intense with a few strands of damp hair hanging down over his brown gaze.

No, she'd never noticed *any* of those things before.

But goddamn …

She noticed now.

"Hey."

Cece dragged in a quick breath, pulling her book against her chest as the soccer ball flew high before dropping down into Juan's waiting hands. He had already turned toward her, flashing his white teeth in a wide grin.

And just like that …

Butterflies beat in her stomach.

She didn't have anything to say.

Couldn't.

And her heart raced.

A crush started in that moment.

Nothing was ever going to be the same.

"Hey," she replied softly.

CHAPTER 6 - CHANGES

Juan POV

14 years old ...

"How? *How*, Miguel?"

Juan shook his head at the table, his younger sisters too busy with the tablet they were currently sharing to watch their favorite YouTubers more important than their mother's fake breakdown. Then again, maybe that was why they didn't care—because they knew it was just their ma acting her usual way again.

"Steph—"

"How do I have a *fourteen-year-old*, Miguel? He was just *five*!"

His mother had been doing this and going on since he first woke up that morning. Since his birthday fell right in the middle of the week this year, he hadn't cared too much about the actual day he turned fourteen. He was more excited for the coming weekend when his parents planned a birthday party he hadn't asked for but would still be fun.

Plus, Cece was flying in with her ma.

He hadn't seen her in three months.

Too long.

He missed his best friend.

"Shit, okay, we're gonna be late," Juan's father said, coming around the kitchen island after dropping a kiss to his wife's forehead. To his mother's benefit, she had finally stopped whining about the fact Juan was no longer a *baby*, but now she was looking at him like she was about to burst into tears.

That?

That was worse.

And Juan wouldn't do that.

He didn't mind indulging his mother's nonsense most of the time. As his father liked to say, it was Stephanie's right as his mother. She brought him into the world, after all, and the least he can do to repay her for that—next to giving her love—was to let her fawn over him in whatever way that pleased her.

Mostly, he tried to do that.

Not if she was gonna cry all over him, though.

Before his mother could get started, Juan shoved the last half of his bagel into his mouth, scooped up his cell phone from the table with one hand, and slung his bookbag up from the floor with the other. He rounded the table, ready to follow after his father because Miguel usually took him to his private high school across town while his mother took his sisters to their lower school.

He didn't even make it to the kitchen entryway before his mother caught up to him. Stephanie caught him from behind, her small arms wrapping tight around his neck so she could draw him into a hug that practically choked him. She dotted the top of his short-cropped hair with kiss after kiss, making Juan cringe even if he did love his ma.

"Stop growing," she told him.

Juan shook his head. "Not really how it works, Ma."

She sighed, arms tightening around him yet again before she dropped one more kiss to the top of his head. "Yeah, I know. Love you, hmm? Be good at school."

"When am I not good, Ma?"

"*Well* ... goddammit, I said I love you. You're not too old to say it back, Juan."

No. He wasn't.

And he never would be.

"Love you, too, Ma."

Her palm patted the back of his head, her silent command for him to head after his father. Juan didn't need to be told again, and by the time he slipped into his father's truck, Miguel was already buckled in, and putting the vehicle into reverse.

"You were good for your ma, right?"

Juan side-eyed his father. "Do you expect me not to be?"

His father smiled. "Never, Juan."

"Hmm."

Before his father could say anything more, the phone in Juan's hand buzzed. He brought the home screen up and checked the incoming text message, smiling at who it was and what the message said.

Cece.

"What's that?" his father asked.

Happy birthday, Juan. See you this weekend.

Accompanied by three heart emojis.

"Juan," Miguel pressed.

He typed back a quick thanks, and that he'd be there waiting to see her once she arrived with her mother on the private airstrip.

Like always.

"Cece," he finally said, "telling me happy birthday."

"Huh."

"What?"

Miguel shrugged, navigating familiar streets with ease. "Oh, nothing. Just thinking."

Juan eyed his father. "Didn't sound like nothing. You said *huh*. You only say *huh* when you have something to say to me, but aren't really sure what to say or how to say it. What would you want to say to me about Cece?"

"Just go right for it, don't you, son?"

Was he wrong, though?

Juan didn't think so.

"What is it?"

"Well, it's … her. Cece."

Juan frowned. "What about her?"

Miguel let out a laugh, but it felt almost … *tense*. Awkward, maybe? Juan thought the only time he'd ever heard his father talk like that was when his twelve-year-old sister started her period and only he and his dad were home to deal with it until his ma got back.

"You know she's got a crush on you, right?"

Juan quieted. "I mean—"

"And that she's going to be thirteen soon—you just turned fourteen. You have to be careful about that, you know? You understand more about things than she does, and it doesn't look good—"

"We're not like that, Papa."

Miguel let out a slow breath, looking at Juan from the side. "*Yet*, Juan. You're not like that yet. But those kinds of things? They change *just like that*. Everything changes in the blink of an eye, and I just want to make sure you understand how to behave appropriately. No, that's wrong. I know you know how to behave. I just want you to tell me you understand everything I am saying right now. That you hear me."

Yeah, he did.

He'd also known that for a while.

About Cece ... and her crush.

At first, he'd kind of thought it was just some innocent thing. Besides, it didn't really matter because Juan still looked at Cece and saw his *friend*. His father talked about that change like it would happen, but Juan didn't know that it would.

And if it did?

If everything changed?

Well, that was the thing.

It hadn't.

Not yet.

CHAPTER 7 - NEVER KNOW

Cece POV

14 years old …

"So, what is even going on with *that*?"

"Yeah, spill the shit."

Cece sighed, tipping her cup of punch up for a drink and trying to ignore two of her cousins who had seemed to pick up on the fact that she was neither in the mood to talk, nor standing right beside Juan during her family's dinner party like she usually would. And since the Marcellos were *known* for being nosy motherfuckers, they decided they couldn't just pretend like they hadn't noticed anything.

No.

They had to drive her crazy.

"*Well?*" Tiffany asked.

Cece passed her cousin a look. "I thought your ma and dad weren't coming in from Toronto this weekend?"

Tiff tossed a blonde curl over her shoulder, shrugging. "Things changed."

"And stop deflecting," Lucky—although his name was Luciano, they'd always just called him by his nickname—added. "What, is Juan being an asshole? Is that it?"

"*No.*"

"Tiffany!"

"Shit," her cousin muttered between Cece and Lucky. She pointed a finger at Cece even as she stepped away from their small group to head for her mother across the room. "I will be back to get all the details. You can't get all red-faced about a guy and then say nothing is going on."

"Nothing *is*," Cece muttered.

And that was half the problem.

Or so she figured.

Well, that and it was really hard to explain this *thing* she and Juan had. This weird place the two of them seemed to find themselves together. Friends, but a little bit closer. Affectionate, but never like *that.* Together, but not a *them.*

None of it made sense.

And they wanted Cece to explain?

Right.

Alone with Lucky in the corner of the living room, Cece tried to focus on the movement happening around her. With her mother's family, and even the other guests who had been invited to the dinner party. Being it was summer, and her ma had some meetings that would be happening between New York and Maine, Juan came down with his father for a couple of weeks which was why they were there, too.

Not in the room at the moment, though.

One good thing.

"You good?" Lucky asked beside her.

She passed him a look, taking in his features that seemed older than his teenaged years for whatever reason. He reminded her a lot of his father, John, but with the compassion of his mother, Siena. Of course, Lucky enjoyed chaos and tended to find himself in trouble more often than not, but he was one of Cece's cousins that she enjoyed spending time with because he was cool with her just being herself.

"Hey," he prodded when she didn't answer right away.

Cece sighed. "I don't know, Lucky."

It took her cousin a second, and then two.

Finally, he nodded, sucking air through his teeth before saying, "Oh, so it's kinda like that, then?"

"What?"

"You and him—Juan, you know? Nothing *is* ... but it also *isn't*, yeah?"

Cece shrugged. "I guess."

Her mom said things like *you've only just turned fourteen.* And her dad made it clear *you're not going out with Juan until you're sixteen.* Her grandmother, Catrina, liked to tell her not to *pine over boys; you've got better ways to spend your time.* And her other nana, Emma, just smiled and promised *everything will work itself out, you're too young to try to understand all this right now.*

Was that really it, though?

Or was it something else?

"It's just me," Cece said, "because Juan doesn't say one way or the other. So it's all in my own head. I'm making nothing into something."

"Doesn't mean it feels good, though."

"Yeah."

"Want me to beat his ass?" Lucky asked. "I'll do it."

Cece pressed her lips together to hide a smile she knew was entirely inappropriate. Besides, Lucky had a terrible habit of taking things like smiles to be signs of encouragement for his bad behavior, or so his father liked to tell everyone whenever her uncle John got to the ends of his rope with his oldest son.

"Well, if you beat him up," Cece said, "then he *really* won't want to be around me."

Probably.

Lucky made a noise under his breath. "Not so sure that's a bad thing."

She laughed, and then smacked her cousin in the stomach with the back of his hand. "Stop it."

He sighed, shrugging one leather-covered shoulder. "Listen, you got lots of time to work this shit out, Cece. And my dad likes to say that as long as something isn't hurting anybody else, and it works for you, then why do you need to change it? Sometimes, he makes good points."

"Maybe."

Lucky smirked. "Besides, you never know … if anything makes sense, it's that nothing ever stays the same, Cece. It can't."

Right.

So, when would things start to change?

Or would they?

*

"Hey."

Cece glanced up from the spot on the porch she'd been lost staring at for the last … well, she didn't even know how long she'd been staring at it. Too long, clearly. Behind her, Juan smiled in that way that she used to think felt like *happiness*. Now, it made her stomach do flipflops and drove her kind of crazy.

In a way, that made her mad.

They'd been *great* before this. Not that they were bad now, because they weren't. They were still just Cece and Juan, except now it was Cece with a crush on Juan, and that made everything entirely different.

"Why did things have to change?" she asked.

Juan blinked, clearly confused. And then all at once, a clarity took over his eyes that said he knew exactly what she meant.

He should.

After all, she'd finally spilled her guts.

Told him the truth.

And all he'd told her yesterday when she did that was *me, too.*

Nothing else.

He took a seat beside her on the back steps, folding his arms over his bent knees while he looked out over the rear property. The two of them stayed quiet for longer than she cared to admit before he broke the silence first.

"It's not fair … to you, I mean," he said, peeking over at her over the line of his forearm. "To be here, and for me to be there. That's a long way, and it's going to be like that for a long time. What, you never wanna go anywhere or do anything with somebody?"

Was he saying what she thought he was?

"But—"

"And when we're like this, I like it," he said. "Just me and you, you know? I like that because I don't have to feel like you're not getting to do whatever you want. Nothing really *changed*, Cece, it just turned into something that had to be different."

"I don't wanna do *whatever.*"

"Not right now, maybe."

"Juan—"

His hand dropped from his knee and found hers on the smooth wood of the porch. Without a word, their fingers tangled tightly together, and before long, Cece found her head resting on his shoulder.

Everything was right, then.

Perfect, even.

"See," he murmured, "just me and you."

Yeah.

Just him and her.

CHAPTER 8 - JEALOUS

Juan POV

16 years old …

I'll text you later, k?

Juan read over Cece's text a third time as he entered the house. The conversation between his mother and father echoed down the hall, but he didn't pay them much attention. He was more concerned with Cece's text because that wasn't like her at all.

All right, he texted back, *later.*

He tried to shake off the strange feeling that settled on his shoulders, if only because he didn't even know why he felt it in the first place. It wasn't like this was the first time he'd ever texted Cece and she blew him off—even if that's not exactly what her text said or did.

"You've got practice in an hour, right?" Juan's father called as he passed the kitchen doorway.

"Yeah."

"Truck will be warm."

"Thanks."

It was kind of pointless for Juan to shower *before* baseball practice when he was just going to need to shower again after, but he didn't care. Using the attached bathroom in his bedroom, he jumped in the shower and made quick work of cleaning away the day. By the time he was done, he'd *almost* forgotten about Cece and the strange text. Gathering all his baseball gear and hauling it downstairs—he'd be happy when soccer season came back around—his father waited out in the driveway next to the truck.

Running, too.

Just like he said.

Juan, on the other hand, was looking at his phone again while he balanced his baseball bag in his other hand and didn't pay the slightest bit of attention to the driveway as he walked across it.

"What are you doing?"

"Checking something," Juan replied.

"Checking *what?*"

He didn't want to say Cece, because Miguel would give him *that* look, so Juan opted to say nothing at all. His father let him toss the baseball bag into the back of the truck, and while Miguel busied himself with getting in the vehicle, Juan took the chance to scroll down through his social media feeds. *Cece* didn't spend a lot of time on social media. She just didn't care, even if that was all every girl around their age seemed to care about.

Her friends, though?

They posted every minute.

Tagged her.

Photos of Cece.

Status or video stories about this, that, or another thing. All pretty typical, and sometimes that was the quicker way for him to find out where Cece was when he wanted to chat, or whatever.

Right then, though, he wasn't finding anything.

And it wasn't really his business to keep looking, he decided. It didn't matter if her text didn't sit well with him, or that he looked forward to talking to her every day that he got home from school. He didn't own Cece—they weren't a thing by his own choice, something she'd reminded him when ever she felt he needed it. Sometimes, that was more than Juan wanted to admit. If she didn't want to talk right then, she didn't want to talk. It was as simple as that.

Or it needed to be.

Juan didn't get a say.

"Come on, we're going to be fucking late!" Miguel shouted from the truck.

Juan jumped in.

And set his phone aside for the time being.

After all, Cece did say *later.*

So, there would be that.

*

"That batting average, son," Miguel said, tone thick with praise as he clapped a hand to the back of Juan's shoulder hard enough to make him almost choke on the water he currently chugged back like it was his only life source. After a hard practice, hydration *was* the only thing that kept him alive sometimes. "Keep that up, and in a year the scouts will be coming around, huh?"

Juan let out a hard breath. "Not playing for college teams."

That quieted his father.

It was a discussion they often went back and forth on with his father wanting him to further his education, and Juan pointing out Miguel never even graduated high school. Which then led his father to say things like *exactly, and I want you to do and be better than me*. Except his father was pretty amazing as he was—worked with one of those dangerous and successful Queen Pins who controlled a good portion of the American market.

Apparently, Juan should just not pay attention to that.

Not be curious.

Like it wasn't *Cece's* mother.

Like Cece wouldn't someday *be* her mother.

Before his father could bring up the conversation and get them going down that road again, Juan grabbed his cell phone sitting atop his bag. Miguel's attention turned back to the field where the coach was currently shouting at one of Juan's teammates to *tuck in that fucking elbow before I break it off*.

Yeah.

Fun times.

Juan's gaze dropped to his phone as he scrolled down through the refreshing social media feed. What he expected to see? The usual mess of teenage life and shit he sometimes engaged in with his friends when he had the time or the give a damn to do so. The thing he wasn't expecting to see?

Cece with a guy.

Juan blinked, and clicked on the picture. The dark background made the house—and party?—she was at nearly indistinguishable. What he could distinguish just fine was how closely tucked into the boy's side Cece was, the fact that the guy's hand was around her waist, *and* that he was kissing her smiling cheek as they lifted solo cups toward the camera.

He had a lot of thoughts then.

Feelings, too, the fucking disgusting things.

Like who the fuck was that guy?

And did he want his arm broken?

What in the hell was Cece doing?

Juan knew what that feeling was, and why it made him have the darkest urge to pick up the phone, call Cece, and let her know he was *well aware* that she was out with a guy.

Jealousy.

He was jealous as *fuck*.

But he shouldn't be.

Didn't have a right to be.

He kept saying while they were like this, her in New York and him in Cali, that they couldn't be a real thing. It wasn't fair. He doubted that was the first boy she went out with—fuck, he went out with girls sometimes, too. This was just the first time it had been so public.

"Hmm."

Juan glanced up to see his father had a perfect view of what was currently on his phone. Juan didn't even bother to try and hide it.

"Bet that's a piss off, yeah?" Miguel asked.

God.

"Just ... why's it on social, you know?"

"Because she's a fifteen-year-old girl. Because she has a life and sometimes, you're not always in it. Because she followed you for the past three years with fucking stars in her eyes, but you had to take the high road every step of the fucking way, Juan. So, maybe it's time you follow her for a while, hmm? Fair is fair, son."

"That doesn't sound right at all."

"Very little about love is."

Juan blinked.

Love.

He remembered the first time he told Cece he loved her - they'd been five and six. He was waving her off when she left with her ma, and he called it out after her. Because that's what his dad always told his ma whenever he left the house. It's what Cece told her ma, and Miguel, too. It felt right.

He'd been saying it ever since.

Still said it.

Just now, that *love* didn't feel the same.

It was different.

More.

"I don't know what to do," Juan muttered.

Except be jealous.

So fucking jealous.

"When she calls later, you ask if she had a good time. Let her know you're around, if she needs anything. Same shit you've always done, Juan, unless you want something different. And if you do, just know now might not be your time. And that's got to be okay, too."

Right, yeah.

It just sucked.

That's what he would do, though.

It's what he did.

CHAPTER 9 - EVERYTHING CHANGES

Cece POV

16 years old …

"Happy birthday to you, happy birthday to …"

Cece had to struggle to look over the top of her cake. That's how tall it was. And considering how packed her parents three-level suburban home currently was, she understood why her mother ordered something that looked fit to be on a wedding display. Because they would need that much, or more, to feed all the guests at her party.

Well, the cake didn't *completely* look like a wedding cake. Three tier high, pale pink and silver trimmings and a large silver *16* on the very top … it was perfect. It matched the rest of the decorations in the house—the home had become a pink and silver wonderland.

She couldn't remember a birthday when her parents *didn't* go all out for her. Maybe it was because around twelve, her brother decided he wanted to stop having parties for his birthdays and so they made up for it when Cece's rolled around.

Who knew?

Either way, she *loved* it.

A proper Donati principessa.

Of course.

And none of these people surrounding her expected anything less. It was the same reason why there was a silver Porsche with a large pink bow sitting out in the driveway. A gift from her father. And a week-long trip to Sicily from her mother to go with her new Versace dresses and Louboutin heels from her grandmother, Catrina.

Some might call her spoiled.

Maybe she was.

Cece just liked to say she was *loved*.

"Make a wish," chanted around the large dining room.

As many people that could had filled the space entirely. All her family—grandparents, aunts and uncles, cousins. Her brother, their parents, and all her friends. Maybe for her sixteenth, she could have done something more grown up for her party … but this was perfect.

The many candles flickering on the cake had shadows dancing on the walls and ceiling. With the lights dimmed down, it made the silver accents on the cake stand out even more. Not that she was paying attention to any of that.

Someone across the table had her attention.

All of it.

Juan stood at the far end of the room, leaning against the wall. Nobody specified the attire for the party, and yet he still showed up in a white silk dress shirt rolled up around to his elbows. It showed off the dark golden tan of his forearms and the ropes of veins she had learned that she liked to trace with her fingertips when the two of them were driving around.

Or … *anytime.*

He smiled her way.

No, that was wrong.

It was more like a smirk.

Entirely *too* attractive.

He knew it, too.

"Make a wish," he mouthed.

Cece cocked a brow, leaned forward so that the flame of the candle she was supposed to blow out was only a few inches away, locked gazes with Juan and then blew out the candle. All the while, she made her wish.

One she'd been thinking about for a while.

She wanted a kiss.

From him.

*

"Cece, your mother is going to want you to open presents!"

She heard the shout of her grandmother, Emma, behind her, but didn't turn around. The hand locked around her wrist kept her attention on the man ahead of her. Juan, that was. And the fact he was steering them toward the back of the house. Before she knew it, the two of them stood out on the back deck.

"You know, I need to be in *there*, right?" she asked.

Juan spun Cece around and leveled her with one of *those* grins. The kind that had her stomach doing flip-flops while her heart only managed to melt into a stupid puddle of *goo*. See, Juan wasn't the first boy to give her attention. She'd *had* boyfriends if that was what someone wanted to call those.

Mostly, they were like toys to her.

Fun to play with.

Cute to look at.

Then, she quickly became bored, and discarded them to someone who might find a better use of them than she did.

But then there was Juan. He couldn't be the same because he'd *never* been the same. The first boy she ever had a crush on, it didn't wane. Not as time passed, boys came and went, and the years went by.

And all it took was a grin from him to remind her exactly *why* that was, too.

"My gift is in there somewhere," he said, "it's that bag you were—"

"The *Hermes* one?"

Juan laughed. "Listen—"

"That's a ten-thousand-dollar bag, Juan."

"And?"

She wasn't going to ask how he came up with the money for that. She knew he'd started to work for his father—and as a by-product—her mother since he turned seventeen. She learned it was better *not* to ask when it came to business unless someone else offered.

As it was, her mother offered her a lot.

Soon, Cece would be with them.

Working.

"Did you bring me out here to tell me about the bag?" she asked.

Juan shook his head and moved in a little closer. Those strong arms of his locked around her waist, and she found herself molded against him. All her soft curves fit into his hard lines, and her heart pounded. She stared up at him, waiting.

They did this a lot.

Just him and her.

It didn't mean very much but it also meant *everything*.

"No, I wanted to tell you happy birthday without an audience," he said.

Cece smiled. "Oh?"

"Yes, so happy birthday, *hermosa*. What did you wish for, by the way?"

A shaky exhale left her lips. "Something silly."

"Doubt it. There's a Porsche in your driveway and the dress you're wearing is an easy five-k. You don't wish for *silly* things. You're too much like your mother and grandmothers for that."

"Hey, now."

Juan shrugged, still grinning. "But I don't *lie*."

Well, he had a point.

"You really want to know what I wished?"

"Yeah, Cece. I know everything about you, right? Why would that be different?"

She swallowed hard.

Right.

But what if this was different?

Because it couldn't be *the same*.

"A kiss. From you. That's what I wished for."

Juan's gaze stayed locked with hers. He didn't tense or act like that surprised him at all.

"All right," he murmured.

"All—"

"Yeah. Let's make that come true."

In the next second, he was kissing her.

It wasn't her first kiss.

Her heart still exploded all the same.

CHAPTER 10 – LITTLE BROTHERS

Juan POV

Eighteen years old …

"So, this is just what you're going to do now?" Cece asked.

Juan grinned her way as he turned the car onto her street. He'd much rather whip the car around—illegal U-turn right there in the suburbs—and take her back to his hotel for the night, but he didn't think that would end well for him all things considered. Her father was lax with a lot of rules as long as he understood what was going to happen. If plans changed, however, then Cross took issue and didn't mind letting Juan know it, either.

But *God*, he missed his girl.

All the time.

"What are we doing?" he asked.

From the passenger seat of his rented Mercedes, Cece gave him a sweet—but still sexy—smile when she said, "*This*, Juan. Flying here for the weekend to take me out and then running back to Cali for the rest of the week. Seems like a lot of time and money—"

"Seems like effort to me," he murmured.

That quieted her.

Not in a bad way, either.

Juan raised a brow, waiting for Cece to respond. She simply kept staring at him with the same smile as before, although it did deepen a little bit to show her pleasure as his words.

"Effort, huh?"

"I was told," Juan said as he came to a stop at the bottom of her parents' driveway, "that when you love someone, it's all about the effort you make to show them you love them rather than everything else in between. That's all."

"And you *love* me."

It wasn't even a question.

She just knew.

He needed her to be sure of it.

Maybe it was strange—here they were with him at eighteen, her at sixteen, and this was how they had come to be. They'd known each other for most of their lives. There had never been any *big changes* that reset the course of their relationship with each other. Everything had always seemed to just fall into place. Even something like love. He'd just *always* loved her for as long as he could remember.

Juan didn't remember falling in love but that didn't make it any less real or strong or absolutely fucking *terrifying*. But he needed it—and her. The same way he wanted the sun on his face every morning and air in his lungs with each breath.

This girl was his.

He would keep her.

"Love you forever," Juan murmured.

Cece's lips split with a grin that showed off her teeth before she leaned over in the seats after unsnapping her seatbelt. He barely even had the chance to put the car in park before she leaned over the middle section and kissed him. The kind of kiss that—once again—had him wishing he'd made different plans with her for the evening than simply a date and bringing her back home. Her lips moved hungry and hard against his own before he finally got a taste of her on his tongue when she opened up for him. In a blink, she sat in his lap, her back tight to the steering wheel while his hands worked to drive the skirt of her dress higher over her thighs.

Because just like that ...

Juan forgot where they were. Who might be watching ...

All of it.

Cece made it easy to forget.

He should really know better, though.

A knock on the driver's window had Cece shrieking and pulling away from Juan before she fell back into the passenger seat. He sent up a quick, silent prayer that when he turned his head, he wouldn't see Cece's father on the outside of his car. Because if there was one thing in this world he was terrified of, it just happened to be Cross fucking Donati.

The man had a way about him. He could make a threat both entertaining *and* scary which was a talent in and of itself. And if there was anything the man cared about more than himself, it was his wife and kids. That's all Juan was saying.

Fortunately, it wasn't Cross.

It was, however, almost as bad.

"Jesus Chris, *Nazio*," Cece snarled under her breath.

Sure enough, Juan turned to his left and found Cece's younger brother smirking from where he now stood on the sidewalk. At least the little fucker wasn't peering into the window, but he was still a little too close for Juan's comfort.

Since he and Cece had become an official *thing*, he'd learned quite a bit about her younger brother. Before, Juan hadn't given Naz much attention or thought because frankly, the kid hadn't mattered to him that much. They didn't make friends, there was quite an age difference, and the two of them seemed fine with that.

Now, however, that Juan was dating Cece ... Naz was up his ass constantly. Like a little bee that he couldn't get rid of.

The kid's due, Juan's father said.

And he'd just have to deal with it.

Right.

"Fucking *ass*," Cece muttered.

She leaned over the seat and gave Juan one more kiss but not before also flipping her middle finger up at her brother while she was at it. A quick goodbye and *love you* later, and Cece stepped out of his car, bitching at her little brother the whole time. Juan watched her head up the drive and step onto the front porch.

Naz, on the other hand, didn't leave the sidewalk. Because of course, not. He couldn't glare at Juan from inside the house. Or at least, Juan couldn't see him do it from there.

Shame, really.

"You want something?" Juan asked, rolling down the window.

Naz shrugged. "Nope, not really."

"Just gonna ... be there, then?"

"All the time," the younger teen replied. "Might as well get used to me, Juan."

Yeah.

Seemed so.

"I mean, all right," Juan said before pulling the car into drive. "Do you, man."

"Wouldn't dream of anything else."

Juan had a feeling this was going to be the rest of his life with Cece.

And Naz.

Fun.

CHAPTER 11 – MARRY HER

Juan POV

20 years old …

"I want to marry Cece."

Beside him, Juan's father stiffened subtly. Of course, it couldn't be noticeable. Not when they were working for the queen, and by all appearances, needed to seem like terrifying statues that would suddenly come alive and move from their shadowed corner if Catherine's—Cece's mom—guest stepped out of line.

A lot of the time, Catherine liked to meet potential clients personally so that she could get a feel for who her girls would be dealing with when they supplied the client with product—usually cocaine, but not always. Anyway, she always made the final call on whether someone made it onto the *list*. At the moment, it didn't look particularly good for the high profile, politician's son who, for whatever damned reason, thought he was God's gift to women and humanity alike.

Juan had news for him.

He wasn't.

He was barely fucking tolerable and Juan hadn't even needed to speak to the guy. But he was entitled, spoke like a fucking prick, and treated everyone around him like a servant meant to please him, and that didn't say very good things for him. Nor was it very promising for his likelihood of getting on Catherine's client list. People often thought that because they had deep pockets and pedigree, they were guaranteed whatever the fuck they wanted.

Not with the queen.

The rich rarely understood the difference between confidence and arrogance. It didn't even surprise Juan anymore, although it annoyed him to no end. Part of him had a good mind to speak up and tell the asshole across the room where he could shove his entitlement, but … well, he knew better. He'd learned while working alongside his father as a personal guard for Catherine—a queen pin to the grossly wealthy and North America's elite—that he was better served when he kept his mouth shut and let the woman do her job.

Catherine could—and *would*—handle herself. She had been doing it for years before he came along, after all. Soon, Juan knew, that would be Cece sitting in the same spot her mother did. Yeah, she was doing the whole college thing—or rather, giving it the old college try, but everybody could already tell … it just wasn't for her.

They'd wait for her to figure it out, too.

She'd yet to say it.

Still dabbled in the family business, though. The girl couldn't change who she was even if she cared to try. Which she didn't. Not that it mattered. Regardless pf what Cece chose to do in the end, Juan was going to be right there following behind her. He didn't know anything different, and he really didn't want to, either.

Finally, after his declaration to his father and the responding minutes of silence that followed, Miguel said, "Say that again."

A faint smile curved his lips while across the room, Catherine looked a few seconds away from telling the snotty politician's son right where he could shove his money and prestige. *Good.* That meant they would be done here soon.

"I want to marry Cece."

Miguel cleared his throat, which drew his Catherine's attention. But when she looked their way, both men had quickly reverted back to their previous still states. She returned to her meeting but not before giving the two of them a look.

A silent *hush*.

The order wasn't missed.

Miguel still opted to test it—then again, Catherine was his best friend. "You thought now was the right time to tell me that—first of all, I should add."

Juan shrugged. "I had to tell someone."

"Secondly," his father continued as though he hadn't said a thing, "the two of you have been on and off for the last couple of years. Are you even *on* right now—did I miss something?"

"Dad—"

Miguel gave Juan a look from the side, stopping him before he could say anything more with, "Not that it mattered—I've known you wanted to marry her since … well, for a long time, Juan."

"Yeah."

"But you're also twenty, and she's only—"

"I'm not saying right now," Juan was quick to say before his father could continue. "But … *someday*."

Miguel let out a soft sigh.

Then, he smiled. "Well, someday, and by that, I mean *before* you think of even asking her, you better make sure you speak to her father."

Juan swallowed hard.

Right.

He'd forgotten about that bit.

CHAPTER 12 – HIM

Juan POV

20 years old …

Nervous did not begin to describe how Juan felt as he moved to stand beside Cross Donati in the man's backyard. He'd decided he would ask Cross for his daughter's hand the next time he had the chance which just happened to be a month after he'd spoken to his own father about it.

With the backyard Donati party long over that evening, Juan decided *now or never* when he noticed Cross outside alone.

"I have something to ask," Juan said.

Cross smirked, giving him a look from the side. "Oh?"

"Not used to having people ask questions, or …?"

"Cute—watch that tone, huh? No, everyone always has something to ask—rarely *you*, though."

It wasn't a lie.

"I don't have a choice. I have to ask this one. And it has to be you that answers it."

Silence covered the dark yard.

Cross stiffened beside him. "Please tell me you're not going to ask *that?*"

"Depends on what *that* is."

The man gave him a burning glance. "You *know*. Don't play stupid. There's only one thing you *have* to ask me for Cece."

Fine.

"Would it be such a bad thing if I did?"

"Yes and no."

Juan didn't plan on asking the man to elaborate on that. "I'll take those odds, Cross. And since you couldn't let me work into it the way I wanted to, I'll just ask. I want to marry your daughter—do I or do I not have your blessing?"

Cross's jaw tightened. If his line of view shot fire, the trees would have been burnt to a crisp.

"I do like you, Juan, I hope you know that," Cross said, shaking his head.

"Sometimes, I do wonder."

"Sometimes, you make it hard to remember *why* I like you."

Yeah, well …

"Same," Juan returned.

"You gotta lot of nerve asking me that when she's only eighteen," Cross muttered, eyeing the dark surroundings of the backyard, then up at the sky before coming back down to the treeline. Looking literally *anywhere* but at Juan. "And you know *why?*"

Juan didn't get a chance to offer a reason.

Cross continued on just as sharply with, "Because I know how much you fucking love her—because we already did this thing once where I threatened you with what would happen if she wasn't treated with the utmost care, and never once—not *one* goddamn time—did you break that promise, *and* you still let her live her life while you did it. You've not given me a single reason to say no to you, Juan, but you ask *now*—when she's still young, and for that, you've got a lot of nerve here."

"I didn't think I was putting you in a bad position."

"Of course, you are. I'd feel like a fuck for asking you to wait—no one should have to wait when it's something they love and adore. I know that better than anyone."

"I—"

"And half the goddamn time, none of us even know if the two of you are *on* or fucking off—it tends to be a clear, obvious thing, you know? Not with the two of you."

He swallowed hard, considering that.

It didn't take him long to formulate a response and when he did, he hoped it made more than just one thing clear to Cross. All the nerves he felt earlier slipped away because out of everything in his life, there was one thing he was most sure of: *Cece*. And he wanted everyone else to know it, too. Including her father.

"I grew up with Cece," Juan said, "and she was my *one* best friend that was constant. And the only thing between her and I that's not really changed even when we got older and the shit we did when we were kids turned into something *different* … I still had my best friend. So, next week I'm taking her to Mumbai—you know about that trip—and we're gonna have a week of just her and I. But last week she spent partying in the Hills and didn't call me until Friday when we were flying back to New York for this thing. I'm not dying about it. I don't need to worry about it when I know what I know. It's not an on or off thing for me and her—we're us, and maybe we don't look like somebody else's thing, but how can it? Everybody else didn't grow up like we did … they're not like we are. It's how we want it. And maybe someday it'll change again and we'll turn into something different."

Juan nodded when Cross's gaze landed back on him again. "So, that's why I'm here. *Someday*, because I have always known where I wanted to be at the end, if it does change, I have done what I needed to do for that, too. I want to marry your daughter—do I or do I not have your blessing?"

He said it the same way.

Posed it no different.

Juan didn't give a time frame of *when* he might ask—because if they changed tomorrow or next week or in three years, he would be happy and ready all the same—how, or otherwise. There was nothing that had changed from the first time he asked Cross that night to the second *except* that he hoped the two men understood each other now when it came to Cece.

See, he'd always understood Cross.

And the man's position.

It was his turn now.

"Is the threat of your worst possible death for her safety and care still well understood between the two of us?" Cross asked gruffly.

Juan nodded. "Of course."

Cross sniffed, shoved his hands in his pockets, and turned to face the treeline of his back property again. "Then, you have my blessing."

"That's all you have to say?"

"Someday, I'll be your father-in-law, Juan. I reserve my right to say *anything* I want *whenever* I want during the duration of your marriage to my daughter. Which we both know will be forever—Catholics don't *do* divorce but for the exceptional few. So, yeah, that's all I have to say."

Arrogant *asshole*.

Yet, Juan respected it.

Because that was him—Cross.

And he made her.

CHAPTER 13 – MOTHER'S DAUGHTER

Cece POV

18 years old …

Mumbai

The hammock rocked back in forth in a breeze that smelled like paradise. Cece wasn't making it move, but she didn't feel unsafe either, considering Juan had her wrapped tight in his arms while he foot on the ground did the work of keeping them moving. The trees blocked most of the bright afternoon son from her line of view, and the heat was just delicious enough to keep her in that tiny white bikini she knew Juan loved to hate and hated to love.

Everybody looked her way when she wore that.

Even him.

"When we get back," she started to say.

"Hmm?"

His hum echoed in her ear, making her smile.

"I don't think I'm returning to college," Cece said.

Juan's arm flexed around her a bit, but he didn't miss a beat in swinging the hammock nor did he give her any sign of how he felt about that statement. "Well, let's be honest, babe, you haven't really spent much time at college at all this last semester. I'm not sure what you're still trying to do with that but—"

"I got bored," she admitted. "I wanted to try *normal*. I tried to explain it to Naz, because he tried to call me out like I was just doing college to *do it*, I guess. He didn't get it—but he's got no interest in being normal. He's always been anything but."

"First, does your brother even have *normal people* struggles, because … I don't think he does. I'm not surprised he didn't get it, Cece."

"Yeah."

"*Secondly*," he said, nipping her shoulder with his teasing teeth, "how did normal work out for you?"

"Like shit."

She laughed.

So did he.

"Everybody let me keep pretending, though," she said in a sigh, "no matter how long I was going to keep it up, it seemed."

"Pretend what?"

Cece shrugged, enjoying Juan's hard lines and warmth that never seemed to be quite close enough … even like this. She would always want more of him—that was a promise. "I guess, that I wasn't my mother's daughter."

Silence saturated the beach.

Juan broke it first when he asked, "But did you ever think you weren't?"

"Not once."

"Then what did it matter what anyone else might have thought?"

Cece laughed under her breath. "I guess it didn't."

His teeth nipped her shoulder *again*. Promising and fun at the same time. "Exactly."

"Hmm."

"Roll over," he demanded.

She did, rocking the hammock dangerously at the same time. He took that chance to steal a kiss from her, but she didn't mind in the least. Especially not when he tasted like that and kissed her the way he did. Hungry and possessive and *pleased*.

It drove her crazy.

Only he could do that.

"You know," he murmured against her lips, "you were never *normal*, Cece."

"Oh, no?"

He shrugged, smirking.

God.

She loved that look on him.

Too damn much.

"No," he said again, "because you can't be normal. Not when you're already exceptional."

And just like that.

Poof.

There went her heart.

But frankly? He'd already taken it long ago.

Nothing and no one on earth could or would ever be *Juan* to Cece.

Facts were facts.

CHAPTER 14 – THE QUEEN

18 years old …

Cece POV

"How was Mumbai?"

Cece sucked air through her teeth and grinned, not at all surprised that her mother knew she was standing in the office doorway before she'd even made a sound. Catherine didn't bother looking up from whatever she was typing into her laptop, either.

"Really good."

"Good, sweetheart." Catherine did look up then, smiling at her daughter from where she sat behind her large desk. Her mother and father often shared an office space for work in their home, and then sometimes, they went through little spats where both of them swore they couldn't stand to work in the same space anymore. Cece didn't know what they were currently doing with that. "And Juan is …?"

"Downstairs having a drink with Daddy."

Catherine nodded. "He's heading back to Cali soon, isn't he?"

"Friday night."

"Hmm."

Her mother went back to whatever work she was doing while Cece stayed in the doorway feeling her nerves climb higher and higher in her throat with every passing second. It wasn't like she had any reason to be nervous. Just like Juan had told her on their vacation, everybody was already expecting this from Cece. It was not a matter of *if* she would follow in her mother's footsteps, but rather, *when*.

When was now.

Cece still wasn't sure how to say it.

"Something wrong?" her mother asked quietly.

Catherine's attention was on her again.

That wasn't a strange feeling, either.

Her whole life had been filled with the attention and loved showered upon her by her parents. She loved them for the freedom they allowed her to have, and room they gave her to grow. There was never a time when she felt like she couldn't go to one of them if she needed something.

This was not going to be the exception to that rule.

"I want to work with the girls," Cece said.

No overthinking it.

No fear.

It just was what it was.

For a moment, her mother said nothing as she watched her from across the room. Cece couldn't really tell if Catherine was trying to search for something Cece wasn't saying out loud, or if her mother was simply giving herself time to think and then speak.

Eventually, Catherine replied, "Do you?"

"Yes."

"Not a *when you feel like it* type of thing, right?"

Cece laughed. "What, like college through the week and dealing on the weekends?"

"Now, you know we call it making a delivery. It's less illegal."

Well ...

Her mother had a point.

"College isn't really my thing," Cece settled on saying.

"And you think this will be?"

Cece really didn't have to think about that at all. Her entire life had been spent under her mother's feet while she ran this *empire*. She idolized Catherine, and maybe not for all the right reasons, but when had that ever mattered?

She was a Donati.

The daughter of criminals.

A princess born from a queen.

"It's what I want to do," she said simply.

Leaning back in her chair, Catherine forgot about her work, steepled her fingers, and watched Cece in that way again. Like she was looking for something.

"Fine—meets with the girls are next week to go over the coming months and what we know for sure is happening. Major events, a few premiers, some other things where I need girls. I believe *you* will have better knowledge of some of the parties up and coming in the Hills seeing as how you manage to hit every single one of them."

Cece laughed. "Was that your sly attempt at shade?"

Catherine grinned. "Queens don't need to be shady, Cece."

Very well.

"I do, however, think your time will be better spent in the Hills for the first while since you know the faces and the people. You have an easy in, and it won't be a stretch when you move on from a guest to a supplier. Juan can follow, act as your guard, he's—"

"One of your personal guards," Cece interjected.

Catherine smiled. "Only because we were waiting for your turn."

Oh.

She hadn't considered that.

"He won't mind," Catherine said. "He's been getting bored sitting in hotels or at restaurant tables when he'd rather be doing something else with someone else."

Her mother's gaze lifted and met hers.

Cece shook her head. "Nice, Ma."

"Yes, well, I do what I can."

"Is ... that it, then?" Cece asked.

"For what?"

Cece smirked. "Well, I guess ... me working for the Queen."

Catherine's smile matched her daughter's. "I suppose it is. Welcome to the family, Cece. Except ... well, you've always been *in*, haven't you?"

Yeah.

She had.

CHAPTER 15 – ALWAYS

Juan POV

20 years old …

"Cece, if you'd just—"

"Right now, I would rather not, Juan."

The sharpness in her tone should have been enough to tell him to back off, but he found that really difficult to do where Cece was concerned. He knew she needed space and all, but whenever she was pissed off at him, there was only one thing he wanted to do about it.

Fix it.

Problem with that—at least this time around because Cece didn't mad at him very often—was that Juan hadn't done anything wrong. In fact, he'd done his fucking job and pulled her from an unsafe situation with a client. Shit, maybe the guy hadn't crossed any obvious lines because Juan had been watching very fucking closely, like he was supposed to do, but that didn't really make a difference to him at the end of the day.

The man's tone said enough.

His *suggestions*.

And the way he looked at Cece when her back was turned?

Fuck all that noise.

The asshole wasn't any different on the surface and on paper than any of Catherine's other clients that were on Cece's list to handle when needed. Too rich for their own good with more money than they knew what to do with. Arrogant to the point that Juan regularly wanted to punch him in the throat. *Overly* privileged.

Nothing new.

Except something was just off.

And he didn't ignore that feeling in his gut. It served him well up until this point in his life, and he highly doubted that was going to change any time soon. Juan was fine with that. It was just Cece that had to get on board with the program.

"Are we going to at least talk about—"

She shot him a burning look over her shoulder in the elevator.

"No."

"But—"

"Juan, I'm over it. It's *fine*."

Ha.

Ha, ha, fucking ha.

It was not fine.

It was never fine when a woman dared to speak the word *fine*. Juan was not so stupid or young enough of a man that he didn't see that shit for exactly what it was.

That was bait.

A trap.

And he wouldn't be the asshole who fell right into it.

"All right," he said, swallowing the next words that threatened to come out of his mouth. No doubt, Cece would eventually come around and they could talk about it.

But *fuck*.

He hated fighting with her.

They didn't fight, really.

Not over shit like this.

And yet ...

Here they were,

Juan remained quiet as the elevator climbed the remaining floors to her LA penthouse. When the doors slid open, she stepped out without so much as looking back over her shoulder at him. He wasn't offended at that and made sure to keep a couple of paces between them as he walked her down the hall to her front door.

Cece fumbled with the keycard for her door, the only real show of her anger now—her fingers wouldn't cooperate. To save her the trouble and more annoyance, he pulled out his own that she'd given him a year ago when she first bought the place. He had his own across town, too, but more often than not ... they woke up together now.

Who knew, though?

That could change.

Things were always changing.

"Thanks," she muttered when the door popped open.

Juan nodded, and waited for Cece to step inside. He, however, didn't follow behind her like he usually would. Instead, he leaned against the wall in the hallway as she kicked off the heels that showed off those long, shapely legs of hers and had been teasing him all goddamn night.

Not that right now was the time for that.

He kind of wished it was.

After she'd shed all the things that she didn't want to wear or carry, Cece turned to him with heavy shoulders that sunk a little too much for his liking and a frown that made him want to kiss right off her pretty face.

With him, she should only smile.

That was his goal.

"I know shit was off," she started, "but I had it handled."

"Maybe that's the problem," he returned, "you know?"

"No, I guess I don't."

And that was another problem.

"You *felt* it—something wasn't right. But you were willing to ignore it for the sake of getting the delivery done to the client, despite the fact he changed the location *and* ended up bringing you into a situation where there would have been no one there except you and him. It *felt* bad and you ignored it. It's intuition talking to you, Cece. Don't pretend like you can't hear it. That's when bad shit happens."

That's why he was there.

"Even if something did go bad—"

"It didn't. And I know you're going to say you can handle it, but that's why I'm there. So it doesn't happen in the first place. I did my fucking job. I won't apologize for it, either."

Her jaw hardened.

Fire came to life in her eyes.

Juan let her have it.

She was due it, after all.

"So, that's how it's going to be working together, then?" she asked.

Juan nodded. "Pretty much."

"Always?"

"If it means you're coming back here every night, even if you're pissed off at me, then yeah. Always."

And she could like it or not.

That was up to her.

Juan was still doing him.

CHAPTER 16 – MARRY HIM

Cece POV

20 years old …

"So, despite how often I hear your father whine and moan about getting you to move back to New York, it's never going to happen, is it?"

Cece grinned at her grandmother's question but hid it well enough when she glanced to the side. That way, she could watch the cars speeding past on the Manhattan street instead of at her grandmother who was *entirely* too perceptive for her own good. Then again, all the women of her family seemed to be that way. It was why she had never been able to get away with shit.

Or maybe it was just because everything she tried to do, they had already done a million and one times over. They knew what to look for.

Either way, she loved them.

And it.

Mostly.

"I … like LA," she settled on saying.

"Let's just call it what it is, Cece," Catrina replied, not unkindly, "and say you're an LA girl and New York just doesn't do it for you."

"That's partly the case."

"Mmhmm. I imagine the man you keep there doesn't hurt, either."

After she said that, Catrina made a point of glancing over her shoulder—not at all with any subtlety—to pass Juan a look who stayed a few paces back from the grandmother and granddaughter duo as they went about their day in upper Manhattan. Which mostly, for them, meant lots and lots of shopping—tens of thousands of dollars spent, a good meal at a Marcello-owned restaurant, and then they would see where the day—or evening—took them from there. As was usually the case whenever she got together with her nan.

She loved Catrina.

Inexplicably.

A lot like her ma.

"To be fair," Cece said, "about the man, I mean … it's not like he's ever said something about it one way or the other. He's not asked me to move to LA or live there. I did that all on my own because it's where I wanted to be."

"Mmhmm."

"It *is*."

Catrina winked with a smile. "I know it is. It was bound to happen. Like your father, though, don't expect me not to occasionally make it known that I wish I could see you more than I do. That's all I'm saying."

Cece laughed. "I know, Grandmama."

"Not that it matters what any of us think."

"Oh?"

Catrina shrugged, fixing her black sun hat as she glanced up at the too-bright sky overhead. "Of course, not, Cece. You're doing great things all on your own and without our input, why the hell should it matter?"

And that was exactly why she loved her nan.

Amongst many other reasons.

She never felt judgement from her grandmother for any of her choices. She could always go to Catrina for anything at all—just to talk, for support, or whatever else she might need. The door was always open. Never closed.

When she needed advice on the business, she came to Catrina … if it was something her ma couldn't handle for her. She kind of felt like, growing up, she had had the best women around her to raise her.

One of them had been her grandmother.

She was grateful.

"Now," her grandmother said, coming to a stop in front of one of their favorite boutiques, "one more shop, I think. Juan, you don't mind carrying another bag or two, do you? We'll call the driver to come around the block."

Behind them, Juan smiled. "Don't mind at all, Catrina."

Though they'd been shopping since the morning.

One more shop was *definitely* a lie.

He still smiled and said yes.

He wouldn't complain a bit.

More than once, he'd told her that he would do anything with or for Cece as long as she was there to do it with him. That was when he had the most fun. Even if it was something as mundane as shopping for hours and carrying her bags. It reminded her of when they were younger, and he would sit beside her on a blanket and do absolutely nothing in the summer while all the other kids played around them.

Her best friend until the end.

He truly was great.

Juan was kind of perfect in that way.

"We appreciate it," Catrina said.

"Of course. Anything for you and Cece."

Turning slightly, her grandmother eyed a black car that passed, and under her breath, too low for Cece to hear, Catrina said, "And if you haven't figured *this* out yet, marry that man. Marry him as soon as you possibly can, Cece. And don't look back."

Cece only smiled.

That was the plan.

Someday.

CHAPTER 17 – AN ANNOUNCEMENT

Juan POV

23 years old …

"Hey, wait a sec."

Cece's hand reaching for the passenger door of Juan's Maserati—the only vehicle he kept stored in New York for their frequent visits—hesitated before opening the latch. She glanced back at him over her shoulder; the nerves in his heart settled the second her gaze landed on him.

He really didn't have any idea why he was nervous in the first fucking place. It wasn't like he'd never done one of her family's large dinners before. All the cars in the gated drive, he pretty well could list every person that owned each one by first and last name.

Still, just glancing up the drive at the familiar three-level home had his heart feeling like it might beat right out of his goddamn chest. His hands might be sweaty, too, but he wasn't going to check when he'd rather just keep gripping the steering wheel like it might save him.

"What?" Cece asked.

"You know this is the first time we're going to *officially* tell your family we're engaged, yeah?"

Cece blinked.

A second passed.

Then, two.

Finally, she simply asked, "And?"

"That doesn't make you nervous at all?"

"I mean, no?"

Then, Cece cocked her head to the side a bit. Her gaze narrowed slightly, drifting from Juan to the home ahead and then back again. It took her another second before she decided to speak, but as she did, an almost *knowing* grin curved her lips.

God.

He loved when she did that.

Teased him.

She was the only female he'd ever let do it, too.

"*You're* nervous?" she asked.

"Don't make a thing out of it. I just had a moment and all. I mean, your family is great … they've always welcomed me in and—"

"Hey," she interjected quickly, leaning across the seats to come far closer than Juan had been expecting. In a blink, she closed the last bit of space between them to press a fast, hard kiss to his lips. Her mouth moved against his—their familiar war coaxing an approving groan from the back of his throat until she pulled away with another one of those smiles of hers that he loved so damn much. "They welcomed you in a long time ago and you know it. Don't be nervous. Besides, now that we have a date for them to save … the next few months are going to be just one big party."

Juan chuckled. "You think?"

"You'd think being around Italians, you might know more about us. Shame … you'll learn."

That time, he grinned.

"I don't mind."

Cece winked. "Are you good?"

He dragged in a heavy lungful of air, nodding with a smile. "Yeah, babe, I'm good."

"Let's go."

Before he could even unbuckle his belt, she was out of the car and heading for the house. Juan had to take a moment to appreciate the sway of her hips in those straight-leg jeans, her loose crop-top of pink silk falling to just below her mid back, giving him a peek at tanned skin. The click-click of her sky-high, strappy heels had him moving out of the car to follow behind as fast as he possibly could.

By the time she reached the front veranda, his hand found her lower back when she moved into step with her. He'd just pressed a kiss to the side of her temple when the front door to the house blew open.

Confetti made of gold and black and silver came out to shower them in color while the gathered people in the house started hollering loud enough that before the night was over, the whole block would know Cece and Juan were engaged.

Congrats were shouted.

Laughter colored up a dark street.

Someone already had bubbly waiting, too.

It sprayed all over the deck.

Juan hadn't been expecting any of that—but the knowing glint in Cece's eye when she looked his way with a happy smile told him that she very well had.

His nerves finally disappeared.

For good.

"How did he propose?" someone called out.

Cece and Juan laughed.

It wasn't an easy answer.

She smiled with a shrug. That smile was enough to tilt his whole world sideways.

"Well, I kind of did? And then he did? Anyway. He broke my necklace—the ring was hidden inside. I guess ... it was always there. Waiting for the right moment."

Any moment would have been right.

They were them, after all.

Still, Juan nodded and said, "Yeah, I was just waiting for that moment."

CHAPTER 18 – WEDDING BELLS

Cece POV

Cece toyed with the delicate lace of her wedding dress. Splayed out over the high curved back of a couch, the gown covered most of the surface and a good portion of the floor. She hadn't known what she wanted for a wedding dress until this one was staring her right in the face. It screamed everything that she was.

Class.

Queenly.

The first time she put it on, she had only fallen more in love with the gown, if that were somehow possible. That was months ago. Now here it was, her wedding day, and Juan would finally be able to see the dress, too.

"Busy?"

The familiar voice had Cece smiling and turning away from her dress. Her mother and grandmother slipped into the private room where she would prepare for the day and her wedding. The makeup artist and hairstylist had yet to arrive, most of the wedding party was already there, and the event planner she'd hired to work with the women of her family that wanted to help were getting everything ready for later.

All she had to do was dress, get pretty, and relax.

It was her day.

Or so everyone kept telling her.

"I wanted a moment with you before everybody gets here," Catrina said, crossing the room first to wrap Cece in a tight hug. "Because I don't think I'll see you again until much later—someone is already blowing up my phone because I'm not helping to decorate like I promised."

That somebody was likely one of her cousins.

Or aunts.

Maybe her other grandmother.

Hell.

Their family was huge.

It could be anybody.

Roses and honey.

That's what her grandmother smelled like.

A different version of home.

Catrina's hand came up to rest against Cece's smiling cheek. She patted the spot affectionately, her gaze softer than usual. "I'm proud of you, hmm?"

"I know, Grandmama."

She never forgot to tell her.

Once, she asked her grandmother why she did that—Catrina's answer hadn't been at all what she expected. Apparently, her nan wished she had told her own daughter more often ... or rather, wished she had recognized earlier what Catherine held the most pride in so that she could do the same.

"And," Catrina said, pulling a black velvet case from her bag to set on the table beside the couch, "because I promised ... that is the jewelry I wore on my wedding day. Taken from the vault just for you—your grandfather had a man follow me there and back and he's still standing outside right now because according to your grandfather, it's the point of the matter ... as if I couldn't make it here without somehow losing or damaging it. But, a promise is a promise, right?"

Cece nodded with a laugh. "Right."

"Keep it safe. They're yours now."

"Thank you."

Catrina winked.

Just as fast, her grandmother brought her in for another tight hug. Catrina's lips found her forehead with a soft kiss. "I will be back later – just to see you before we all have to get in our chairs later."

"You better."

She took another quick hug from her grandmother before Catrina said her goodbyes. Once the door clicked close, Catherine finally pushed up from the chair near the door where she had found a place to sit while her mother had been in the room.

Her smile matched her mother's.

Catherine sighed as her gaze found the wedding dress spread out across the large couch. "He's going to love it—and your father, too."

"I hope so."

"They will."

Once her mother had crossed the room and stood in front of her,

Cece sniffed to try and hide the emotions that suddenly came to lodge in her throat. Unlike her grandmother, Catherine made sure that she was going to be with her daughter the entire day because that's what Cece asked for. Something about that just felt right. Spending the day with her mother before she officially became a married woman was ... *appropriate*.

"Do you remember when you thought he didn't even notice you?" Catherine asked. "When you were too young ... and you thought he couldn't even see you when he looked your way? Things were a lot more innocent then, I imagine."

"Something like that."

"Did you figure it out?"

"Figure out what, Ma?"

"The only person he ever saw was you, Cece."

Later, when the wedding bells would ring, and she found herself standing at the end of the aisle with Juan across from her ... she'd remember what her mother said. Amongst many other things about her wedding day that stayed forefront in her memories, that one stood out the most.

Because Catherine had been right.

She usually was.

GODFATHER

"So, what does this even mean?"

The priest, fully dressed in his robes, and ready to go over one last time how this ceremony was going to happen, turned to give Zeke a look. "Pardon?"

"This *godfather* thing. What does it even mean?"

The man's gaze dropped to the bundle of white in Zeke's arm. Little Cece Donati. He decided to give her mother and father a break after they had their regular mass, and the baby girl cried nearly the *whole* time. Maybe because she knew in about an hour, she was going to get her forehead splashed with holy water, and wasn't in the mood.

She looked a lot like her ma, sure.

But acted more like her father.

Even as a newborn.

"Bit late to be asking the purpose of a godparent, isn't it?" the priest asked.

His arms tightened around the baby. Cece was really the *only* newborn he could remember holding in … well, ever. He adored her, though. She came from his best friend, and from day one, all he wanted to do was help protect the baby girl.

"I just never really thought about it," Zeke replied. "What it *means*, I guess."

The priest smiled a bit, his hand coming up to rest along the white cap Cece wore for her Christening that matched her baby gown. "It is a great responsibility, Zeke. See, many have turned *godparents* into something else—a coveted title for their favorite people. And in doing that, they forgot the purpose of a godparent."

"Which is what?"

Because the priest wasn't wrong.

Zeke could admit that.

In their culture, picking godparents for a child was as expected as going to church every Sunday. People waited with baited breath to find out *who* the parents would pick amongst their group of family and friends to do the job. And then once it was said and done, the baby had its Christening, and the deal was finished … the rest was forgotten.

The point of a godparent was lost.

Except at birthdays and holidays in which gifts were given, and someone always thought to mention, *that's from your godparents.*

But there had to be more to it than that?

Right?

"To be a godparent means a lifelong commitment to the child," the priest said, running the edge of his thumb down the slope of little Cece's nose. She didn't seem to mind the priest's attention, as she continued happily sleeping away. "Because you see, it is your job to educate this child on her purpose in life where God is concerned. You're promising her parents, that should something unthinkable happen to them, you will be the person who steps up to continue her guidance in the spiritual aspects. And in some cases, they may even expect you to take an active stance on her religious teachings even while they are around."

"Huh."

"You are her spiritual guide—that is what you agree to by becoming a godparent. And of course, it is her parents' right to ask other duties of you, because this is what you've agreed to, but that is a case by case basis, and I only step in when asked to help direct you."

Zeke peeked down at the sleeping baby. "I can do that."

"Not so scary, hmm?"

Nothing about little Cece was *scary.*

Just new.

And he was still learning.

"How about we get this baby Christened?"

"Yes," the priest agreed, "let's do that."

*

2 years later …

"*Pretty*," Cece said, holding up a dandelion she ripped from the grass. "*Pretty.*"

Zeke didn't have the heart to tell the girl that her mother paid a lot of money to keep those goddamn dandelion weeds off her grass, and

Catherine did not think they were pretty at all. All Cece saw was a flower. Bright yellow, with it's sticky green stem.

And to her, it was pretty.

"Pretty," he agreed.

She picked a handful more, and proceeded to dump them right in his lap. Zeke didn't mind. While she enjoyed herself, he went to work braiding the dandelions into a crown. If there was anything to be known about Cece Donati, it was the fact she was a *principessa*.

A princess.

Already.

At only two years old, the girl loved everything pretty, pink, or sparkly. Even better if it was a mixture of all those things together. She had a row of shoes that rivaled her mother's. Her father regularly came home with bags of pretty things just for her. And even Zeke, though girl had more than enough, was known to randomly buy pretty things he saw on his days out just because he knew it would make Cece smile.

Was she spoiled?

Ab-so-fucking-lutely.

That changed nothing.

"Look what I made," he told her.

Big, happy brown eyes looked up at him, and her lips curved into a wide smile at the sight of the flower crown in his hands. Pleased as could be, she let him put the flower crown in her hair, and then proceeded to sit like a pretty little princess on her throne of gross for him to admire his work.

Zeke could only laugh.

God, he loved this kid.

"I pretty," she said, in her childish tone.

Zeke nodded. "Beautiful."

"Like Ma."

Well ...

Zeke knew better than to pay Catherine too many compliments, because even if he only meant them in the best way, Cross was a terribly jealous fucker about his wife. Simple as that, and he didn't like to play with fire.

"Yep," he settled on saying.

All at once, Cece fell back to the grass, and stared up at the sky. Zeke followed her lead because why not? He tried to spend one day a week with the girl—one day a week that he dedicated most of his time in the day for her. Sometimes, he took her out for lunch and dessert, or to the park, and sometimes, they did *this*.

Nothing but sit together and play.

Cece loved it either way.

So did he.

"What's there?"

He glanced over to find Cece was currently pointing at the sky. Overhear, big, fluffy white clouds filled the blue canvas. "The sky?"

"Yeah, there. What's there?"

He thought about that.

The most obvious answer was *heaven*. Whenever people prayed, they looked to the sky as if that's where the heavens would someday open for them to welcome them home. He didn't know if that was the case. Was heaven an actual *place*, or more a state of mind? Was eternal happiness in heaven a thing created by religion to have people check their faith, and what they worked toward, or was it just something to calm people for their fear of death?

As if something *worth it* was waiting.

He didn't know.

"Anything," he told her, "and everything. That's what's up there."

"Oh." Cece hummed under her breath, kicking her little legs before rolling to her side so she could stare at Zeke. "Go there?"

"Can *you* go there?"

She nodded.

He had to think about that one, too.

And then, his answer came easily, all at once, and so sure. "You can do whatever you want to do, Cece."

They would all make sure of it.

FOUR QUEENS

A streak of muted yellow warmed a streak of the bundle wrapped in soft, off-white muslin. The ray of sunlight peeked through the slate in the hotel room's blinds. It was early enough that just three weeks ago, Cece wouldn't have dreamed of rolling over in bed. Now, she was usually up before the sun even thought to say hello.

For good reason.

One she didn't mind.

"Shhhh," she said, a soft murmur as much as the sound was musical at the same time. She kept the sway of her body moving side to side as well, something her newborn daughter seemed to like after every single feeding because it helped to soothe little Catherina Cecelia back to sleep. At first, Cece hadn't really considered breastfeeding beyond the first two weeks, but here they were at three and she hadn't found a reason to stop yet. Even if it meant she was the one getting up hour after hour in the night to care for her and Juan's first child—he would if he could, she knew, and as it was, he already did *so much*.

She struck it lucky that way.

They both did, really.

"Hey," Cece whispered when Catherina's dark eyes fluttered open before quickly falling closed all over again. She was nearly there—almost in her sweet dreamland. Cece didn't have the first clue what a baby might dream about, never mind a newborn like her daughter, but she was fascinated with it all the same. "Mommy loves you, *bambina*."

And she did.

More than the girl would ever know.

Mostly, she'd never considered having children. If someone asked did she want them, Cece used to shrug and say *sure*. But that was as far as her mind ever went down that particular road. Then, a few short months after she married Juan, something was just … *different*. It'd been two days before what would have been a missed cycle, and yet Cece just knew. She took a test early—wasn't at all surprised when it showed she was pregnant.

Now that her daughter was here, she couldn't imagine going back to life where having children and being a mom was something she only considered in passing. Everything changed the moment she found out she was pregnant.

She learned *a lot*.

One—it was possible to love someone you never met.

Two—this was not easy.

Three—she wouldn't change it for the world.

"Hey."

The sleepy call had Cece turning away from the window that overlooked the busy Manhattan street below. They were using the penthouse suite in the Waldorf that her grandparents had rented for decades just because they liked to have it on hand in case they or someone else might need to use it. Like Cece and Juan when they came into town for a weekend to visit. This was their first trip to New York after the birth of Catherina.

"Hey," Cece said.

Juan grinned from the mess of sheets. "Could have woke me up."

His gaze drifted to the baby.

She'd finally fallen back asleep.

"I have her," Cece said. "All's good."

Besides, she was just starting to get used to this whole little sleep thing. Juan helped by letting her nap in the daytime—soon, though, she would be heading back to work as she'd only taken the month. That was going to be interesting. Her mother made it seem like it was just another thing Cece would figure out, the sae way she did everything else.

We all did it, too, Catherine said.

Cece kept that in mind.

"Everything's perfect," she told Juan.

"Yeah?"

"I got it—no worries."

Juan smiled sleepy, humming under his breath, "Queens always do."

*

Juan didn't know it, but his words lingered with Cece long into the day. She remembered them while she hung back to show off her daughter to her cousins while her grandmother managed the kitchen, readying to feed their very large family like she did it every single day of her life. And later, she thought about his words while she watched her mother fuss over and herd each family within their large unit, all the kids included, for family portraits because Catherine had managed to get her favorite photographer into town that weekend.

Dinner and a show, really.

Two birds, one stone.

Women got shit done.

That's what Juan meant.

That's why his words didn't leave her.

"One more picture," the photog called to Catherine from across the room. "Since we've got all the ladies here to do it."

"Which one is that?" her mother asked.

"The four queens—we can do another when Catherina's old enough to stand but let's get one of her brand new with her great-grandmother, grandmother, and mother. On the grand staircase, I think."

Catherine smiled Cece's way. "What do you think?"

Was there ever really any question?

"Absolutely."

BABIES

The scariest part of any flight was always the landing. For Cece, anyway. The plane hit the ground, and the lurch that followed always had her heart dropping into her stomach as though she were about to meet her maker. Oh, the fear was entirely pointless. Her pilot—as she only flew private unless she absolutely *couldn't*—had never even had an incident. The jet was practically brand new, considering she'd replaced it a couple of years earlier with the newest model from the company. There were all kinds of safety features to keep them *safer*.

And yet … the safer things became and the happier Cece seemed to be in her life—like now that she was a wife and had a daughter who reminded her of herself more often than she didn't—that fear became worse. Like she had things more things to lose and her heart wasn't about to let her forget it for even *one* single flight.

So be it.

In the leather seat next to hers, Juan's hand came across the flipped-down armrest so that his fingers could find hers. His digits wove tightly with hers—the softness of his hands belied the rough pads of his fingertips that stroked over her skin. He didn't say a single thing while he held her hand and calmed her down. The jet continued taxing and Cece absolutely refused to open the shade on the port window until the jet had stopped moving completely and the pilot came out to stand at the door in front of the cockpit.

"It's irrational how much worse this has gotten the last few years," she muttered to her husband.

Juan glanced her way with a chuckle. "I think it's cute."

That had her narrowing her eyes. To his benefit, her husband didn't even look bothered by her show of attitude. Not that it was anything unusual for him. Always her perfect match, no matter what. Everything was always so easy for them.

Not that it made up for his comment.

She'd not forgotten that.

"What, *why*? Why is me being scared, *cute*?"

Cece would give him a minute to answer. He was owed that. Depending on the way he answered would determine how she reacted. Fair was fair. Right?

Juan chuckled as the plane came to a jerky stop. All at once, he tipped his head sideways to stare at her that way—all amused and not at all bothered by her attitude. "The powerful queen pin scared of flying?"

"I'm not scared of flying!"

"No, just the landing. Like we could avoid that, Cece."

"Stop it."

Juan grinned. "It's only really bad when Catherina's not with us."

He wasn't wrong.

It was the only thing that made Cece think … maybe her fears were more about her anxiety at being separated from her child than it was being scared of the plane crashing. The fears barely made themselves known when their daughter came along on trips. This time, however, Catherina had school. Juan's parents were keeping an eye on her. Cece and Juan would be home before their daughter even laid her head back down to sleep on her pillow tomorrow night. This wasn't a work-trip.

More a social call.

"New York, Mrs.," the pilot said as he came to stand in front of the door of his cockpit. His familiar smile greeted Juan and Cece while the one flight attendant they kept on call came out of the cockpit as well to finish up the tasks she had started before landing. "Say hello to your family for me—and congratulations to your brother, of course."

Cece felt better already.

"I will, thank you."

Leaning over her, Juan reached for the port window and lifted it for them to look outside. Unsurprisingly, a black car sat there ready with lights on.

"Better get going," Juan said, winking her way. "Nobody keeps those Donatis waiting."

He wasn't wrong.

*

"Here he is," Naz said.

Cece turned at her younger brother's voice to watch him enter his living room where she and Juan currently sat with Roz—her brother's wife. The bundle of white cashmere in his cradled arms was the first thing to gain her attention, really.

"Cross," Naz introduced, "my son."

Cece had been all the way across the country when her brother's first child was born. She was one of the first people he called to announce Roz was in labor, however. And she immediately started making plans to leave Cali for a trip to New York to visit and see the new baby. It was times like these when she seriously considered moving back to New York to be closer to her family but at the same time ...

Cali really was home.

They just made do with what they could.

"Oh, my ... bring him here," Cece said, giving Roz a wide smile before standing with her arms already outstretched to take the baby. Little Cross—named for her and Naz's father—was sleeping happily when he switched arms from his father to aunt. He didn't even stir a bit. She stared down into the face of her newborn nephew and completely melted. "He's perfect."

"He is," Roz echoed from the couch.

Fell in love.

Just like that.

Babies had that effect.

Knowing exactly how her sister-in-law must be feeling as a new mother, Cece kept one arm tight to the newborn baby, and then leaned down to hug Roz while she whispered in her ear, "Congratulations—welcome to the club, huh?"

Roz laughed under her breath with a nod. "Thank you."

Sometimes people forgot in the chaos of a new baby being born that there was a woman who brought that baby into the world. A woman whose entire life would never be the same because now they were a mother.

A beautiful change, to be sure.

It was still a lot.

Cece went back to her nephew, the sway of her body keeping the baby settled and happy as her husband came to stand by her side. The two of them *ohh'd* and *ahh'd* over the baby as they should. Seeing little Cross reminded her all over again about her own child and what it had been like to become a new mother.

"Planning a second anytime soon?" Naz asked where he leaned against the entry to the living room. "Ma and Dad would like that."

Cece wanted to laugh.

She wanted to say *nope*.

One and done.

That had been her plan. Juan never said anything different. Life was busy. Crazy. They were always moving. Nonstop. She never complained about it, but that didn't make it any less true. Yet, the longer she stood there with her nephew, the more she felt like ... *maybe*.

Cece smiled at her brother, shrugging. "You never know. We might."

ONE MORE TIME

"Are you looking, Ma? Are you watching?"

The shouts of her sweet girl had Cece lifting her gaze from the thread that she'd been picking at on the blanket keeping her safe from the sand. She found her daughter running across the beach, each step sending sand flying up around her bare feet. She would never understand why she kept trying to keep the sand out when frankly, it always found a way in. Like right from her daughter's feet.

She really didn't mind.

Juan was quick on Catherina's heels, ready to catch their daughter, or the kite she had finally managed to get into the air, should he need to. He came to a stop when it was clear their girl had everything handled. Her kite flew higher and *higher* … until it was probably at the end of its string. The wide smile that stretched across her daughter's face matched her father's while the two stared up at the cloudy sky.

For once, she was thankful that the sun decided to hide behind the clouds. They could appreciate all Catherina's practice finally coming to fruition now that her kite was up in the air and actually staying there. Every day this week, they walked down to the beach with Catherina's new kite in hand. She wanted to do it herself, though. She didn't want her parents to make the kite fly for her.

They always gave the girl what she wanted.

Especially when it was something like this.

Already, she was learning to be independent.

The beach was their happy place. It didn't matter if it was a beach in Cali, one across the country in New York, or even a beach in an entirely different country … Cece's family found happiness in warm sand and whispering waves.

"I see you!" Cece called back.

Catherina kept one hand tight on the spool attached to the string but used her other to wave wildly at her ma.

"Hold on a sec, Ma," Cece said to her own mother who'd she had been having a conversation with while her kid tried for the fourth time this week to get the kite into the air. "I gotta take a picture of this."

She could hear her mother's question even as she took the phone away from her ear and held it out with the camera up to snap a quick photo of Juan overlooking their *very* proud daughter flying her kite.

"Did she get it up in the air?" Catherine asked.

Cece laughed.

Even her parents had been invested in this moment. From afar, of course. They were always on one call or another, either with her mom, dad, or brother. *Someone* from back home. It was the only way they could feel present despite living in California.

"She did," Cece said when she brought the phone back. "Just the right gust of wind, I think. I was distracted for a second and missed it going up into the air."

Catherine sighed on the phone. "Motherhood in a nutshell. We spent immeasurable time teaching you things that you finally learn to do when we're not watching. She'll fly it again, no worries."

Wasn't that the truth?

Then, Cece's mother asked another question. One that had her attention drifting away from her still smiling daughter and husband.

"Have you told him yet?"

"Today," she replied, offering nothing else. "I bought him a gift to tell him."

"Oh?"

"He'll love it."

She swore she could see her mother smile when Catherine replied, "Oh, I have no doubt. Love you, hmm?"

"Forever and ever, Ma."

Cece hung up the phone and tossed it aside on the blanket knowing good and well she would likely be back on the phone with someone from New York before the evening was out. Smiling to herself, she didn't even hear Juan's approach until he dropped down beside her on the blanket.

Bringing sand with him.

Because *of course*.

Cece's laughter was quickly swallowed up by the kiss Juan leaned over to plant on her lips. All over again, she was reminded why she loved the beach and this man so much as sand tickled over her feet and legs while her husband kissed the very breath out of her lungs.

"Look, look!"

Cece and Juan broke apart to watch Catherina run down the beach in the opposite direction with her kite trailing behind high in the air.

She was still just as proud as could be.

Juan resituated himself on the blanket, using his arm and elbow as a prop to watch their girl. With his attention distracted, Cece took the chance to grab the little white box with the gold bow that she'd kept hidden at her back. Setting it directly in front of Juan's line of vision, she took great pleasure in watching him notice the small box.

His gaze lifted to hers.

"What's that?"

She winked. "Open it and see."

He didn't need to be told twice. Soon, he had the top of the box pulled off. The pretty satin bow was discarded with the rest as he pulled out the smallest pair of Nike runners. All white with golden *swooshes* on the side, the baby shoes matched the current ones Juan liked to wear day in and day out when he didn't have to throw on a pair of loafers or something else to better fit one of his many suits.

"*Cece*," he murmured, his fingers reaching for the little card dangling from a small piece of leather tied to the strap of the Nike baby shoe. He read the note aloud, "*Are you ready to do this one more time?*"

He laughed.

Cece shrugged. "I thought you might like that."

Juan nodded, pushing up from the blanket again to cross the space between them. His lips found hers as their daughter shouted down the beach and ran their way. His lips whispered over her grinning mouth when he said, "I like it very much."

NAZ AND ROZ | PENNY

5 Years Later …

Roz POV

Spinning around in her apartment, Roz looked for the box she'd just walked away from not three minutes ago. It was the one with the papers stacked close to the top, and according to the doctor's office that just called … the information she was seeking had been in a file they mailed over the week before.

Unfortunately, her entire place was just *boxes* right now. Boxes to the left, and boxes to the damn right. Problem was, while most of the lower section of boxes had been packed and taped up properly, the ones on top were not. So it could be any number of boxes, and Roz just *really* didn't have time to try and go through each box right now because—

The chiming of her phone in the other room had her sighing. That right there was why she didn't have time, probably. She expected it to be one of her handlers for the company calling to make sure she was still on time and didn't need them to send over a driver to bring her to the Hall. Running to catch the phone, she picked it up on the fourth ring just before it would go to her voicemail. Pressing it to her ear, she let out a breathless, "Hello?"

"How interested are you in making a stop in England before heading back to the states, anyway?"

Roz blinked. "*Kyle?*"

Silence answered her back on the other line before the man asked, "How many English people call you with a request to stop in England, Roz?"

It took her entirely too long to blink away the confusion settling in her mind and reply to him. Not that she wasn't happy to hear from her old mentor—she was. Like she would always be whenever Kyle took time out of his *very* busy life to send little old her a message. Roz was getting better and better with this sarcasm thing.

Really, her former mentor didn't call a lot. Usually once a year, but he might call twice if he heard news of something big happening in her career. She knew he kept up with everything—hell, he knew about things happening to her before it was even announced in the upscale music circles. But for the most part, Kyle didn't call a lot and he let Roz have her space. After all, he wasn't her mentor anymore— she had made it to the top of her career like she wanted to be, and he helped her to get her foot through the door.

And now ...

Roz turned around to look through the entryway of the kitchen, and peer into the living room where the boxes were stacked up high. A reminder that she had finally decided to choose a different path, now. Something that would take her back home where she wanted to be the very most.

Back to New York.

Back to *him*.

God, she missed Naz all the time.

"Did you hangup completely, or what?" Kyle asked.

Roz rolled her eyes, and went back to the conversation. "How do you know I'm leaving Australia? You haven't called in eight months, and I only made this announcement two months ago."

"Do I have to call you everytime you do something I disagree with, or ...?"

Jesus.

"Kyle—"

"I didn't call to argue about you leaving the Australian company. And even though I don't agree with it," her former mentor quickly added, "I understand your need to do something different. But that's the thing, isn't it? I called a couple of companies in New York when I had a minute last week, and guess what I found out?"

"Probably nothing that I care to hear."

Kyle let out a sigh. "Like I said, I called a couple of companies. The only companies that I know would be worthy of *you* and your talents. Yet, none of the owners of those companies had even heard from you—mind you, they let me knew I should pass along the message that if you're looking for a new company, one closer to home, they are very willing to bring you into the company. You just have to make a phone call to get it done."

That was the thing, though. Five years later, and Roz wasn't sure what she wanted to do. When she played show after show, it started to become the same thing over and over again. The bright lights wore off, a lot like the everything else. Her name had been in lights and was able to shine.

But here she was at twenty-three, and she didn't know if she wanted to keep doing this. What she wanted to do, like she had from the moment she stepped foot on Australian soil, was go home. Constant homesickness wasn't cured by a stage, a shined piano, and a beautiful dress.

She needed Naz more than she got him. He never said a word edgewise to her—never once asked her to come back. Over the last five years, they worked it out. He flew to her, or she flew to him. When he had a job that took him out of country and closer to her, she made sure to head his way if he couldn't come to her. They took vacations to different spots. But typically, they were only able to see each other a handful of times a year, and for the most part, it might only be three or four days at a time.

The last time they had got together for a spread of days was two months earlier during a vacation to Barbados. That was really when Roz cemented her decision to leave the Australian company and head back home. Naz hadn't said one thing about it when she called to tell him after arriving back in Australia. He simply told her to do whatever she needed to do. Her company, on the other hand, tried to convince her to stay a little while longer.

She couldn't ...

It might have affected them—she loved him just as much now as she had when she was a stupid eighteen year old girl; she was faithful, and she never questioned if he gave her the same respect because she knew he did. But at the same time, she needed to close some of that distance now.

It'd been too long.

"How about you let me worry about my career?" Roz asked her old mentor. "And you worry about ... whatever it is you're doing with your career lately."

"Oh, nasty."

Yeah, well.

Sometimes that was the only way to get your point across to Kyle. He didn't understand anything else. She had to do what she had to do. Simple as that.

"What's in England?" Roz asked, folding her arms over her chest, and heading into the living room. Her gaze skimmed over the tops of open boxes while she still had time, trying to find that fucking *file*. "Because I can promise you it's nothing that will interest me enough to make me stay there, either."

"A prodigy, actually," Kyle said.

Roz stiffened in place. "What?"

"She's sixteen. Typical sixteen-year-old, too. Moody, snappy, and impatient. She doesn't follow direction well, and she's already been expelled from two other prep schools for the musically gifted. Heathrow Prep was her last stop. If she gets kicked out of here— very likely that's going to happen—then she's going to be sent back to New Jersey where her parents have no idea what to do with her. Thing is, it'll be a might waste of talent, Roz. She just needs the right person to—"

"Why can't that be *you?*"

"Because I'm a man. She doesn't like … men," Kyle said, his voice dipping a bit. "Seems everyone around this girl is more interested in trying to correct her behavior than trying to figure out *why* she's behaving the way she is. Not that I think for even a second she would talk to me about it, that's not why I'm calling. I thought …"

"You mean for me to mentor her?"

"Roz, it would be a terrible waste of talent."

"There's more to life than what someone can do with an instrument," she shot back.

Kyle scoffed. "Maybe in your life. Anyway, make the stop in England. Do whatever you gotta do to get your tickets switched around. It'll be what, a couple of extra days on your trip? I'm sure your gangster boyfriend won't mind."

Roz clenched her teeth. "Don't call him that."

"I was kidding."

"Well, *don't.*"

Kyle acted like she hadn't said a thing. "Okay, so England is a go, then?"

"Fuck you, Kyle."

He knew she wouldn't refuse. That's why the bastard called. But it didn't even matter. The asshole hung up before Roz could say anything more about the situation. Like a refusal to mentor a girl who sounded like she was troubled, and needed someone to help her more than she needed someone to further her musical career.

Roz stared at the dead phone in her hands, and glared. *Asshole.* Was that even something she wanted to do, really? Sure, it kind of felt like she had hit an early peak in her career, but was she so *done* with it all that all Kyle thought she was good for now would be mentoring the next young pianist prodigy?

Fuck.

Hormones were a bitch.

Speaking of which ...

Roz's eye finally caught sight of the box in question that she had lost earlier, and the file sitting right at the top from the doctor's office. When she's gotten off stage one night, and prompty puked into a trash can, her handler called in one of the doctor's who worked on call for the company. He came in, drew blood between sets, and sent her back out on the stage to finish her set. The results had been mailed in, but Roz had kind of passed over the file because well, she felt fine mostly. She figured maybe she ate something bad that day, and never gave it another thought.

And then her period was late.

And then she realized no, it'd actually been late for two months.

Since that vacation with Naz.

Picking up the folder, Roz opened it up, and flipped through to the page the doctor's office had told her she would find the information she was looking for. And sure enough, there it was printed in big, bold letters.

PREGNANCY CONFIRMED.

NEW PLANS

"Aren't you supposed to be up in the air right now? Why do I hear—"

"Little change in plans," Roz said.

Naz glanced up from the bathroom sink where he'd been flicking his razor into the basin—fuck, here he was at twenty-five, and his father still bitched when his face wasn't clean shaven. *Made men can't have that, shave it*, Cross would bark. Drove him crazy. "What do you mean, a change in plans?"

"I agreed to make a quick pitstop in England for—"

"Kyle," Naz said dully.

That asshole.

All these years, and Naz still thought Roz's former mentor was a bit of a prick. Not that the guy had ever overstepped his boundaries, or anything, because that wasn't the case. Naz just figured the guy's cocky attitude was little too much to take even when he was in a good mood, never mind when he wasn't. And that was saying a lot considering his father was Cross Donati, and Naz was ... well, himself. Cut from the very cloth that made his father, too.

"What did Kyle want that you were willing to entirely change your plans, switch flights, and ... when exactly are you going to get into New York, then?"

Because *fuck*, he'd had shit planned to be there to pick up Roz, not some random driver with a car. *He* wanted to be the one to pick his woman up after not seeing her for a little more than two months. Not to mention ... being separated by the world for five goddamn years. This was supposed to be their time—she was finally come back to stay.

He was ready for that, even if he didn't give her an impression that he cared either way. Naz let her know he was happy that she was coming home—because fuck yeah, he was. But he didn't tell her she *had* to come home, and certainly not for him. He refused to step in or step on her dreams in anyway. If she wanted to further her career beyond what she had already accomplished, then he was going to be the first person to tell her to do that.

Even if what he wanted the most was for her to be with him.

"I'm not sure," Roz said. "I switched out the final flight to detour into England. I planned on getting a ticket when I went back to the airport. I really don't plan to stay here very long. A couple hours, maybe. Just long enough to appease Kyle, and then I'm on my way to you, Naz."

He smiled a bit at that.

Still …

Fucking Kyle.

"What did he want, anyway?" Naz asked.

"Uh …"

"Roz."

She sighed. "I guess there's a girl he's found that needs a good mentor behind her. She's from New Jersey, but he's been placed at the same school I attended until graduation. They don't think she's going to stay there for very long though. Seems she gets kicked out of every school her parents send her to."

Naz straightened against the sink, and considered her words for a minute before replying. "Sounds like maybe someone's parents should stop sending their kid to someone else to take care of, and start taking care of her themselves. But what the fuck do I know?"

Roz cleared her throat. "I looked into them—called Kyla back the next day to get some information. They're old money from Jersey, and yeah. It could be rich-kid syndrome, but that also just means they have enough money to satisfy a spoiled kid, Naz. Which you know, is exactly what people do when they don't want to deal with a kid they can't handle. They send them away to prep school, and give them enough money to keep them quiet until they're old enough to get them out of their hair altogether. Instead, she's been sent to schools for the arts—and they don't bring her home at all. That doesn't explain anything to me. Not why she's rebelling like she's hurting, anyway."

Naz shook his head because yeah, she had a point. And this right here was Roz in a nutshell. He knew now why she stopped in England, and whether she wanted to admit it or not, it probably had very little to do with Kyle. More like, his sweet woman found someone she thought needed help, and just being who she was, couldn't walk away without seeing if *she* could be the one who might be able to help the girl.

How was he supposed to get mad about that?

He couldn't, really.

"All right," Naz finally murmured, staring at himself in the mirror. A few extra hours, that's all. He just had a few more hours than he was expecting to have to wait before he'd have this woman back in his arms—they could start this thing called life together, finally. What were a couple more hours in the grand scheme of things? He could wait that long, surely. "Just call me whenever you're on a flight on the way *here*. So I know, babe."

"You got it." Roz laughed nervously, adding, "I might have a little surprise for you, by the way."

"Might? Either you do or you don't, Roz." Naz chuckled. "Not that I need anything, babe. Just having you back in New York is going to be enough for me, if that's what you want, too."

"Of course, that's what I want."

"Then that's enough for me."

"Well, we don't really get a choice in this surprise. It's coming one way or the other."

"What—"

"Oh, there's a cab. Okay, I'll call you in a couple hours to let you know the new flight time, okay?"

Naz was still trying to figure out what her *other* words meant. "Roz—"

"Love you, Naz."

He could figure it out later.

"Love you, Roz."

THE SURPRISE

Naz POV

"I thought Roz was supposed to be getting in sometime this evening," his father said to his right. "I know it was tonight because you made it *very clear* that if I called your phone at any point in the next seventy-two hours, you were going to come over here and …" Cross made air quotes as he said, "… *personally gut me like a pig.*"

Not that the threat really fazed his father. Nothing ever did. Naz still tried to give his father a warning every once in a while.

Cross glanced over at Naz with an arched brow. "That is what you told me, wasn't it?"

Why wash is father such a prick?

"Rub salt in the wound, Dad," Naz muttered. "I told Ma why Roz was going to be late, so don't act like she didn't tell your nosy ass the first second she could."

"First of all—"

"You are nosy," Naz interjected.

Cross scowled. "And secondly—"

"You gossip like a fourteen-year-old girl at her first dance," Naz said.

"I don't know where you get that mouth from. It doesn't come from me."

Naz laughed. "*Lies.*"

"All lies," the man in the wicker chair to Naz's left said with a smirk around the cigar in his mouth. Zeke side-eyed Cross like he was waiting for his friend to punch him for that comment. "You should have seen your father when you were all of maybe … *five*, Naz, and you told the neighbor to *fuck right off, then* when he wouldn't throw your ball back across the street for you. Your mother was horrified—your father?"

Cross grinned. "I remember that."

Zeke shook his head. "Cross laughed, and told the asshole the same thing you did before he took you to the mall and bought you a whole bag of balls to throw in the guy's yard. We sat on the porch and watched while you threw your balls across the street, and he called the cops on a five-year-old. So, there's that."

"Good times," Cross said to himself.

"He knows exactly where you get it from."

Naz found it slightly amusing how the two of them could converse with him, each other, and also pretend like they were having a conversation with themselves all at the same time. He was used to this kind of shit from his father, and Cross's best friend, though.

That was funny, too.

He'd been with Roz for five years, and he still didn't see Zeke as her father first. He still just saw his Godfather as his father's best friend, and her father second. He supposed that was because Zeke never stepped in on Naz's relationship with Roz. He just stepped back, and let the two of them figure out whatever in the hell they needed to figure out.

He appreciated it, really.

Cross looked over at Naz. "Do you know when she's getting in, then?"

Naz sighed, and shook his head. Resting back in the wicker chair, he stared up at the blue sky and wished he was on his way to the fucking airport right now to pick Roz up. After all these years apart … this was supposed to be *their* time.

"No," Naz said, trying hard not to grumble.

And failed like a fucker, too.

"From what I know," Zeke started to say.

"Nobody asked you."

Cross reached over and smacked Naz hard right in the middle of his chest. "Watch your fucking mouth, there."

Naz rubbed the aching spot and scowled. "What were you going to say Zeke?"

Roz's father chuckled. "I was saying … that from what I know, she won't be too long in England, right? Just a pit stop. She'll be back in New York before you even know what's going on. You are not the only one here who wants to have her back in the States, Naz."

Felt like it sometimes.

He didn't say that out loud.

The thing was, Naz didn't mind letting the two of them think he was just sour over the fact that he was going to have to wait a bit longer before Roz was back in the states. That actually wasn't his biggest issue with this whole thing at all. He was more concerned with his last conversation with her, and how she kind of left him wondering about something she'd said rather flippantly.

Yet, it stuck in his head.

Well, we don't really get a choice in this surprise. It's coming one way or the other.

He didn't know what in the hell that meant, and it wouldn't leave him alone. It had stayed in the back of his mind ever since he hung up the phone with her. If she had something to tell him—a surprise, right, so that must mean it was *good*—then he wanted to know it.

Naz wasn't fucking known for his patience.

To say the least.

Something else he got from his dad.

"I have a question," Naz said.

"Hmm?" Cross glanced over at him over the top of the beer bottle he'd tipped up for a drink. "What's that, now?"

"What kind of surprise just comes, and you don't really get a say in it one way or another?"

He didn't actually expect his father to know what in the hell he was talking about. He figured Cross would just give him one of *those looks*. Like his dad was silently telling him to stop acting like a fucking idiot. It wasn't like he gave any context to the question to explain it, but nonetheless, he wondered if he might get an answer that would … well, give him something more to go on about Roz's statement.

"Like a happy surprise?" Cross asked.

Naz shrugged. "Yeah, sure, why not."

"Uh," Cross said, his brow raising. "I can only think of one thing, really."

Zeke laughed and blew out a heavy cloud of cigar smoke. "Me, too."

The two friends passed a look between one another.

"You thinking the same?" Cross asked Zeke.

"I mean, I got two, just like you."

Cross nodded. "Yeah, we're thinking the same, then."

Naz's brow knotted in his confusion. "Then why can't I figure out what that kind of a surprise it would be?"

"Because you've never experienced it, Naz."

His father's words sounded so simple.

He didn't think it was.

"So what is it?" Naz asked.

"A baby," Cross murmured. "That's the only kind of surprise that ever came for me when I wasn't expecting it, and didn't get a choice one way or the other."

"Me, too," Zeke echoed.

Naz froze.

His gaze zoned in on the wall of trees at the other side of the back of his parents' property, and silence surrounded him. Actually, he could hear Zeke and Cross talking ... but he wasn't really *listening*.

Was that what it was?

Was Roz ...

Pregnant?

He knew it was possible, but unlikely. And he was only saying that because he knew she kept up on her shots, and the last time they had been together was two months ago on their vacation. But at the same time, he knew that didn't actually make a difference. It took *once* for a birth control to fail. It took one time to get pregnant.

That's what happened when people had sex.

Babies.

He was a fucking genius.

He knew how bodies worked and what happened when people had sex. He was very well aware that for any number of reasons, no matter how perfectly birth control had worked previous times, that it could fail. He also knew that there were a number of reasons someone might not have realized they were pregnant right away. He knew all of these things, but he didn't want to think about them unless he was looking at Roz, and she was *confirming* it.

Pregnant ...

It was always a possibility.

"Naz?" he heard his father ask. "You all right?"

He couldn't get out of that chair fast enough, saying, "I gotta go."

"Wait, what the hell—"

"I gotta go," he repeated, already heading across the back yard and leaving his father and Zeke behind him. "Later."

"Naz, what is wrong with you?"

"I gotta go!"

Was that what it was?

Was she pregnant?

Naz needed to know *now*.

ENGLAND

Roz POV

"Took you long enough."

Roz openly glared at the man standing behind the door of his flat. She didn't even try to hide the fact that she was annoyed, *and* holding two pieces of luggage. "No, Kyle, the appropriate way to greet someone at your door is with a *hello*, and then you take my fucking luggage off my hands. Try that."

Okay, wow, hormones.

Roz was not the type to be snappish, but apparently today was not the day to test that theory out. To be fair, she had just spent far too many hours in the sky, in a tin box, flying through clouds with an angry baby—poor kid—a few rows back, and a man beside her who wouldn't quit talking even when she basically put her headphones in and turned her music up loud enough that the flight attendant asked her to turn it down.

Add onto that the fact that she had barely made it through the entire flight without puking her guts out because it seemed now that she *knew* she was actually pregnant, her morning sickness seemed ready to make itself known again. Which didn't make any sense because most of her flight had not even been *in* the morning.

But that was pregnancy, apparently. Nothing was like you thought it would be. Well, according to the book she downloaded on her e-reader to read during the long flight. All it really did was scare the shit out of her for a number of reasons. Fun, huh?

It hadn't been a good flight.

To say the least.

Kyle leaned against the doorway, and arched a brow. "What bee crawled up your ass?"

Roz sighed. "Just … take my bags, will you?"

He did as she said, but gave her a look all the while. He kept that up until he'd dragged her shit inside the flat, and had it resting against a wall.

"Why did you lug those with you, anyway?" he asked.

Roz shrugged. "Because I don't intend to stay here, Kyle. I wasn't getting a hotel for the night when I knew that it would be pointless. I want to be on another flight before the sun sets here. Got it?"

"Listen, this prodigy—"

"Sounds like a troubled girl who needs a therapist and a good support system, not someone to put her in front of the piano and make her play, Kyle."

He scowled. "Listen, we're not the same."

"I have no idea—"

"*Artists*, Roz," Kyle said, clearly over her attitude. "we're not the same. Sometimes, what he need is an *outlet*. And our outlets are not like other people's outlets. We don't beat out our problems in a gym, or drown it in food while he binge watched a television show. We have something *better*—the chance to use that pain or whatever it is and create something amazing."

"I've never used my music for that."

Kyle rolled his eyes as he turned his back to her and headed for the kitchen area of the loft. "Of course, you didn't. I didn't say *all* artists are the same, Roz. Just because you haven't experienced something traumatic in your life to focus your music on doesn't mean the rest of us are going to be the same."

She stilled and considered his words.

"Is that what you think it is?"

"What?"

Roz followed Kyle into the kitchen and watched him as he pulled a glass goblet from the cupboard. Then, he went in search of something else. Alcohol, it seemed, if the crystal bottle he pulled from a top shelf in his cupboard was to be believed.

He poured himself a glass and downed it in one go. Roz raised her brow in silence, half amused, and half concerned. With Kyle, sometimes, it could go either way. For as long as she had known him, he had … well, most people would just call them demons, maybe. Something that never left his mind and left him troubled day in and day out. He dealt with it the best he could, but that didn't change the fact *something* had happened to this man.

Kyle waved at the bottle of bourbon. "You want a drink?"

"First, not on my worst days would I drink bourbon," she returned, "you all act like that tastes good when really, it tastes like death. And secondly, I can't drink, so no."

"Why can't you dr—"

"We're not talking about me here."

Nope.

She wasn't talking about that with him. Kyle was *not* going to be the first person besides her and the doctor to know she was pregnant. She had a man all the way across the world who deserved to know he was going to be a father before the rest of the world knew it. Roz owed Naz that much.

"So, is that what you think it is with her, then?" Roz asked.

Kyle cleared his throat. "What?"

"Trauma. You think she's been through some trau—"

"I don't make assumptions about others or what they've been through," Kyle said, and then quieter, he added, "but there's a look— all of us who have been through some shit can see it. It's not like everybody else, Roz. We just ... *know.*"

Huh.

She wondered ... was it true what people said, that lost people found other lost people? Did they just see a reflection of their own experiences and pain in someone else, and *know?*

She didn't have a clue.

It wasn't the time to ask.

Kyle slapped a hand to the counter, and gave her a charming smile. It wasn't lost on her how two seconds ago, the man had looked dark and entirely lost in his head. It was like he put his mask on for her, and just like that, he was fine again.

Or ... he looked that way.

In a way, Roz found that concerning. That Kyle was so good at pretending he was okay to everyone else that he didn't even have to *try* to make people believe it, really. He probably had years to perfect his ... mask.

And wasn't that kind of sad?

She thought so.

"Her name is Penny," Kyle said, "and we can go see her anytime."

Roz chewed on her inner cheek. "And then what, Kyle? What happens after I meet her, huh?"

"Guess we're gonna see."

Great.

That didn't sound problematic at all.

ENGLAND: PART 2

Naz POV

"Business or pleasure, sir?"

Naz looked up from the line he'd been standing in for well over an hour to see a custom's agent arching a brow at him. Apparently, he was the next to go through—*finally*, why did customs always have to take forever no matter which country you were traveling into?—the line to get his shit checked.

"Pleasure," Naz replied, smirking just a bit.

Yeah, pleasure seemed like the right way to say it. He certainly had business in this part of the world, but that had *nothing* to do with why he was here right now. In fact, he might regret this split decision later, but right now, he seriously doubted it.

"Bag on the table—open it up," the agent said with a gloved-wave. "And get your passport out for me, too."

Naz couldn't count the amount of times he had gone through customs in his life. Okay, that was a lie—he absolutely could count it. His genius brain didn't let him forget. He also knew the exact number of countries he had traveled into over the years, too.

It was a lot.

Fun, right?

Not so much.

Naz hefted his small carry-on up to the table, and fished his passport out of the back of his pocket, and tossed it over for the man to open up and look it over. He didn't notice the look the agent was shooting him until he'd unzipped his bag, and looked up at the man.

"What?" he asked. "There a problem?"

That was the tricky thing about being who he was, and by that, he meant a *criminal*. Naz had a rotating folder of identities he used to run guns, but that didn't mean somewhere ... in some fucking country, he hadn't gotten caught in some way. Smart authorities wouldn't plaster his picture and real name all over the place. No, they'd just send his information through Interpol, and let it do the work of waiting for him to show up somewhere again.

It was always a risk.

He took it.

The agent raised a brow, and set his passport down. "You don't have very many bags if you're visiting the country for pleasure, sir, that's all."

Naz chuckled, and nodded. "Well, I don't plan to stay longer than it takes me to find my girlfriend and ask her if she's pregnant."

The agent blinked.

Naz smiled.

His father liked to say the best way to put a person off balance was to hit them with the last thing they expected you to say. Naz figured this had done exactly that for the guy across the table. *One step closer to Roz.*

Without even looking through his bag other than a quick, cursory check, the man brought out the items needed, stamped Naz's passport, and nodded at him. "You be on your way, then. Good luck; you're gonna need it one way or another."

Naz laughed. "Thanks."

He pulled his phone out of his pocket as he headed out of the customs area. A quick check of the screen told him what he expected—Roz was still here in England, and she hadn't left yet. She'd been keeping him updated on what she was doing here, and when she expected to leave. She should have left the night before, but apparently, something made her stay.

Naz believed it was the prodigy.

Penny, Roz had texted her name.

That was fine.

Fine and good, really.

Naz was here now, though. Because they had other things to handle—he needed to know if the surprise she was supposed to share with him was the fact that she was pregnant. There was no way in fucking *hell* he was waiting for her to fly over to his side of the pond to do it.

Nope. He was here now.

*

Roz POV

"She didn't react well yesterday, what makes you think she'll be better today?"

Kyle passed Roz a look, and shrugged. "Hope and blind faith?"

Roz let out a heavy sigh. "You're an idiot."

"And you're not in a good mood *again*. What is wrong with you?"

Oh, other than the fact she'd barely slept a wink because she knew she should have been in New York by now, and not still in England? Besides the fact that she had a whole freak out moment about the fact she was pregnant because she couldn't even remember holding a baby before? Besides the fact that she hadn't been able to keep down her breakfast this morning?

And that was before Roz got into … Penny.

The prodigy.

The *girl*.

Something was not right with that young woman, and Roz didn't mean that in a bad way. She meant it in a way that she just thought … she needed help. She was in a bad place and holding onto a ledge by the very tips of her fingers. She didn't know *how* she knew it, but she did.

That was concerning.

Penny barely spoke, and when she did? God, the girl was *angry*. Confrontational, mean, and rude. She hadn't even bothered to get out of bed the day before despite knowing they were coming over to visit her. The head of the dorm happened to mention to Kyle and Roz that Penny had almost got into a fight with a girl across the hall, and they were planning a search of her room because they believed she had drugs hidden somewhere in her dorm.

Bad news.

The girl wasn't *trouble*.

She was in trouble.

Roz didn't know how to explain that to Kyle, though. He figured he girl just needed the right mentor in her life—someone to put her back on the right track and find the reason to make her sit in front of a piano and do the damn thing again.

That wasn't what she needed.

She needed *help*.

Something was wrong.

It was only once they were inside the dorm and standing in front of Penny's room that Kyle turned to Roz with a frown.

"You know, I can practically feel what you're thinking," Kyle muttered.

"Can you?"

He nodded.

"Then, you won't be surprised when I say this girl needs help that we can't give her," Roz returned. "Ivory, wood, and gloss isn't going to fix the parts of her that have been broken by someone or something else."

"She doesn't have *anyone*, Roz."

Yeah, she figured that out. Somewhere between the many prep schools the girl had been sent to, and the fact her parents were just willing to keep sending their daughter away instead of bringing her home and getting her help ... Roz knew Penny had no one.

"Can we figure out something for her?" Roz asked. "Something to get her ... in a place where she can be helped, *and* do music?"

"Where would you suggest we move her?"

That was the thing ... she didn't know.

They weren't Penny's guardians. They couldn't make legal choices for her. They couldn't even bring in a doctor for the young woman without permission to do so. They had very few moves they could make to help her.

It was sad, really.

"Let's just see how she's doing today," Roz said.

Kyle nodded, and knocked on Penny's dorm room door. At the same time, the phone in Roz's pocket started to buzz. She pulled out the phone as Kyle knocked a little harder on the door.

Roz checked the text message from Naz as Kyle continued knocking, and when he didn't get a response from Penny, tried to jiggle the knob.

"It's unlocked. She knew we were coming, I just talked to her an hour ago," he muttered.

Roz nodded, but was still reading Naz's text.

I decided to meet you halfway, babe. I'm at your hotel room. Surprise. See you when you get back. —Naz

He came here?

Jesus.

The man must have been going stir crazy, but just didn't want to tell her.

Roz was about to reply to Naz when Kyle pushed the dorm door open, and peeked his head in, saying, "Penny, are you up, or what?"

"Don't open her door without her permission, that's—"

Kyle's face went white when he opened the door a little more.

"Oh, my God," Kyle mumbled, shoving the door all the way open. Before Roz could even see what was waiting for them behind the door, he shouted at her to, "Call for emergency services!"

She saw what was behind the door, then.

A blue teenager.

Bare arms that she'd keot covered the day before with a long sleeve were now naked, giving Roz full access to see the crisscross patterns of white, pink, and red marks. Old scars, new scars, and fresh marks.

Cuts.

A ripped bedsheet tied to the pipe across the ceiling.

And a toppled over chair.

"Penny! *Penny?*"

ENGLAND: PART 3

Naz POV

The thing Naz hated the most about countries he wasn't familiar with? The fact that he didn't know where *anything* was. He swore it felt like the cab he had managed to hail just drove around aimlessly for twenty minutes even though he knew the driver was actually taking him to the hospital. But to him, because he didn't know any of these streets or where to go for the hospital, it just seemed like the guy was driving aimlessly.

It was only made worse by the fact that Naz didn't actually know what in the hell was going on. He'd gotten a text from Roz with the name of a hospital and she told him to *get here now*. He came to England to surprise her, and to get answers ... he didn't think his first stop after waiting for her at the hotel would be a fucking hospital.

Was it for her?

Had something happened?

Was someone going to die because they hurt her?

All possible things.

The cab pulled up to the drop off lane at the hospital and put the car into park. Already, Naz's heart felt like it was in his fucking throat. The panic had been ever constant, and all too present. No matter what he tried to get it to leave, it just wouldn't go. He was the calm one in the storm—that's just how it worked for him.

Not right now.

Not when it came to Roz.

He couldn't be *anything* when he thought something might be wrong with her. That's just not how his brain worked. All the logical shit was there, sure, but it didn't factor into the way he felt at all.

"That'll be—"

Naz threw a handful of bills over the front seat, saying, "There you go."

"Sir, that's too much money."

"Keep it."

Naz didn't even care.

Once he stepped out of the cab, that pressure in his chest got worse. His heart felt like it was about to explode right out of his fucking chest. A car blew its horn at him when he walked in front of it without looking first, but Naz just tossed his hand up as if to say, *yeah, yeah, fuck off.* He had other things on his mind right now.

He couldn't get into the hospital fast enough. He went right into the emergency section because he figured that's where Roz would have come in if something happened … it wasn't like she had a doctor here to visit, right?

The emergency room was full—not that it was any surprise. It seemed like that didn't matter what country someone was in. The hospital was always at capacity, and overflowing. Wait times for fucking *days.*

Naz was planning on going right up to one of the receptionists, giving Roz's name, and seeing where that got him. All it took was a quick sweep of the people sitting in the waiting chairs for him to find her, instead.

Roz had tucked herself into the corner of the waiting room near a window. She might have seen him coming into the hospital, except she was currently using her propped up arm as a pillow to rest her cheek on her palm. Her eyes were closed, and she'd used a windbreaker to cover herself up. Even her knees were tucked in close to her chest.

Naz might have let her rest her eyes, if she was that tired, considering it was only twelve in the afternoon and she was sleeping in bright daylight. But he couldn't because this very moment was the first time he realized she was *actually okay.* It clearly wasn't her that needed to be brought into the hospital if she was just sitting there sleeping.

"Roz," he murmured, approaching her.

She didn't move until he was kneeling down in front of her, and had both of his hands on her tucked up knees. He squeezed her legs gently, and her eyes fluttered open. It took Roz a few seconds of blinking to realize she was awake, where she was, and the fact that she was now looking Naz right in the face.

He smiled a bit. "Hey, babe."

Roz wiped a hand over her face. "Hey."

"Pretty sure this wasn't in the plans when you decided to make a stop in England, huh?"

She laughed bleakly. "No."

Naz tipped his head to the side. "What happened?"

She sniffled, and he didn't miss the way her gaze filled with water before she tried to blink it away. Not that it worked. She shook her head when Naz reached up to stroke her cheek with his fingertips, and then brushed a few strands of her hair behind her ear. It wasn't like Roz to get emotional, really. She had her shit under control—it was one of the things he loved the most about her, but when she *did* let the emotion through ... he knew something was up.

Always.

"The girl Kyle wanted me to come meet to possibly mentor?" she asked.

Naz arched a brow. "Yeah, what about her?"

"She's ... not well," Roz said, and then she frowned. "And not like physically sick, but ... in her mind, Naz. She's got something going on that she's not telling people. I knew it when I met her yesterday, and then today ... it just confirmed what I thought."

"I don't understand—"

"She tried to hang herself this morning. We found her in her dorm."

Naz blinked, and his hands tightened on her legs. "I'm sorry."

Roz shrugged. "I think someone needs to tell her that, you know?"

Yeah, he did.

Naz let out a heavy sigh. "*Fuck.* I thought this was about you, or maybe ..."

She eyed him from the side. "Or maybe *what?*"

"Nothing."

"Naz."

Just the tone of her voice had him chuckling. This woman knew all of his secrets. She could tell when he was trying to hide something, or just avoid it altogether. There was no way for him to *ever* pull something over on her. His mother liked to say that was the universe's way of kicking Naz in the ass for all the shit he pulled over the years.

And hell, maybe it was.

He loved Roz for it, though.

Instead of telling Roz his suspicions about what he thought her *news* happened to be, he just looked at her and asked, "Listen, do you have anything you want to tell me right now?"

Roz pressed her lips together. "Maybe, yeah."

"Okay, well *maybe* that's why I came all the way here. I didn't want to wait."

She laughed, but shook her head. "I shouldn't be happy right now. This is not the time to be—"

"You're human, which means you can feel multiple things at the same time. You can feel pain for someone else at the same time you feel joy for yourself for an entirely different reason. That's *normal*, babe."

She nodded again. "Okay."

"So, any news?"

"Well …"

"Hmm?"

Roz winked. "Seems I'm pregnant."

Naz grinned. *There it was.*

He'd been right, and while he had pushed it to the back of his mind to let *her* tell him so he could feel all that happiness and joy because she told him … now, he was just over the fucking *moon*.

"Yeah?" he asked.

Roz laughed. "Like eight weeks, I'd say."

"Barbados, then," he murmured.

"Guess so."

His heart was hurting again, but it wasn't for the same reason from earlier. Now, it was because something amazing was happening in his life. This woman was about to give him something incredible.

"I love you," he told her.

"I know—I love you, too."

Naz finally got to do what he'd been wanting to do for two months, then. He pulled Roz into a tight hug, and hid her away from the rest of the world. That's how he liked her best, after all. Tucked into his arms, and *safe*.

She tipped her head back, and that smile of hers clouded his vision. He dropped a kiss to her grinning lips, and then another and another. Until she was smiling against his kiss.

"So, what happens now?" he asked.

"About what?"

"The girl. Kyle. *You*."

"I don't know, Naz."

Yeah, him either.

THE AFTERMATH (OF ENGLAND): PART 1

Roz POV

Naz was funny in the way he would much rather rent an Airbnb, even if he was only staying in a place for a couple of days, than a hotel room. Roz never understood why, but that's how it worked for him. She thought it was probably because he didn't feel at home in a hotel room, or maybe because over the years, he'd stayed in *a lot* of hotels when he traveled. But who was to say?

Nonetheless, when he figured out she wasn't going to be leaving England for at least another week, the first thing he did was call back home, and get things settled there. The second thing he did was get on the laptop, and rent them an Airbnb because as he said, he *wasn't sleeping in a fucking hotel.*

Roz let him do what he wanted. It was easier, and she really didn't care as long as she had a bed to sleep in. Even better because he was there to sleep in it with her. But Roz also knew Naz wouldn't be able to stay in England more than a week—people were waiting on him back in New York. Responsibilities and duties were waiting on him to get back to what he did best. She didn't fault him for that.

"Okay," Naz said, hanging up the phone he'd been talking into for the last half hour as he came into the kitchen. "All done, babe."

She peered over her shoulder at him. "Great."

"Two weeks from now on Monday, eleven in the morning."

Roz gave him a look.

Naz arched his brow right back. "What?"

"I thought you were going to make the doctor's appointment for a month from now? What if I'm still *here*, Naz?"

He shrugged. "This was the closest opening that the office in New York had. If you're still here, then we'll figure something out for a doctor here until you get back home again. Okay?"

She smiled.

He really was something else, this man. She was well aware that he wanted her home *more than anything.* He wanted to put her on a flight today, and get her back to New York where they could finally start their life together. She wanted that, too, more than he could possibly know. But there was still a part of her that needed to see things through here first. She needed to make sure that Penny was going to be okay ... or she was going to help the young woman to get to that place in her life.

Naz was just ... going to let Roz do her thing.

She loved him for that.

Naz slipped around the island, and came to stand at her back. One of his arms drifted around her waist, and his hand laid flat to her stomach before he dropped a kiss to the top of her head. She felt her smile grow the longer his kiss lingered. Finally, she tipped her head back, and he dropped a quick kiss to her lips, too.

"How're you feeling today?" he asked.

She shrugged. "Better—I didn't throw up yet."

Yet being the keyword.

It could still happen.

Morning sickness didn't discriminate.

"You need *anything*, then you tell me, got it?"

Roz winked. "Got it, Naz."

He grinned, and dropped another kiss to her lips. Only this time, he wasn't ask quick to pull away. This time, that kiss lingered long enough to burn her from the inside out. Just like that, the flames of her lust had been stoked in the right way—enough to make her want to pull this man back to the bedroom, and find all sorts of fun ways to spend their morning.

She suspected Naz was feeling the same way given his hands tangled into her loose hair, and tugged gently as his tongue struck out against the seam of her lips, demanding she open up for him. *God*, she loved that, too. Loved the way their kiss always felt like a way when their lips worked against one another, and their tongues tangled to get a taste.

And then a knock echoed through the house.

Naz lifted up, pulling away from her kiss with narrowed eyes as he looked toward the hallway that led to the front door. She might have laughed at his annoyance at having been interrupted with her, but she couldn't.

The knocking continued.

Fuck.

Naz gave her a look. "How much do you want to bet that's—"

"Anybody home?"

"Kyle," Naz muttered.

Naz let her go just as footsteps echoed in the hallway of the house they had rented. She gave Naz a look, silently telling him to *stay in line*. Not that she needed to remind him, but she also knew there was something about Kyle that often put Naz on edge.

She thought it might be because Kyle was the one who constantly reminded Roz that love could come *anytime*. Her career in music, however, had a time limit on it. There was an expiry date to her talent—something could take away her ability to play, or she may simply just become irrelevant in the world as a pianist.

But love?

Love would always be waiting.

Thing was ... Kyle wasn't wrong. She tried *not* to put love last the best she could—she constantly tried to keep Naz as the center in her life, the one thing that continued to ground her and remind her what was important.

That didn't mean Kyle had been wrong, though.

"There you are," Kyle said as he came into the kitchen, looking only at Roz. "Did you get a visit like I did this morning?"

Roz passed Naz a glance. "No?"

Kyle scowled. "At all?"

"No. What's going on?"

"The Bobbies came around," he said.

Roz's brow dipped. "The *what*?"

"English police," Naz said from his new spot behind the island. "Better question is why are they making a visit to *you*, Kyle?"

Kyle stared hard at Naz. "I don't know—you're better acquainted with the police than I am, aren't you? Why don't you tell me why they do the shit they do?"

Roz didn't need to look at Naz to know he was tense, and probably ready to jump across the counter at Kyle. She quickly stepped in to stop that from happening. "Well, you *must* know why they came around to talk to you—they *talked* to you, didn't they?"

"It was about Penny."

Okay, that had Roz's attention. She turned around on the stool entirely so that she could face Kyle for this conversation. She had a feeling, just by the way his tone turned thick, that she was going to need to be sitting down and staring at him for whatever he was about to say.

"And?" she asked quietly.

"They wanted to know if she'd ever … uh, talked to me about her father," he muttered.

Roz took a second before she asked, "Why would they ask about that?"

"She's made allegations while in the ward."

She was cold, now.

Entirely cold.

Too fucking cold.

"What kind of allegations?" Roz asked.

She didn't want to ask.

She didn't want to know.

Still, she felt like she had to.

"That … uh," Kyle struggled, refusing to meet Roz's stare.

"*That* kind of allegations?" Roz asked.

"Sexual abuse?" Naz spoke up behind her.

Kyle swore under his breath, and scrubbed a hand down his jaw. "Yeah, that's what it sounded like to me. She made some serious allegations when the Bobbies were brought in to talk to her about an investigation they have for something she did in the dorms against another girl who she had beaten up in the communal showers."

Roz straightened. "Why did she beat up a girl?"

"I don't know. Maybe she said something that triggered her?"

She looked over her shoulder at Naz, but he was staring hard at Kyle. She could tell by the tension in his shoulders, and the hardness of his gaze, that he wasn't pleased. And not because of Kyle, but because of the rest of the information they had right now.

"They don't think she's saying that just because of the investigation about the girl, right?" Roz asked Kyle.

"I don't think so … but the bigger problem is this isn't their territory," Kyle said, shrugging and looking helpless. "This happened in America—they can't bring charges against an American for something that happened in America. They're referring the case on, but she's underage. They're going to send her home, she'll be in the care of CPS until they get this figured out and—"

"No," Roz said, firmly.

"What?"

"She doesn't need to be in the care of CPS. We can figure something else out for that. She can stay with me and Naz, even.

Right?" She looked back at Naz who met her stare, but said nothing. When he stayed quiet, she pressed again, asking, "*Right?*"

"Roz, that girl probably needs a lot of help and—"

"Okay, then we get her what she needs, Naz."

"She might not be comfortable with a man there."

"We don't know that if we don't *ask*."

"Okay," he murmured, clearly not wanting to fight.

Kyle cleared his throat, bringing their attention back to him. "They kept sending her home, Roz. She'd act out, and they'd send her *back*. Where he was waiting. I got the impression that the allegations she made indicated it had been a regular thing until she left for school, but it continued through the years. So ..."

"Every time she got sent back," Roz whispered.

What kind of *father* ...

What kind of *monster*?

Roz felt Naz's had find her back, and he said nothing as he stroked her just below the neckline of her shirt. Like *she* was the one who needed to be comforted then. It wasn't her that needed someone to love them and protect them at all.

She had *always* had people to do that.

Penny, though?

Clearly never had anyone.

THE AFTERMATH (OF ENGLAND): PART 2

Roz POV

The sixteen-year-old tucked into the window bench, overlooking the backyard of the infirmary where she had been placed—a temporary hold until, one, she was no longer a threat to herself, and two, they figured out what to do with her by placing her somewhere *safe*—didn't even acknowledge Roz when she approached. She didn't take it personally. It was quite obvious that Penny Masterson had plenty of things on her plate to deal with it, and Roz bet she was simply a *very* small portion of that.

"I noticed they have a music room down the hall," Roz said.

Penny didn't look away from the window.

Roz didn't let the silence bother her too much. Stuffing her hands into the pocket of her dress, she peered around the quiet room that seemed to be some type of area for communal gathering for the patients. Stark white, the walls and floors gleamed. The light fixtures above were the same bright white and flush with the ceiling. A setting of couches and chairs had been set up in one corner next to a row of bookshelves, and another sitting section in the other corner faced a large flat-screen television. Toward the west side of the room, hallways leading further into the complex showcased a few scattered people moving from what seemed to be different rooms.

A single woman wearing gray scrubs came out of the hallway, but didn't even pass Roz a look before she disappeared behind a door where a wall of Plexiglas windows gave them a clear view of the *many* medications sitting on shelves.

That was the only indication this place was something different than it appeared on the surface. Specifically, the institution handled teenagers from thirteen to eighteen—on their eighteenth birthday, if still here, they were transferred to a different institutions with adults—dealing with mental illness.

Those illnesses ranged from behavior, eating, and other disorders, not limiting it to just that, they also handled cases like Penny.

"Why are you here?"

Roz jumped a bit at the question, surprised the teenager had even spoken to her at all. She came to visit three times in the last week, and each time, Penny said nothing. Each time, she sat in this same window, stared out the window, and stayed *silent*.

She wasn't willing to give up, though.

"And where is your shadow?" Penny asked when Roz didn't answer her right away.

"My shadow?"

"Tall guy," Penny said, "dark hair, never leaves your side when you're here, and glared at a guy when he checked you out."

Roz blinked.

Had Naz done that?

Because only Naz had come with Roz to visit Penny, although he stayed back as to not intrude on their conversation ... or rather, the total fucking lack of it, for the most part.

"Naz ... he's my boyfriend," Roz said. "And he thought maybe it would help if he didn't *shadow* me, as you might say. Because maybe he was making you uncomfortable."

Penny made a face, and looked back to the window. It struck Roz, then, how *childlike* Penny seemed in a lot of ways. She was small featured, and small-bodied. With her hand propped up to use it as a rest for her chin while she stared out the window, she almost seemed like a little girl. Put her in a white dress, and wipe the red lipstick stain from her lips, and she could probably pass for a twelve-year-old.

It was disconcerting.

"He doesn't bother me," Penny said, "I can tell when they're ... bad. I *see* it in them. There's a way they look at you. They're all the same, you know."

"I don't, actually."

She couldn't imagine the horrors this girl had gone through. She couldn't begin to *consider* what it was like to look at every strange face that passed you by, and think, *is he like one of them; is he a monster, too?*

"I haven't used the music room," Penny said.

So, she *had* been listening to Roz. That made her wonder, what else did the girl listen to when people thought she wasn't paying attention?

"Why not? Their baby grand is *beautiful.*"

"Needs a good tuning," Penny replied dryly.

Roz laughed. "I am sure Kyle could come in and—"

"He's not *like them*, but he's the same as them in that he wants something from me. It might not be the same thing—he's not like *that*," Penny said, looking back at Roz with her wide, blue eyes that just always seemed *so fucking haunted*. "He's not like that, but he wants something from me, he's only interested in what he can get from me."

She blinked.

"And what is that?"

"For me to play," Penny said simply. "The piano, I mean. That's all he's focused on. It isn't the same thing as the rest of them, but it's still *something*."

"I promise Kyle isn't *only* interested in making you play. That was a big factor that drew him to you, and he would still love to see you play at a piano, but it's not at all the *only* thing he cares about, Penny."

"Mmm."

The noncommittal sound made Roz sigh quietly.

"But you," Penny said, looking Roz over with a pensive stare, "I don't know about you. I can't figure *you* out. Everybody always wants something from me—they don't care how they get it, but I can't find what it is you want. And I don't like that."

"Nothing," Roz whispered.

Penny raised a brow in silent question.

Roz shrugged. "I just want to help, Penny."

That was the reason she was *still in this fucking country*. Instead of being at home, telling her parents they were going to be grandparents again, or letting Naz share the news with his parents. It was why she had allowed Naz to buy tickets that he had to cancel last minute because she couldn't zipper up her luggage knowing this young woman was stuck in this place, hurting and *broken*.

"I'm angry," Penny said.

Roz nodded. "I don't doubt that."

"No, you don't get it. I'm *mad*, Roz. At everything—at the *world*. All the time, it never leaves. It's right under my skin every waking moment of my life. I tried to cut it out, and I can't get it to leave. I look at people like *you*—happy and *good*. There's not things in your head that aren't right. There aren't people in your life who hurt you when they were supposed to love you. And I'm so fucking bitter about it. I look at you, and all I see is everything I can't ever be. And that makes me angry. I don't want to be angry anymore. I don't want to be *anything* anymore."

"Penny—"

"And you think you can *help*?"

"I think you need someone who is willing to try," Roz replied. "So here I am, willing to *try*. I'm not asking for your permission to do it because if it was left up to you, I don't think you would let anyone help. And yeah, I'm here whether you want me to be or not."

That quieted the girl.

Finally, Penny muttered, "They're saying I have to go back to the States ... for a lot of reasons."

Yeah, Roz knew that, too.

Because Penny needed to bring charges in the country where the assaults happened. Because she wasn't a citizen of this country, she couldn't be *placed* with a family or conservatorship here. And there were more details that just ... muddied all of this up.

"I applied to foster you when they bring you back to the states," Roz said quietly.

Penny's head snapped up. "*What?*"

"It was me, or a random family. A random foster home. I am here to help," Roz said again, "whether you want me to or not."

"Oh, I bet Kyle will *love* that," Penny sneered under her breath. "Put the prodigy in with the washed-up prodigy, and he gets exactly what he wants."

Roz brushed the girl's attitude off.

Mostly.

"I have spent the last several years headlining one of the biggest orchestra companies in the world, and I chose to leave the company because I want to begin my life with a man who waited for me despite all the odds," Roz said, "and I truly don't give a single shit if you never put your fingers back on the ivory again, Penny, but in case you haven't figured it out yet, lashing out to hurt me doesn't actually fix *you*."

Penny wouldn't look at her, but her shoulders sunk a bit. "Sorry."

Roz decided to go in a different direction with the girl. "How are you feeling about the fact they're going to make a second formal statement about your father's abuse to US officials once you're back home? I imagine you don't want to go through that a second time."

Something akin to a bitter sneer curved the girl's lips.

"What is that for?" Roz asked.

"You think it was *just* my dad?" Penny gave Roz a look over her shoulder, and in that moment, it felt like her heart fell to the floor and shattered. "It's more than just *him*. There are a *group* of them, Roz. It's a network. And I am not the only one they did it to. We're a commodity to them … something to be traded, kept, or borrowed. He only sent me away because I was getting too old, my body changed, and I was getting *louder*. I was causing problems—I *was* a problem. That's why they started sending me away."

She felt sick.

"I haven't broken the surface yet," Penny continued, "but when I do, nothing is ever going to be the same, and *that* is what scares me."

"A network," Roz echoed.

Because she was still stuck on that.

Why would this girl *lie*?

"They're everywhere. But you're not like me, so you can't see them. Monsters are very good at hiding in plain sight."

NEW YORK: PART 1

Naz POV

"And this is the room where Penny will be staying, correct?" the woman CPS had sent in to do a walk-through of Naz's Manhattan penthouse. Now, *Roz's* penthouse, too.

"That's right," Roz said. "She's sixteen—she needs privacy, and her own space to be alone in when she feels the need, doesn't she?"

"Being that she's a suicide risk—"

"She is still sixteen."

The woman nodded, and scratched something on the paper in her hands before looking back up at Roz. Then, her gaze drifted to where Naz was lingering at the end of the hallway, closer to the sitting room in the penthouse. The wall of glass windows behind him sat in front of a baby grand that had once been his grandfather's.

Naz tried not to feel edgy when the woman looked him over, but it still made him feel uncomfortable all the same. He didn't know why, but her stare was just a little *too* pensive. Like she was considering something about him, but the problem was, she didn't know *fuck all* about him to know anything. Anything she thought were all conclusions she had drawn on her own, and he wasn't here for that shit.

"And this man—Nazio Donati, yes?—will also be living in the residence," the woman said.

"He owns the penthouse?" Roz's question came out slightly sarcastic, and yet still annoyed at the same time. "He's also been my long-term boyfriend for over—"

"Not *husband*," the woman interjected.

Naz blinked.

Roz quieted.

"Because that could present a problem. The girl will need to be brought into a stable household. We consider that to be, more often than not when presented, a couple that has proven their—"

"The only reason she isn't my wife is because she has spent the last several years on an entirely different continent than me," Naz said sharply, "and I thought it wasn't appropriate to marry someone when

564

we couldn't begin an actual marriage together in the same house, let alone *country*, but okay."

That made the woman clear her throat. Roz, to her benefit, shot Naz a small smile. This whole fucking charade was getting on his goddamn nerves, and Naz wasn't the type to let small things get to him like this, but here they were … doing exactly that.

From the paperwork … to the officials being in and out of his goddamn house, to this bitch trying to insinuate that their home wouldn't be an appropriate place for Penny to be fostered until she was eighteen, or something else came about that would mean she needed to be moved. It all just pissed him off spectacularly.

He never asked for this.

None of it.

But Penny didn't ask for her life to be the way it was, either. And Roz couldn't help that she had a heart of gold. Which meant Naz was going to do whatever he needed to do for Roz, including getting Penny under their roof.

The woman cleared her throat—frankly, Naz could have asked her to repeat her name, but she wasn't important enough for him to give a shit to know it. "All right, well, Rosalynn, I will get all of this filled out, and put into the system so we can … hopefully have Penny with you as soon as possible. From what I understand, she has asked to be allowed to live with you as well, and judges often consider older teenager's requests when needed."

"She … did?"

"I'm sorry?"

"Penny," Roz clarified, "she asked to live with me?"

"Apparently. Have a good day."

It was only once the woman was gone from their penthouse, and Naz had followed Roz into the kitchen where she could pick up the bottle of water, she'd discarded earlier did he finally speak to her.

"So, if they're going to push that line," he said, "we'll get married."

Roz, standing at the island with her back turned to him, spun around to face him with wide eyes. "What did you just say?"

"If they push the line about the fact we're not married or common law, then we can get married, Roz. It takes twenty-four hours after getting a marriage license to get married at the City Clerk's office. It's not a big deal."

"Not a—"

"No, it isn't," Naz said. "It's easily fixed. They won't fuck us around with her because of *that*, I assure you."

He'd make sure of it. Also, his family, and Roz's, had deep pockets and a lot of fucking contacts to use. Some money shoved into the right hands, and all these issues were going to go away, anyway.

A small smile played at the edges of Roz's lips. "So, you're telling me that despite the fact we haven't even told our parents that we're expecting a baby ... or that we're bringing a sixteen-year-old girl into our home to live with us, we should get married and add *that* to the pile, too."

Well, when she put it like that ...

Naz shrugged. "They would understand."

Or not.

It didn't matter.

"I don't think we'll need to do that," Roz said. "We *are* the best choice for her, and like Rebecca said, Penny did ask to live with me."

Yeah, Rebecca.

That was the bitch's name.

All right.

Naz filed that away for later. "So, does that mean you don't want to do that at all, then?"

Because that was *really* going to fuck up the plans he'd been working on from the moment he knew she was coming home to him—long before he even knew about the pregnancy, too. He'd scrap those plans if they needed to jump into marriage for the sake of Penny, but that was a different thing.

"What, get married?"

"Yeah, babe," Naz said, shrugging.

Roz gave him a look from the side. "You've never asked, Naz."

"Yet," he returned, "I have not asked *yet*."

His girl grinned. "Exactly."

Naz nodded at her water. "Take that prenatal vitamin, too, while you're at it. You didn't take it this morning."

She had so many things to think about, he was picking up the slack in other areas for her. He didn't mind, though. Wasn't that the whole point of loving someone? When they needed you, no matter what, you were there?

Because that's what Naz had been taught.

That's what he knew from his parents.

This was the only way he knew how to love Roz.

"Yeah, I will," she said, giving him a wink. "And what are you dressed up for?"

By dressed up, she meant the fact he'd shrugged on his leather jacket, and had his Doc Martens laced around the back, ready to go out.

"I need to meet up with Luca," he said. "Business stuff, you know."

Roz nodded. "Okay. And then dinner tomorrow at your parents with everybody, right?"

Naz grinned. "To share the news, yep."

He couldn't fucking wait.

She came across the kitchen, pushed up on her tiptoes, and pressed a sweet, lingering kiss to his lips. "I better call across the pond, and see if Penny wants to talk today."

Naz swept his thumb across her cheek. "She'll talk for you."

Roz was literally the *only* person Penny cared to talk to on a personal level, now. Anything beyond giving a few words to police or her therapist, and Penny shut the fuck down. She also didn't have a problem meeting Naz's gaze on the few times they met, but she wouldn't say a single word to him.

Not even *hi*.

"Okay, go play with my brother," Roz said, patting him on his cheek.

Naz chuckled. "*Play*, right."

She could believe that.

He didn't mind letting her.

After all, the second Roz had told him about one of her last meetings with Penny before they left England where the girl explained a network of people were involved in this ... *thing* that victimized Penny, well, time started ticking down.

Naz was about to really get started.

Some people just deserved to die.

Roz didn't need to know that, though.

For now.

NEW YORK: PART 2

Naz POV

"Are you fucking *serious?*"

"If you're going to hover over my shoulder," Naz snapped at Luca, "then do us both a favor and *fuck off* somewhere."

"Naz, this is—"

"The only reason I came over to your place is because I couldn't very well get my system up and running without Roz watching me do it. I don't want her to worry about this. Got it?"

Luca paced behind Naz's chair as several PC screens came to life in front of him. On his lap, the laptop was already booted up and ready to take a trip onto the black web where he knew with a few clicks and the right keywords, he was going to find forums.

"Give me a username," Naz said.

Luca rolled his eyes and glared at the ceiling. "This is *stupid.*"

"It isn't. And you're going to help me round them up."

Like pigs to the slaughter.

Naz didn't add that part out loud.

"Do you realize how large these *networks* are?" Luca asked. "They span *continents*, Naz. So what, you pick off a few of them *here*, and then what happens you come across a fucking video of some little kid in Asia somewhere being—"

Naz let out a sound that ached when it came out of him. "Then, the next time I am in Asia, I will take a side trip."

His friend cursed a blue streak under his breath. "You are *inviting in* trouble. If those fucks attention wasn't on you or us before, they will be now. Is that what you want—when you have kids, do you wanna go on the dark web and find pictures of them being distributed because they're a *target?* I hear two hearts inside each other, depending on the color stamped on the picture, means which gender they prefer. They're pretty cool with listing the *ages* of preference right beside it, too."

That made Naz hesitate as he found a forum called *Little Dreams*. Sickness welled in his gut because that was a lot more than he wanted to understand, but he had a feeling that wasn't even the tip of the goddamn iceberg. Once he went down this rabbit hole, there was going to be no coming back from it—a picture of a kid as a target would be the *least* disturbing thing, to be sure.

Did he really want *that?*

"And what happens when they figure it out?" Luca asked. "What happens when they start putting it together than the man in the forum is the one *hunting them down?"*

"I actually like the sound of that, so don't use it to discourage me."

They were animals.

He didn't mind hunting them like one.

"My point is, which you completely fucking missed, is that they'll *go underground,"* Luca said.

"More than dark web forums and secret networks that even *we* don't know about?" Naz returned.

"Exactly, Naz."

"I hear what you're saying."

"Do you? Do you *really?* Because if you put me or mine in danger for this, I will gut you. Do you hear me?"

"I hear you."

And he understood that, too.

"Good. Make sure of it."

Luca turned to leave the secondary office space Naz had set up in his friend's home as a backup just in case, for some circumstance or another, he couldn't use the one in his own place. Naz spoke up to say one thing before Luca could leave entirely.

"Her father is a multi-billionaire," Naz said.

Luca hesitated. "What?"

"Penny. Her father is a billionaire from Jersey. Made his money through an investments company that worked *overseas.* You mean to tell me that some *fuck* from down the street on these forums have the kind of connections and money that man does to network like her father would? I bet ... I bet it's a tiered thing, Luca. On the lower end, you've got people distributing the porn—videos, pictures, or whatever. And in the middle, you've got those who are a little better off, and maybe they have something to *offer."*

Naz twisted that word because saying what it really meant made him want to fucking puke. Still, he continued on to drive the point home, adding, "They're the people the lower fucks who can afford it are going to, and the top tier? They're the ones using the middle of the spectrum when they find something *specific* … and I wouldn't doubt for a second that they have their own—" Naz made another noise under his throat. "Like Penny … like *Penny*, Luca."

"Naz, I get it's fucking horrifying, okay? I *get it*."

"No, you really don't. Do you know what she told Roz?"

"God, don't make me ask. I don't want—"

"Just because it is not in your home, affecting *your* life does not mean you have the right to ignore it happening to someone else."

Luca's gaze handed as he looked back at Naz. "What did she tell Roz?"

"She was four—her virginity was auctioned off by her father. Three quarters of a million. She was flown to Hong Kong to deliver for the buyer. *Four*, Luca."

Luca was quiet for longer than Naz cared to admit. As his friend chewed on those words, and decided what he wanted to do with it, Naz turned back to the screen. Without warning, the username he wanted to use on the forum came to his mind, and before he could think better of it, he created an account.

At the doorway, Luca still hadn't moved to leave.

"You can't hunt them all down, it'll be impossible," Luca muttered.

Naz didn't need to be told, although it hurt his chest like nothing else. "I know."

"You're going to chase a rabbit hole, Naz."

"What if …"

"What?"

"What if I made a program, Luca, that traced every picture, and every person in these forums. It'd have to be advanced … *crazy* advanced, right? I can code it to run information through other databases."

"*Hack*, databases, you mean," Luca countered.

Naz shrugged. "But I've done that before—I've been in government databases and back out with no one knowing I was even there. It's not impossible. I could do it again … if I could match information from profiles or pictures to *real* kids with *real* parents or the people doing this to them … it could be anonymously delivered to police across the globe. Everything is on the internet now. Everything has security cameras with facial recognition. I could make a fucking program—I could *do it*."

"A program like that, one that could actually grab information when everything from IPs to … shit, everything and everyone on the dark web use proxy servers and VPNs, Naz. That's *before* the fail safes put into place by the people running the forums and … You know it's not that easy, *we* use it for gunrunning."

"I know how they work, I made one, remember?"

A whole online, deep web network for the gun trafficking side of his father's business. Yeah, Naz knew how it worked.

"But nothing is perfect and all I need is the right program to get *past* those safe guards," Naz said. "I could do that—I could make it."

Luca made a noise under his breath. "… fuck, Naz, that could take—"

"Years, I know." Naz frowned at the screen in front of him as he scrolled through a forum topic that described the grooming and sale of a child from Alabama. *Holy fucking shit.* "But I don't have years, Luca. I have nine months."

"What?"

"I have seven or so months before my baby is born. I don't *have years to do this.*"

Because he couldn't imagine his child coming into the world when this was all around them. And if he didn't do *something*, then what good was he?

"Is Roz—"

"Dinner tomorrow," Naz interjected. "You should come and hear the news like everyone else."

"Shit."

"And these kids … they don't have years, either. Once was one too many. I can't hunt them all, but I can get rid of a lot of them."

"Except they keep coming back," Luca replied, "it's not something you can eradicate like a diseased animal, or something. When these ones are gone, someone else will take their place. Just like with anything else. All you can do is protect your kids from it the best you can, Naz."

He didn't need the reminder, but he still had to do something. For now, he would settle on doing this until he figure something else out.

But the ones at the *very* top? Ones like Penny's father?

Naz would save those as a lesson—a lesson that would *really* hurt when he drove it home—for the rest that somehow managed to escape his notice. Someone was watching them, and someone was coming for them. Every fucking one of them.

NEW YORK: PART 3

Naz POV

The chatter at the table continued on despite the fact Roz had looked to Naz with an arched brow as if to silently ask, *Now?* He shrugged, letting the choice be up to her. They had spent the first *hour* of this family dinner explaining to the important people from both their families that a teenage girl would be living with them, and very little else. The whys wasn't important, not was it their business to share the things that Penny had gone through over the years. They answered as many questions as they were asked, but when it came right down to it, they actually said very little about it.

This was their choice.

Or rather, Roz's.

Naz was just here to let her do what she needed and wanted.

"Should I go get it, then?" Roz asked.

Naz grinned. "*I* will go get it. You should grab another plate of that lasagna your ma made. It was good."

"Because I need a second plate."

He was already standing from the chair, ignoring the curious gazes of their family that drifted his way when he did so. Dropping a kiss to the top of Roz's head, he said, "Who said anything about need? It's all about what you *want.*"

She grinned.

He winked.

"Where are you going?" his father called from the head of the table.

Naz passed his father a look as he headed for the entryway of the dining room. In his captain chair, Cross never looked happier to Naz. There was something about being surrounded by his entire family that made his father *most* happy. Well, his family and his friends, when it came to Roz's family. And they were *all* happy to finally have Roz back home, even if they were a tad bit worried about the new circumstances with Penny.

They might not have been voicing those concerns *loudly*—if only because they didn't want to say the wrong thing or step on someone's

outtakes vol 2: the commission world

toes—but Naz could still tell. He wasn't stupid, but he appreciated his parents', and Roz's parents', effort to let them figure this shit out on their own. He didn't doubt for a second that once everyone knew the *second* piece of their news, that concern would ratchet up a bit.

Oh, well.

"I have something to grab in the car," Naz told his father.

"What?"

"Well, if we wanted you to know that when we first arrived, then you would have known, no?"

Cross smirked. "Oh, you're in *that* kind of mood today, huh?"

"Let the man go, Cross," Zeke said from across the table.

"Let me needle him. No one else does."

"Except he acts just like you, and we know where that *leads*."

"Did I ask—"

Okay, that was enough for Naz. Zeke and Cross were only joking around with each other, but they could continue to do that without him standing right there to listen to it. He had other, more important things, to be doing.

"I'll be back," Naz said as he slipped out of the dining room.

He heard his father shout after him, but he was already halfway down the hallway by then. Outside, their car was parked at the far end of the driveway because they arrived later than everyone else. A product of living in Manhattan when his parents still lived far outside the city limits. In the trunk of the car, Naz found the item they had kept hidden. Or rather, *items*. One was a cake Roz had decided to make, and despite the fact she wasn't exactly a *baker*, she had full with it. It looked like it was going to make his teeth ache, too, what with the thick, white chocolate icing that looked like soft waves covering the cake, but apparently, she hadn't intended for it to be eaten at all.

The other two items, small, matching boxes with white bows keeping the tops firmly on were his idea ... just because. He ran around the city half of the evening the day before to find the things he needed to put *inside* those damn boxes when the cake probably would have been far more than enough, but hey.

His mother was a Marcello.

His father, a Donati.

They didn't go halfway.

They went *all the way*.

By the time Naz got back inside the house, the table had been mostly cleared but for a couple of bottles of wine that were being passed around. Roz passed on hers, but nobody seemed to think that was out of the ordinary. Naz took a glass for himself after setting the cake in the very middle of the table, and passing his mother one of the two boxes, as well as a box for Roz's mother, too.

"What's this?" his mother asked, passing a sly smile to Katya, Roz's mother. "Gifts, Naz?"

He chuckled. "Something like that."

Sitting back in his chair, he sipped on the bitter wine as he tossed his arm around Roz's shoulders. It was Italian tradition—rich, fatty, rich, fatty, sweet, rich, sweet, fatty ... that's how the meals went at an Italian's table. And then they *always* finished it off with something bitter to remind them of the sadness in life because the sadness was usually the most important. It was where the *growth* came. And it made them all the more grateful to be alive for it. Or, that's what his parents always explained.

Naz didn't know if it was true.

But he drank the bitter wine.

"And a cake?" Cross asked.

Naz waved a finger between the cake, and his father, as well as Zeke. "We thought while ma and Katya opened their boxes, you and Zeke could ... cut the cake for us."

Zeke's brow dipped as he passed Naz a scowl. "Are you high? Who needs two people to cut a cake?"

Roz laughed. "Just do it. It's all in good fun, Daddy."

"Stop wasting time," Naz said, "cut the cake—and Ma, don't open that box until they're cutting."

"Why not?" Catherine said, her tone suspiciously whiney.

Naz only shook his head.

Nope.

They would find out soon enough.

Cross finished his wine with a huff, and set the glass to the table as he gave his son a wag of his finger before lifting from his chair. That was another thing his father didn't like—standing from his chair before someone else at the table. He preferred to be the last person to leave a dinner, following right behind his wife.

That was just their way.

At the other side of the table, Zeke stood from his chair as well, but he kept a hold on the crystal glass with his remaining bit of wine.

Two knives were picked up from the middle of the table, left over from dinner. As the two men popped the plastic cover from the cake holder, Catherine and Katya had their boxes ready to go.

It was only as two knives were cut through the cake did their mothers pull the bows from the boxes. It was timed almost perfectly—Catherine gasped first at the sight of two little gold crowns, one with pink gems embedded in the band, and one with blue, and Katya soon followed with a shout of happiness. The hollers from their fathers came right after as Cross and Zeke pulled two pieces of cake out with the knives, one with the middle colored in blue on one side, and one colored in pink.

Cross stared across to his son, a smile drifted over his face. "Another grandbaby?"

Naz nodded. "Yeah, Dad."

"Oh, Naz," Catherine whispered.

He shrugged.

Their pride was clear.

So was their *love*.

What else could he do?

Beside him, Zeke and Katya had already rounded the table with enough noise to break the windows to celebrate with them, too. A hand hit his back hard before Zeke bent down to hug his daughter. Kayta did the same. Under the table, Naz kept a hand on Roz's thigh because he knew this was probably a bit overwhelming.

"A baby," his father said again.

Naz laughed. "It's going to be a busy year."

"But a *good* one."

That, too.

THE DONATIS

"Done," Naz grumbled, wishing he had taken his grandmother's offer of her flowery garden gloves to protect his hands because *fuck.* He had so much dirt under his fingernails that it was going to take hours to get out. And not to mention, yeah, he was known to occasionally work with his hands, but not typically like *this.* He didn't get on his hands and knees in a fucking garden to pull weeds for hours.

Oh, he wasn't joking.

Not exaggerating.

Not even a little.

His father had suckered him into helping Emma get her garden ready for planting because *she misses you, and she doesn't get to see you enough.* Right. What his father didn't say was that Cross just didn't want to be the one here on his hands and knees, ruining very expensive clothes, to pull out weeds that would, no doubt, grow back in a couple of weeks.

Because they were weeds!

"Oh, we're not done," Emma said, poking her head up over the shrubbery bush. "We have to till the soil again, and add in a bit of the fertilizer to mix it again. Then, we'll get the rows ready over there for the new roses I want to put in."

Oh, my God.

Naz knew work.

He *did.*

He loved to work on cars. He was good with grease, and oil. He worked out morning and night to keep his body in shape. And yet, on his knees under the hot August sun after pulling weeds for several hours, since almost the moment he woke up that morning considering this was the first place he came after he ate breakfast, he was tired.

Exhausted.

"Grandmama?"

"Hmm?"

Emma's bright smile came his way, and his shoulders dropped a bit. She was happy—*so fucking happy.* His father probably hadn't lied, all things considered. His life was constantly chaotic, even if that was how he liked it best. He did great things under immense pressure, after all. Nonetheless, it kept him on the move, nonstop. The only time he really got to sit down with his grandmother was every other Sunday for family dinner at her house.

The other Sundays, they went to his mother's family.

In those seconds, with his grandmother staring his way and waiting for him to speak, Naz decided it didn't fucking matter what he felt. So what if he was tired. Who gave a shit if it was way too hot. He didn't have a green thumb, and he didn't give a shit what roses needed to grow as beautiful as they could be, but whatever.

Emma was smiling.

Because of him.

"Would you like something to drink?" he asked her.

Emma nodded. "I think we should. A break would be good."

Naz agreed. "Find some shade, and I'll bring it out to you, Grandmama."

His grandmother pulled the glove from her hand. Reaching across the shrubbery bush that kept them separated, Emma patted Naz on the cheek with her warm, weathered palm. "You're a good boy, hmm?"

Twenty, and he was still a boy to her.

Like he was to his ma, too.

Naz didn't mind.

"Is there anything else you want me to get you, Grandmama?"

Emma grinned conspiratorially. "*Well*, if you think we could use an extra pair of hands out here, I am sure you could convince your grandfather to join us."

Right.

Nazio seriously doubted that. Calisto was a lot of things, but a man who worked with his hands was not one of them. He blamed it on the fact that his grandfather had always held a special love for the piano, and that meant taking care of his hands as much as possible.

"I'll see what I can do," he told Emma.

She nodded, and pulled one last weed as he stood up. He was quick to help her up to her feet as well, but without waiting for her to ask. Once his grandmother was situated in the shade under her favorite sitting area, Naz headed for the house.

He was just pulling a picture of iced tea from the fridge when his grandfather came to lean in the entryway of the kitchen with a knowing smile.

"What?" Naz asked.

"Has she tired you out yet?"

"Very much."

Calisto chuckled. "She does love that garden."

"She better for all the work she puts into it."

"And you, too."

"Hmm?"

Naz glanced back at his grandfather as he pulled two glass cups from the cupboard, and then proceeded to set them down on the island to fill with the iced tea. "What do you mean?" ·

"She loves you, Naz," his grandfather explained. "She would have been happy had you came and took her out for lunch, but I know she appreciates this more than she'll say."

Huh.

"I know," he said.

"Thank you for not complaining, and indulging her."

Naz shrugged. "Why wouldn't I, Grandpapa?"

Calisto nodded. "Exactly, Naz."

Family was everything.

That lesson had started with Calisto.

He passed it onto Cross.

And now it was Naz's turn to carry it on.

"Good men aren't born," Calisto told his grandson.

Naz nodded. "They're made."

THE MARCELLO SIDE

"All right, kid, there you are," Ronnie said.

In the backseat of his enforcer's Hummer, Naz did his best *not* to roll his eyes at being called *kid* by a guy who couldn't be more than twenty-five. Even if he had a good ten years on Naz, he just didn't understand why the asshole insisted on calling him a kid all the time when it was clear Naz didn't like it. He only made the effort not to roll his eyes because—usually—he did actually like this enforcer. He didn't want a new one because he opened his stupid mouth and caused a problem. Plus, Ronnie let him get away with more shit than the last one did.

All wins in Naz's book.

"Stop calling me that," Naz muttered, shoving open the back door.

His feet had just hit the paved driveway leading up to his grandparents' three-level home when the enforcer in the front seat replied, "You might be a fucking genius, Naz, but you're still just a fifteen-year-old boy to me. Call me when you're ready to leave, you hear me?"

Naz sighed. "Yeah, I hear you."

So was his life.

"And wipe that scowl off your motherfucking face, too, kid. You know better than to walk around looking sour being who you are and all."

Dammit.

Naz fixed his face.

If only because he didn't want to keep going a round with his enforcer. He swore Ronnie acted like his keeper, babysitter, and mentor just as much as he did his guard. Naz didn't entirely think that was his job, but since nobody ever corrected the guy, well, what could he do or say?

Nothing.

That's just how it worked.

Despite his irritation with the enforcer, when Ronnie waved to him as he headed for his grandparents' house, Naz waved back. After all, even if Ronnie parented him way more than he should, he still liked the fucker.

Naz climbed the stairs to the entrance of the large home, not at all surprised to find his Grandpapa, Dante, already waiting for him in the opened doorway. Even if there were a million other things he'd rather be doing on a Friday night, seeing his grandfather waiting had him grinning to match Dante's smile.

"What was that all about, huh?" his grandfather asked.

"What?"

Dante nodded to somewhere behind Naz, still not moving from the doorway so the two of them had to stay standing like they were with him on the porch and his grandfather in the doorway. "You and your driver."

Oh, *that*.

"He just gets on my nerves."

Dante arched a brow. "How so?"

"Does it matter?"

"Maybe. Won't know unless you tell me why."

Naz sighed. "He just ribs me all the time. You know? Won't let shit go. Puts me on the spot. Always on my damn ass."

Dante nodded, tipping his chin up as though he'd heard that exact sentiment before. "In a bad way, though, or in a way that teaches you how to keep control of yourself through building your character?"

Well, that made Naz think.

"I'm not sure," he finally muttered.

"Yeah, it's usually later that you figure it out. Probably a little harder on you than it was for me," Dante noted, cocking his head to the side, "because see, I had two brothers going through the same shit with their own enforcers. It's a rite of passage, Naz ... because if they don't get on your nerves and teach you how to hide it, then you'll never fucking learn."

"Dad never said his enforcer—"

His grandfather barked out a laugh. "*His?* His was ten times worse—would taunt him non-stop, smacked him in the back of the head whenever he could get away with it, drove him up the fucking wall constantly. Whenever Cross went into one of his moods and took off, who do you think hunted his ass down and brought him home? And do you know where that enforcer is today?"

Naz really had to consider that.

"Dead?"

Because that's where he probably should be.

Dante smiled. "No, he's your father's consigliere. Has been since Cross took over the family. Because as much as he hated that man growing up, he was still one of his closest, most trusted people."

"Ronnie isn't *that* bad," Naz muttered.

"Maybe he doesn't have to be … or maybe your dad just knew who would work best for you, hmm?" Dante shrugged, and then reached out to clap a hand on Naz's shoulder before he pulled him into the familiar house. "We all had the same shit to handle, Naz, and so will you. Your grandmother is in the kitchen. She's making lasagna and garlic bread."

Which meant he needed to help.

Naz heard what Dante didn't say.

"Got it."

Naz found his grandmother in the kitchen, just like Dante said he would. However, his grandfather hadn't been entirely right because Catrina wasn't actually cooking. She had simply pulled out some pots and dishes, all the groceries needed to make supper, and put them on the counter.

"Waiting for me?" he asked.

Catrina turned on him with a smile. There was a familiarity about his grandmother's face that always made him feel welcomed—his mother looked so much like her mother. And even his sister took those same, pretty feminine features.

"Actually," Catrina said, "I'm not going to be cooking today."

"But—"

"You are."

Naz laughed. "You want *me* to cook? Alone?"

"Why not? I think I've cooked for you more than enough, no? It's only fair that you cook me a nice dinner, *and* entertain me while you do it."

Naz grinned.

That was typical for his grandmother.

Always keeping him on his toes.

"And what if I fuck it all up?"

"You won't. You can't. I'm here."

DONATI SHORTS

CAL AND THE PRINCESS

Emma moved through the house with Midnight fast on her heels. She could hear the quiet murmurings coming from the back of the house—near Calisto's office. It couldn't be Cross and his father. Cross had gone with Wolf and his wife for the weekend for a visit to Canada.

Business, likely.

Sometimes, Emma wondered if their son was still too young for business, but she didn't think on it for long. Cross wasn't always seeing business when he traveled with his father, or Wolf. Sometimes, it was just to let him go with his Godfather, and get him off their hands for a while.

A break was good.

Once in a while.

"No, Daddy, like *this,*" Emma heard their three-year-old daughter say.

"Ah, okay. I see."

"Yes!" Tiny hands clapped loudly. "Good job, Daddy!"

Emma scooped Midnight up off the floor to keep him from barking. He settled happily into her arms, and sniffed around as she walked the rest of the way down the hall. Peeking her head into the office, she found a sight that melted her heart in an instant.

Calisto had moved practically everything from his desk for Camilla to set all of her makeup—children's makeup, of course—on the top. Everything from her lipglosses, to her compact blushes, and even her nail polishes.

And God knew ... the girl had a collection.

Frankly, she had more makeup than her mother, and that was saying something.

It looked like Camilla had brought down each and every damn piece of makeup she owned to set on her father's desk. It covered just about the whole top. Calisto had even brought the mirror from the hallway into the office, and set it up next to the desk.

He and Cam, on the other hand, sat on the floor together in front of the mirror.

"So, how do we do this one?" Calisto asked, holding up what looked like a small eyeshadow pallet.

Of *neon* colors.

Jesus.

Emma pressed her lips together to keep from laughing out loud. This was, frankly, way too fucking good to pass up. Calisto did everything for his children. He was the best father. The *very* best. He never shied away from duties, and he was hands on with every aspect of their raising.

And she loved him for that.

She knew this day was coming, though. This day when Calisto having his own little girl would catch up to him, and the manly man he was found himself reduced to either a princess to please Camilla, or her very own personal guinea pig willing to do all the girly things she loved.

Because *yes*, their daughter loved all of that nonsense. From the frilly dresses, to the clicky shoes. The makeup, and her hair in curls. She loved pink, purple, and anything sparkly.

And at the same time, she also loved wearing jeans, getting dirty, and trying to beat the hell out of her brother when she thought she was fast enough to pull it on him.

What were little sisters for, anyway?

"Well," Camilla said, maintaining the most serious expression she could manage, "you just take it like this, and go like that."

Basically, she had taken the cheap little brush from the eyeshadow pallet, rubbed a whole bunch of puke colored green onto the tip, and then smooshed it against her father's eyelid. Calisto stayed perfectly still, and let her do just that, too.

Oh, God.

This was perfect.

Too perfect, really.

Quietly, Emma slipped the phone out of her pocket as Camilla moved onto the next thing. Lipgloss, it looked like. Or some lip paint—who fucking knew?

It was a terrible shade of red, and that was saying something considering how much Emma loved her red lipstick. And yet, Calisto didn't say a word as his daughter painted his lips with that horrible, awful color.

Actually, he smiled for her.

"You want to help me now?" Camilla asked.

Calisto grinned, and opened his eyes. "Yeah, I'll help you, *principessa.*"

Emma held up her phone, and got the two in the shot as she readied to take a picture of their moment. Maybe she would show Calisto someday, but maybe she would keep it just for her, too.

Who knew?

Moments like these were special, and she didn't like to share. Sometimes, she didn't get to see these moments with Calisto and their children because their lives were so busy, and it felt like they were just strangers passing each other by occasionally.

So yeah, this was *important.*

Special.

And … well, funny, too.

Calisto was painting his daughter's lips with the same shade of red when Emma took the picture. Thankfully, he didn't seem to hear the shutter click on the phone camera—stupid thing, why did it even do that?

"See," Camilla said, "I told you Daddies could play, too. Not *just* Ma for makeup, Daddy."

Calisto chuckled. "Well, no … this daddy doesn't like to play with makeup, *but* I will for you."

Camilla peered up at her father. "Promise?"

"You know it, *principessa.* Whatever makes you smile."

Emma backed away from the doorway, and let the two have their private moment. So was the way with fathers and daughters. They always seemed to have a special sort of bond, and the last thing she wanted to do was interrupt their time.

It was the relationship Emma *wished* she had been able to have with her own father, but instead, she was given what she was given. It had been years, and she still hadn't spoken with either of her parents. She knew they were alive, but not much else.

That was fine with her.

She'd cared about them enough.

She didn't anymore.

It was later in the evening—after supper, and after Camilla's face was washed free of makeup, her hair brushed, and she was put to bed that Calisto gave Emma *that* look.

The one he always gave her when he knew she was up to one of her tricks.

"Why are you looking at me like that?" she asked. "I'm just washing dishes."

Calisto cocked a brow, and nodded. "Right *now*, maybe. Where's your phone?"

"On the counter. Why?"

Then, a realization dawned on her as Calisto headed for the counter, and reached to grab her phone. Emma was quicker, and grabbed it despite her hands being soapy and wet.

"No way," she told him, laughing. "I am keeping that *forever*, Cal! How did you even see me?"

"I knew you were home the moment you walked through the door—Midnight would only leave Camilla if that meant you were home. Give me that phone."

"Yes, but *how*?" Emma stuck her tongue out at him. "And *no*, you can't have it. It's mine, thank you."

Calisto rounded the island, and came closer. She saw his determination with every step, and he kept coming despite the fact she kept walking backwards.

"I am not giving this to you," she told him, "but maybe we could make a deal."

"I don't make deals with terrorists."

Emma gasped. "I am not terrorizing you, Cal!"

"You have a picture that could very well terrorize me, *bella*. Give it to me right now."

"Nope."

"Emma."

She shivered at his growl.

"I hope you know when you sound like that, it only turns me on," she told him.

Calisto smirked. "Give me the phone, and I will make you a very happy woman."

Emma hugged it to her chest. "But ... it makes me happy, too, Cal."

He finally stopped walking.

She stopped, too.

"Someday," she said, "they're going to be all grown up, or too old to do this kind of stuff, and this is what we're going to have left of it, you know? They won't even remember these days, Cal. But I want to."

"Do you really need a picture of me done up in makeup?"

She shrugged. "I have one of you wearing a tiara and having tea, too."

Calisto groaned and glanced up at the ceiling. "*Why?*"

"I just told you why—they make me happy, too."

He pressed his lips together and eyed her from the side. "That's unfair."

"I never said I played a clean game."

"True." Calisto sucked in a deep breath and said, "Fine, keep your pictures."

"Like you were ever going to take them from me, anyway."

Calisto *meh'd* under his breath. "And for the record, they're going to remember these days, Emma. That's why I do it. So, they have what we didn't."

Yes.

Good parents.

Good memories.

Love.

Their children had everything that they didn't.

And she was so grateful.

ALL HALLOWS' EVE

Calisto glanced over his shoulder, chuckling at the sight of his son doing his best to look … well, *tough* wasn't quite the right word. More like … indifferent. Eight-year-old Cross loved Halloween. Just like his sister, Cam. Really, they took that from their parents. The one night of the year when he and his wife could let go a bit, have some fun … scare the whole fucking block, even. All that sweetness his wife retained throughout the year could disappear in a blink when someone gave her a vat of fake blood and told her to have some fun.

It wasn't a surprise their kids followed the tradition. Cross just liked to take things one step further—with their haunted house done for the year, and final night of Halloween there, Emma and Cal took their kids through their gated community for the usual trick or treating.

Except Cross had to make a whole show of it.

Or rather, a *story* around it.

The kid had an imagination, that was for sure. Hence why he walked behind them looking unbothered with bloodstained hands, a spattered leather jacket, and a pair of black jeans that had seen better days where the knees were concerned.

Black on black.

Hair slicked back.

"Are you really going to walk behind the *whole* time?" Camilla asked her brother.

"Why not?"

"Because … I don't know."

Cross shrugged. "You just don't get it, Cam."

Before the two could start a whole new argument—they'd had four before the four of them left the house earlier; well five, if you counted the enforcer staying thirty yards back—Emma was quick to step in with a bloodied, battered face looking sideways at her kids in *that* way.

All mothers had the look.

The kids shut up just like that.

It was a little disconcerting when Emma's *look* only made her FX makeup seem all the more terrible and scary. The white dress she wore to complete her costume, ripped and tattered, was just as bloodstained as the rest of them.

Cal's was just a suit.

Camilla wore her ballerina outfit.

With blood, of course.

Some scars.

Gory shit.

It wasn't Halloween without a little gore.

Or in their family's case, *a lot*.

"That's enough," Emma said. "First house."

That was that.

Camilla skipped ahead of her mother on the dimly lit path to head for the front door of one of their neighbors. The same one that had about pissed himself the week before when he walked through the Donatis' haunted house.

Fun times.

She pressed the doorbell, and then quickly came back to stand next to her mother. Calisto wasn't far behind, and neither was Cross. Although, as was the kid's plan, he stayed a bit back because he didn't want to look entirely *with* them, apparently.

The neighbor opened the door with a bowl of candy in hand—the usual Halloween shit, just a different year.

"Calisto, Emma," the man greeted. Then, his gaze darted to a bloodied Camilla before finding Cross aa few paces back. "I sense a theme." He pointed at Cam, saying, "Dead ballerina."

"Yep."

"Dead … wife?" the man asked Emma.

She shrugged. "Or mother."

The man nodded, but looked to Cal saying, "Same, then?"

"Pretty much."

"Did you all have to make it look so … *real?*"

"That's the best part," Calisto returned.

"Is it?"

Absolutely.

Then, the neighbor gave Cross a second look.

"And what are you supposed to be, Cross?" the neighbor asked. "You don't look as … dead as the rest of them."

Still standing back from his family, all bloodstained and unbothered, Cross showed his bloodied palms and shrugged, saying in monotone, "Well, obviously the one that killed them."

The man took a second.

Then, choked out a sound. "*Well*, huh."

Emma laughed. Camilla smiled, her murdered ballerina getup a little more devilish when she looked as sweet and innocent as she did. Cross, though, still appeared unfazed.

Yeah, a whole production.

Calisto grinned. "Trick or treat, man."

ABOUT THE AUTHOR

The author of too many novels to count, Bethany-Kris is a Canadian, lover of much, and mother to four sons, a glaring of cats, and a pack of dogs. A small town in Eastern Canada where she was born and raised is where she has always called home. With her boys under her feet, a snuggling cat, barking dogs, and a spouse calling over his shoulder, she is nearly always writing something ... when she can find the time.

Find where to follow BK and keep up to date with all her book news at www.bethanykris.com.

www.ingramcontent.com/pod-product-compliance
Lightning Source LLC
Chambersburg PA
CBHW050119030726
47505CB00007B/1937